MW01009871

Honor for Sale

Gerald E. Kelly

Honor
for
Sale

SP

SHARON PUBLISHING
NEW YORK

Published by Sharon Publishing, New York.
Distributed by Independent Publishers Group, Chicago.

ISBN: 0-9669973-0-1

Manufactured in the United States of America

10 9 8 7 6 5 4 3 2 1

Contents

For my wife,
who never said, "I told you so."

Author's Note

The essential events in this book are factual and a matter of public record. Most characters are authentic. However, the names of several people as well as identifiable details and dates have been changed to disguise and to protect the guilty and their families from retribution, and to afford anonymity to others. Some scenes and dialogue are invented. But the story is true. This is the way it was. Nobody was innocent. God bless them. I loved them.

The Sixties

Turbulent times. Tumultuous years. Missiles in Cuba. Camelot died. JFK, King, Bobby. Dreams shattered. Vietnam. My Lai. Killing fields. A Chicago convention. Abbie Hoffman. Kent State. Black Panthers. Tremors of revolution. Riots. Watts. Civil rights marches. Hate. Not only Mississippi was burning. Men on the moon. The Beat Generation. Hard rock. Woodstock. The Age of Aquarius. Sexual freedom. The Stonewall rebellion. Towers of tradition cracked, tumbled. Cynicism grew out of the debris. Anger. And Drugs. Uppers, downers, LSD, marijuana, cocaine, heroin. Tons of drugs. Addicts. Drug money. Thousands. Millions. Temptation. Greed. Corruption. Death.

The Stage

The honor of New York's Finest was always for sale. Theodore Roosevelt condemned the oldest municipal police force in America as steeped in "venality and blackmail," "utterly demoralized" and "the most corrupt department in New York." That was 100 years ago. The former cattle rancher was summoned to become President of New York's Police Board in 1895 to clear out the ethical sewage after the political establishment could no longer suppress the fact that operators of the city's brothels paid generously for police protection.

In the thirties, the young prosecutor Thomas E. Dewey investigated graft and corruption in New York's political and legal institutions. He tied hundreds of law enforcement officers to the public pillory for pocketing two salaries, one from the city and another from prominent Prohibition era crime hoodlums such as Lucky Luciano and Dutch Schultz.

The price for dishonesty kept pace with inflation. The gambler Harry Gross had to dish out a million bucks a year to protect his illegal operation. "Dirty Harry" had channeled his bribes to the top guns of the police hierarchy. The Police Commissioner resigned as a sacrificial token to appease public indignation and anger. Several of the indicted officers committed suicide.

The most recent chapter of the long *chronique scandaleuse* was written by corrupt cops in the summer of '98. It was discovered that about twenty officers of the Midtown South Precinct had for many years received cash and services from a Manhattan madam and her prostitutes for not seeing, hearing or saying anything regarding their business.

Not an affair to kick up a great fuss about, but the investigation of the copulating cops illuminated another durable element of police culture, the "Blue Wall." Bob Herbert in a *New York Times* Op-Ed piece described it as "The Stone Wall of Silence" erected by the 37,700 members of the New York Police Department to shield it from outside scrutiny. This code of honor is as strictly observed from the rookie officer up through the ranks to the Four Star Chief of Operations, as the law of the *omerta* is by the Mafia. Adds Herbert, "The Police Department will never voluntarily open its doors and let the public in on the full extent of corruption, brutality and other criminal activity in its ranks. Every now and then the door is forced open and we get a whiff of the stench within. But that's all."

Should a cop cooperate with a DA who is prosecuting a fellow officer for brutality, or stand up for a female colleague who has been sexually harassed by a superior, or report corruption or call a crime a crime even though the perpetrator wears a shield, he will be stigmatized and crucified for the rest of his life in uniform by his fellow cops. He may not even live long enough to regret his actions. No cop wants to be branded a rat.

When Frank Serpico, that rare species of principled and unblemished policeman who took his oath seriously and would not tolerate corruption by cops (portrayed by Al Pacino in Sidney Lumet's film *Serpico*), was shot by drug dealers in February 1971 and needed a blood transfusion, not one of New York's Finest volunteered. Sympathy, protection, if not complicity by the civilian supervisors, the Commissioners—and the Mayor—is an adhesive ingredient cementing the ring of resistance. Us against Them. Them being us, the people.

In his book *Cop Hunter*, Vincent Murano, a former investigator of the NYPD Internal Affairs Division, writes: "I was . . . tracking NYPD officers who were burglars, armed robbers, gun dealers, drug smugglers, fences, arsonists, kidnappers, terrorists, and murderers." Murano adds, "A police department is a closed society, maybe more so than the military because it is smaller and restricted by geography. The world is divided into cops and non-cops, and it does not take long to develop a 'good guys versus bad guys' mentality. The outside world seems to be filled with bad guys; the world inside the force becomes a treasured haven, populated by your colleagues, men and women who have vowed to fight and die at your side."

". . . the existence of the Blue Wall seems to dictate that one simply does not rat on one's fellow officers. This is an article of gospel among most of my colleagues in the NYPD and in every other police force in the nation. The penalty for breaching the Blue Wall is ostracism, petty retribution, retaliation, and, in extreme cases, death."

The traditional investors in police corruption were gamblers, bookmakers, pimps and prostitutes, racketeers and union bosses. In the sixties, new and powerful players appeared on the field, the drug dealers. The cartels. They radically changed the rules, and the prices. A totally new and gigantic market for illegal police activity and revenue was generated. A paradise for all men and women in Blue who put income before integrity, dollars before dignity, sullied the badge and risked their careers. Holding up the streetcorner pimp might generate $100 in additional revenue for the rogue on patrol, but shaking down a cocaine courier from Latin America or France could net 25 grand or more.

The changing criminal environment was conclusively described by the French journalists Pierre Galente and Louis Sapin in *The Marseilles Mafia—The Truth Behind the World of Drug Trafficking*: "In the sixties, with an increase in demand from the American market . . . the number of addicts continued to rise. The problem spread throughout the United States, affecting all social classes. In the wake of marijuana and LSD, heroin swept through the university campuses. Several factors were behind the sudden expansion of the problem: first there was the Vietnam war; then growing reservations about the 'American way of life'; and, corollaries of both of these factors, sexual liberation and the rebellion of the young. For a whole generation of adolescents, drugs became the symbol of flight from the adult world. The epidemic soon affected other countries, spread particularly by the 'hippies.' It reached a point when civilization itself seemed to hang in the balance."

The authors of a narcotics report prepared for New York Congressman Charles B. Rangel in 1972 delivered a rude wake-up call. "The magnitude and nature of heroin smuggling combine to pose a complex, as yet, unsolved problem. Traffic in heroin brings lucrative profits. The demand from an estimated 559,000 addicts nationwide (about half are located in the New York City area) can be translated into as much as $17 million in daily sales. Although it is uncertain how much heroin enters the country directly through New York City, it appears that most of it enters, or passes through, the city along various routes from other nations and from within the United States. Should a heroin smuggler choose New York City as a point of entry, he has available to him a choice of smuggling techniques limited only by his imagination."

Gold rush fever. The New York City Police Narcotics Division, never known for honesty or lawfulness, rotted to the core. Standing order of the day: shake down the scumbags. Thefts, murders, extortions, beatings, frame-ups, drug pushing. Crime within the Department exceeded epidemic proportions. It became standard procedure, a way of life. Policemen stole the streets blind, and went home to families without remorse. After all, the only people getting hurt were criminals anyway, right?

During the early 1960s, the NYPD Narcotics Bureau was headed up by Deputy Inspector Edward F. Carey. He commanded a loosely knit group of some forty undisciplined detectives who were arresting junkies and small-time drug pushers in all five boroughs of the Big Apple. But it was one particular case in 1962 that really put the Narcotics Bureau on the map, the case that came to be known as the "French Connection." In October 1961, two smart undercover agents, Detective First Grade Edward "Popeye" Egan and his partner, Detective Second Grade Salvatore "Sonny" Grosso, discovered and followed the trail of the Tuminaros, a Mafia family importing drugs from Marseilles. The four-and-a-half-month investigation ended with two spectacular seizures totaling 112 pounds of pure heroin, a world record at the time.

The first occurred on February 19, 1962. Joseph Fuco, a seasoned mobster, was arrested in his Brooklyn brownstone, where he had hidden twenty-four pounds of heroin in the basement ceiling. A week later his son, Tony "Patsy" Fuco, was caught in an apartment building in the Bronx with two suitcases, one filled with fifty-seven and the other with thirty-one pounds of top-quality heroin. The worldwide attention sparked by the case spurred the formation of a NYPD Narcotics Task Force, for which only a handful of elite detectives were selected.

The spectacular heist elevated Egan, a burly Irish redhead and a tough, vicious pit bull of a man who would take on anyone anytime, and Grosso, a laid-back, patient and quiet Italian-American whose Narcotics Bureau code name was "Cloudy," to international prominence. The author Robin Moore started the legend with his best-seller *The French Connection* and Hollywood followed with William Friedkin's slam-bang thriller, which collected five Academy Awards in 1971, including Best Picture, Best Director and Best Actor—Gene Hackman as Egan's film alter ego, "Popeye" Doyle.

Yet Popeye and his partner's superiors did not join in the celebration. By traditional standards, both detectives should have been rewarded accordingly, but it was not to be. Egan's abrasiveness and penchant for publicity incurred the wrath of the NYPD brass. A few weeks after the "French Connection" story made headlines, Egan appeared again on the front page of the *New York Daily News*—in a Santa Claus outfit. He had just made another impressive arrest for two kilos of heroin. For the record, he told the interviewer, "Thank God me and Sonny are out there. Nobody else seems to know there's a narcotic problem, certainly not the police higher-ups." The higher-ups did not appreciate Egan's commentary. He and Grosso were soon separated, pushed out of the Narcotics Bureau and exiled to different precincts. Grosso took his transfer to the "Seven-Five" stoically, whereas Egan was crushed by his reassignment to Brooklyn's 81st.

The "French Connection" was a milestone in the history of the NYPD Narcotics Bureau. The Task Force established in the aftermath of the front-page case formed the nucleus of the Special Investigating Unit (SIU), the sharp spearhead of the rapidly expanding Narcotics Bureau which targeted high-volume dealers. By 1965, with the drug scourge spilling out into white suburban communities, the NB had expanded to 110 men, grouped into five field teams. Three years later the New York City Police Department Narcotics Bureau was the largest drug enforcement agency in the world, with 330 men and woman in its ranks. The NB shared the Old Slip station house in lower Manhattan with the First Precinct, uncomfortably squeezed onto the third floor of the turn-of-the-century building. The Special Investigating Unit was lodged in an attic-type room on the fourth floor.

Edward Carey's successor as NB chief, Inspector Ira Bluth, assigned only the best and brightest detectives to this special section, under the direct supervision of his friend and longtime aide, Lieutenant Vinnie Hawkes, and Lieutenant Pasquale Intrieri. Every member of the SIU worked nonstop to try to top Egan and Grosso's "French Connection" blockbuster. These well-dressed and meticulously groomed detectives, whose number swelled to seventy-four in its "golden days," had city-wide jurisdiction and worked on cases they alone considered important.

The regular field teams, used to handling insignificant "nickel baggers," regarded the SIU bigshots with awe.

But in reality, the SIU investigators were marauders who preyed on Italian and Latin American drug importers and wreaked havoc on their organizations. An SIU detective's most prized weapon was his tape recorder. Night and day, hidden recorders noiselessly taped conversations between dealers, buyers, associates and girlfriends. The detectives were invariably rewarded with arrests, seizures, and, most importantly, scores, which meant illegally confiscating what money or drugs they found for themselves. "Popeye" Egan, who never made it into the SIU, liked to brag, "Good detectives can hit a financial home run every month if they want, but great ones like me can hit grand slams every day. "

Shakedowns of pushers were by no means confined to the Narcotics Bureau. Dealers were looked upon as fair game, and scoring by uniformed cops was commonplace on the streets of black and Hispanic precincts. It didn't matter what time of day it was, nor was it a precondition that the cop saw something "going down" or not. The officer simply walked up to a dealer and held out his hand. The dealer paid. It went with the territory.

Banter in precinct locker rooms and stairwells generally concerned the amount of money made on the previous day's tour. Several uniformed cops bought Long Island and Westchester homes that many Wall Street executives of the day couldn't afford. Transfers out of the Harlem or Bedford-Stuyvesant precincts were considered a financial catastrophe, to be avoided at all cost. Beat cops paid sergeants, sergeants paid lieutenants, lieutenants paid captains, captains paid inspectors, inspectors paid . . .

In the fall of 1968 two minor earthquakes rattled the narcs' paradise. In October two detectives were arrested for the sale of heroin. The damage could have been contained within the NYPD, but unfortunately Federal agents had a hand in the messy affair. A month later the commander of the Undercover Unit complained that $1,200 had been stolen from his desk. The department's boss, Ira Bluth, shrugged him off, and so did the Internal Affairs Division which the enraged captain had informed. When the whistleblower was deported to the newly formed Data Processing Unit a week later, he fired off a letter to the *New York*

Times. He was subsequently interviewed and his story considered "News That's Fit to Print." The article stated, "An unidentified police captain, formerly with the Narcotics Division, asserts the entire Narcotics Division is riddled with corruption."

The tremors of the two incidents threw the police establishment temporarily off balance. The Commissioner and his closest aides ordered some face-saving cosmetic surgery. First Ira Bluth was replaced by the head of the Bronx Patrol Force, the ramrod-straight Assistant Chief Inspector Thomas Renahan. To lead the Department's crown jewel, the SIU, they handpicked Captain Daniel Tange as its commanding officer.

The thirty-six-year-old Tange, a politically astute insider, was the youngest captain on the job. His record was unblemished—the right choice to guarantee a smooth and trouble-free operation. On the day of his inauguration he was told, "The chief selected you for this job because he knows you will instill some discipline. He won't tolerate another fiasco. Do a good job and he'll take care of you." But Tange's superiors never explained to him what their definition of a "good job" was.

The corruption permeating the NYPD was also working its way through the local Federal Bureau of Narcotics and Dangerous Drugs (BNDD). In November 1968, Attorney General Ramsey Clark dispatched a handpicked team of attorneys and law enforcement agents from Washington to the rotting Big Apple to investigate allegations of "significant corruption" spiced by suspicion that four Federal detectives had framed and murdered two black drug dealers. The inquiry ended with the conviction of 36 federal agents for perjury, extortion and selling of narcotics.

For a few years, the paths of Washington's BNDD and New York City's top guns of the Special Investigating Unit ran parallel, only occasionally crossing the tracks without disturbance. The SIU untouchables never considered the Feds equal rivals or a threat to the supreme control of their turf. They dominated the stage, the rest had to play cameo parts. James Lardner illuminated the situation in his police chronicle *Crusader:* "The detectives assigned to SIU tended to live far beyond their police salaries. Fancy vacations were a tradition in their unit—a way of celebrating major collars. A number of SIU men had impressive houses well outside the usual police neighborhoods of

Queens and Staten Island. Anyone looking for evidence of something wrong would not have to look very far. But in 1969 and 1970 no one was looking. . . ."

In *Prince of the City* author Robert Daley confirmed: "They were not ordinary detectives, not even ordinary narcotics detectives. They were SIU detectives . . . Their appearance was special, their prisoners were special, and their evidence was special . . . They seldom mixed with other cops. In the police world they were as celebrated as film stars, and they were aware of this . . . They had style; also, obviously they had money, more money than cops were supposed to have. But for a long time no one in authority noticed this, or wondered where the money might be coming from . . . That they worked hard was never questioned . . . They were hunters . . . They had citywide jurisdiction. They chose their own target and roamed New York at will . . . they operated with the impunity, and sometimes with the arrogance, of Renaissance princes."

David Durk, a New York City cop, shunned by most of his former buddies as a "rat," was never challenged by authorities for statements in his kill-and-tell-biography, *The Pleasant Avenue Connection*. He wrote: "By 1969, SIU and much of the New York City Police Department's Narcotics Division had become a kind of heroin brokerage . . . In 1970, SIU, a unit of only seventy men, seized more heroin or other illicit drugs than were seized by all customs, border patrol, and Federal narcotics agents working throughout the country . . . But no one was looking too closely at how these seizures were made and what happened to the seized narcotics . . . By 1969, there were two major marketing operations of heroin in New York City. One operated out of Pleasant Avenue; the other operated out of the fourth floor of the First Precinct station house in lower Manhattan—the headquarters of the Special Investigating Unit . . . This was the heyday of SIU. It was steak or lobster every night. Officers who were ripping off narcotics dealers generally carried self-addressed, stamped envelopes with them for making 'night deposits' in the mailbox soon after seizing large sums of money."

Such was the setting and the ensemble of players on the stage on which our drama unfolds in January 1969. It is the tale of the most incredible, outrageous, ingenious criminal case in the twelve-year existence of the infamous Special Investigating Unit. The chronology of a criminal masterpiece. One of the darkest chapters in the long history of the New York City Police Department. An affair which jolted the Federal and New York City law enforcement communities and sent tremors through Mayor John Lindsay's City Hall and Nelson Rockefeller's gubernatorial mansion. It was the crime which ultimately led to the dramatic downfall and ruin of the SIU. It all started—and ended— with the "French Connection." It is the story of a crime which has never been solved. Until now.

It is also the most intimate and illuminating report about the men and women of the SIU and the NYPD Narcotics Division to date. This author is not a curious outsider looking in. He *was* inside. He did not need to search for clues, he did not need to retain a coach to teach him "cop-ese." He knows how police officers talk, what they feel. He knows because he *was* a cop. He worked undercover in the most dangerous neighborhoods of Knee-Jerk-City. He did not need to track down witnesses and rummage through archives and dusty administration folders. He only had to recount, recall faces and events forever burned in his memory preventing distortion or oblivion. He knows the territory and the players. They were his friends, his partners. He was an SIU detective, one of the chosen, one of the "hunters," a "prince of the city." When the principality built on the shifting sands of hubris collapsed, he was nearly buried, but escaped, untarnished. Looking back fills him with pride and torments him with pain. *Honor for Sale* is also his story, told in his own words.

The Story

Jerry Lynch crouched in the basement of a six-story apartment building in Queens. The SIU detective was changing the tape on a wiretap monitoring Vincent Capra's home phone. Two months earlier, he had received a tip from a reliable source: "Capra is doing heavy drugs with a group of guineas from the Bronx." For the last six weeks, Lynch and his team had conducted an unauthorized and illegal wiretap surveillance of the reputed mobster.

The tape recorder was hidden in the corner of a utility room near an unbelievably putrid garbage compactor. A large rat colony infested the area. The aggressive rodents intimidated the detectives so much that one day an unnerved Lynch showed up with a borrowed Irish Terrier in tow. He shrieked each time the fierce little dog snapped a rat's spine; it killed eleven beasts in two hours. In gratitude, Lynch ran out of the basement and bought two pounds of rare roast beef for the dog in a nearby delicatessen. The moment the terrier smelled the meat, it bit Lynch in the ankle. Lynch pulled out his blackjack and smashed the dog's skull.

After reviewing the tape, a frustrated Lynch called his boss at home. Within the hour, Lieutenant Pat Beninati pulled up in front of the building. When Lynch opened the door, Beninati gagged. "Holy Mother of God, Jerry. It smells worse than month-old shit down here."

"This is nothing. Wait till you come to this place after a weekend," Lynch muttered.

He stepped back and let his superior enter the room. Shocked, Beninati jumped. "You Irish cocksucker. Look at all these stinking rats!"

Lynch laughed. "You should have been here an hour ago when they tried to eat me."

"How did you get them?"

"I strangled them."

Beninati suddenly recoiled and pointed across the room. "Jerry, look at the size of that rat in the corner! That's a monster."

"That's a dog," Lynch answered.

"A dog? The rats got a dog?"

"You had to be here. The little prick put up some fight."

Lynch picked up a broken broomstick, put it against the side of a dead rat lying in the middle of the floor and propelled it across the room. Tossing away the stick, Lynch removed the empty tissue box covering the tape recorder. "Lieutenant, check it out yourself. It's a complete waste of time."

"Then forget it, Jerry. What's the big deal? You've got plenty of cases."

Lynch stared at the recorder. "It's just that I know this bastard is moving a lot of shit, and I want to get him."

Lynch and the lieutenant left the building and drove to the Neptune Diner on Thirty-first Street and Astoria Boulevard. After both ordered sandwiches, Lynch picked up the topic again. "Loo, this is one cute scumbag. Not only does he stay off the phone, but he drives with his head in the rearview mirror. He's impossible to follow."

"Forget it, Jerry. It's over. If we had time and money like the Feds, we could wait him out and slap him with a conspiracy."

Lynch leaned back in his chair, lit a cigar and while fanning the smoke away with one hand, his face lit up with a big grin. "That's not a bad idea, Loo. As a matter of fact, I think it's a great idea."

"What's a great idea?"

"Let's jump Capra. Tell him we have a conspiracy on him. That we're going to lock his ass up unless he comes across with some bread."

Beninati frowned. "I don't know, Jerry. It could be tricky."

"Lieutenant, six weeks in this rotten rat hole. All for nothing? I say we do it."

Beninati sipped his coffee and smiled at Lynch. "How stupid of me. I must have lost my mind. For a minute I thought I was the boss. I don't know what came over me." He paused, slapped mustard on the mountain of hot pastrami in front of him. "Go for it."

"Loo, I'm not going for it with the kids I work with, Cascio and Keaveney. They just came up from the field. I barely know them. I'll need some heavy-duty backup. And since you just made me boss, I'm taking you with me."

Jerry Lynch was a paunchy six-footer. Physically out of shape, but not soft, he was a powerfully built man. One of the first things that impressed an observer was the fact that Lynch wore a twenty-inch collar. He was a two-fisted drinker, yet never seemed completely be-fuddled. He was melonheaded, balding, with small rheumy light-blue eyes, a veined, rummy nose, tobacco-stained teeth and an unhealthy pallor. A sloppy dresser, he looked like he slept in his rumpled clothes. Lynch chewed on cigars while smoking them. He constantly spat brown globs of tobacco juice, and he wasn't too particular where the mess landed. If someone had the misfortune to sit near him, he would place the hot end of his cigar near the back of the person's hand until he jumped from the shock of heat. Lynch laughingly called it his "attention-getter."

In contrast to Lynch's proletarian attire, clothes were Lieutenant Beninati's trademark. A sharp, preppy dresser, he wore fingertip-length leather jackets, always over a shirt and tie. His shoes were always polished to a high gloss. He was fastidious about his appearance; he never had a hair out of place. He was ruggedly handsome, with sky-blue eyes, of medium height, and strongly built. Second-in-command of the SIU and very sharp, he would consider any deal that might line his pocket.

LATE THE FOLLOWING EVENING, LYNCH met Beninati at the Astoria Diner. After a quick cup of coffee, they drove to Capra's home. It was a middle-class house, in a middle-class neighborhood, complete with a middle-class wife inside. Everything was middle-class about it except its owner.

Vincent Capra was a fifty-six-year-old, gray-haired tire company pro-prietor, who could always be trusted to keep his mouth shut. His bottom line was, "My word is my bond." He had nineteen arrests and three narcotics convictions on his record, and was known by local and Fed-eral cops as a "standup guy." A prosecutor who had once indicted him recalled: "Capra was a sweetheart of a guy. He wasn't a drinker and he didn't cheat on his wife the way most of those guys do. His only problem is that every once in awhile he would import between fifty and one hundred kilos of heroin."

The almost-perfect model citizen kept a low profile, an attribute which endeared him to his Mafia trading partners. Capra had two passions in life: his home and the Astoria Colts Social Club, which was located in an unobtrusive-looking building a few minutes away. He spent a great deal of time in both places. At the club, as at home, Capra was lord of all he surveyed. Any deal of consequence required his personal blessing. Capra had rules which were followed to the letter, without question.

Not spotting Capra's Oldsmobile in front of his house, Lynch and Beninati drove directly to the Astoria Colts Social Club. Capra's car was double-parked. Lynch and Beninati positioned themselves a block away and waited patiently for their man to come out. At 3:30 A.M., Capra appeared in the doorway, a light vicuna overcoat draped over his shoulders. After shaking hands with two men the detectives did not recognize, Capra drove off alone. Three blocks from his home, he stopped for a red light. It was all the opportunity Lynch needed. He swiftly pulled his car alongside Capra's vehicle on the driver's side.

"Police. Pull over." Beninati flashed his gold shield.

Capra looked mildly annoyed. "Whadda I do, officer?"

Alert for a possible hit, Capra clutched the .38 calibre revolver he kept next to him on the passenger seat. "Wait a minute. How do I know you're cops? Anybody could have a badge."

Lynch slid over into the passenger seat that Beninati had vacated. Leaning forward so that Capra could see his face, Lynch pointed his revolver at Capra's head. "Hey, fucko, do I look like some guinea hit man?"

Capra said calmly, "You could be one of those Irish hit men. A no-good Westie."

Lynch laughed, "Well, if I was a Westie, it'd be too late for your guinea ass. My friend on the other side would have already put a hole in your head."

Capra hesitated, then smiled faintly. "OK, I believe you're cops. What'd I do wrong?"After Lieutenant Beninati searched Capra and confiscated his weapon, he ordered him into the back of Lynch's car and got in beside him. The detectives left Capra's Oldsmobile parked on the street and drove down a quiet side street.

Capra watched in silent amusement as Lynch continually checked the rearview mirror to see if they were being followed. Ten blocks away from the club, Lynch pulled over and parked.

Lynch half turned around and mockingly said, "Vinnie, we got some ba-a-a-d news for you. You've been moving some big packages."

"Not me. You've got the wrong guy."

"Bullshit. We've got it all here," said Lynch, holding up a couple of tapes. "We've been sitting on your house and the club for months. I'm meeting with the Feds next Tuesday and we're going to put a waterproof Conspiracy on you."

"Then why all this show? Just lock me up."

Lynch tried to move his torso around to get a better look at Capra, but it hurt his side, and he muttered, "Got to loose some weight." He got out of the car and climbed back in the driver's seat, kneeling and facing Capra. "Vinnie, like I said, we've been on you for months. We've listened to you night and day. You're moving big shit."

Capra smirked. "I ain't moving shit and I know you've got nothing on me."

Lynch grimaced and slapped Capra lightly in the face. "Let me finish, willya?"

Capra sat back, unfazed. "Go ahead." He knew where this was going; it was not the first time he had been shaken down.

Lynch spat a wad of phlegm out the open window and wiped his chin with the back of his hand. "Look, Capra, we've gotten to know you. We like you. We think you're a square shooter."

"What does that mean?"

"It means if you want to talk business with us, we'll talk business. If you want us to give you ten in the can for conspiracy to sell narcotics, we'll give you ten in the can."

"Plus the pound you'll do for the gun," Beninati interjected.

"How much?" Capra asked icily.

"Fifty large," Beninati replied.

Capra shook his head from side to side. "No good. Twenty-five."

Beninati bargained. "Forty."

Capra again shook his head. "Twenty-five."

Beninati shot back, "When?"

"Drive me back to my car. Give me an hour and meet me back here." Lynch growled, "Capra, if you try to fuck us, you're one dead guinea, so help me God!"

"Hey, I'm not going to screw you. But I do know I'm getting screwed. I figure it this way: I might need your help someday, and you'll earn the twenty-five. You can never be too sure about these things. Maybe one day, you'll see my name on a report or hear someone ratting on me. Then, you let me know. OK?"

Lynch shook Capra's hand. "You've got a deal, Vinnie."

The two SIU men drove Capra back to his car and watched him drive off. As soon as he was out of sight, they raced back to the basement where the recorder was still installed. "Better safe than sorry, lieutenant. Let's make sure he doesn't call anyone. We'll sit on him until he leaves," Lynch said.

Just as a large gray rat sniffed its way across the room, the voice-activated recorder came alive. Capra's voice was loud and clear. "Gentlemen, I'm leaving the house now. Don't keep me waiting." The machine clicked off.

Lynch threw back his head and laughed, "Hey, Lieutenant, this is one sharp sonofabitch. I'd love to have him as a partner."

AT 7:02 THAT MORNING, BENINATI was sound asleep when his telephone rang. His wife stirred as he reached out for the end table and fumbled for the phone.

Vincent Catalano, a narcotics detective with the Group Three Field Team, was on the other end. "Lieutenant, it's important that I see you and Lynch this morning."

Beninati immediately sat up. "Is there a problem, Vinnie?"

"No. No problem. I just want to talk to you about a mutual friend. You met him last night with Ugly."

Beninati looked at his watch. "Why don't we meet at the Olympic Diner at 9:30?"

He grimaced when Catalano responded, "That's a good spot. For a minute I thought you were going to say we should meet in front of the Astoria Colts Club."

*   *   *

VINCENT CATALANO WAS A SHORT, muscular, second-generation Italian-American cop. Though his parents spoke perfect English, Catalano affected a thick Italian accent. He also enjoyed the reputation of being one mean tough guy. When Catalano worked Harlem, he delighted in meting out his own personal justice to blacks, which he justified by saying, "Who gives a fuck? They're only dumb, ugly apes."

Like many white cops of his day, Catalano loved hurting blacks. While a rookie patrolman in Harlem, he spotted a black drunk helplessly sprawled on the sidewalk. Catalano got out of his patrol car and jumped repeatedly on the man's leg until it snapped. He left the man writhing and screaming in agony.

On another occasion, a petite black female waitress in a diner put a check in front of a uniformed Catalano, who brushed it off the counter with, "Hey, nigger, cops don't pay here." The waitress picked up the check and put it near his empty coffee cup. Catalano punched her viciously in the mouth, shattering several of her teeth. During the departmental hearing that followed, he maintained, "I was trying to swat a fly out of the air when the woman jumped in front of my hand."

Catalano could afford to march to the beat of a brutal drummer. His uncle, also named Vincent Catalano, was the influential Manhattan Republican Party Chairman, riding the wave of a Republican resurgence in this heavily Democratic city. Indeed, it was Vincent Catalano who guided candidate John Lindsay's successful mayoral campaign. After Lindsay swept into office, Catalano the cop basked in his uncle's success, and he made sure everyone was aware of the family relationship.

I GOT IT." THE WAITRESS slid the order check under the plastic ketchup bottle. "Bacon and eggs over easy. I'll get you your coffee."

Promptly at 9:30 A.M., a disheveled and tired-looking Lynch and Beninati met Catalano. They sat in a booth at the rear of the restaurant. After the waitress took their order Beninati asked, "What's up, Vincent?"

Catalano smiled and inquired sarcastically, "Was that you who jumped my good friend Vincent Capra last night?"

"Yeah. What about it?" Lynch snarled.

"He's good people, that's what about it. Real good people. He's curious to know if you guys are good people too."

"We are!" Lynch said.

Catalano sneered. "Yeah, $25,000 worth."

Beninati waited until the waitress finished pouring coffee before speaking. "Vincent, if we had known Capra was with you, we wouldn't have bothered him. You know that."

"I don't know that, but what's done is done. He expects for that kind of money, you'll watch out for his ass in SIU."

"Tell him not to worry. We will."

"Good. He'll be glad to hear that." Catalano ripped the paper off two cubes of sugar. "I also want to talk to you guys about something else. As I said to you before, Capra is good people. I swear to you, the best. A stand-up guy. You understand?"

"We understand," Lynch and Beninati answered in unison. Both men waited for Catalano to drop the other shoe.

"I'll get right to the point with you guys. I've laid down a couple of packages with Capra. He's very good people. As you know, he never speaks on the phone. He knows cops sit on him and listen in on his calls. So what I'm saying is, if you guys ever got some shit and want to get rid of it, let me know. This is one beautiful man. Whatever you get, he can handle. Big or little. Understand?" Beninati and Lynch nodded in agreement. Catalano sipped his coffee. "Should I tell him we have a deal?"

Beninati reached across the table and shook Catalano's hand. "Tell him we have a deal, and that we'll watch out for him in SIU."

Mid-January 1969

THIS IS BULLSHIT. PURE, UNADULTERATED bullshit!" The five detectives gathered in the SIU office stared at Lieutenant Beninati in disbelief. "Transferred. To Homicide. Can you believe this shit?" He glared at Captain Hughes's office. "That rotten motherfucker hasn't got the balls to tell me like a man. He makes them send me paper. God-damn him!"

Later that afternoon, Beninati composed himself and confronted Captain Hughes. "Why, Captain? Why are you transferring me?"

"Because I want my own man. I've known Lieutenant Ryan for years."

"But why didn't you tell me?"

"Because I didn't want you in here every day trying to change my mind."

"What's the real reason? I worked hard for this unit."

Hughes looked Beninati in the eye. "Lieutenant, besides the fact that I don't like you personally, I know this unit is corrupt. I'm going to clean it up. I've heard lots of things about a lot of people around here, including you, lieutenant. I've only been here a short time and I hear it, constantly. You've been here a long time but you don't seem to hear ever. If I was you, Lieutenant, I'd consider myself fortunate. In fact, you're one lucky son of a bitch. In another unit, your ass would probably be carted off to jail. Now get out of my office before I really get pissed off."

There was no going-away party for Beninati, as was the custom when someone of his stature was transferred. He was in no mood for one anyway after his encounter with Hughes. He cleaned out his desk unceremoniously and two friends helped carry his personal effects to his car. A number of detectives who had been out in the field when news of Beninati's transfer broke gathered in the office to wish him good luck. All the senior detectives were there—Bob Bucci, Carl Redmond, Drew Belfry, Jack McDuff, Joe Novack, Carl Ramos, Joe Graziano, and Jerry Lynch.

The men lined up to say good-bye. Beninati hugged each of them as he went down the line. Embracing Lynch he whispered, "Meet me tonight and bring Joe."

Captain Hughes and his new "whip," Lieutenant John Ryan, a thirty-three-year NYPD veteran with a shock of white hair and Santa Claus-rosy cheeks, observed the ceremony from Hughes's office behind half-drawn venetian blinds. Hughes said quietly, "Watch those last two, lieutenant. Lynch and Graziano are bad."

Beninati stood in the middle of the detectives' room and seethed as Ryan walked into his former office. Ryan sensed Beninati watching him, but when he looked out into the detectives' room after seating himself behind the desk, Beninati had vanished.

Ryan shoved aside the stack of daily team reports on his desk, leaned back in his chair, crossed both hands behind his head and stared at the ceiling. " 'Watch Lynch and Graziano,' he says. He isn't fit to carry their jockstraps," he thought.

RYAN HAD FIRST HEARD OF Joe Graziano when he worked at the Chief of Detectives' office several years earlier. Graziano, then a mounted cop, had been involved in a shootout with three suspects in lower Manhattan. He killed one, but was shot once in the arm and once in the thigh, and his horse, "Say Hey," named in honor of Graziano's baseball idol "Say Hey" Willie Mays, was shot twice and died.

A couple of days after the incident Inspector Warren Creighton and Chief Walter Crane asked Ryan to drive them to the piers at West Twenty-third Street. When they arrived, about 100 men, in and out of uniform, cops to captains, waited in line to board a boat to shuttle them to a barge anchored in the middle of the Hudson River. Captain Alexander Symington of the Mounted Patrol welcomed them onto the barge. "I thought you'd want to be here."

"Thank you." Chief Crane shook Symington's hand and surveyed the scene, "Where's Stephen?" He was referring to his son, who was assigned to the mounted police.

"He's getting Graziano."

"I thought Graziano wasn't supposed to get out of the hospital till the end of the week."

"That's correct, chief. They're just borrowing him for a couple of hours."

Crane smiled, then turned serious. "Captain, if it wasn't for Graziano, Stephen wouldn't be here today."

Symington bristled, "Have you forgotten, chief? Cops do that for cops."

A couple of months before Graziano was shot, a deranged man had attacked Sergeant Crane while he was eating dinner in a midtown restaurant and held a gun to his head, threatening to kill "the fucking cop." Graziano, on patrol nearby, was alarmed by screaming patrons running onto the street. He got off his horse, ripped off his helmet and uniform jacket and donned an onlooker's overcoat. He then walked coolly into the restaurant. Getting within seven feet of the gunman he shot the assailant three times in the head.

Captain Symington turned and saluted when Graziano, visibly in pain, was helped by Sergeant Crane and two other officers off a small launch onto the barge, where by now several hundred cops of all ranks stood at attention.

"Are you guys crazy?" Graziano's eyes moistened. "You'll all get in trouble for this."

Symington raised his arm and several members of the Emerald Society bagpipers marched forward with bagpipes blaring, followed by sixteen officers holding a taut tarpaulin which supported Graziano's dead horse. Graziano, tears now running down his face, haltingly walked over and kissed his horse. He then turned and saluted the officers. Sergeant Fernandez of the Forty-first Precinct blew "Taps" as "Say Hey" was slowly lowered into the Hudson River.

Chief Crane hugged Graziano and informed him that the Police Commissioner had promoted him to Detective Third Grade and that he would be assigned to Narcotics as soon as he was well.

THAT NIGHT, HUGHES EMBARKED ON his reign of terror. He called an 8:00 P.M. meeting, attendance mandatory. To a man, the entire SIU unit assembled in the Detectives' Room. Hughes stood atop an old wooden desk.

"I can smell you people. You stink. You're rotten. Corrupt."

He paused several seconds for effect. "The games stop tonight. As of now, if I hear of anyone doing anything illegal, I'm going to lock them up personally. If you think I'm bullshitting, try me. One out-of-line step and you're history. If you even look wrong, you're going to jail. Understand? With the scumbags you put away after you robbed them. And when you get there, I'm going to help the scumbags lay out the welcome mat for you. Get the picture?" Hughes jumped to the floor and walked through the crowd. "By the end of the week, I will have reviewed all team cases. I'm also going to review the dossier of every member in this unit. Expect changes. Radical changes. Any questions?"

The men stared at him silently. Murderously.

After Hughes's blustery declaration of war, Lynch and Graziano set off for Beninati's home. Graziano was the consummate detective. In his mid-thirties, tall, well-built and movie-star handsome, he commanded attention merely by walking into a room. He had earned the reputation of being entirely trustworthy and loyal to a fault. Hardened veteran cops and rookies alike were eager to be associated with him. Graziano exuded confidence. He was an excellent investigator, one of the SIU's golden boys.

As Lynch drove uptown towards the Battery Tunnel, he used the dashboard lighter to fire up his cigar and asked, "What did you think of the jerk, Joe?"

"He's a grandstanding moron. A loudmouthed clown. He hasn't even found the shithouse yet, and he has the balls to tell us how he's going to run the place." Graziano opened the window a couple of inches and fanned the air. "How the hell can you smoke those things?"

"Men smoke cigars. Pussies like you smoke cigarettes." Graziano ignored the playful barb as Lynch tailgated a Cadillac limousine into the tunnel.

"What's your opinion of Hughes, Jerry?"

"He could be dangerous. He's a vindictive prick. Look what he did to Pat."

"I agree. Did you see the way he eyeballed us tonight when he said he knows some guys are scoring people?"

"Don't get paranoid, Joe. Everyone must have thought he was looking at them. How are you going to play it?"

"I'm going to ignore him. I'm going to sit on my hands just like I've been doing the past couple of months. I'm not going to make any arrests. Sooner or later, he's going to get heat from the PC's office."

"How long you figure before the Chief jumps on his ass?"

"A month or two. They'll straighten him out. They'll miss their money." Lynch shook his head. "It's a goddamn shame Beninati had to take a beating on account of this guy."

"You're right. Incidentally, what's with the Lieutenant tonight? Why does he want to see us?"

"As luck would have it, Loo and I scored a wiseguy a couple of nights ago. Turns out he's good people and can move a lot of shit. So Loo's going to tell you if you get stuff, we can move it for you. Act surprised when he brings the subject up. If he ever thought you and me moved packages before, he'd shit himself. At the very least, he'd want his share ipso facto. Whatever ipso facto means."

IN THE PAST, GRAZIANO AND Lynch had moved small packages of heroin and cocaine through Conrad Green, a Jamaican, who was the owner of the Sky Room nightclub in East Elmhurst, Queens. From the beginning, Lynch didn't like dealing with Green because he was uneasy about Green's relationship with many of the club's white female patrons. "This spear chucker thinks he's one of us. He doesn't want to know any of his own. That bothers me. The only reason I let you deal with this nigger is because we haven't got a choice."

Once when Graziano was about to bring cocaine into the club, Lynch grabbed his arm. "I'm going inside with you. I want to talk to him. I want him to know if he ever mentions he's doing business with us, I'll blow his club up."

"Jerry, calm down. He's never said anything. He's good people."

"I want to make sure he stays that way. I want him to know if he ever says anything, I'll kill his fuckin' kids."

Graziano teased, "He won't give a shit. He doesn't have any kids."

"Come on, Joe. All niggers have kids. They're born with kids, for Christ's sake. Why do you think there's so many of them? And if it happens Green is that one nigger in a zillion who doesn't have a kid, I'm going to adopt him one, wait until he has it tree-trained, and then I'm going to whack it." Both men burst into laughter.

BENINATI LED LYNCH AND GRAZIANO into his spacious kitchen and said they wouldn't be disturbed, as his wife and kids were at the movies. He opened the refrigerator and removed three bottles of Budweiser. After handing a bottle to Graziano, Beninati apologized. "Joe, I hate to be rude, but I need to spend a minute with Jerry."

"No problem. I'll help myself if I want anything." Beninati and Lynch held a quick conversation in the living room and returned to the kitchen.

"Joe, sorry, but I had to clear it with Jerry one more time. He agreed we could talk about it."

"What's it about?" said Graziano, feigning agitation.

"Don't get nervous, Joe. It's nothing bad."

"Unnerve me then, Lieutenant."

"A few days ago, Jerry and I scored a guinea. A good guinea, a stand-up guy. We've bullshitted with him a couple of times since, and he says he can move packages for us. I trust him. So what it boils down to is this: if you ever grab any shit, we can move it for you."

"That's good to know."

Beninati continued, "To be honest, Joe, Jerry and I never moved shit before. Even before the Feds nailed Ignesi and Hurley, I always made sure I stayed straight and narrow as far as selling drugs."

"Same as me, Loo. But just for curiosity's sake, how much can this guy do?"

"Ten, maybe twenty keys."

"Probably more," Lynch offered.

"Why don't you guys find out for sure what he can do?" Graziano went over to the refrigerator and took out another beer. He raised the bottle and said in a flawless Irish brogue, "Who knows? Maybe we can do business, me lads."

THREE DAYS AFTER THAT EVENING, Graziano invited Robert Bucci to dinner at Stella's Restaurant in Rego Park, Queens. Cherub-faced Bucci, a fellow SIU detective, owed his entry into the upper class of New York's narcotics cops to a recommendation by Graziano. Respected by his peers, he had the reputation of being smart, a tough cookie—resourceful and reliable.

Bucci sat down opposite Graziano. "What's a-matter, do we have a problem, Joe?"

"No problem."

"Then why did you call me?"

Graziano laughed. "Can't a guy call his best friend and invite him to dinner?"

"Stop playing games, Joe. Why'd you want to see me?"

"Have patience." Graziano sipped his Dewar's and soda. "All right since you want me to come right to the point, I will. I want us to steal the 'French Connection.' "

Bucci became angry "Steal what? 'The French Connection'? Are you crazy?"

"It'd be easy."

"Joe, you've finally flipped!"

"Hear me out, Bob . . ."

"No. I'm not going to hear you out." Bucci stood up and stepped around to Graziano's seat. Aware that patrons were watching him, he knelt on the floor and pressed his nose against the side of Graziano's cheek. His lips no more than a half inch from Graziano's ear, he whispered, "Joe, I don't ever want you to bring up the subject again. There's no way I would do that. Selling an ounce or two is one thing, stealing a hundred pounds of shit is another. Can you imagine what would happen if we got caught? They'd hang us up by our pricks!"

"Robert . . ."

"Don't 'Robert' me. I don't want to hear it." Bucci returned to his seat and acknowledged several amused diners by waving his hand.

Graziano's expression never changed. "Give it some thought."

"No."

"Please. I can get rid of it right away."

"No!"

"Please, just give it some thought, that's all I ask," Graziano pleaded.

"All right. I'll give it some thought, if it makes you happy, but I'll never do it. I'm on the record."

"That's all I wanted to hear." Graziano giggled and rubbed his hands together gleefully. "Bob, it's a cinch. I'll put it all together."

"Bullshit. If it was a cinch, it would have been stolen a long time ago."

"That's the only thing that bothers me. Maybe it has been," Graziano said, his smile fading.

Mid-February 1969

GRAZIANO'S TEAM SCORED A MAJOR package. They hit a bodega in the South Bronx, pocketed twenty-eight thousand dollars, and confiscated four kilos of heroin. Graziano explained to his partners, Carrera and McDuff, that he could move the package, but he refused to tell them who he was going to move it through. McDuff said, "Partners tell partners everything. There are no secrets."

"Sorry, but that's the way it has to be."

"Joe, for the record, I don't like it one bit."

"I don't like it either, but I gave my word."

Initially, Graziano had considered using Conrad Green. But the more he thought about it, the more attractive the alternative of using Lynch and Beninati's new buyer appeared to him. Graziano reasoned Green was good for small packages, but wasn't sure if he could handle a package this size. Graziano also wanted to see if Lynch and Beninati could deliver.

LYNCH SLID INTO THE PASSENGER side of Graziano's car. He adjusted the rearview mirror and looked at what was left of his hair. He licked his hand and tried to flatten his hair down. "You wanted to see me?"

Graziano smiled. "I got four keys of H for sale."

"Beautiful."

Graziano asked impishly, "How much?"

Lynch fidgeted for a second. "I figure nine or ten a key."

Graziano laughed out loud. "Are you kidding me? I got two partners. We need at least thirteen. We should be getting fifteen. For nine or ten, I'd rather dump the shit on 125th Street and let the jigs party."

"Wait, Joe. Listen. Loo and I have to make a few bucks too. How about taking eleven?"

Graziano waved his hand at Lynch in disgust. "No way. Thirteen."

Lynch sighed, "All right. We'll get you twelve."

Graziano smiled. "That's a lot better than nine or ten."

Lynch extended his hand towards Graziano and they shook hands. "All right, we have a deal then, Joe. But I hope you kept up your end."

"What's that?"

"That you didn't tell that Irish harpie McDuff that you were doing business with me. I hate that fag douchebag."

"I swear I never said a word. And, believe me, if McDuff ever knew I was selling the shit to you, he'd go nuts."

Lynch grimaced. "I don't know how you can work with that prick after he tried to hold out on us."

Graziano's eyes dropped defensively. "Jerry, Jack isn't really bad people. He made a mistake. Anyway, you cost him $1,100 in dental bills when you punched him in the mouth."

"Joe, you can't trust him. How can you forget that he tried to hold out $10,000 on us? If you died tomorrow, he'd pick your pockets clean while you were on your way to the morgue. Your other partner, Carrera, is a gentleman. I don't know how you guys can stand that donkey McDuff."

"I can't believe what I'm hearing, Jerry. McDuff always speaks so well of you."

Lynch smirked. "Sure he does. I'd take book on that. But if you don't mind, let's change the subject. The thought of that fag turns my stomach." Lynch rapped on the windshield and waved at two parochial school teenagers walking in front of the car. "Jesus, that's nice. And with brand new tits."

Graziano grimaced. "You're sick."

"That's prime stuff." The girls returned Lynch's wave. "See."

"You are one perverse son of a bitch. Now, what's the story with your man?"

"There's no story. He says he can handle a hundred keys. Easy. All he needs is a couple of weeks' notice."

"Notice? Where does he want me to keep the shit in the meantime? In my desk?"

"I know, I know. I'm just saying if you get the chance, give us some notice."

Lynch got out of Graziano's car. When the door slammed, Graziano leaned over, rolled down the window and yelled, "Notice! Wait till McDuff hears your guinea wants notice."

"Get lost," Lynch screamed back, kicking the side of Graziano's car as it sped away. Lynch stood in the middle of the street and laughed, then lit a cigar.

February 23, 1969

CAPTAIN HUGHES AND HIS ATTRACTIVE subordinate, Brogan Conner, one of the few female detectives in the SIU, followed the four men down the unlit stairs of a Brooklyn apartment building and trailed them outside to the garbage-strewn street. At a double-parked car, they waited impatiently as Detectives Richie Belfry and Doug Redmond guided the handcuffed prisoners into the backseat.

After Redmond slammed the door shut, Captain Hughes approached him. "There's no need for Brogan to go to the precinct. You guys can handle this."

As Belfry and Redmond drove away down the darkened street with the two arrested drug dealers, Conner embraced Hughes from behind, kissed the back of his neck and whispered, "I'm horny as hell."

Back at Brogan's apartment, the fevered couple made love deep into the night. As the early morning sun peeked through the venetian blinds, they embraced and went to sleep. Pigeons cooed on the window-sill.

LATER THAT MORNING, A WHISTLING Hughes sauntered into the SIU office. Bernie McClellan, the freckled, red-haired clerical man, looked up from his desk and shouted, "Captain! Jesus, am I glad you're here. Inspector Creighton and your wife have been trying to reach you all morning!"

"My wife! Why would she call? I told her I'd be working all night and wouldn't be in the office till noon."

McClellan looked at Hughes sheepishly. "After the Inspector called, I tried to reach you at home. Your wife said you were working and she wanted to know how come I didn't know that? Then she suggested I try to reach you at Conner's."

"Shit!"

"She's been calling all morning, sir."

"Shit again!"

Hughes went into his office and called home. After a heated

exchange, he banged down the phone and was startled when it rang immediately. It was Deputy Inspector Creighton.

"Where for Christ's sake have you been, Dan?" I've been trying to reach you for hours. I'm here with Inspector McLoughlin. We want to see you right away."

ON THE FOURTH FLOOR OF Police Headquarters, Hughes was promptly ushered into Deputy Inspector Creighton's office by a uniformed sergeant. Deputy Chief Inspector McLoughlin of the Police Commissioner's Office was seated across from Creighton. Both men stood up and shook hands with Hughes. Creighton said, "Have a seat, Dan."

After sitting down, an apprehensive Hughes asked Creighton, "Is there anything wrong, Inspector?"

"Dan, I'll come right to the point. You've got all of SIU jittery. They don't trust you. They think you'd lock them up if you got a chance. Morale stinks. Arrests are way down. Seizures compared to two months ago are off seventy-five percent. And we haven't seen a single dime in months."

"Well, almost nothing" mused McLoughlin. "Thank God, Ryan's up there. He's given us a little taste."

Creighton intervened. "Dan, $1,200 from Ryan in two months ain't gonna cut it. The guys here miss their taste and they're getting antsy. If the well stays dry, they are going to get nasty. When you bounced Beninati, we let it go through because we thought you had a hard-on for the guy. To be honest, we didn't like the guinea either. But he was good for $20,000 a month. Now, it's zilch."

Beads of perspiration appeared on Hughes's forehead. His lips moved soundlessly. Then he blurted, "I didn't know. I misunderstood."

McLoughlin got up and walked over to Hughes. "Come on, Dan. You're a big boy."

"I wasn't sure. I thought after the Feds got Hurley and Ignesi, everything was on hold."

"Dan, nothing's on hold."

"I'll take care of everything right away." Hughes jumped to his feet. "As a matter of fact, I've got a great idea. Why don't we bring back Beninati?"

Creighton shook his head. "That's impossible, Dan. Once you're out of SIU, you're out. Anyway, we don't need Beninati."

"I'll straighten everything out."

"That won't be necessary, Dan. The men don't trust you. Ryan will straighten them out. He knows what to do. Most of the men already trust him. As a matter of fact, several of them have already approached him about doing a little business."

Hughes sat down. "What are you saying, that you want me to sit in my office all day and let Ryan run the whole show?"

Creighton laughed, "No, that's not what we're saying. We've got a better idea than that." Creighton extended his hand. "Congratulations, captain."

Hughes looked suspiciously at Creighton, but put out his hand.

"Congratulations for what?"

"Dan, you've been selected by Chief Crane and the PC to represent the Department at the FBI Academy in Quantico, Virginia."

"What are you talking about?"

"The PC wants you to go to the new FBI school in Virginia," Creighton said more slowly.

"When?"

"Immediately. It's a six-month course."

"A six-month course at the FBI Academy? That's bullshit!"

Creighton laughed. "Dan, it's not bull, and don't get in such a huff. You're not joining the FBI, for Christ's sake. You're just going to go through their academy. They've invited the Commissioner to send down his best man from the department to attend, and he's chosen you. It's a first."

"I don't want to go."

"You *have* to go."

"What about SIU? I just got there. I don't want to leave."

Creighton shook his head. "You're not leaving SIU forever. You'll be back there in six months."

"You're kicking me out of SIU, aren't you?" Hughes said.

Creighton again laughed. "Nothing could be further from the truth. When you finish the academy, it'll be a feather in your cap. The first New York police official to ever attend the FBI Academy!"

"Who's taking my place in SIU? Ryan?"

McLoughlin spoke up. "Nobody's taking your place. Ryan will run SIU in your absence. When you're done in Quantico, you'll be put back into SIU. The FBI thing is only a temporary transfer."

"You just said nobody gets back into SIU."

"That's if you're permanently transferred. Yours is a temporary assignment."

McLoughlin walked over and put his arm around Hughes. "Dan, this is about the long run. Your career. The PC has tons of captains ahead of you waiting to be promoted. If you do the FBI thing, it'll give him something to hang his hat on when he promotes you to DI. Here's his plan. Six months at the academy. Six months back in SIU. Six months in a precinct. And whacko, you're a Deputy Inspector."

Hughes laughed. "That's 'presto' chief."

McLoughlin gave Hughes a blank look. "Huh?"

"Nothing, chief."

McLoughlin shook Hughes's hand. "Good luck, Dan." Creighton and McLoughlin turned and started towards the door. Suddenly Creighton stopped. "Incidentally, we've instructed Ryan to tell the men you're really good people, and he's been told to hold out a full share for you while you're gone. This way you'll be earning while you're at the FBI Academy. Now go give Brogan a hug and kiss from me and then go home to your wife."

"Sir, I'm not doing anything with Brogan," Hughes blurted out too quickly.

McLoughlin held the door open for Hughes, and sighed after the captain had left.

"I wish I were screwing Brogan Conner. Those long legs must lead to heaven."

March 10, 1969

GRAZIANO MET BUCCI AT THE Part I Bar and Grill in Forest Hills, Queens, for lunch. It was cold; the wind chill factor pushed the temperature down towards zero. Bucci, who couldn't find a parking place near the restaurant, was half-frozen when he pushed open the front door.

Graziano, standing at the bar across from a smooching middle-aged couple, laughed as he watched Bucci gingerly stomp his feet on the floor. "Bob, if you don't start wearing the right clothes, you're going to freeze to death."

Bucci rubbed his hands together and followed his friend to the dining area. "Don't worry about me freezing to death. You're going to give me a heart attack if you don't stop calling me in the middle of the night and telling me we have to meet. It scares the shit out of me."

"Come on, relax. If it was bad news I'd have let you know right away."

"So what's the good news?"

"First things first. Your lovely wife told me that she hates you being in Narcotics. She doesn't see you anymore."

Bucci waved his hand in disgust, "She drives me up the wall. That's all I hear, 'Get out of Narcotics, get out of Narcotics.' But she also loves her mink coat."

"I hear you bumped into Sonny Grosso at a party the other day. I haven't talked to him in ages. Are the rumors true? They're going to make a movie out of the book?"

"It looks that way. Sonny thinks that a deal is close. The lawyers just have to cross the T's and dot the I's."

"That's wonderful. I'm truly happy for him. For the jerk, I'm not so happy." They both smiled at Graziano's reference to Eddie Egan. "Well now, they'll be rich and famous."

"Maybe. But, you know, the movie people make most of the money."

"What kind of a deal did the guys make for themselves?"

"I don't know the details, but they're supposed to get $75,000 for the movie rights, plus be technical advisors. They've also been promised minor parts in the picture."

"Terrific. What about . . ."

"Joe, hold on a second. You didn't call me to talk about the movie. What's the story?"

Graziano chuckled, "Come on, superstar. You know why I called you. I'm ready to steal the 'French Connection'."

"Jesus Christ! I told you before I don't want any part of it. I can't believe you're for real!"

"Don't get yourself in an uproar. Calm down before you really do have a heart attack."

"You're the one that's going to give it to me!"

"You told me you would listen when I was ready."

"I was just joking."

"Whatever. Hear me out."

Bucci closed his eyes. "Go ahead."

"I got the guy who can handle it. He just moved four keys for me."

"Oh my God. You're crazy."

"I'm not crazy. We're crazy if we don't do it. The shit is waiting for us at the Property Clerk's office."

"Joe, you scare me. I don't want any part of it."

"All right. You don't have to be a part of it. Just calm down."

"I'll calm down when I'm good and ready!" "God knows, I owe you— and I am grateful. But sometimes you have to take no for an answer."

"Bob, I'm talking megabucks."

"Why don't you offer this once-in-a-lifetime opportunity to your partners Carrera and McDuff?"

"Because you know McDuff. When I say left, he says right. When I say white, he says black. When I say up, he says down. This job has to be like clockwork. Bam, bam, bam. I can't have somebody questioning every move I make."

The waitress served the soup. Two cups. New England clam chowder. Steaming hot.

Bucci covered his face with both hands. He did not move or say a word. A minute, two minutes, an eternity. Graziano did not dare to break the silence.

Finally Bucci put his hands on the table and lifted himself out of the chair. He looked down at Graziano. "You didn't listen to a word I said. I'll pray for you, Joe. Thanks for the invitation." Without looking back he walked out of the restaurant, shivering as a gust of icy wind hit him.

Graziano sat motionless for awhile, staring in his soup bowl. Then he smiled and thought, *I am going with the kid.*

March 12, 1969

THE PHONE RANG AS GRAZIANO was watching the Knicks play the Bullets on Channel 9, with less than a minute to go in the game.

He yelled, "Can you get that, honey?"

Anne Graziano covered the receiver, "It's a Detective Klyne. Are you home ?"

"It's the wrong time . . . but yap, I'll take it. Thanks." Graziano turned the volume down.

"Hey, kid. Hang on a few seconds. I want to see the end of this game." He moaned as Dave DeBusschere's shot at the buzzer hit the rim. "Now I'm with you, kid. How are things going? You got my message . . .

"Sorry I didn't call earlier, I was out for a few days."

"You ok?"

"I'm fine. I was in Boston for my sister's wedding."

"So you gained a few pounds."

"You bet, lots of corned beef . . . and pasta."

"What a combination . . ."

"She married an Italian."

"A good choice." Graziano reached for a bowl of popcorn which his wife had brought from the kitchen. "Klyne, I have to talk to you. Business."

"I can meet you in front of the First Precinct tomorrow morning."

"That's not the right place. We need some privacy."

"Do you want to come to my place? I'm in Woodside."

"Thanks, but why don't you come here? My wife makes the best gnocchi outside of Italy. Is tomorrow evening OK?"

"No problem."

"Get a pencil, I'll give you the address."

After he had hung up, Graziano surprised his wife with the news. "We have a guest for dinner tomorrow. Can you make some of your world famous gnocchi, or do you have some in the freezer?" Graziano added kiddingly.

Ann feigned annoyance. "Are you trying to insult me? Gnocchi out of the freezer? Not in this house. But who is coming? This . . . Klyne? Never heard of him."

"He's a young guy, twenty-four or twenty-five. Sharp . . . Was transferred to Narcotics a year ago. Works Harlem, Group Three. I'm thinking of getting him into SIU. I'd like to work with him."

*   *   *

GRAZIANO HAD BEEN INTRODUCED TO the young police officer Patrick Klyne at The Suite, a Queens hotspot, owned by the mobster Vincent Squillante. Among the many patrons were usually a dozen or so narcotics cops who partied deep into the night with female groupies who would do anything for a cop.

Patrick Klyne had the looks and the demeanor of the "boy next door," the species readily described as "the man every mother would like to have as a son-in-law." Rusty blond, brown eyes, about six feet, slim. A three-sports high school student. When, at the senior-year athletic banquet the team captains handed out little fun gifts to the players addressing their idiosyncrasies, they could not find anything typical for Klyne. "He is just so normal," his buddies conceded, and presented him with a Beach Boys record, showing how middle-of-the-road he was. But the boyish exterior camouflaged a steely energy and toughness.

Graziano and Klyne operated on different social levels. Graziano was the star detective, respected by his peers, admired, always the center of attention; Klyne was the rookie, an unknown quantity, "Klyne who?" He would not approach the elder, not talk to him until summoned.

The distance separating the two men shortened a bit after a brief episode at the Criminal Court on 100 Centre Street.

GRAZIANO HAD BUMPED INTO A distracted Klyne and his instincts, always on high alert, signaled him that something was wrong.

"Hey, kid, what's the matter?"

Klyne shook his head, "Nothing."

Graziano grabbed Klyne's arm, "I said, what's the matter?"

"Nothing."

Graziano leaned forward, his face now an inch from Klyne's. "Kid, if you don't tell me what the problem is, I'm going to kick you in the balls."

Klyne, with the expression of a penitent, started his confession. "I locked up a junkie a couple of months ago on 103rd and Central Park West with nine bags, but in my report I moved the arrest location to 111th and 8th Avenue, which is in Group Three. My group. You know how fussy they get when you make a collar outside your territory."

Graziano laughed, "And what's the problem?"

"Now we're going to trial and the nigger's lawyer is screaming to the judge that I perjured the complaint, and that he can prove it . . . I'm worried, man."

"Let me get this right, will ya?"

"OK."

"Who was there when you locked him up ?"

"Me and my two partners."

"Where was the nigger's lawyer standing while you were locking him up?"

Klyne shook his head and laughed. "He wasn't there."

"I know and all that shithead Jew lawyer knows is what his junkie tells him. Right? So get your ass back in court and wallop that nigger's ass."

PATRICK KLYNE HAD RECORDED THE scene and the successful turn of the trial (the judge dismissed the lawyer's motion) in his diary, which he had kept since he scored his first touchdown in high school. Now sitting on the kitchen table in his small bachelor's apartment, he scribbled in a new entry: "March 12. Graziano wants to see me. His Majesty himself. No idea what this is all about. Business ???"

Klyne closed the brown cardboard paperbound ledger, whose brass lock clasp had been broken for years, and recalled the events which marked a turning point in his career and his life. Again, it was Joseph Graziano who had directed the traffic at the young officer's crossroads.

In August 1968 Patrick Klyne and his Group Three Field Team partners, Billy Caputo and Jack Kiernan, had caught the owner of a beauty salon in Harlem, Elaine Jackson and four companions, with four kilos of heroin in a shopping bag while driving on Lenox Avenue. While Detectives Kiernan and Caputo escorted the apprehended quintet to the station house of the Twenty-eighth precinct, Klyne held on to the narcotics and parked Elaine Jackson's 1967 Buick near the precinct. Going up the stairs at the station house later, shopping bag in hand, Klyne met Graziano on his way down.

"Congratulations. I heard your team made a big collar. A key."

Klyne, with a broad smile, lifted the bag. "Four kilos."

Graziano laughed, "Kid, I know. One key, four keys, what's the difference? Both are great collars." He looked up the stairs behind him and back towards Klyne. "Pat, tonight I want you to do me a favor. Don't say anything to your partners, just make sure that *you're* the one who brings the narcotics to the lab. Tonight I'll teach you how one key becomes two and four keys become eight, and how you make a lot of money. I'll be back in a couple of hours. Make sure you don't leave." In passing, Graziano asked, "Are you guys planning to hit Elaine's apartment on Garden Street? If you are, watch out for her Dobermans."

"No, we're not going to hit the place," Klyne answered, and thought, How does he know all that? Her address. About her dogs. This guy really is the king."

"Good. Sneak the keys out of her purse or get them somehow, but get her keys and give them to me later. Don't let your partners know."

Ninety minutes later, Caputo and Kiernan had left to take the prisoners to the Centre Street holding facility where they would be lodged overnight. With shopping bag in hand, Klyne waited outside the precinct when Graziano drove up. "Get in, kid."

Graziano drove to the Paris Hotel at Ninety-seventh Street and West End Avenue. There they took the elevator to the sixth floor. Graziano had the key to room 609. On the bed were two five-pound bags of Gold Medal Flour and some empty glassine bags. Without fanfare, Graziano took the shopping bag from Klyne, opened the eight bags of heroin and poured the contents into several large glassine bags. Whistling to himself, he poured the flour into the original bags until they were three-quarters full. Graziano then carefully added heroin from the glassine bags into each of the original bags until they were filled. When the operation was concluded, he sealed, vigorously shook each bag until the substances were thoroughly mixed. He then turned to Klyne. "You see, that wasn't hard at all. Now you bring these bags to the lab—and you still have a four-kilo collar."

"But—"

"Don't worry. It works." Graziano put his hands on Klyne's shoulders. "Kid, sometimes we have to pay the devil his due."

As Klyne was about to get up with his drug-and-flour-mixture, Graziano asked, "I nearly forgot, did you get the keys?"

"The keys?"

"The keys to Elaine's apartment."

"Oh, yeah." Klyne reached into his pocket and handed Graziano a ring of keys which he had taken from the salon owner's purse. Graziano read the engraving on the little silver pendant dangling from the key ring, "Take Care of Business."

He laughed. "You bet I will."

Three weeks later Graziano handed Klyne a brown paper bag containing forty-three thousand dollars. He explained that he had sold the four confiscated kilos and two more he had found in Elaine Jackson's apartment for $12,000 a key and also split the fourteen thousand dollars cash he had taken from her home, while she was in custody.

FORTY-THREE THOUSAND DOLLARS IN CASH was the price for Patrick Klyne's honor. A small fortune for a young police officer from a poor family, born without a passport to wealth and financial security. He had crossed the line, leaving behind his ideals, his honesty, his pride. It was all so easy. Ever since that day in September when he counted the $100 bills on his kitchen table, doubt and guilt gnawed in him. A few weeks later at his parents' home, his father, a retired public-school janitor who had worked a second job as a night watchman at the Brooklyn Navy Yard until the arthritis crippling his hands prevented him from turning the keys of the heavy metal gates, referring to a newspaper story about two narcotics detectives who were arrested for shaking down a drug dealer, growled, "Shame on those scoundrels. They stole blood-money from that bum. You can't trust anybody anymore." He looked over at Patrick. "Son, if you would ever do a thing like this, I would kill you—and then myself. I could not live with that disgrace."

After dinner that night, Klyne sat in his car in front of his parents' house with the motor running and and tears streaming down his face. Graziano, one of New York's top narcotics detectives, had reached out for him, and invited him to his house. That's like going to the White House, he thought, storing the rest of his Chinese take-out food in his refrigerator.

March 13, 1969

ANN GRAZIANO'S GNOCCHI, SERVED WITH a delicate tomato- and roasted-pepper sauce, was heavenly. After she excused herself for the night, her husband brought their guest down to earth. Bluntly, without losing much time Graziano informed Klyne about his plan, to steal the heroin seized in the "French Connection" from the Property Clerk's Office and sell it.

"I don't know, Joe. Isn't this like stealing gold from Fort Knox?"

"We'll do them next. Seriously, kid, it's a piece of cake. I've arranged everything, including a buyer who's got the money. It's all set."

"Sounds like you don't need me."

"Of course I need you. You play a very important part."

"I'm not checking the shit out from the Property Clerk, am I?"

"No. I am. Just listen to me. Here's what I want you to do. Starting tomorrow afternoon about 4:00, I want you to wait at LeSane's."

"LeSane's?"

"Yeah, the bar down the street from the office."

"Why do you want me to wait there?"

"Let me finish, willya? I'm going to be upstairs in SIU. When there are no bosses there, I'm going to come down to LeSane's and let you know. Wait ten minutes until I can get back upstairs. Then call SIU. OK?"

Klyne nodded. "OK."

"Ask for the clerical man, McClellan."

"By name?"

"No, of course not. Just ask for the clerical man. As a matter of fact, McClellan will probably answer the phone. When he does, make believe you're ADA Goldberg from the Manhattan DA's Office. Tell him you need a detective to deliver evidence from the Property Clerk to your office." Klyne's eyes narrowed. "Go on."

"Ask him to have voucher number M544-62 delivered to your office."

Klyne's face lit up. "By any chance, is that the voucher number for the 'French Connection' narcotics?"

"Bingo! The first seizure. Twenty-four pounds."

"And is it possible that you'll be standing there with McClellan when I call and you'll volunteer to bring it over to the DA's Office?"

"Exactly."

"Now I understand why you don't want any bosses up there."

"Of course. That would mess everything up. McClellan would give the call to the boss, and the boss would refer the call downstairs."

"Joe, suppose one of the bosses stays up till after McClellan leaves?"

"We'll just have to wait until the next day or the day after. Sooner or later McClellan is going to be alone up there, and that's when you call."

Klyne cleared his throat. "This might sound silly, but something else bothers me. What happens if you're stopped by Internal Affairs when you're carrying the junk out of the Property Clerk?"

"Pat, forgive me. I'm a poor host. I'll get you another beer and then I'll answer all your questions and tell you the rest of the plan."

March 20, 1969

EARLY THURSDAY EVENING, SERGEANT O'BRIEN slipped on his overcoat and headed towards the front door. "Good night, men." Graziano, McClellan and the two other detectives in the SIU office looked up from their desks.

"Good night, boss."

"Good night, Sarge."

A few minutes later, Graziano pushed back from his desk and headed towards the door. "Bernie, I'll be back in a minute. I gotta take a leak. If McDuff calls, tell him I'll be right back." McClellan glanced at Graziano and acknowledged his directive by waving his hand. Once outside the SIU office, Graziano scurried down the stairs to the first floor. Leaving the building, he weaved his way across the rush-hour-filled street and headed for LeSane's.

Inside, he pushed through the packed happy-hour crowd and located Klyne pressed against the bar. Graziano grabbed him by the arm. "Come on, kid. It's a go."

Graziano led Klyne down a flight of stairs to where the bathrooms and phones were located and shoved him into one of the phone booths. "Stay in here. Don't leave. We don't want any of these drunks tying up the phone. McClellan is up there with two new guys. He should pick up the phone. But in case he's taking a leak or something and one of the assholes answers, insist on talking to the clerical man. Now, give me ten minutes to get back up there."

GRAZIANO WAS DISAGREEING WITH McCLELLAN about the playoff chances of the Knickerbockers when the phone rang. "SIU, Mc-Clellan." On the other end of the line, Klyne identified himself as Manhattan Assistant District Attorney Goldberg, muffling his voice by holding a handkerchief over the phone's mouthpiece. He told McClellan he needed someone to bring narcotics evidence from the Property Clerk to his office the following afternoon. Graziano got up from his desk and moved closer to McClellan's desk when he saw McClellan frown.

"There's no one here to help you. I'm going to put you on hold while I switch this call downstairs to the field teams. Maybe they can help." As McClellan was about to transfer the call, Graziano leaned across the desk and touched his arm.

"What's the problem, Bernie? Can I help?"

McClellan cupped the phone's mouthpiece. "It's some stupid ADA who wants some shit from the Property Clerk brought to his office."

"What borough?"

"Manhattan, I think. Let me check with him again . . . What borough?"

McClellan pushed the hold button and repeated to Graziano, "Manhattan."

"I'm going to be over there tomorrow. I'll pick it up for him."

McClellan with a disgusted expression on his face dangled the receiver in the wastebasket. "Jew schmuck. Who does he think we are, errand boys? He makes less money than us and thinks he's hot shit ordering us around."

The two other recently assigned detectives looked up from their paperwork and snickered. Graziano suddenly realized he had caught a break. He now had two witnesses who were aware a conversation had taken place between an ADA and McClellan requesting evidence be brought from the Property Clerk to the DA's Office. The alibi could prove invaluable in case he was ever stopped at the Property Clerk's Office while checking out the evidence.

Graziano bent forward. "It's no big deal, Bernie. I can always use a friend in court. Get a voucher number from him."

Taking the phone off hold, McClellan took a deep breath and asked irritably, "Do you have a voucher number?"

"M544-62," Klyne recited.

"M544-62," McClellan repeated as he wrote the number down on his yellow pad. "That's right."

"Tell me exactly where you want this delivered to."

"Fifty-five Leonard Street tomorrow, sixth floor. Ask for ADA Goldberg."

McClellan finished writing the information. "Detective Graziano will see you tomorrow." Shaking his head slowly from side to side, McClellan hung up the phone and handed Graziano the sheet of paper with the information on it. "Know what's the matter with you, Joe? You're too good a guy. Too good a guy."

Fifteen minutes later, Graziano hugged Klyne at LeSane's. "Patrick, you were terrific! He went for it hook, line and sinker." Graziano ordered a scotch and soda. He raised his drink and winked at Klyne. "Like clockwork." He took a sip. "I better get moving. There's a lot to do. I'll see you tonight."

THIRTY MINUTES BEFORE MIDNIGHT, KLYNE parked under the dimly lit street behind the two-story Travelers' Hotel. Getting out of his car, he could see the bright lights of LaGuardia Airport in the background. He slipped into the hotel through the rear entrance, took the back stairs two at a time to the second floor and cautiously peeked around the corner to make sure there were no guests in the hallway before walking hurriedly to Room 237.

He stopped and listened at the door for a couple of seconds before knocking softly. His heart pounded as Graziano let him into the large double room.

On the badly soiled carpet in the middle of the room lay two A&P shopping bags. One contained several packages of flour. The other held strainers, mixing bowls, long rubber kitchen gloves, large glassine bags, a small scale, surgical masks, and a bedsheet.

Seeing the scale and strainers sticking out of the bag shocked Klyne. "Holy shit, Joe. Suppose somebody walks in here?"

"Are you expecting company?" Graziano grinned.

"I don't think we should be taking any chances."

"Boy, if you think this is taking a chance, what do you call tomorrow?"

Klyne, fingering a strainer, looked up. "Tomorrow is suicide."

March 21, 1969

BOTH MEN STAYED AT THE hotel overnight. At 5:00 A.M. the alarm clock awakened them. They quickly showered and dressed in silence. Graziano grabbed the shopping bags. "I hate dragging this stuff around with us, but the last thing we need is some curious maid finding it."

Graziano told Klyne to go downstairs and start the car. He waited a minute, turned off the TV and lights, opened the drapes and watched Klyne get into the car. He hurried down the back stairs to the parking lot. Klyne pulled the car up to the door. Looking in the passenger window, Graziano observed Klyne fiddling with the radio dial. Impatient, he tapped on the glass and hissed, "Stop fooling around. Open the trunk, for Christ's sake."

Both men knew they had reached the point of no return. Klyne took the Grand Central Parkway and headed for Manhattan. Cursing, he navigated the potholed, dirty streets of Queens to the Fifty-ninth Street Bridge while Graziano listened to the WINS news. In lower Manhattan, a hungry Graziano nudged Klyne and pointed to an all-night deli on Canal Street. "Pull over. Let's get something to eat."

Klyne remained behind the wheel. "Don't get me anything. How can you eat at a time like this"

"Easy. I'm starving."

After Graziano returned with a large brown bag and newspapers under his arm, Klyne headed for the Property Clerk's Office on Centre and Broome Streets and pulled down a side street. Graziano handed

Klyne a container of coffee and a buttered roll. "The *News* or the *Times*?" Klyne selected the *Times* and opened his coffee container. Graziano turned to the sports section of the *Daily News* and read Dick Young's column. Klyne tapped on Graziano's paper. "Let's go over it one more time, Joe."

"Jesus, we went over it a hundred times last night."

"Practice makes perfect. Please."

"Yes, there is an ADA Goldberg. Yes, we have the right voucher number. Yes, I'll put my shield down as 3484. Yes, I'll sign it right-handed. Yes, I'll spell Graziano with two "z's" and an "a" at the end. Now stop worrying. It's going to work!"

"Joe, tell me again. Slowly, please?"

Graziano rolled up his newspaper and playfully hit Klyne on the head with it.

AT 8:45 A.M., KLYNE CIRCLED 400 Broome Street. "Can you believe the size of this building? A whole city block. It's like a fortress . A squad of tanks couldn't knock it down." Klyne found a vacant metered parking space a block away and pulled in. Graziano started to get out of the car.

"Where are you going?"

"Wait here and watch the car. I'm going to take a look upstairs."

"I'm going up there with you."

"Stay here. I'm only going to check the place out. I'll be back in a couple of minutes."

"Joe, I want to check out the place too."

"Wait in the car. We got that stuff in the trunk."

"We're legally parked. Nobody's going to bother the car. Anyway, my eyes are as good as yours, and I'd like to see what's going on. Don't forget, my ass is on the line too."

Klyne's apprehension was beginning to grate on Graziano's nerves. "Jesus, Pat. You got a bad habit of breaking balls at the worst time. Take a look if it makes you feel any better. But after this, stick with the program."

When Klyne and Graziano walked into the Property Clerk's Office, it was business as usual—complete chaos. Uniformed cops, sloppily

dressed Narcs and well-dressed plainclothes detectives, and special-
ized squads milled in front of an iron-mesh cage. The two openings
in the cage were manned by four surly, unkempt longshoremen-type
policemen wearing faded blue police shirts and worn dungarees. Inside the one hundred- by fifty-foot cage, unmarked boxes, crates,
paper bags, suitcases, canvas athletic bags and oversized purses
were scattered around the room. Sixty-plus policemen moved in and
out of two snake-like lines in front of the evidence windows. Cops
clutched evidence seized from all sorts of arrests, as well as clothing
and personal belongings of DOA victims. Despite the deafening din,
cops held intelligible conversations with other cops in front or behind
them as well as with cops on line beside them. The lines shifted
constantly, and cops in one line automatically adjusted when the
other line moved forward. No one missed a word of what the other
was saying. Confusion abounded, yet each cop knew his exact
spot.

Klyne looked around, stared at the hand-printed signs hung on the
cage: "All Handguns & Narcotics, Before 9:00 A.M. New Property To
Be Invoiced Before 9 A.M."

Klyne whispered to Graziano, "Look at those suckers in the cage.
Just because they got a shield, they think they're real cops."

Graziano nodded in agreement. Klyne continued, "Most of those
assholes in the cage are either in the rubber-gun squad or are drunks.
The jerk-offs out here are getting shot at, stabbed, having bricks
dropped on their heads, junkies throwing up in the back of their cars,
and they still have to take this shit from these meatballs." Klyne was
referring to the treatment the cops would get from the clerk-cops if their
paperwork was not properly prepared. "Cops are dopes," he muttered,
glancing at the long lines of New York's Finest.

Graziano tapped Klyne. "Let's go back to the car. I'll give it an hour."

As they turned to leave, a giant in uniform grabbed Graziano by the
arm. "Graziano, you old horse thief. You look terrific, Joe. I mean terrific."

Graziano quickly regained his composure. "Gene Wisco! You're the
one who looks great. How are things going? The Mounted Unit still the
best job on the force?"

"The best, Joe. As a matter of fact, the guys still talk about you.

Swindel always tells the story of you meeting that fag streaker in the park."

"Jesus, that was some wild night. His boyfriend went nuts."

Another hand slapped Graziano on the back. "If it isn't the old guinea crime fighter himself, Joseph Graziano!" Detective Dominick Gatti of Safe and Loft yelled to the crowd, "In case you don't know, this is the pride of the SIU."

Minutes later, Graziano followed an extremely agitated Klyne up the street. "Take it easy, kiddo. It's not the end of the world."

"You're too well-known. It'll never work."

Graziano caught Klyne's arm and spun him around. "Patrick, you're making a big deal out of nothing. Forget about it. I bumped into some old friends, that's all."

Graziano and Klyne sat in the car and waited silently. Graziano thumbed through the *Daily News* while Klyne watched passersby. A little after 10:00 A.M., Graziano folded the newspaper. Klyne leaned back in his seat, inhaled deeply and slowly exhaled. Graziano reached into the inside pocket of his leather jacket and pulled out a piece of paper with the voucher number M544-62 written on it and read it aloud. Klyne pursed his lips and nodded.

While Klyne waited in the car, slumped against the driver's door, Graziano walked slowly to the Property Clerk's Office. Once inside the building, he declined the black elevator operator's invitation of "Hey, Mr. Grazzio. Take a ride with me." Climbing the nineteen steps to the second floor, his legs grew heavier with each step. By the time he had reached the second floor landing, he had broken out in a cold sweat.

To his relief, the place was quiet. At 10:14 A.M., the scene was totally different than earlier that morning. Seven uniformed cops waited patiently in two lines in front of the evidence windows. Graziano got on the shorter line and glanced around. No one looked familiar. From his vantage point, he could partially see into the Commanding Officer's office. Someone was reading a newspaper at a desk. Inside the cage, two clerks were handling requests.

Graziano thought, *Say what you want about them, they sure got rid of that horde from this morning.*

He looked past the clerks at the special thirty-by-thirty-foot wire enclosure in the background which housed narcotics, cash and well-reviewed pornography. In disbelief, his eyes scanned row after row of shelves reaching from the floor to the ceiling. Thousands of manila envelopes and containers stuffed with evidence were jammed haphazardly on every shelf, without apparent pattern or system. Graziano's immediate mental reaction was, *I'm dead. They'll never find anything in that mess.*

Within minutes, the line to Graziano's left disappeared and the clerk serving it closed the window indifferently. Graziano had only one cop left in front of him when two black uniformed cops entered the room and lined up behind him. He reached into his left-hand pocket and pinned his gold shield to the jacket. For a brief moment Graziano wondered if he should partially hide the shield with his lapel. He concluded it would be a mistake, as it might focus attention on the numbers. A second later, he was face to face with the clerk. Graziano slipped him the piece of paper with the voucher number on it.

The clerk lifted his eyes from the paper and looked at Graziano's gold shield. "Detective, where's your voucher sheet?"

"I don't have one. I was told by my office that a Manhattan DA wants this evidence to be delivered to him. All they gave me was the voucher number."

Not wanting to get into a hassle with a gold shield, the clerk took the note and slowly walked away. Halfway to the special cage, he stopped, stared at the slip of paper and returned to the window shaking his head.

"Detective, I don't think this is the right number." He held up the slip to Graziano.

"That's the right number. It's an old case."

"Seven years old?"

"Time flies."

"Are you sure this shit hasn't been destroyed?"

"Positive."

"Hmmph. Standby. This is going to take a few minutes." The clerk left the window and Graziano watched him enter the special cage. He stared incredulously as the clerk climbed a ladder and struggled with various containers and suitcases on two-foot-high shelves. No luck. Then the clerk brought the ladder to another section of shelves. He was about to repeat his high-ladder act when property piled carelessly in the corner caught his eye. The clerk decided to check these items before proceeding further. He tossed, wrestled and kicked dozens of packages all over the floor. Irritated, he grabbed a briefcase and fris-beed it to the other side of the cage.

By now, fifteen minutes had elapsed. One of the bored uniformed cops standing behind Graziano started to play catch with his hat. The second cop spun his baton. Graziano bit his lip when two plainclothes cops came into the room and stood on line. Sweat seeped from his armpits.

The clerk returned to the window. "Detective, I can't find the damn thing. Are you sure it's here?"

Graziano, struggling to control of his frayed nerves, answered, "It must be in there."

"OK, let me take care of the guys behind you. Then I'll get the boss to help me find it."

Graziano remained outwardly calm. "Sure, knock these guys off first. I got plenty of time. Then, if it's OK with you, take another look. Don't rush. You're not under a gun." The last thing Graziano wanted was a group of clerks led by the commanding officer tearing the place apart.

Graziano prayed silently. *Just find the stuff. No inquiries. No inter-rogations. No one remembering me. Just find the fucking thing.*

It took the clerk less than five minutes to check in evidence from the two patrolmen and the two plainclothesmen. "All right, Detective, I'm ready for another look-see. If it's OK with you, it's OK with me. I got all day."

"Do your thing."

After the clerk left, Graziano took out a handkerchief and dabbed his brow. Steps coming up the stairs startled him. It was Klyne peeking around the corner. Graziano grimaced and hand-motioned Klyne to get back downstairs just as the clerk who earlier closed the first line came out of the commander's office, walked into the special cage and con-ferred with his colleague helping Graziano. They both looked up at him dubiously. Graziano smiled back at them. The second clerk glanced at the voucher number. He scratched his head and stared at the com-mander's office. Suddenly he walked briskly to another section of the cage. Graziano closed his eyes and held his breath.

Can you believe this? he thought.

Within minutes, the second clerk emerged from the section with an old blue suitcase. He called his buddy and dropped the suitcase. Both clerks rechecked the voucher number. The second clerk left the special cage and went into the CO's office. Graziano expected the boss to come storming out of the office any second.

The first clerk went to the cage opening. "Detective? Are you ready?"

Graziano was contemplating the answers he would be giving the commanding officer if questioned.

"Detective?"

"Oh! I'm sorry, Officer. My mind's a million miles from here." Graziano put his head into the cage opening. "My wife's having lunch with my girlfriend this afternoon and I was wondering what they're going to talk about."

The clerk laughed. "Barbecued ass, I'd say. If I was you, I'd call home before I showed up tonight. Take her temperature long distance." The clerk spun around the large green-bound ledger for Graziano to sign.

"That's not a bad idea. Might save myself a trip." Graziano took out his pen and, as rehearsed hundreds of times, signed with his right hand, "Grazziana, 3484." Graziano removed the shield from his jacket. "Officer, I know I gave you a lot of work this morning, and I appreciate your help. First time I catch you at Brophy's, the drinks are on me."

"Peace. Let me know how you make out tonight."

"If I survive."

As the clerk lifted the suitcase onto the counter, a man with rolled-up sleeves came out of the CO's office and opened the side gate. He headed towards the stairs calling out to the clerk, "I've got to crank one out. I'll be back in ten."

Graziano frowned as he took the suitcase in hand. "Is that the boss?"

"In the flesh."

GRAZIANO HAD JUST PLACED THE suitcase on the backseat when Klyne jerked the car forward.

"Hey, kid, let me get in the car, willya?"

The car slammed to a halt and Graziano got in and closed the door.

Klyne drove ten blocks to the Manhattan District Attorney's Office. The building in sight, he pulled over to a telephone booth, where

Graziano got out and called the DA's Office. The operator answered immediately and Graziano asked to speak with Assistant District Attorney Goldberg. He was told to hold.

Seconds later, an abrasive voice responded, "ADA Goldberg's office." Graziano thought, *I know this ugly black cocksucker. She's the Ubangi that thinks she's God's gift.*

He politely inquired if he could speak with ADA Goldberg.

The receptionist said, "ADA Goldberg is in court. He won't be available until one o'clock."

"Will he be there all afternoon?"

"No. He has to be back in court at two and then he won't available again until after five."

Graziano gently cradled the receiver and returned to the car. "Let's get over there. Relax. Everything's going to be fine." Graziano took the suitcase from the backseat and got out again. He bent over and looked in the window at Klyne. "I'll be back in a few minutes."

The vestibule was unusually quiet when he entered the building. The lone policeman standing guard by the elevator bank, whom Graziano knew from his many visits to the DA's office, smiled. "Hi Joe, how's the hammer hanging?"

Graziano shook the guard's hand, stepped into an empty elevator and pressed the sixth-floor button. He went directly to the Homicide Bureau and stopped at the reception desk. Graziano identified himself and told the same black woman he had spoken to on the phone only minutes before that he wanted to see ADA Goldberg. She said brusquely, "ADA Goldberg's in court and he'll be back at one. If you don't catch him then, you'll have to wait until five."

Graziano pointedly looked up at the wall clock which read 11:34 A.M. and ignored what he just heard. "Tell Goldberg the detective from Narcotics is here with the stuff he wanted from the Property Clerk's Office."

Annoyed, the receptionist took a deep breath. "I just told you when you axed me that ADA Goldberg is in court. He's only available between one and two and then after five."

"I know what you told me. Just give him the message. Tell him I was here at 11:30 A.M. and I'll be back around five." Graziano nodded curtly, turned and headed back to the elevator.

Graziano had more than five hours to kill before he returned to the District Attorney's Office. A hyperventilating Klyne drove them back to the Travelers' Hotel, and parked in the rear of the hotel where they could observe the car from their room window. The men left the shopping bags containing the paraphernalia and flour in the trunk of the car, and Graziano carried the blue suitcase to their room. Once the door was locked behind them, he put the suitcase on top of the bed, undid the straps, pushed down two half-inch levers and opened it. He stared at the large, white plastic bags. "In a minute we know the score, kid. Wouldn't it be a sharp stick in the eye if somebody beat us to the punch?"

Kyne didn't answer. Ever since he accepted, without hesitation, Graziano's offer to be an active partner in this crazy and dangerous venture, he acted as though he were under a spell, like a marionette manipulated by the puppeteer's hand. He was aware that he was balancing on a highwire and he was scared. He had asked himself more then once, "Is it the money? Greed? Is it because everybody else is doing it?" But he did not wait for the answer, he just went along for the ride. He belonged. He was promoted. He finally played in the Big Leagues now. He was— like Graziano. And this feeling was stronger then fear and paralyzed his conscience.

GRAZIANO REMOVED THREE MARQUIS REAGENT tester kits from the inside pocket of his leather jacket and handed them to Klyne. All narcotics detectives were supposed to carry them around in case they arrested a person who possessed suspected heroin; they could test the substance immediately for content and quality. Each kit contained a vial partially filled with Mencizes fluid and a plastic spoon. If a small amount of tested powder, mixed with the fluid, turned pink, it was heroin; if it turned bright red, it was high-quality heroin.

Graziano counted twenty-two plastic bags in all. He randomly selected one of the bags from the bottom layer, still wrapped in the original black-red-and-green-striped friction tape the smugglers used when shipping the drugs from Marseilles to New York in the hollow fenders of Monsieur Angelvin's 1960 Buick Invecta.

Graziano made a pinhole opening in the bag with a small stiletto, enlarged the hole slightly and removed a minute amount of the substance with the tip of the knife. He carefully passed the knife to Klyne who mixed the substance with the fluid from the vial. The fluid turned pink immediately, then bright red. Klyne whispered, "Nobody's touched this shit. It's pure heroin." Graziano deliberately placed the bag on the bed with the puncture upward. He applied scotch tape over the hole and returned the bag to the suitcase.

Klyne took out another Marquis tester. "Do you want to test another one?"

"No need to. It's all there." Graziano's eyes caressed the plastic bags. "Kid, that's $165,000 for us." He closed the suitcase and re-strapped it as Klyne turned on the TV. Graziano went over to the window and glanced down at the car. "Pat, check the car every now and then. I'm going to flop for a couple of hours."

"Jesus, how can you sleep at a time like this?"

"Hey, I'm tired. I've been up since five. Besides, you're going to be awake." Graziano grinned as he lay down on the bed. "Make sure I'm up by three-thirty."

At 4:55 P.M. PRECISELY, GRAZIANO walked into the reception area of the District Attorney's Homicide Bureau. The receptionist was not at her desk, and it appeared she was gone for the day. Graziano walked passed her desk and proceeded down a long corridor. It was paramount he actually see ADA Goldberg, or at the very least, one of the clerical personnel who would remember that Graziano had attempted to deliver the suitcase. Walking down the narrow hallway, he spotted Goldberg's nameplate affixed to the wall. A horrible thought crossed his mind: "Wouldn't it be a bummer if Goldberg said he was expecting me and to leave the suitcase in his office?"

Graziano stood in Assistant District Attorney Goldberg's open doorway and cleared his throat. "Are you ADA Goldberg?"

The middle-aged heavyset man at the desk took off his glasses. "Yes."

"I'm Detective Graziano from Narcotics. I've got the evidence you requested."

"Evidence? What evidence?"

"Didn't you call the Narcotics Bureau yesterday and ask that evidence be delivered to you?"

"Certainly not. Why would I want narcotics evidence? I'm in Homicide."

"Beats me. Is there another ADA Goldberg up here?"

"No, but there is an ADA Greenberg down the hall. He's in Homicide too. You can ask him."

Graziano thanked Goldberg and shook his head walking down the corridor. "A Greenberg on the same floor. Not even I could come up with something like that. A double alibi. Somebody is watching out for me." Greenberg occupied a corner office. Graziano smiled before knocking on the door.

A voice answered, "Come in."

Three men looked up at him as he entered the office. Startled, Graziano recognized two of the men, Inspector Johnson and Captain Comperiati. They both worked in Internal Affairs. Graziano's alarm sensors signaled highest alert. *Oh shit! I need this like pneumonia.*

"ADA Greenberg?" Graziano asked nervously.

"Here," Greenberg acknowledged from behind the desk.

"I've got the narcotics evidence you asked to be delivered."

"What evidence? What narcotics evidence did I want?"

"I got a message yesterday you wanted this evidence delivered here."

Inspector Johnson looked up at Graziano. "What evidence is that?"

Graziano hesitated. "I dunno. Some old narcotics case."

Comperiati turned to Greenberg. "Stan, did you order any narcotics evidence?"

"No. Obviously a mistake's been made. This probably belongs to ADA Goldberg down the hall. People mix us up all the time."

Graziano picked up the suitcase from the floor. "Where do I find him?" He quickly left the Homicide Bureau and rushed to the elevator bank, where he bumped into Eileen McManus and another typist he recognized. An already crowded elevator transported the trio to the lobby. In the street, he bade the ladies farewell and walked up the block to where Klyne was waiting in the car. "How'd it go?"

Graziano put the suitcase on the backseat. "Beautiful. Everything went beautiful."

In heavy traffic, Klyne cautiously navigated the car uptown towards the Property Clerk's Office where he parked the car a block from the building. Graziano looked at his watch: 5:29 P.M. He reached over to the backseat and pulled the *Daily News* from underneath the suitcase.

"Let's give it another few minutes, kid. I'd hate to run up there and have someone still there."

"It closes at five."

"I know. But with our luck someone will be working overtime and wanna check in the shit."

After waiting twenty minutes, Graziano shifted in his place and lifted the suitcase to the front seat. He opened the door and turned to Klyne. "I'll be back in a few." Graziano got out of the car with the suitcase in hand and walked down the street to 400 Broome. Entering the building he turned right and crept up the stairs towards the second floor. Graziano thought, *If this stinking place is open, I'll just turn around and walk out.* Nearing the top step, he noticed the door to the reception area ajar. Graziano stood on the staircase landing, paused and looked into the dimly lit room. Taking a deep breath, he stepped inside.

The two evidence windows were shut. Two large green signs were set in front of each window indicating: "Office hours: 8:00 A.M. to 5:00 P.M." The relieved Graziano was about to turn and leave when he heard a cough. He went up to the counter and peered into the cage.

In the middle of the cage under a naked lightbulb sat a massive black man thumbing through a pornographic magazine. Graziano wasn't sure if the man was a cop or a janitor but he thought, *I've caught another break. A witness that can say I tried to return the stuff.* He yelled into the enclosure, "Hey, in there. Are you open?"

The black man put down the magazine and shuffled towards Graziano. Sorry, brother. I can't help you. Tomorrow, 8:00 in the morning."

ONLY SCANT REMNANTS of the heavy rush-hour traffic remained as Graziano and Klyne exited the Grand Central Parkway, and headed for the Travelers' Hotel. Behind the hotel, Klyne found a parking spot and cut the engine. While he was removing the two shopping bags from the trunk, Graziano got out of the car and carried the blue suitcase to the rear entrance of the hotel. As had become their custom, the men took the back stairs to the second floor. Once inside Room 237, Klyne put down the shopping bags and made a beeline for the TV as Graziano shut the door. He pressed the off/on button, switched stations to Channel 7 and waited for the picture to appear. A slightly inebriated Tex Antoine was drawing a rain hat atop Uncle Weatherbee's bald head with a grease crayon. "I love when this guy gives the weather. Look at him. He's drunk as a skunk."

Graziano grinned, put the blue suitcase on the bed and started unstrapping it. When an Ipana toothpaste commercial began on the TV, Klyne turned around. "Can I do anything, Joe?"

Graziano pointed to the closet. "Do me a favor and get the other suitcase from the closet."

"Suitcase? What suitcase?"

"The one I checked in with."

"Oh." Klyne went to the closet, removed a brown suitcase and brought it over to Graziano, who indicated a spot in the middle of the room. "Leave it there. We'll put the shit inside." He turned and looked at the two shopping bags by the door. "Get the sheet out of the bag and spread it on the floor. Then put everything else on the sheet."

Klyne opened one of the shopping bags, shifted the scale and strainers and took out the sheet. He returned to the middle of the room, unfolded the sheet and spread it neatly on the carpet. He then retrieved the two shopping bags with the paraphernalia and flour, removed the contents and put all the materials on one side of the sheet. Graziano lifted the open blue suitcase filled with heroin off the bed and carefully put it next to the packages of flour. Both men knelt on the sheet, shook hands and donned surgical masks and rubber gloves.

Graziano reached into the blue suitcase and removed a half-kilo bag of the "French Connection" heroin. He cautiously pulled away some of the friction tape that prevented the bag from rupturing and unsealed the opening. Facing Graziano, Klyne awkwardly opened up a new plastic bag. With workmanlike precision, Graziano unerringly poured the contents of his bag into the empty bag being held open by Klyne. When the exchange was completed, Klyne gingerly put his bag on the sheet, then placed a five-pound package of Gold Medal flour be-tween his knees and tore open the top. He lifted the flour and slowly poured approximately one pound into the now empty bag be-ing held by Graziano. Finished, Graziano put the bag he was hold-ing on the sheet in front of him and picked up a teaspoon. Klyne, seeing Graziano pick up a teaspoon, also picked one up. Graziano dipped his spoon into the bag in front of him and removed a spoon-ful of flour. He reached over and poured the flour into the left side of the open bag in front of Klyne. Klyne took his spoon and took a small spoonful of heroin from the right side of the bag and poured it into the bag of flour in front of Graziano.

Graziano then reached over and took a large yellow Tupperware bowl off the sheet and put it in front of him. He poured the contents of his bag into the bowl and thoroughly mixed it with a flour sifter. Klyne reached over, picked up the bag Graziano had placed on the sheet and held it open as Graziano meticulously poured the contents of the bowl back into the bag. Klyne handed Graziano the bag, reached into his shirt pocket and removed a Marquis tester kit. He opened the kit and waited while Graziano removed a small amount of white powder from his bag with the tip of the spoon. Klyne broke open the vial and watched as Graziano poured the powder onto the translucent fluid. Seconds later he pointed at the tester. "Jesus, Joe. We better give this shit another hit. Maybe we should put in a tablespoon."

"Why? It's red."

Klyne's brow wrinkled. "It only looks a little pink to me."

Graziano waved his hand. "That's good enough. No sense wasting the stuff."

"Suppose they test it?"

"So what? It'll come back narcotics."

"Suppose they test it in a year or two? Will it still give a read-ing?"

"Probably not, but who's going to test it a year from now?"

Graziano intertwined his fingers and stretched his arms in the air. "Here we are on the verge of committing the perfect crime and nobody will ever know. Whatashame." Graziano put down his arms. "What do you think, kid, are we so smart or are they just so dumb?"

It took the two men less than an hour to complete the process. Five of the bags they didn't even bother to lace with narcotics. When all the bags were sealed, Klyne put the bogus heroin in the blue suitcase, and Graziano packed the "French Connection" heroin in the brown suitcase. Afterwards, the detectives put the paraphernalia and empty flour bags into the shopping bags. While Klyne inspected the room, Graziano went to the lobby to use the public telephone. He called the Narcotics Bureau switchboard and asked the operator to check his box for messages. There was a message from McDuff to call him at home that night.

Five minutes later, Graziano returned to the room with two cans of Pepsi. He handed one to his partner. "Pat, why don't you take off? There's no sense in both of us hanging around."

"Are you sure?"

"Positive."

Klyne removed the tab from his soda can and immediately took three swigs. He wiped his mouth with his sleeve. "What time are you picking me up in the morning?"

Graziano put his arm around Klyne's shoulder. "Nine sharp. I want us to be at the Property Clerk's Office by ten. By the way, I hope you've given some thought to where you're going to bury your money. You shouldn't leave it around the house."

Klyne turned and threw his empty can on the bed. "I got a good spot. Nobody will ever find it. What about you?"

"A few weeks ago, I rented some storage space at a place in Long Island City under an assumed name and address. They don't check ID. All you have to do is pay the rent. One hundred-fifty dollars for five years. Round-the-clock security, and I'm the only one with the key. I keep all my money and the extra junk there."

"Jesus, you can't beat that. Maybe I should rent space there too."

"That's up to you, but just be prepared to hide your money in the morning when I come by. If everything goes right tonight you should be sitting on eighty-two five."

"Are you sure it's a go?"

"Positive. Everything's set."

Klyne picked up the blue suitcase, walked to the door and turned around. Graziano went over to him, put his left hand on the back of his head and kissed his cheek. "Kiddo, don't get caught with that bag. If you do, we'll have a lot of explaining to do."

March 22, 1969

A LITTLE AFTER 2:15 A.M., Graziano picked up the brown suitcase and the paper bags. Twenty minutes later, on the Lower East Side, he stopped his car and called Jerry Lynch from a telephone booth with smashed-out windows. "It's a go. I'll see you at three."

The meeting place had been prearranged. All Graziano needed to do was mention the time. On the way, Graziano frequently checked the rearview mirror. Satisfied he wasn't being followed, he pulled over to a corner sewer and disposed of the shopping bag with the crumpled flour bags. At a construction site a few blocks away, he tossed the shopping bag with the paraphernalia into a half-filled dumpster.

Graziano spotted Lynch's car parked in front of the 1st Precinct, pulled alongside, tapped his horn and signaled for Lynch and Beninati to follow. Eight blocks away from the station house, the men parked in a dark section of the Fulton Fish Market underneath the East Side Highway. As Graziano opened the back door of Lynch's car to get in, he froze. Vincent Catalano was in the backseat.

Graziano masked his immediate flush of anger, got into the backseat and passed the suitcase up to Beninati.

"Joe, that better be good shit," Catalano said coldly.

"Catalano, this shit is better than good. It's dynamite. The junkies are going to drop like flies."

Lynch laughed. "Good. But let's not kill all of them. We'd put ourselves out of a job."

Graziano leaned forward. "Jerry, why is Catalano here?"

Lynch half-turned. "He's representing the buyer."

"I thought you guys were."

"We are, but Vinnie's his personal friend."

Beninati spun around abruptly. "Come on, Joe. It's no big deal. Let's get going. The money is in the attaché case next to Catalano."

"Is it all there?"

"Yep, $165,000."

As Graziano attempted to lift the attaché case, Catalano put his elbow on top of it. "Joe, my man don't like to pay now and pray later. This better be Dom Perignon."

"Keep your guinea theatrics to yourself, showoff. I'm not some nigger cunt you can punch in the face."

Beninati reached back and touched Graziano's knee. "Easy, Joe, he means no harm."

"It's been a long night, and I don't need this clown's bullshit." Graziano growled.

GRAZIANO CARRIED A SUITCASE UP to Klyne's apartment and rang the bell. A split second later the door opened, and Klyne signaled him to come inside. Graziano entered and handed him the suitcase. "Your half's inside."

Klyne gave Graziano the thumbs-up sign. "I can't believe it. We did it." He opened the suitcase, stared at the bundles of bank notes. "No, you did it." He closed the suitcase and shoved it under the bed. "Joe, we better hurry. You know how it is at the Property Clerk on Saturdays. It's only open till noon. With most of the courts closed, there'll probably be only one guy checking in. If there's no business, he's liable to close the joint early."

"Relax. We'll be there by ten o'clock."

Graziano drove the car into Manhattan and parked a block away from the Property Clerk's building entrance. Opening the car door, he pinched Klyne on the cheek and took the suitcase from his white-knuckled hands. "Wish me luck, sweetheart." Klyne watched apprehensively as Graziano walked down the street and disappeared into 400 Broome.

What a difference twenty-four hours make, Graziano thought as he stepped into the empty Property Clerk reception area. *A weekday, it's a madhouse; Saturday, a mausoleum.* He stood at the open but unattended evidence window. "Hello in there! Anybody home?"

A moment later, the same clerk who helped Graziano check out the suitcase the day before appeared. "I'll be a son of a bitch. You're alive and kicking. What did the wife say?"

"The ladies made a deal. They're going to share me. This way they each get six inches." The clerk laughed as Graziano lifted the suitcase onto the counter. He turned the green log book for Graziano to sign. Once again, Graziano took the pen in his right hand and signed, "Grazziana, Shield Number 3484."

June 1969

VINNIE CATALANO WAS IN FOR a bad night. Earlier in the week, he had sold two keys of heroin, pilfered during a Harlem raid, to Rudy Santobella, a big-time Bronx Mafioso. Now, Santobella demanded a face-to-face meeting at Santobella's private club, The Chez Joey, in the Williamsbridge section of the Bronx.

Four women in their mid-twenties were cha-cha-ing to the beat of Latin music when Catalano came in the front door. He scanned the twenty-odd patrons in the room. Five of Santobella's goons were playing cards at a table. Nothing struck Catalano as unusual, but he remained jumpy. Santobella was known for his mercurial temper and unpredictability, albeit smart enough not to mess around with a cop.

Catalano sauntered cockily up to the bar where two of Santobella's whores stood next to one another. He pecked both blondes on the cheek and lightly patted their backsides. Neither girl reacted, but Santobella's "boys" seethed. Joey Fasanella gave the 'Va fangul' sign and started to get up, but his friends restrained him. They not only hated Catalano for being a cop, but they loathed his toughguy arrogance. Tommy Aquino, a Santobella lieutenant, came out a back door, greeted the detective indifferently and escorted him to the back office.

Santobella looked up from his desk. "Sit down, Vinnie. We got a problem, and I want you to fix it." Aquino moved away from Catalano and stood with arms crossed in front of the door.

"What is it, Rudy?"

"Those two keys you sold to me the other day was shit. No fucking good."

"Bullshit. It was dynamite. I tested it personally. It was the best."

"You're a liar, Vinnie. My man said it was shit, and I want my money back."

"I never gave you bad shit, Rudy. I think you're trying to rip me off.

Who do you think you're dealing with? One of your dumb wops?" Catalano stood up, walked to the door and brutally shoved Aquino aside. In the open doorway, he turned and faced Santobella.

"I hope you try something, scumbag. If you do, I'll put a bullet up your mother's ass." He slammed the office door shut.

An ashen Santobella jumped to his feet trembling with rage and screamed at Aquino, "Kill that no good motherfucker! Right now!"

Catalano stood at the bar between the two blondes. "Sal, buy the girls a drink." He waited until the girls were served and, as usual, he left the club without paying. He was pleased with himself. They're all pussies, he thought.

About twenty feet from his car, he heard an empty bottle rolling out of the alley to his left. He immediately went for the off-duty revolver he wore concealed in an ankle holster, but it was too late. Tommy Aquino stepped out of the darkness and fired two shots at him with a .22 caliber revolver. Catalano was hurled backwards from the impact of the bullets. As he lay writhing in agony on the wet pavement, Aquino fired three more shots, then disappeared.

Police officers responding to the shooting started questioning the barely conscious detective as ambulance attendants worked on him feverishly. Catalano opened his eyes. One EMS medic, a young black woman, smiled, "I know you must think you're in heaven, but I got bad news for you, gunslinger. You're going to have to stay on earth another few years. Good thing the shooter only had a .22."

WHILE CATALANO WAS BEING OPERATED on in Montefiore Hospital, Captain Timothy Hanley searched his blood-soaked clothing. He pulled a small red address book from the inside jacket pocket. Once he read the names and telephone numbers of Vincent Capra, Rene Texeiera, Louis Cirillo, Robby Stepney and Hollywood Harold—all prominent organized crime figures—he immediately contacted Internal Affairs.

Inspector William Bonacum, a soft-spoken, distinguished-looking widower in his mid-forties, was assigned to head up the investigation of Vincent Catalano's past and present activities. Bonacum had a reputation of being a maverick, an unapproachable loner who would lock up his best friend. This made him "untrustworthy" in the eyes of most of the police hierarchy.

During Catalano's convalescence in the hospital and later at home, Bonacum questioned him repeatedly about the shooting and the address book. The battle-hardened detective insisted he knew nothing about either. Bonacum remained skeptical and later muttered to a subordinate, "This guy's story has more holes in it than he does." He was not only sure Catalano knew who shot him, and why, but he was also convinced that he had close illicit ties to the Mafia.

Over the next several weeks only two members of the department visited the shooting victim in the hospital—Lynch and Beninati. As soon as Catalano was discharged, both he and Santobella were subpoenaed before a Bronx grand jury. Again and again they denied knowing one another. Catalano maintained, "I never met a Rudy Santobella. I never saw a Rudy Santobella. And I don't know a Rudy Santobella."

When asked by the grand jury to explain the red address book, Catalano brazenly claimed: "The District Attorney's Office must have planted it on me. They're Democrats. Everybody knows they have a personal vendetta against my uncle because he's a Republican, and he ran Mayor Lindsay's campaign."

Catalano loved the ring of his story. He repeated it loudly and often.

WHILE CATALANO RECUPERATED AT HOME, Inspector Bonacum had a court-ordered wiretap installed on his phone and assigned a task force of no fewer than twenty-two detectives to keep their suspicious colleague under observation around the clock. After being home about a week, Catalano received a midnight telephone call. An obviously disguised male voice said staccato, "Meet me at the nest and watch your back." The detective monitoring the phone alerted the two surveillance teams watching Catalano's home.

Dressing quickly, Catalano stepped out of his house, mockingly bowed to the detectives hiding in the dark and got into his car. He slowly headed up the street. Two blocks away, he unexpectedly made a U-turn and waved at the two cars following him. He floored the accelerator, sped down a one-way street, raced through several red lights and stop signs, jumped a highway divider and swung onto the Triborough Bridge. After he had paid the toll, he checked the rearview mirror and smiled.

Five minutes later, the hell driver was seated in the Delightful Diner in Manhattan with Lynch and Beninati. The Lieutenant chewed his turkey-club sandwich. "How many cops are sitting on you?"

"At least a coupla hundred."

Lynch needled,"We figured it was a shitload. I guess that's why it took you so long to get here."

Catalano laughed. "Whaddaya mean took me so long? I shook'em in two minutes." He signaled for the waitress. "Anyway, what's up?"

Beninati leaned forward, "Vinnie, you've got to continue to lay low and under no circumstances go near Capra. Some cops are sitting on him."

"He never said nothing to me."

"I know. I told him not to talk with you."

"So what are you trying to do, cut me out?"

"No. You're a partner in everything me and Jerry do with him. You have my word. I'm going to hold your share."

Lynch suggested," Vinnie, after you eat, why don't you go home and take up gardening for the next few months?"

Catalano was not to be deterred. "I wish it were that easy, but Bonacum is insisting I go back to work."

Lynch sneered. "He's a scumbag."

"Yeah, but a smart scumbag. He wants me to go see a Department doctor. He figures if he can get me back to work, he can get me assigned to his office and break my balls every day. He figures sooner or later I'll try and punch his lights out and he'll get me fired."

Lynch yawned. "What are you going to do?"

Catalano winked. "What do you think I'm going to do? I'm going to go home and garden. And for Chrissakes, wipe that ketchup off your chin."

THE NEXT MORNING, CATALANO WAS hoeing the soil around a rosebush when Bonacum's telephone call summoned him downtown.

In a musical voice the IAD boss began, "You broke the rules last night, Vincent."

Catalano picked up the melody, "What are you talking about, Inspector?"

"You're supposed to be on sick leave. You went out of the house last night for more than three hours." Catalano continued to sing, "You're full of shit. I never left the house. It musta been someone else." Bonacum's voice sharpened. "Stop the nonsense. You went out. As far as I'm concerned, you're ready to go back on duty."

"No way, Inspector. I'm still hurting."

"Detective Catalano, I'm going to have your ass in my office every day until you go back to work."

"Fine with me, as long as you pay for the cab or send somebody up here to get me. I'm too sick to drive. And, incidentally, somebody will have to bring me home.

Five days a week, Bonacum dispatched a radio car to pick up the obstinate officer and bring him to Police Headquarters. On most occasions, Catalano refused to report, claiming he was too ill to see anyone, but when the mood struck him, he would cheerily go see his nemesis. The street-smart scoundrel knew he was getting under Bonacum's skin, and he deliberately goaded him at every opportunity.

The Inspector lost his cool when Catalano strode into his office one day with, "Hey, boss. Those six assholes outside look like the same shitheads that have been sitting on my house all week. They look beat." He took out a thick roll of bills and nonchalantly tossed a twenty on Bonacum's desk. "Buy the guys some coffee. It's on me"

Bonacum angrily brushed the money to the floor. "Catalano, you and your smart-ass mouth are going back to work immediately."

Catalano shook his head. "No way, Inspector. I'm not well."

"We'll see about that. I've set up an appointment for you to see the Police Surgeon today at 1300 hours."

"To hell with you and your jerk-off doctors. They can't tell me about my pain."

"Be there. Doctor Levy's at 160-47 Queens Boulevard. You're going back on duty tonight."

"Inspector, before I go back to work, a nigger will be Mayor."

"Listen to me, you clown. If you're a no-show at the doctor's, I'll bring you up on departmental charges and take your pension away."

*   *   *

DOCTOR STANLEY LEVY REMOVED HIS glasses and put them on his desk. " Officer, I've just talked with Inspector Bonacum, and I've advised him you're ready to go back on duty." Levy squirmed in his seat as he saw Catalano's face contort.

"Fuckhead, is the Inspector your consulting physician?"

"No. It's my professional opinion, that . . ."

Catalano abruptly swept his right arm across Levy's desk, knocking papers, the telephone and a lamp to the floor. "You're a liar, Jew boy. Bonacum told you to put me back to work."

"No. That's not true. It's my medical opinion that you're fit for duty."

"Well, here's my medical opinion on you. *You're* going to need a doctor. A *bone* doctor." Catalano came around the desk, viciously slapped Levy's face, jerked him out of his chair and slammed his face against the wall twice. Levy buckled and fell down.

Catalano stood over him. "Hey, scumbag. Find me another bastard that's working out there that's been shot five times and I'll go back to work tomorrow. I don't give a shit what kind of a deal you've made with Bonacum. I'm telling you I'm too sick to work, and you're going to retire me right now!"

He grabbed the back of Levy's head. "See that picture of your wife and kids?" Levy watched in terror as Catalano ground his heel into the picture frame and the glass shattered. "If you don't retire me today, I'm going to retire you, your old lady and your kids. Permanently."

Within minutes, Levy had submitted his recommendation to the Medical Bureau that Detective Vincent Catalano be allowed to retire on a medical disability. The doctor's recommendation entitled Catalano to three-quarters retirement pay for the rest of his life. Bonacum had lost.

July 1969

THE POPULAR, FASHION-CONSCIOUS detective-duo of Dick Belfry and Doug Redmond was greeted by a loud chorus of hoots and catcalls as they swaggered into the SIU office. Seated at a corner desk,

Brogan Conner laughed as they curtsied to the dozen detectives. An amused Lieutenant Ryan shook his head as Belfry and Redmond hugged most of their colleagues.

McDuff grabbed Redmond's arm. "Nice jacket, Doug. The leather is as soft as a baby's ass."

"I just got it yesterday."

"Must have cost a fortune."

"Not a penny. It's a present from the PC. A reward for the great work I'm doing."

The audience laughed, and Belfry took over. "Guys, did you hear the story of the year?"

Of course, nobody did but everybody wanted to know. "What story?" asked Detective Malloy.

"The story about Jack D'Arpe of the twenty-fifth squad."

"What about Jack?" Jiminez was curious. "Did his wife find out about the blonde at the nail salon?"

"Worse. She found his stash in the garage. Seventeen grand. Evidently she is some sort of Holy Roller. She took the money and handed it over to their parish priest. When Jack found out what she did, he went over to the rectory to get the money back. The priest told him 'No good,' that he wasn't giving it back, that Jack's wife had confessed, the money was 'evil.' "

Jiminez covered his eyes. "Oh, my God, he musta kicked her ass."

"Naw. You know D'Arpe. He said he's going to get another $17,000 but this time he's going to hide it at his girlfriend's place."

"Amen!" shouted McClellan from his desk.

Belfry and Redmond followed Conner into Ryan's office. After the group exchanged amenities, Conner put an attaché case on her lap and crossed her legs. Ryan, catching a glimpse of thigh, smiled appreciatively. Conner took out a brown folder and handed it to Ryan. "Lieutenant, we'd like to open a case folder on Vincent Capra. Then we'd like your permission to apply for a legal wiretap."

Ryan looked up from the folder. "Brogan, you can't open a folder on

Capra. Jerry Lynch already has one open. He's been working on Capra for months." Conner slumped back in her chair.

"I'm sorry, Brogan. You know the rules. Whoever opens up the case folder first, it's their case."

"Oh, I know, Lieutenant. It's not that. I'm just a little disappointed. I didn't think anyone was working on him."

"Perhaps you can help Lynch. Tell him what you've got."

Conner glanced at Belfry, who was whispering to Redmond. She and Ryan waited patiently until they finished their conversation. Seconds later Belfry spoke up, "Lieutenant, set up a meet with Lynch. We'll let him know what we have."

AT DONOHUE'S BAR AND GRILL, Ryan informed Lynch over dinner that Belfry's team had approached him about opening a folder on Capra.

"I hope you told them I was working on him."

"Of course I did, but you know those greedy cocksuckers. Now they know you're on Capra and probably smell there's money to be made."

After Lynch left the restaurant, he drove straight to the Astoria Colts Club. Capra's car was parked outside.

A few hours later, a bored Lynch saw Capra leave the club and drive away. He followed him a short distance, and when satisfied they weren't being tailed, blinked his headlights once, then twice in rapid succession. Recognizing the signal, Capra slowed and let Lynch pull in front of him. A few side streets away, Lynch pulled his car over to the curb, followed by Capra. Capra got into Lynch's vehicle.

"I just found out a team of detectives from my office have been working on you. I don't know what they have, but I do know they've had your phones bugged for a couple of weeks. I'm supposed to meet them later this week and find out what they have," Lynch said.

"I appreciate you watching out for me, Jerry. But, believe me, I haven't done much since I laid down that package with you. If it's all right with you, I'd like you to give them a little something for their troubles."

"That's a good idea."

"If you don't mind, I'd like you to wait here a few minutes and I'll be right back." Capra opened the door and hesitated. "By the way, Jerry. I'm ready for another package."

AT 9:00 P.M. THE FOLLOWING evening, Lynch was seated in Ryan's office when Belfry and Redmond arrived. Both men, noting Lynch's lighted cigar, jockeyed for position to avoid sitting next to him. Ryan looked out his office window. "Where's Brogan?"

Belfry sat down. "Downstairs, parking the car. She'll be up in a minute."

Lynch put his soggy, half-chewed cigar on the corner of Ryan's desk, reached into his rumpled jacket and took out an envelope. "I want to give you this before she gets here. I don't trust her."

Belfry countered. "She's good people."

"Good people or not, I don't trust her." He handed the envelope to Redmond. "There's twenty-five thousand dollars. It's from Capra. He'd like you to stay away from him."

Redmond hefted the money. "We appreciate this, Jerry. But it isn't necessary. All you had to do was ask us to stay away."

"I know, but my man insisted on giving you a taste."

Redmond opened the envelope and removed the rubber bands from the money. "How much of this is for you, Jerry?"

"None of it. It's all yours. Split it anyway you want. The only thing I want to know is, do you have anything on Capra?"

"Not really. All we did was put a sneak on him."

"I hope you're not holding back on me."

"No. We have nothing on him except a stool who says that Capra is doing. That's all."

"What's the stool's name?"

Belfry laughed. "Come on, Jerry. We can't tell you that. He'd be dead in the morning."

Lynch stood up to leave. "There might be another twenty-five in it for you if you let me know."

Redmond looked at Belfry, who shrugged. He turned back to Lynch. "Capra shouldn't turn his back on 'Crazy Al Salerno.' "

Lynch left the SIU office and met Brogan as she was coming up the staircase. "Brogan, you look terrific tonight."

"Jerry, you better not try to burn me with that cigar."

"Come on, Brogan. Don't you trust me?"

"About as far as I can throw you."

"You sure know how to hurt a guy," Lynch grinned.

When Conner went into Ryan's office, she saw Redmond counting two stacks of money. He pushed the two piles of fifty $100 bills over to Ryan. "Lieutenant, there's ten thousand dollars here. We'll keep fifteen. Take care of Captain Hughes when he gets back."

Conner flushed. "Gentlemen, if you don't mind, I'm going to wait downstairs."

Redmond put the rest of the money in his pocket and a minute later, left Ryan's office with Belfry. Going down the stairs, he handed Belfry fifteen thousand dollars. "When you get a chance, whack this in two, Dickie. That's seven thousand five hundred dollars each."

Belfry's face lit up. "What about Conner?"

"You saw her. She doesn't want any part of this."

September 18, 1969

LYNCH AND BENINATI GULPED THEIR beers and fans cheered as shortstop Buddy Harrelson grabbed a dying line drive for the final out in the top of the ninth inning. Wiping his mouth with his bare arm, the perspiring Lynch complained, "Graziano, you must be nuts having us meet you at a dumb baseball game."

"Hey, this is where the action is. The Mets are going all the way."

"I hope they lose every game from now on and next time, get us seats in the shade. You know I hate getting sun on my head."

Pittsburgh's reliever Nelson Briles delivered a slow curve for a strike. Lynch turned to Graziano, "Let's get down to business. When can you get us the forty keys, Joe?"

"Didn't you get the message I left in your box? I sold it."

Lynch shrilled, "You *what?!*"

Everybody around them leaped up as a pop foul headed in their direction but wound up in the upper deck.

"Jerry, calm down. I'm only kidding, for Christ's sake."

Lynch squeezed back into his seat. "Don't kid around about stuff like that."

As the crowd was settling down, Beninati suddenly piped up, "Where are you keeping it, Joe?"

"Keeping what?"

"The shit."

"Wouldn't you ugly cocksuckers love to know."

A solid single up the middle by Rusty Staub opened the bottom of the ninth for the Mets, the score still tied nothing-nothing.

Beninati started again. "Come on, Joe. You can tell us where the shit is. Suppose something happens to you?"

"Loo, If I told you guys where it was, something would happen to me for sure."

Beninati faked disgust. "And another thing, Graziano. You're a lousy thief. Eighteen thousand a key."

"Hey, it's dry out there."

"But eighteen thousand is highway robbery."

Graziano jumped up with the crowd and cheered when Duffy Dyer smashed a fastball into left field and Rusty, not New York's fastest man, beat Richie Zisk's throw to home plate and slid past Pirate catcher Manny Sanguillen. Sitting down, he turned to Beninati. "You guys are going to sell it for twenty-two, twenty-three thousand. Maybe twenty-four. Ain't a working stiff entitled to a few bucks?"

"When do we get the junk?"

"Soon."

"How soon?"

"Do you have the $720,000?"

"We have it."

As the delirious Met fans celebrated the 1:0 win over the Pirates, Graziano said, "Then let's shoot for next week."

September 29, 1969

PATRICK KLYNE PARKED HIS CAR a block away from the Property Clerk. He turned and looked at Graziano. "Joe, I think you're crazy going in there and checking out that shit without an excuse to bring it someplace. Suppose you're stopped?"

Graziano half-opened the car door. "Don't worry, kid. Nobody's going to stop me."

Fifteen cops formed two lines checking in property or returning evidence when Graziano reached the second-floor landing. An inordinate amount of empty cigarette packages, ground-out butts and crumpled candy wrappers littered the floor, mute proof that Monday was the Property Clerk's busiest day of the week. Graziano got in line and looked to see if the two clerks who inadvertently helped him pull off the first theft were there. If either of them was in attendance, he was going to make light of the fact that the DA was still working on old cases. If a new clerk experienced difficulty finding the evidence, he planned to direct him to the section of the cage where the narcotics had been located previously.

Both lines moved rapidly, and Graziano found himself facing a loud, heavyset man in his mid-fifties whom he had never seen before.

"Good afternoon," Graziano said, handing the clerk a slip of paper with the voucher number M573-62 on it.

"Where's your voucher sheet?" the clerk asked irritably.

"I don't have one. I was told by my office to bring this evidence to the DA's Office."

The clerk looked at the number. "This is bullshit. How am I supposed to find a 1962 case at three o'clock in the afternoon?"

"Officer, I don't make the rules. I follow them. All I know is that the DA wants this evidence. By the way, there are two suitcases. Now, that shouldn't be too difficult to find. Or is it?"

The clerk took a step back and yelled, "Ambrose! Ambrose!"

"What?"

"Take my window for a year while I try to find some old stuff." The angry clerk went into the special cage. Graziano watched him chew on a dead cigar as he furiously pushed and tossed bags and packages aside. Graziano couldn't bear to watch. He paced the reception room kicking candy wrappers and empty cigarette packages. Twenty minutes later, the clerk removed two gray suitcases from the highest shelf on the rack, and carried them to the evidence window where Ambrose was pinch-hitting. Ambrose stepped aside. The clerk scratched his groin, relit his cigar, made some entries in the voucher book and turned it around for Graziano to sign. Graziano took the pen in his right hand and signed "Grazziana."

Then Graziano drew a blank.

He couldn't remember the shield number he used the first time. Impulsively, he scribbled the numbers "3495." The clerk reversed the book, looked at the name and raised his eyes to Graziano's shield. Graziano realized his shield, with different numbers on it, was still pinned to his jacket.

"How long have you been a gold shield?"

"About six years," Graziano replied, removing his shield.

"I was a gold shield ten years ago. In the two-eight. But ten of us got flopped." The clerk extended his hand through the window. "Sorry I was sharp with you before. I hate Mondays."

"Think nothing of it," Graziano smiled, shaking his hand.

As the clerk passed the suitcases out to Graziano through the window, Graziano put them on the floor. Suddenly, the same commanding officer who was present during the first theft came bustling out of his office, with a newspaper in one hand and a container of coffee in the other. He stopped and looked at Graziano. "Officer, you look familiar. Did you ever work for me?"

"I don't think so."

"What about the George Wallace presidential rally at Madison Square Garden last year? I was in command."

"No, I wasn't there, but I sure wish he was elected." Both the Captain and the clerk agreed. "What's this?" the Captain asked, nudging one of the suitcases with his foot.

"An old case," replied Graziano.

"Where are you parked, officer?"

"Right downstairs, sir."

The captain turned to the clerk, "Get someone to give him a hand, O'Mara."

"That's all right, sir. My partner will be right up," Graziano said quickly.

"Just trying to be helpful." The Captain waved good-bye with his newspaper and scooted off. Graziano picked up both suitcases and walked towards the stairwell. He chuckled and thought to himself, *Here I am a poor dumb Italian boy, with all the luck of the Irish.*

December 5, 1969

AN IRRITATED MCDUFF SPAT. "WAITING for these spicks to do something is boring."

"Jack, take it easy. You're going to wear a hole in the rug," Graziano advised.

"This is a waste of time. We've been here close to a month, and Fernandez hasn't done a goddamn thing except screw those two broads silly and run back and forth to his safety deposit box."

"Just take it easy, something's going to happen."

"Joe, nothing's going to happen, and even if it did, we'd never know. We can't even put a sneak on his phone or bug his room." McDuff sat on the edge of the bed. "It wouldn't be so bad if we could bug his room, but he always makes one of the broads stay up there while he wanders all over town without a care in the world."

"Gilberto says it's going down any day now."

"Gilberto again? You think your stools know everything. He's been wrong before, plenty of times."

"Jack, gimme a break and stop whining. We're all tired of sitting on the prick, but Gil insists this guy is waiting for a package." Graziano pulled the window drapes aside and looked out from their room in the Americana Hotel onto Seventh Avenue. "What do you think, Ray?"

Carrera, sprawled out on the bed, replied, "I know there's something happening. That scumbag checks his box twice a day. He's got something in there. It must be loaded with bread. I say we stick it out."

THE FOLLOWING AFTERNOON, MCDUFF CALLED downstairs and requested the switchboard operator to page Carrera, who was standing by the house phones in the ornately decorated lobby. Carrera picked up the phone at once. "What's up?"

"Ray, Fernandez is on his way down. One of the girls is with him."

"I got him. He just came out of the elevator, with the broad I like."

Carrera watched the expensively dressed couple get into a waiting limousine. He hailed a cab and followed them to the McAlpin Hotel on West Thirty-fourth Street, where Fernandez rented a room. Carrera watched him pocket the room key and walk with the woman to the elevator bank. As one of the elevator doors opened, Fernandez quickly glanced around, took the woman's arm and hurried outside the hotel to a cab. Carrera, fearful he might had been made, decided not to follow them, instead he went over to the front desk clerk, flashed his shield and identified himself.

"Can you tell me what room that couple just rented?"

The young clerk looked at Carrera for a second and nervously answered, "Room 612, officer."

As Carrera turned from the counter, the desk clerk asked, "By the way, do you know a Detective Degman? He's in the two-four squad."

Carrera leaned across the counter. "Richie Degman?"

The clerk smiled. "Yeah."

"I know him well. How do you know him?"

"He's my older brother. I'm John Degman. I'm going on the job in a couple of months."

"Congratulations, kid. You're going to love it. Tell Richie 'Spanish Ray' sends his best regards. He'll know who it is." Carrera paused. "John, I need a favor. Is there any chance I can get a room near 612?"

The clerk checked the room chart. "I can give you one opposite 612 or right beside it."

"The room next door would be perfect."

"That's Room 610. Do you want me to ask the manager if I can give it to you on the arm?"

"Let me pay for the room tonight. If we need it any longer, we'll let you know. Could you do me another favor?"

"What's that?"

"I'd like a key to 612."

GRAZIANO MET CARRERA IN ROOM 610. "What's happening, Ray?"

"I'm not sure if that sucker made me or not. Like I told you on the phone, it was a wild move. He went to the elevator, but never went upstairs. He grabbed the bimbo and got a cab."

"Where are they now?"

"McDuff is sitting on them at the Americana. And is he pissed! You know how he hates sitting in that stinking room."

"That's tough. It goes with the territory." Graziano took off his leather jacket and put it on the back of a chair. "Let me call him and find out what gives." Graziano dialed the Americana and asked to be put through to Room 402.

McDuff answered gruffly, "Yeah."

"Are they still in there?"

"Where else would they be?"

"OK. Call me if anything changes. Ray's going next door now. As soon as he finishes, I'll come up and relieve you."

CARRERA LEFT THE ROOM AND unlocked the door to Room 612. It took him less than a minute to install a miniaturized listening device to the top of a large picture frame centered over the queen-sized bed. He placed a second device on top of the inside bathroom door frame. Pleased, Carrera quietly returned to Room 610. He put on a headset and told Graziano to call Room 612. A moment later, a smile lit up Carrera's face as he heard the phone in Room 612 ring loud and clear. "You can hear a flea fart in there, Joe."

"Terrific." Graziano stood up and rubbed his stubbly chin. "Ray, you look tired. Why don't you crap out here for awhile? I'll shoot up to the Americana and relieve McDuff for a couple of hours. If anything happens, I'll call you."

"Good idea." Carrera sat down on the bed and kicked off his shoes. "Maybe we should bring in Belfry and Redmond to give us a hand. We're really stretched thin."

"Forget those thieves. If we're going to get anybody to give us a hand, let's get Ramos and Novack. At least they speak Spanish." Graziano put on his leather coat. "Anyway, I think we should wait and give it another day or two before we bring anyone in. No sense in having two more mouths to feed."

"When do I see you next?"

"Probably tomorrow afternoon. I have to go to school in the morning. My kid's been acting up again. Then I'm going to run down to the office and bring Ryan up to date."

ANNE GRAZIANO OPENED THE FRONT door of her house. "Sonny, Eddie, what are you doing here? Is everything OK?"

Sonny Grosso took off his hat. "Everything's fine, Anne. Is Joe awake?"

Anne Graziano tightened her robe and welcomed the men inside. "He's asleep. He was out most of the night." She led the men into the living room. "I'm supposed to wake him in an hour because he's got to go to Joey's school. But if it's important, I'll get him up now."

Eddie Egan draped his overcoat over a chair. "It is important, Anne. But if you don't mind, we'd like to wake him up. We have a surprise for him."

"Good news, I hope."

"It's great news. Come on upstairs with us. I want you to see his face."

"Let me put a pot of coffee on."

"No, it'll wait. This is too important. Come on up with us."

Anne watched both men take off their shoes and tiptoe up the carpeted stairs to the bedroom.

Egan and Grosso crept noiselessly into the room and stood at the foot of the bed. Anne observed the scene from the doorway.

Grosso tickled the bottom of Graziano's foot and in singsong voice chanted, "Jooooeeeeeyyyy. Oh, Jooooeeeeeyyyy. Wake up, sweetheart. Jooooeeeeeyyyyy."

Graziano stirred, propped himself up on an elbow and adjusted his eyes. "What the hell . . . ?"

Both Egan and Grosso started tap dancing clumsily while singing, "Hoooray For Holllleeeeewood!"

A wide smile creased Graziano's face. "Congratulations, you bums. That's terrific."

Egan raced over to the side of the bed and tousled Graziano's disheveled hair. "Isn't it the greatest? Two New York cops going to Hollywood. It's unbelievable. We're taking a year's leave of absence to be technical advisors. As a matter of fact, we're even going to be in the picture! Sonny's part is small, but I get to do a lot of talking."

"I'm thrilled for you guys. Truly thrilled. Isn't it great, Anne?"

"It's wonderful. I couldn't be happier."

Grosso hugged Anne and said, "Tell him, Popeye."

Egan stiffened uncomfortably. "You do it."

"You're the bigshot with the talking part. You tell him."

Egan moved to the side of the bed. "Joe, none of this would have been possible without your help. Without you pushing and helping us with Moore, there'd have been no story. We can't thank you enough."

"Cut the shit. If it wasn't me it would have been someone else."

Grosso moved to Egan's side. "Know what breaks my heart, Joe? I'm sorry it's not the three of us."

"Don't worry. I'll be fine."

After the aspiring movie stars had left, Anne sat down on the side of her husband's bed."Come on, Joe, be honest. You must be upset. It's your book as much as it's theirs. Wouldn't you have loved to go to Hollywood? All the glory . . . and the girls."

"Sure." He paused. "I just have to get my share of the 'French Connection' some other way."

"At least they can give us tickets for the opening gala." Anne got up. "You have plenty of time. Stay. I'll bring you some coffee." She turned at the door. "Joe, we're getting a new car?"

Graziano pulled the pillow up behind his head. "Yeah, but who told you? I wanted it to be a surprise. Anne, it's a beauty."

"But can we afford it? The orthodontist bill was over three thousand dollars."

"You are the eternal worrier, Anne. Yes, we can afford it."

"You know, Joe, I always remember what my mother said. 'If everything is too good, look twice. Maybe something is wrong.' " She closed the door gently behind her.

Joseph Graziano closed his eyes. His wife's concern did not bother him. His conscience was already hardened and sealed, his moral arteries clogged by easy cash.

*   *   *

GRAZIANO WHISTLED 'HOORAY FOR HOLLYWOOD' as he walked down the hallway of the McAlpin Hotel to Room 610. He was about to knock on the door when McDuff swung it open. "How did you do that?"

"Do what?" hissed McDuff.

"Open the door without me knocking."

"Women's intuition," yelled Carrera from behind McDuff through a mouthful of a ham and cheese sandwich.

McDuff whipped around and glared at Carrera who was wearing a headset. "Shut up, Ray. They're right next door."

McDuff refocused on Graziano and whispered, "Where for Christ's sake have you been? Fernandez got two guys in there with him. You were supposed to be here at one o'clock. We've been leaving messages for you all over the place. When we couldn't reach you, we got Ramos and Novack to watch the broads at the Americana. In case you're interested, it's a go. The package is coming tonight."

"Are you sure?"

"Positive. Carrera picked it up this morning. It's coming in from Chile. They're bringing it here to the hotel."

At 7:30 P.M., Carrera yanked off his headset. "Jack! Joe! Get ready."

McDuff jumped off the bed and went over to Carrera, who held one of the earphones against his ear.

"What's up?"

"They're going downstairs to get a bite to eat in a few minutes. Then they're going to wait for them in the lobby."

"Ray, you stay up here and listen. Joe and I'll go downstairs and wait. As soon as we get to the lobby, I'll call you and find out what's happening."

Moments later, McDuff called Carrera from the house phone. "Did they leave yet?"

"Any second now. One of them is taking a leak."

Graziano and Mcduff watched the three men step out of the elevator and go into the hotel's coffee shop. The taller of the two men with Fernandez carried an oversized gray Samsonite attaché case. After eating, they came out of the shop, took seats in the lobby and chatted excitedly in Spanish. Within a half hour, two disheveled Latins wearing rumpled sport jackets struggled into the lobby carrying a cumbersome rectangular wicker container. Graziano glanced over at McDuff, who was standing by the house phones, and nodded. McDuff watched the five men greet each other boisterously. As the group slowly inched towards the elevator, McDuff dialed Room 610. "Ray, it's beautiful down here. They'll be up in a minute."

As the men neared the elevators, McDuff raced up the fire stairs two at a time to the sixth floor. In the lobby, Graziano helpfully held the elevator door open for the two Chileans jockeying the heavy wicker basket. He waited for the five men to enter the elevator, pushed the button for the seventh floor and stood off to the side. Fernandez glanced at him and pushed the button for the sixth floor. The elevator started and five pairs of eyes were riveted on Graziano as he stared up at the floor indicator. The elevator stopped on the sixth floor and the five men got off without speaking. Graziano sensed their collective sigh of relief as the elevator door closed.

Through the slight opening of the fire-exit door, McDuff observed the men making their way down the hallway. The last two with the heavy wicker basket momentarily stopped for a rest. Graziano quietly came down the fire stairs behind McDuff and put his hand on his shoulder. They both watched Fernandez open the door to Room 612. As he stepped inside and switched on the lights, McDuff and Graziano pushed open the fire door and pounced.

Fernandez froze in the doorway. Carrera, his .38 drawn, beckoned him forward. "*Raoul, entra por favor. Estra por favorti.*" Graziano and McDuff came up behind the other four men and shoved them into the room. In Spanish, Carrera ordered the five to lie face down on the floor and extend their arms. Graziano frisked the men for weapons while Carrera and McDuff kept them covered. He relieved them of their wallets, and he also took the safe-deposit box and room keys from Fernandez. He picked up the Samsonite attaché case that had been dropped on the rug and opened it. It was filled with stacks of fifty and one hundred dollar bills.

"Whose is this?" Carrera translated Graziano's question in rapid-fire Spanish.

There was no response.

Graziano said, "Perhaps you didn't hear me. Who owns this attaché case?"

Carrera rattled off the question once more in Spanish. No response. Graziano grinned. "Then I guess it's mine. Is that right?"

Carrera smiled as he repeated Graziano's question. Again, there was no response. Graziano winked and showed the contents of the case to Carrera and McDuff. In Spanish, Carrera continued, "Thank you for your honesty, gentlemen. I wouldn't want you to say something was yours when it wasn't."

Graziano closed the case and tossed it on the bed. He then walked over to the wicker basket. "What have we here?"

No response. Graziano poked Fernandez with his foot. "Fernandez, this is yours, right?"

Fernandez lifted his head off the floor, twisted his neck and stared up at Graziano. In a heavily accented voice, he said, "Nooo, sir."

"Whose is it?"

"I no know, sir."

Graziano turned to Carrera. "Ask them in Spanish if anybody owns the basket."

Carrera bent his knees and squatted. *"Hay una persona que posea la canasta?"*

The five men chorused, "No, sir."

McDuff ripped open the wicker basket. Heavy matted straw protected four ten-gallon jugs of Concha y Toro wine. McDuff reached down and removed one of the dark-green glass jugs from the basket.

"Holy shit. Feel the weight of this thing."

"Bring it into the bathroom. We'll open it in the tub," Graziano ordered.

McDuff tilted the bottle towards Graziano. "What are we going to open it with? Look at the size of the cork!"

Graziano took the bottle from McDuff. "Go downstairs and get a corkscrew from the maître' d. In the meantime, I'll take the money next door and count it."

"Joe, hold on. I was born at night, but not last night. You run downstairs and get the corkscrew, and I count the money."

"It sounds like you don't trust me," Graziano said softly.

"I trust you, Joe. But promise you'll wait here with Ray until I get back. Then we'll count it together."

"That's a promise."

A perspiring McDuff returned with a heavy corkscrew. It took a herculean effort on his part to pull the cork out of the bottle. He sniffed the cork. "This stuff smells pretty good. Want a drink?"

Graziano frowned. "Cut it out. Just find out what's in there."

McDuff tilted the jug and slowly poured the wine into the tub. But soon, too soon, the flow became a trickle. McDuff shook the last drops out of the bottle. "What a shame. I coulda used a drink."

Graziano moved closer. "Can you see inside?"

McDuff hoisted the bottle above his shoulders to the bright vanity lights. "I can't see a damn thing—oops, wait a second. There is something. It looks like a divider."

"Stick your finger in there. See if you feel anything."

"My finger's not that long. We should have brought Cahill with us. He coulda dropped his cock in there and probably hit bottom."

They both laughed. McDuff volunteered, "Damn, I'm going to run downstairs to Maintenance and get a screwdriver."

"Get a hammer while you're down there. We might have to break the thing open. And see if you can borrow a flashlight."

McDuff paused in the bathroom doorway. "Same conditions apply, Joe. No counting the money until I come back."

Ten minutes later McDuff sat on the toilet bowl seat, jug between his knees, holding a flashlight close to the bottle's mouth.

Graziano, standing in the tub, inquired, "Jack, can you see anything?"

"It looks like some sort of wax or something."

Graziano handed McDuff a long screwdriver. "Stick this into it."

McDuff probed the material with the screwdriver. "It's kinda soft. I think I can make a hole in it." He worked the tip of the screwdriver deeper into the wax and widened the hole with circular motion. "I'm through."

"Can you see anything yet?"

"Give me another second." McDuff took the flashlight and peered into the bottle. "Jesus Christ! There's gotta be ten keys here! How did those two gold-toothed crooks ever get this dope through customs? It's a national disgrace!"

Graziano took the flashlight and looked for himself. "Their loss is our gain."

After checking that the other three wine bottles also contained high-quality cocaine, Graziano called Carrera into the bathroom while McDuff guarded the prisoners. "Ray, stay here and watch these guys. Jack and I are going next door to count the money. When we're finished, we're going to the Americana and take a look in Fernandez's safety deposit box. OK?"

"OK."

"Before we leave, I'll let you know how much is in the case."

"I appreciate that." As Graziano opened the bathroom door Carrera inquired, "What about the girls in Fernandez's room?"

"Jack and I will hit their room with Ramos and Novack."

"Sounds good. Keep in touch."

"I'll call you from the Americana and let you know what's going on."

Graziano and McDuff took the attaché case to Room 610 and counted the money by wrappers. Before leaving for the Americana, Graziano knocked on the door of Room 612 and quietly told Carrera, "$220,000."

GRAZIANO CARRIED AN EMPTY BRIEFCASE into the Americana Hotel and walked straight to the front desk. McDuff sank in a soft-cushioned chair in the lobby with the attaché case containing close to a quarter-million in U.S. currency on his lap. He watched Graziano hand Fernandez's safety-deposit-box key to the desk clerk, who indicated a side door adjacent to the front desk and requested Graziano to come in. Once Graziano closed the door behind him, the desk clerk opened a small vault and removed a long, thin safety-deposit box, then discreetly returned to the front desk.

Alone, Graziano teased the steel lid open slightly. A glimpse of green, a smile of greed. Packets of hundred-dollar bills lined the box from end to end. Graziano checked the money straps and estimated their was eighty thousand dollars in all. He stuffed the straps into the briefcase, called to the clerk and said he was finished. She placed the box in the vault and returned the key to Graziano.

Graziano left the hotel by a side entrance on Fifty-third Street and waited in the cold air for the trailing McDuff. He handed McDuff the briefcase. "Jack, take all the money home. We'll split it later. Take out six thousand for Novack and Ramos."

"What about Ryan?"

"Shit. I forgot about him. Give me a second. Take out twenty-two thousand dollars."

"How much is in the briefcase?"

"I just skimmed it. Around eighty thousand dollars."

"Ah-ha. You don't know for sure, do you?"

"I have a pretty good idea."

"Better you have to trust me than the other way around."

BUENOS NOCHES, SENORITAS." DETECTIVE JOE NOVACK pushed opened the door to Room 404. Two women jumped off the bed, one holding a blouse to her bare chest. The taller of the two women snapped, "Who are you people?"

Graziano pushed her backwards. "Friends of Raoul."

"No, you're not. I know his friends."

"You're wrong. Look, he gave us the key."

"You're the police. I can tell."

"You're quick, honey. Raoul sure could have used you on an elevator a couple of hours ago."

"What?"

"Forget it. Both of you get your asses against the wall and stay there."

Within a minute, Ramos removed a suitcase from under the bed. He lifted the suitcase onto a chair and opened it. "Joe, take a look at this. You're going to like what you see."

Graziano stepped away from the closet he was searching, went over to Ramos, and saw rows of plastic bags containing white powder. He lifted one of them out of the suitcase. "Oh, my, my, ladies. What have we here?"

"We don't know what it is. We never saw it before."

Graziano carefully opened a bag and removed a pinch of the substance. He rubbed the powder between his fingers and touched it with the tip of his tongue. He grimaced and spit, "Ladies, you have a big problem. You're going to jail."

WHAT A GIGANTIC COLLAR!" CARRERA crowed. "Forty-four keys of cocaine and sixteen keys of heroin! What do you think, lieutenant? Aren't we the best?"

"It's good, but I've seen better," Ryan grunted.

Carrera shot back, "You must be referring to our *last* collar, Lieutenant." The men were laughing as McDuff entered the squad room of the Eighteenth Precinct and handed Graziano a briefcase and small gym bag. Graziano gave a sign to Ramos and Novack to follow him. Walking them down the stairs, he gave Ramos the gym bag which had six thousand dollars in it, thanked them both, and advised them he would handle everything from then on and returned to the squad room. "Lieutenant, do you have a minute?"

In the men's room, Graziano made sure all the stalls were empty and locked the door before handing the briefcase to Ryan.

"How much is here, Joe?"

"Twenty-two thousand dollars."

Ryan shook his head. "I'm very, very disappointed, Joe. I thought it was going to be a lot more. Carrera told me there was a lot of money in that attaché case you grabbed at the McAlpin. And what about the safety deposit box at the Americana you've been bullshitting me about for the last month? How much was in there?"

"All together, it was sixty-one thousand dollars. We gave Novack and Ramos three thousand each. We took eleven apiece for us, and there's that famous double cut for you and downtown."

Ryan's face reddened. "Joe, we go back a long way. You've been like a son to me. I can take a lot of things, Joe, but I won't take anyone cheating me. This means you, your team, anybody. You're shortchanging me now. I'm telling you this once, don't ever do it again. If you do, you're out of SIU."

April 17, 1970

"STEP DOWN, DETECTIVE GRAZIANO." As Graziano started to get out of the chair, Judge Rothman continued, "I would like to say in passing, Detective, that the Court appreciates the clarity and conciseness of your testimony at this suppression hearing."

"Thank you, Your Honor." Graziano stepped down from the witness stand and stood by two valises and a suitcase. McDuff, seated in the front row of the courtroom, rose and stood beside Graziano.

Judge Rothman directed his attention to ADA Hannon and a battery of Hispanic attorneys who were defending Fernandez and his associates. "Today is April 17th. I'm going to set the trial date for May 21st. Be prepared."

"May I approach the bench, Your Honor?" asked Raphael Gonzalez, the attorney for Fernandez.

"No. Anything you have to say can be said from there."

"Your Honor, there are many attorneys involved in this case. All of us are very busy, and we have other commitments. We were hoping you would start the trial in September. This way, my fellow counselors and I could have the summer to get ready for the case."

"Please, counselor, spare me. You've had months to prepare. May 21st it is. Be here, and be ready for trial."

AT THE AMERICANA HOTEL Graziano, carrying two leather valises filled with nearly ninety-seven pounds of cocaine and McDuff, following with a suitcase containing thirty-five pounds of heroin, got off the elevator on the fourth floor. McDuff laughed as he watched Graziano stumble and recover his balance. "Graziano, you look worse than those two dumb Chileans."

Graziano opened the door to the fire stairs. "I might look worse than those spicks, but I'm a lot smarter. At least I check stairwells."

The men moved down the hall to Room 404. Just as McDuff was about to knock on the door, Carrera flung open the door.

Startled, McDuff asked, "How did you do that?"

"What?"

"Open the door without me knocking."

Graziano and Carrera giggled at McDuff. "Women's intuition!"

Carrera took one of the valises from Graziano and admitted the men into the room. "Joe, of all places, why this hotel, why this floor?"

"Because lightning never strikes twice in the same place. Besides, it's one of the few hotels in the city where you can take the elevator directly from the garage to the room floor."

Carrera stepped back and pointed to the five-pound packages of flour and glassine bags on the sheet "We're all set."

As Graziano moved forward, McDuff grabbed his arm. "Joe, for the last time, Ray and I would like to know who you're selling this to."

Graziano whirled on him. "We've been through this before, Jack. I can't tell you."

"That's bullshit. Partners tell partners. There are no secrets between partners."

"I gave my word, and that's it."

"Go ahead then, and make your crummy secret deals. But you're wrong and you know it. Ray and I should know who you're selling this shit to. We helped you get it."

April 25, 1970

GRAZIANO PARKED HIS NEW BRIGHT-RED Buick convertible next to Dino's Pizza Parlor, in Douglaston, Queens. Several women, all wearing green T-shirts, chatting outside, waved. Inside, a dozen excited and noisy Little Leaguers, brown and green stains on their uniforms, hats on backwards, screamed "We're number one!" One of the mothers grabbed Graziano by the arm and escorted him to Coach Ciliano. "Maybe you can help him control the crowd." Michelle Graziano and her male teammates cheered when slices and sodas arrived. A rolled-up paper napkin bounced off the side of Joe Graziano's head.

As he reached down to pick up the napkin, Graziano noticed the headline of a discarded, sauce-splattered *New York Times* lying on a nearby chair. His eyes narrowed as he read the headline: "GRAFT PAID TO POLICE HERE SAID TO RUN INTO MILLIONS."

He grabbed the paper and started to read, electrified. "Narcotics dealers, gamblers and businessmen make illicit payments of millions of dollars a year to the policemen of New York, according to law enforcement experts and New Yorkers who make such payments themselves. Despite such widespread corruption, officials in both the Lindsay administration and the Police Department have failed to investigate a number of cases of corruption brought to their attention. The policemen and private citizens who talked to the *Times* described situations in which payoffs by gamblers to policemen are almost commonplace, in which some policemen accept bribes from narcotics dealers, in which businessmen throughout the city are subjected to extortion to cover up infractions of law and in which internal payoffs among policemen seem to have become institutionalized. One of the policemen who came to the *Times* discussed the effect of the departmental attitude toward corruption on the individual policeman. 'I believe that 90 percent of the cops would prefer to be honest, but they see so much corruption around them that they feel it is pointless not to go along.' "

Graziano skimmed through the rest of the article to see if the Narcotics Division and the SIU were mentioned. Satisfied the article was general in nature, with more focus on bribes and payoffs to cops in the Gambling Division, Graziano folded the newspaper and pushed it into the white trash receptacle. He strolled over to the coach's table, sat down and rehashed the kids' surprising 17-8 victory. When the check came, Graziano snapped it up. He peeled off a hundred-dollar bill from a large wad and paid the $11.45 tab.

April 28, 1970

NEW YORK MAYOR JOHN LINDSAY convened an emergency closed-door meeting at City Hall with his top advisors and several upper-echelon police officials. The administration aides, including Deputy Mayor Richard Aurelio, sat on one side of a massive mahogany conference table, while Police Commissioner Howard R. Leary and three deputy commissioners were placed across from them. Lindsay, jacketless and looking troubled tossed a folded newspaper he was carrying onto the table and dropped into his chair.

"Richard, how many of those rotten vultures are out there? It looks like a small army."

"Mr. Mayor, you told me to call a press conference."

"Yes, but I didn't expect you to invite the foreign press corps." Lindsay shoved his *New York Times* across the table. It stopped within inches of Leary's right arm. "What the hell is going on, Howard?"

"Mr. Mayor, much of that article is old hat. Last year, a cop named Frank Serpico beefed to Headquarters that plainclothesmen assigned to the Seventh Division in the Bronx were on the take. We thoroughly investigated his allegations and brought the matter to the attention of the Bronx DA's Office. They later indicted several plainclothesmen. Don't you remember? It was a big deal." Leary attempted to placate the Mayor. "Don't worry, we did everything according to Hoyle."

"Who?"

"Hoyle. It's just an expression, sir."

"Oh. *That* Hoyle. I thought you were talking about some DA." Lindsay loosened his tie, leaned back and closed his eyes. "I remember the incident well, Howard, but that's not the point. Serpico is now saying the Seventh Division is just a microcosm of the entire Police Department's corruption. He says all the Gambling units in the city are corrupt." Lindsay opened his eyes and sat up straight. "The man is specifically quoted as saying, 'It's not just a few rotten apples in a barrel. The whole barrel is rotten.' He said these practices have been going on since the 1800s, and no one has ever done anything to stop it."

"How would he know? He wasn't even on the job in the 1800s unless he's a lot older than he looks." The police personnel with Leary snickered politely, while the politicians fidgeted and stared at Lindsay.

"Howard, you may think this is a joke, but in twenty minutes I have to meet with a very hostile press."

"Your Honor, I know it's not a joke. I just think things are being blown out of proportion."

"Out of proportion or not, that's what's being said about your department. And to be frank, Howard, there's been a lot of rumbling lately.

Not only from this cop in the Bronx, but rumors are flying around City Hall that many of the men in the Narcotics Division are on the take."

"Excuse my French, Mr. Mayor, but that's bullshit."

"Again, BS or not, the public perceives the Department to be out of control and completely corrupt. And you know as well as I do, in the eye of the beholder, perception is truth."

"Granted, Mr. Mayor. There have been a few isolated incidents of misdeeds, but we're on top of them. For the record, the Gambling and Narcotics Divisions are comprised of hard-working, honest, dedicated men."

"Say what you may, Howard, but last week I had Congressman Rangel from Harlem in my office. He was very frank with me. Are you ready for this, Howard?"

"Yes."

"Rangel claimed a number of policemen have requested he intervene on their behalf and get them transferred to the Harlem Narcotics Squad, because, and I quote, 'that's where all the money is.' "

"Rangel's a liar and a rabble-rouser."

"Most Democrats are, Howard, but you're missing the point. He's also been talking to the *Times*. And with this morning's article screaming for wholesale changes, I have to demonstrate we're not afraid to take bold remedial action."

Leary sighed, "What do you have in mind, Your Honor?"

"Howard, I've already instructed Richard here to form a search committee to find a group of respectable New Yorkers, with impeccable credentials, who can be impaneled as a commission to investigate corruption in the Police Department."

"Your Honor, that's unnecessary. I can assure you, Internal Affairs is working diligently to ferret out corruption in the Department. The last thing they need is a group of power-hungry civilians looking over their shoulder and usurping their authority."

"I appreciate what you're saying, Commissioner, but I got word the *Times* is going to call for some sort of independent commission to look into police corruption. So for once in my life, I'm going to beat those slimy hypocrites to the punch."

* * *

FLANKED BY COMMISSIONER LEARY AND Deputy Mayor Aurelio, John Lindsay stood smiling and waving in front of a battery of cameras and microphones. The mayor cleared his throat twice and read his prepared statement. "Reports in the *Times* of rampant police corruption are extremely serious and go to the heart of the effectiveness of law enforcement in our city. These allegations must be investigated thoroughly and prompt action must be taken to change any general practices that can lead to misconduct. This government is committed to rooting out corruption and wrongdoing with every means at its command. That is why I have appointed Deputy Mayor Richard Aurelio to head a search committee to seek a group of able New Yorkers qualified to investigate all allegations of police corruption in this city. I've instructed Deputy Mayor Aurelio to have a list of twenty-five names submitted to me by the end of the month."

Gabe Pressman, a TV reporter from NBC, interrupted. "Mr. Mayor, does that mean—"

Annoyed, Lindsay looked up from his notes. "Mr. Pressman, please let me finish my statement. Then I'll be glad to answer your questions. OK?" Lindsay continued, "This commission will have the full cooperation of the New York City Police Department. It will be a completely independent unit with the power to subpoena."

"Mr. Mayor!"

"Please, Mr. Pressman, hold your question just a few seconds more. Now, where was I?"

Aurelio prompted in a low voice, "Power to subpoena."

"Er . . . Thank you, Richard. As to the specific charges in the *New York Times,* Police Commissioner Leary has assured me the allegations in this story came from only one particular policeman. The Commissioner insists the allegations were fully investigated at the time. Furthermore, if this officer has any additional information, the Commissioner will be only too happy to go over it with him and review his charges personally."

Lindsay looked out into the sea of gathered reporters. He deliberately avoided the waving Gabe Pressman and pointed to Robert Crane, a reporter from the *Daily News.* "Yes, Bob."

"Mr. Mayor, I'd like to ask Commissioner Leary a question if I may."

"Certainly." Lindsay stepped back. Leary nervously adjusted a microphone.

"Yes, Bob? You have a question?"

"Commissioner, with these serious allegations of corruption now surfacing, do you see yourself staying in New York on weekends? Or are you going to continue your practice of going home to Philadelphia to visit your wife and family?"

"Bob, this Philadelphia issue was put to rest years ago when I first became Commissioner. I'm disappointed you're raising it again. Four years ago, the Mayor and I struck an accommodation whereby I could go to Philadelphia on weekends to stay with my family. In a case of emergency, I am less than ninety minutes away by car. Seconds by phone. Nothing has changed since to warrant my staying here on weekends."

"I'm sorry if I've upset you, Commissioner," Crane continued. "Let me frame my question another way. With the public demanding that this corruption issue be addressed at the earliest possible moment, will you be spending any weekends here?"

"No. It's been my experience very little corruption takes place on weekends."

Startled, several reporters laughed. Crane scratched the side of his head. "Excuse me, Commissioner. Did I hear you right? Very little corruption occurs on a weekend?"

"Yes, you heard me correctly, Bob. But you know I was only kidding. However, I see nothing at the moment what would warrant a change in my personal arrangements."

As an ill-at-ease Leary stepped back from the microphones, Lindsay whispered to Aurelio. "Find me a new Commissioner. One without foot-in-mouth disease. And make damn sure he wants to live in New York."

May 1970

BERNIE MCCLELLAN OPENED HIS DESK drawer and removed a pair of well-used scissors. He spread out the *New York Times* and carefully cut out an article. He then walked to the back of the office and tacked the clipping on the bulletin board. Detectives Jimmy Canavan and Dave Cody pushed away from their desks, went over to the brown corkboard and read the article impassively: "LINDSAY APPOINTS CORRUPTION UNIT. Mayor Lindsay announced yesterday the appointment of a special five-man commission to investigate charges of widespread police corruption in New York City. The group also is to develop methods to prevent departmental corruption.

'Official corruption and rumors of corruption harm our Police Department as well as the public,' Mayor Lindsay said in a statement announcing the new commission. 'Corruption is devastating on police morale, police recruitment and police effectiveness, as well as public confidence.' The corruption commission will be headed by Whitman Knapp, a sixty-one-year old Wall Street lawyer who served in the Manhattan District Attorney's Office during the 1950s.

"Mayor Lindsay announced that to provide the commission 'unquestioned legal authority' he would ask the City Council to grant it power to subpoena witnesses. The mandate of the new commission, as defined by the executive order creating it, was extremely broad. It said the commission should investigate the extent of police corruption, evaluate the existing procedures for investigating corruption, recommend stronger safeguards against corruption and to hold whatever hearings, public or . . ."

Canavan ripped the article from the board, crumpled it into a ball and made a jump shot into the wastepaper basket.

September 1970

"NINETY-SEVEN DEGREES. I HATE New York summers. Thank God for air-conditioning, huh, Stanley?"

The graying black butler nodded and led Commissioner Leary into Gracie Mansion. "You returning to Philadelphia tonight, suh?"

"I hadn't planned to. Why? Do you know something I don't know?"

"No, suh. I forgot. I thought today was Friday."

The servant opened the door to the library and announced, "Commissioner Leary."

Mayor Lindsay and Deputy Mayor Aurelio started out of their chairs. "Hello, Howard. Would you like a drink before dinner?"

"Sounds good, Your Honor." Leary turned back to the butler. "I'll have a tall gin and tonic, Stanley. A twist of lemon instead of lime, if I may."

Lindsay motioned to an oversized couch. "Take a seat, Howard. How did it go today?"

"Just another long day, Mr. Mayor."

"Last night was pretty rough."

"Are you referring to Gabe's editorial on Channel 4?"

"It certainly wasn't very flattering. He's out for your scalp."

"There's not much I can do about it, Mr. Mayor."

Lindsay took a deep breath. "If it was me, Howard, I'd seriously consider resigning."

There was a pause, Leary digesting the mayor's bait. "Resigning? You want me to resign? You're throwing me to the wolves?"

"Please, Howard. This pains me very much. No one has served this administration with more dedication and loyalty than you. In fact, I consider you one of my closest personal friends. The last thing I would do is throw you to the wolves. Or is it lions?"

Aurelio assisted, "Wolves!"

"Thank you, Richard. I thought so." Lindsay sat down next to Leary. "Howard, I honestly have no choice. It's not only the media that's killing us. I had breakfast with the five members of the Knapp Commission this morning. They shared their preliminary report with me, and it's highly critical of the Department. In a nutshell, they believe you and your staff haven't shown enough initiative in fighting corruption. In fact, they blame your administration for perpetuating it."

"That's a goddam lie!" Leary answered, his voice rising. "They're making me a scapegoat to appease the media. And you're siding with them!"

"Howard, don't say that. We've been through a lot together over the years, and I've always stuck with you."

"But you're caving in to the press now!"

"Just the opposite, Howard. Trust me. The shit is going to hit the fan in a few months. It's going to be rough, real rough. As a friend, I want you long out of here. Incidentally, you're not leaving here hat in hand by any stretch of the imagination. You're getting a terrific pension and benefits package."

"Well, if it's all right with you, I'd like to leave as soon as possible. How much time do you need before you get someone to replace me?"

"To be honest, we don't need any time. Patrick Murphy, the Detroit Police Commissioner, accepted the position last week."

"Last week?"

"Yes."

"I wonder if he'd jump into my grave as quickly? Where's that drink, Stanley?"

"Howard, we had to move fast on this." Lindsay said gently.

Leary accepted the drink from the knowing butler and raised it slightly. "Thank you, Stanley. Mr. Mayor, if you don't mind, I'd like to skip dinner with you and Richard tonight. I'd rather head home for Philadelphia and talk to my wife before she reads about it in the newspapers."

WHEN THE OFFICIAL WORD CAME down that Murphy was the new Police Commissioner, a cautious Lt. John Ryan called Inspector Warren Creighton at his home in Valley Stream, Long Island. "Warren, I guess everything's on hold with Murphy coming in."

Creighton shot back, "Nothing's on hold, John. Nothing's going to change. You just do what you do best and meet me once a month. I've known Murphy a long time. He's a pompous, idealistic pain in the tail who keeps his head in the clouds. What you and me do is none of his business."

December 1970

"GOD ALMIGHTY, IT'S COLDER THAN a whore's heart out there," the razor-thin Eduardo Cortez said as he slammed the door of Detective Bob Bucci's car.

Bucci, who had been reassigned out of the SIU seven months earlier, rubbed his hands together. "Come on, Danny, it's not that cold. What are you trying to do? Make me feel bad?"

"That's easy for you to say. You've got your heater on full blast. I've been waiting out there for over an hour."

"It's all in your mind, Danny. If you think it's cold, it's cold. If you think it's hot, it's hot."

"Bullshit, Baby Face. It's twenty degrees out there. I don't think it's cold, I know it's cold. I can't even find my prick."

"I couldn't help it. I got stuck."

"You're always getting stuck. Let me see it."

Bucci reached into the pocket of his short black leather jacket, took out a packet wrapped in aluminum foil and carefully unwrapped it.

Cortez looked at the four ounces of heroin admiringly. "Beautiful." He lifted himself up slightly off the car seat, reached into his pants pocket and pulled out a large roll of ones, fives and tens.

"Here's the money. When do I see you again, Baby Face?"

"I'll be in touch."

" 'I'll be in touch.' That's all you ever say. Can ya gimme a ride to the subway?"

"I can't. I'm heading out to the Island. I'm going to hop on the highway right here at Cross Bay Boulevard."

"For Christ's sake! The subway's less than five minutes from here."

"Sorry, Danny Boy. I've got to get home. I'll catch you next time." He reached across Cortez and opened the passenger door of the Buick.

Cortez' right leg submerged in the icy slush. A fresh Arctic blast bit through his thin slacks. He turned to Bucci. "How do you think hot in this weather?"

"Concentrate. Make believe you're in Puerto Rico."

Cortez was about to close the car door when a hand shot out and held the door open. A flat-nosed, broad-shouldered man quickly seated himself beside Bucci. Caught off guard, Bucci whirled around to the sound of metal tapping his window. A revolver was pointed at his left eye. He turned very slowly and looked at the man now in the seat beside him. "What's going on?"

"I'm Agent Nick Spina from the Knapp Commission. The man outside is Captain Ivarone of the New York City Police Department. We've got bad news for you, Detective Bucci. You're under arrest."

BUCCI WAS DRIVEN TO A tired old office building in lower Manhattan, home to the Knapp Commission. The rooms were uncomfortably cold, as the building's heat was lowered on weekends. Capt. Donald Ivarone took Bucci into a sparsely furnished waiting room while Spina went into an adjoining office and called Knapp and the Commission's Counsel, Michael Carpenter, at their respective homes. Carpenter arrived at the office first, followed minutes later by Whitman Knapp. Each man wore a broad smile.

Knapp was ebullient as he embraced Spina. "Good man, Nick. This is big, isn't it?"

"It couldn't be bigger, sir. Anytime you catch a former narcotics detective selling drugs, it's big. But this is special: this guy used to work in SIU."

"What's SIU?"

"The Special Investigating Unit. They're the guys assigned to track down major drug dealers. They're the heavyweights."

Knapp hugged Spina again. "I'm so proud of you, Nick. Our first fish, and you catch Moby Dick!"

"Thank you, Mr. Knapp. But please don't forget Captain Ivarone. He worked hard on this too."

"I won't." Knapp offered Spina a Marlboro. "How did you men do it?"

Spina declined the cigarette and opened his attaché case. "We finally caught a break last week. A drug dealer named Eduardo Cortez walked into the office and said, 'I can give you a cop selling drugs. I do business with him all the time.' I asked him why he was turning him in and he said, 'For the last four or five times we did business, he's been short-weighting me.' I challenged him and asked if he would be willing to wear a wire the next time he met this cop, and he agreed."

"Nick, you're an attorney. Is there any way he can claim entrapment?"

"Not a chance, Mr. Knapp. We strip-searched Cortez to make sure he wasn't carrying any drugs before we left the office. Then we wired him and gave him marked buy money. Don and I drove him to the location where he was to meet the detective. He wasn't out of our sight for one second. We watched him stand on a corner until Bucci pulled up. He got into the car, and we recorded their conversation. Cortez got out of the car and handed me the drugs. I retrieved the money from Bucci's jacket."

"I assume that's Bucci in the anteroom with Captain Ivarone?"

"Yes, sir. How do you suggest we handle it? Should we arrest him or give him a chance to cooperate?"

"I don't know. What do you think?"

"Mr. Knapp, I think we should try and turn him. We could make a big splash for a day or two if we arrest him. But if we're able to turn him, it may enable us to get at the heart of corruption in the Department."

"Then let's try and get him to cooperate."

"Thank you, sir. When we get him inside, I'll play the tape for him and see how he reacts."

"OK. Set it up in Michael's office."

Spina went to the closet and removed a new Akai tape recorder while Carpenter told Ivarone to bring Bucci into his office. While the four men watched Spina clumsily threaded the tape onto the recorder's sprockets, Knapp addressed Bucci.

"Detective Bucci, my name is Whitman Knapp. Seated to my right is Michael Carpenter, the Commission's Counsel. I know you've met Spina and Ivarone under very unfortunate circumstances. The four of us, including Captain Ivarone, are members of the bar, and it truly distresses us to be here tonight, because we all have the utmost respect for the law and the New York City Police Department. Before we proceed further, I want you to listen to this recording. Are you ready, Nick?"

"Anytime you are, sir."

"Go ahead then."

Spina pushed the play button and the five men leaned forward.

" 'God Almighty, it's colder than a whore's heart out there! Come on, Danny, it's not that cold. What are you trying to do? Make me feel bad? Easy for you to say. You've got your bbbbrrrrrrr blast. I've been waiting out there for over an hour. It's bbbbbbbnrrn Danny. If you think it's cold, it's cold. If you think it's hot bbbbbbbrrrn rrrrrrrrrffrrffpp twenty degrees out bbbn-rppp.' "

Spina pushed the stop button and fiddled with the sprockets and tape heads.

"What is it, Nick?" asked Knapp, irritated.

"I have no idea. It's probably because the machine is new."

Carpenter said, "Let me try something." He fiddled with the tape head. Annoyed, Spina said, "I just did that."

"Try it now, Nick."

Spina pushed the play button . . . "There. 'I don't think it's cold, I know it's cold. I can't even find my prick. I couldn't bbbrrrr got stuck. You're always getting bbbrrrr see it. Beautiful. How bbbbbbbbiiiiii pp. What you bbbbrrnpppp ounces. Here's bbbbbbbbiiriiiirnTrrrrppppp again, Babyface?"

"Turn if off. Turn that goddamn thing off! " screamed Carpenter. "Get another machine that doesn't malfunction. And get this sleazy drug pusher out of my sight."

ABOUT AN HOUR LATER, SPINA came out into the waiting room. "Put your coat on, Bucci." Both Bucci and Captain Ivarone stood up as Spina closed the door.

"Where are you taking me?"

"To the First Precinct. You're under arrest."

"For what?"

"For the sale of narcotics."

"You can't lock me up for selling. That tape's no good! It's all messed up."

"Bucci, you don't know if that tape is messed up or not. But for argument's sake, let's assume the tape is messed up. It doesn't make any difference. Captain Ivarone and I heard the deal go down. We have the guy you sold it to, and he's ready to say you sold it to him. We have the drugs you sold, and the marked money he paid you with. That's more than enough to get you ten years in jail."

"Mr. Spina, you deliberately altered that tape. You people would do anything to make a case against a cop."

"You know that isn't true, Bucci."

"All I know is that you messed up that tape deliberately. No jury in the world would convict me after they hear that tape. Everyone knows this commission would do anything to get a cop, including framing him!"

"You disappoint me, Bucci. I thought you were a bright guy. I honestly thought you'd be trying to cooperate with us. Because by tomorrow morning, all of New York is going to know your name. Can't you see the headlines now, Bob? 'KNAPP COMMISSION NABS DRUG DEALING COP.' Imagine the television coverage. What a number they're going to do on you. Imagine your wife. Your kids. Your friends. Bob Bucci, a lousy dope dealer. It's not going to be a pretty picture. And even if you survive all this, you'd never survive a departmental trial. You're fired. Washed up. Everything you've ever worked for . . . gone."

"That's a chance I'll have to take."

"You're wrong. That's not a chance you have to take. There are alternatives."

"Like what? Me being a stinking rat?"

"Bob, there's no question a lot of corrupt cops would say you're a rat. Does that matter? Is that really important to you? What about the good cops? I'm asking you to think about them. Good cops like you once were. We're talking about saving the Department. You can be in on the ground floor."

Bucci bit his lip. "What do you want me to do?"

"Help us get those drug dealers in the Narcotics Bureau. Especially SIU."

"Impossible. I don't work there anymore."

"Nothing's impossible. If you agree to work with us, we'll get you transferred back."

"*Nobody* gets transferred back! They'll know something's wrong!"

"Don't worry about it. We can arrange it." Spina took off his jacket and put it over the back of a chair. "I agree with you. In the beginning, it'll be rough. You'll just have to tough it out."

"What's in it for me?"

Spina leaned over and spoke quietly into Bucci's ear. "You help us, and no one will ever know about this night. Nobody will ever know we caught you. Everybody will be told you voluntarily came forth to help us root out corruption."

Knapp, Carpenter, Spina and Ivarone debriefed Bucci at length. They talked extensively with him about his career, experiences and the rumors of rampant corruption throughout the Narcotics Bureau. All the while, he maintained his own past misdeeds in the Narcotics Bureau were limited to only five instances of stealing money and "a few times selling drugs."

Michael Carpenter slammed the palm of his hand on the table. "I find that hard to believe, Bucci. It seems to me you're a seasoned corrupt cop."

"That's not true, Mr. Carpenter. I never got involved. I never believed in it. And if you don't believe me, lock me up now."

Worried that Bucci's agitation would blow his willingness to cooperate, Knapp changed the subject. "Bob, how does it all start? I don't mean you personally, with the other men. How do they become involved in corruption? After all, they're sworn to uphold the law."

Bucci pondered a long moment. "How does it start? It starts when most of the guys are first assigned to the Narcotics Bureau. They're assigned to work with experienced detectives they've never seen before. The detectives want to know if the new guy is willing to go along with the program, so they test him."

Spina interrupted, "Test him?"

"Yeah. Say, he meets with his new partners and they're sitting in a car with a stool. They chat with the stool awhile, then one of the new guy's partners tells the stool to get out of the car and wait across the street. When he leaves, one of the partners reaches into his pocket and takes out two nickel bags of heroin. He hands them to the new guy and says, 'Do me a favor, kid. I forgot to give this to the stool. Go over there and give it to him.' The new guy knows it's wrong. He knows he's committing a crime if he gives it to him. He knows he's as guilty as the nigger who's selling drugs out of his apartment in Harlem. But he really doesn't have a choice. If he wants his gold shield, he goes along. Whether he likes it or not, he's just become a drug dealer. He can't complain to anyone, because he's just committed a felony."

"Then what?"

"He graduates. One day he's one of the experienced detectives and some new kid wanting to get his gold shield is sitting in the car with him and his partner. He says, 'Kid, I forgot to give this to the stool. Go over there and give this to him.' He hands the kid a couple of packets of heroin, and the cycle starts all over again."

Knapp toyed with a pencil. "Jesus, that's frightening. Does anyone ever say no?"

"Never. If they did, they'd be branded as untrustworthy and sent back to uniform patrol. No matter what, they'd never be given another detail."

Carpenter demanded, "And you were never confronted with this? You never had to give drugs to anybody to prove that you were trustworthy?"

"No. I was lucky. When I first was assigned to Narcotics, I was assigned to a coupla good guys." Bucci laughed. "Real honest to goodness crime-fighting cops. They did everything by the book. They knew what was going on. They constantly reminded me when we saw other cops flashing a roll that it wasn't worth losing the job over and going to jail. So even after I started my own team, I made sure my guys stayed on the straight and narrow."

Carpenter shook his head in disbelief. "How did you get into SIU then? I heard you had to be corrupt to get in there."

"That's not true. You had to be a goddamn good detective and have a rabbi."

"A rabbi?"

"Someone who would recommend you. In my case, I had a good friend working in SIU."

"Who was that?"

"Detective Joe Graziano."

"How'd you know Graziano?"

"When I was in the field team in Brooklyn, my stool told me about this drug dealer on Marcy Street who was doing heavy shit. Instead of sending the info up to SIU, my boss put me on special assignment. He gave me a chance to catch the guy. But as it turned out Graziano was already working on him. My boss was a good guy, he went to Graziano's boss and asked him if my team could work the case with Graziano. Graziano's boss spoke to Graziano, and he said, 'Sure. No problem.' We met, we worked together and we became friends. When the case was over, he got me into SIU. That simple."

Knapp reached over and put his hand on Bucci's. "Robert, if I can get you back into SIU, are you willing to help us rid the Narcotics Bureau of corruption?"

"I've already told Mr. Spina I would. But I warn you, under no circumstances will I set up any of my friends or former partners."

A FEW DAYS LATER, SPINA knocked on the clouded-glass panel door of Whitman Knapp's office. It was 11:00 A.M. Still euphoric over the recent turn of events, the Chairman greeted Spina warmly. "I still can't believe it, Nick. A former SIU detective."

Spina grew uneasy. "Sir, may I speak frankly?"

"Of course."

"I don't want this to be taken the wrong way, sir."

"What is it, Nick?"

"I think Bucci is too big for us."

Michael Carpenter, who had been on the phone, slammed the receiver down. "What do you mean 'too big for us'? Who the hell are you to tell Mr. Knapp he's too big for us?"

"Mr. Carpenter, please bear with me."

"I think you're—"

Knapp held up his hand and interrupted the lawyer. "Michael, let him speak his mind. Go ahead, Nick."

"Mr. Chairman, even though Bucci has committed relatively few acts of corruption during his career—"

"That's his version," interrupted Carpenter.

". . . he knows all the nuances of how corruption works. He claims if we can get him back into SIU, he can get us a lot of corrupt cops, not only from SIU and the Narcotics Division but from other squads. He also says he can get us dozens of lawyers, bail bondsmen and judges. That's why I think it's too big for us. We're talking about investigating hundreds of people. We don't have the resources. It's going to take dozens of investigators and attorneys working around the clock just to put a dent in this thing. Right now, we can't even begin to do this case justice. If we're going to do this right, we'll need a lot of help."

"What are you suggesting, Nick?"

"Bringing in the Feds. When I was an ADA in Manhattan, I worked on some corruption cases with a Federal attorney named Harrison Parker. He's now the number one man in the Federal Bureau of Narcotics and Dangerous Drugs. His specialty is police corruption. He would be more than interested in Bucci."

Carpenter protested, "What do we get out of it? This is our first and only case, for Christ's sake. And you want to give it away!"

"No. Not give it away. I suggest we cooperate with the Feds and make it a joint venture. There's enough glory here for everyone. We can have our cake and eat it too."

Knapp went to the window and looked down onto the slow-moving traffic. Spina walked over and stood alongside him.

"Sir, besides all their resources, they also have clout. If they tell Commissioner Murphy to put Bucci back into SIU, he'll jump."

"Nick, if I tell Patrick to put Bucci back into SIU, he will. He's been very cooperative to date."

"Sir, with all due respect, if you tell the Commissioner we want Bucci back in SIU, within a week every foot patrolman in the Department will know Bucci's working for us."

"Hogwash, Nick. I'll instruct the Commissioner to keep it confidential."

"That's not the way it works, sir. Someone in the PC's office will leak it. Once that happens, it'll be all over the Department."

"So how could Parker prevent that from happening?"

"Sir, do you mind if I use the word 'prick'?"

"Of course not."

"Parker is a Class-A prick. What he'll do is invite the Commissioner down to Washington, and tell him in no uncertain terms to put Bucci back in SIU. He'll also tell Murphy he wants it kept strictly confidential, and if one word leaks out, he'll personally seek an indictment against the individual responsible for subverting justice."

January 3, 1971

TELL ME MORE," PARKER SAID, adjusting himself in his seat.

Spina loosened his tie. "Mr. Parker, it was not an easy decision for Mr. Knapp to let me come down to Washington to see you. He's under a lot of pressure to produce. He could have kept Bucci all to himself, gotten a great deal of publicity and justified our existence for the next year or two."

"How did you get this guy?"

Spina thought about his promise to Bucci, that if he cooperated with the Commission nobody would ever know he was caught selling drugs. "It was unbelievable. Bucci just walked into our office a couple of weeks ago and told us his brother was a junkie, and he was sick and tired of seeing corrupt cops shaking down drug dealers. He told us he had done a few things in the past himself, was ashamed and he wanted to help us clean up the department."

"So why are you here?"

"I told Mr. Knapp we didn't have the resources to properly address the situation. I told him we worked well together in the past, that you were a square shooter, and perhaps we could achive our mutual objectives by forming a joint venture, so to speak."

"You told him I was a prick, didn't you?"

"Yes" said Spina. "But I also told him you were the best corruption fighter I ever met."

"You're right on both counts, Nick. You have to be a prick in this business. It's not a popularity contest."

"I know that."

"Mr. Knapp's pretty cagey. He wants me to commit an army and do all the work while he gets half the credit. What does he commit?"

"He commits me. And a fantastic opportunity for you. It will probably be the biggest corruption case your department has ever handled."

"Perhaps. What's in it for you?"

"I want to work for you. I want you to make me a Special Agent in charge of the Bucci investigation. You can assign anyone you like to work with me, and we'll take our orders directly from you."

Parker walked around his desk and sat in the chair beside Spina. "You must think you have some case."

"It's going to be colossal."

"All right, Nick, I'm sold. I'll contact US Attorney Madison Pierpoint in New York and tell him I've just made you a Special Agent. I want him to help you get this project structured properly and off to a running start. I have to make sure the appropriate resources are put against this. You'll report to Pierpoint directly, and he'll report to me directly. Anything else?"

"Yes, sir. I would like to arrange for Mr. Knapp, Carpenter and myself to meet with you to confirm our agreement."

"No problem. Have my secretary set a date."

"There is one more thing.. We want you to talk to Commissioner Murphy. We want Bucci put back in SIU."

Late January 1971

IT HAD BEEN A LONG, hectic day, culminating in the execution of a search warrant on a fourth-floor walk-up in the Washington Heights section of northern Manhattan. Lieutenant Ryan supervised the arrest of three Cuban dealers for possessing four kilos of cocaine. A search of their apartment uncovered forty thousand five hundred dollars in cash hidden in a bedspring. The money was divided into five equal shares. Ryan took his and downtown's share while the three-man SIU team divided the remaining twenty-four thousand three hundred dollars among themselves.

It was a little after 11:00 P.M. when a bone-tired Ryan drove up his graveled driveway in lower Westchester and parked. It was pitch black save for the lone light shining above the entrance to his home. Ryan closed his eyes for a few seconds and slumped behind the wheel of his car. Then he looked up at a darkened bedroom window and wondered how much time he had left with his terminally ill wife.

He reached over and took a brown paper bag containing sixteen thousand two hundred dollars from the passenger seat. His heart skipped a beat when he heard a voice whisper, "John . . . John."

Ryan froze. "Who is it?"

"It's me. Chief McLoughlin. Inspector Creighton is with me." Ryan was startled to see the two men materialize outside his car.

Ryan regained his composure. "What are you guys trying to do? Give me a heart attack?"

"I'm sorry, John, we didn't mean to startle you. We called your office and they told us you were hitting a search warrant tonight. We knew you were going to be late, so we decided to come up here and wait for you."

"What's up?"

"We have to talk. There may be a problem."

"What about?"

"That's the funny thing. We're not sure. But an ounce of prevention always beats a pound of cure."

"What's that supposed to mean? Come on inside. I'll fix us a drink."

"No, John. Let's stay out here. I hear Eadie is still under the weather, and we don't want to disturb her. This will only take a minute. We want your opinion about something."

"What's that?"

"This afternoon, the Commissioner comes back from Washington. When I asked him what went down, he ignores me. Later, he brings me into his office and tells me to call the Orders Section and have a detective transferred to SIU from the Six-Seven Squad. It took me completely by surprise because it's the first time Murphy ever personally intervened on anyone's behalf. Another thing, to get into SIU, you have to come out of the field teams. Right?"

"Right."

"Murphy's order seemed odd to me, so I called Pat Skelly over in Personnel, and he tells me this guy was in SIU before."

"Who's the guy?"

"A Detective Bucci. Robert Bucci. Know him?"

"I sure do. He worked for me in SIU. He was good people. About six months ago, he came to me and said his wife was complaining about his being gone so much. He asked me to get him transferred before she divorced him. I helped get him transferred to the Six-Seven."

Creighton asked, "You ever do business with him?"

"Yeah, several times. What are you telling me?"

"I'm telling you to be careful. Don't do anymore business with him. This whole thing doesn't add up."

"When can I expect to see him?"

"He's to report this Monday, but I understand he's on vacation until Wednesday. Be careful, John. I can feel something wrong about this one in my gut."

"I appreciate the warning, Mac. I know you guys wouldn't have come up here unless this really bothered you. Don't worry, I'll keep clear of him"

"Good. Give me a couple of weeks and I'll find out from Murphy what gives with this guy."

"Incidentally, you gentlemen saved me a trip to your offices tomorrow."

"How's that?"

"The search warrant I hit tonight?"

"Yeah?"

"Good news. You guys made four thousand dollars."

Early February 1971

BUCCI HEARD THE UNDERCURRENT OF voices as he sauntered through the SIU Detectives' Room. He recognized a few faces, half-waved at them and knocked on Lieutenant Ryan's door. Ryan avoided shaking hands with Bucci by remaining seated behind his desk. "Bob, you're the last person I expected to be reassigned to SIU. You said your wife hated the hours."

"I know, but I missed Narcotics, Lieutenant. This is where the action is. I'm not cut out to be a precinct detective. It's too boring. I had to pull a hell of a lot of strings and cash in my IOUs to get back in here."

"I think it was a bad move on your part. I can tell you up front that none of the old-timers will work with you. You know what the grapevine is like. The rumor is you're hot. That you're with the Knapp Commission."

"Boss, we go back a long time. I can assure you I'm not with the Commission."

"I'd like to believe that. But a basic rule of SIU has been broken. Once you're out, you're out."

"I've never seen that written anywhere."

"It doesn't have to be written anywhere, Bob. Dozens of guys have tried to get back in here before and none of them could ever pull it off. No one, including me, understands how you did it."

"There's always gotta be a first time. I guess I got lucky."

"Lucky or not, the men don't trust you. They think something's in the wind."

"They're entitled to their opinions, Lieutenant. If I was them, I'd probably feel the same way. But believe me, there's nothing wrong. However, since the guys feel that way about it, assign me to some of the new men."

"Bob, as I told you, I have no choice. You have to work with new guys. None of the old-timers will touch you."

As LIEUTENANT RYAN PREDICTED, the veterans shunned Bucci. The word was out: "Bucci's a rat. He's working for Knapp." Detectives stated it openly, within earshot of Bucci, occasionally to his face. But Bucci ignored the taunts. He concentrated his efforts on convincing his newly assigned partners that he wasn't a double agent. His engaging personality, and knowledge of narcotics trafficking soon won them over.

A close camaraderie quickly developed between Bucci and his team. Before long, both new partners took exception to the barbs directed at Bucci. On several occasions, heated arguments and shoving matches broke out in the SIU Detectives Room between members of Bucci's team and the other men. Twice, superior officers had to intercede and threaten the combatants with disciplinary action.

During this time, one of Bucci's informants told him that he could buy drugs from a Bronx drug dealer named Joseph Andretta. Bucci suggested to his team they put an illegal wiretap on him. "Once we put the wire on, we'll have my stool order an eighth of a key from him, and see if he uses the phone to reach out for his connection."

The next week, Bucci and his team cowered in the basement of Andretta's apartment house and listened as Bucci's informant called Andretta. Hanging up on Bucci's stool, Andretta telephoned Viola's Poolroom and ordered an "eighth of a tire" from someone named Joe.

The following night Bucci and his team followed Andretta to a pre-arranged meeting place on a secluded street off the Boston Post Road. They watched Andretta get out of his car and get into another car parked in the shadows. The detectives rushed the car, ordered everyone out of the vehicle and found a package of white powder under the front seat.

Joseph Marchese, a known drug dealer who had been in the car with Andretta, made a pitch. "I'll give you seventeen thousand dollars to let me and Andretta walk."

Bucci's partners conferred with him. "What should we do, Bob?"

Bucci backed off. "It's up to you guys."

A GLEEFUL BUCCI PLAYFULLY ROUGHHOUSED in the elevator with Federal Agent John Grimes on the way up to their undercover apartment on East 52nd Street. Amused, the three agents with them laughed as Bucci feinted a left hook to Grimes's jaw and threw a light right to his stomach. Grimes enveloped Bucci in a bear hug, lifted him a foot off the ground, and walked him off the elevator. Grimes continued down the hallway with Bucci pinned to his chest and kicked the door to apartment 6E. Grinning, Spina let the men into the sedately furnished living room.

"John, are you guys crazy? The neighbors are going to think a herd of elephants is on the loose!"

"Forget the neighbors! They've got nothing to celebrate. How many of them ever got crooked cops on tape?"

"Who's got the tape?"

"Vernon."

Spina turned to the tall, lean Southerner who removed a reel of tape from a white box and extended it to him. "Did you play it yet?"

"Several times. Everybody's dirty. You can hear them taking the seventeen thousand dollars and stealing the drugs."

"How's the clarity?"

"Perfect."

"Good. I can't wait to hear it." Spina walked over to the coffee table and turned on a recorder. Bucci punched Grimes's arm. "Nick, it was like taking candy from a baby."

"That may be, Bob, but I don't think it will be as easy with some of the old-timers."

"They're starting to come around. This morning O'Sullivan asked me to hit a search warrant with him tonight. I told him that we were busy with our own thing."

"Too bad you couldn't do it."

"I would have loved to, but we had this thing all set up. Don't worry, he'll ask again."

"Great."

"It's even better than that. As I'm leaving the office, that old hairbag Koonce asked me to join his team."

"Are you kidding?"

"Swear to God."

"Are you going to do it?"

"Of course not. Everyone would really know something's going on if I started working with niggers."

Moments later, Bucci accepted Spina's congratulations as the tape rewound. Spina rewound the tape and returned it to the box. "One day these creeps are going to be the most surprised sons of bitches in the world when we lock them up."

June 1971

As THE WEEKS PASSED, Graziano steadfastly assured his old buddies that Bucci was as right as rain: "He's good people. For Christ's sake, I've known the guy for years." Most listened dutifully, but were unsure of Graziano's opinion and kept Bucci at arm's length. Exasperated by Graziano's pro-Bucci campaign Lieutenant Ryan summoned Graziano and his team. As the detectives neared Ryan's office he intercepted them. "These walls have ears. Walk with me."

Ryan led the trio out of the building, marched them across South Street and under the FDR Drive to a low guard railing by the East River. He stood in front of the men with his back to the water, his white hair dancing in the cool breeze.

"Joe, I hear you've been sticking up for Bucci again. I've warned you before to cut it out. I am telling you a last time, the guy is bad."

"Lieutenant, we have a difference of opinion."

"Fuck your difference of opinion, Graziano. Can't you see what's happening? How he's sucking in the new kids? Why do you think he's working with them? One day, those poor idiots are all going to jail."

"Boss, nobody's going to jail. Bucci's OK, believe me. I've known him for years. I was the one who brought him into SIU."

"That means nothing to me. He's working for the Commission."

"No way."

"Joe, hear me out. Loud and clear: Bucci is a stool!"

"That's not fair, Lieutenant. Just because the guy came back to SIU, everyone bad mouths him. I never understood what the big deal was anyway."

"Joe, this isn't about a guy who happened to just come back to SIU. This is about a rat. I've heard from several reliable sources that the guy is no good. He's working for Knapp and his jerks! They caught him red-handed, shaking down a junkie in Queens. For him it was the slammer or giving up his old friends at SIU."

"That's bullshit!"

"Joe, it ain't bullshit. You hear me? *It ain't bullshit.* I've gotten it from several people in the know. Can't you get it through that thick guinea skull of yours that he's a rat? I'm not saying I think he's a rat. I'm telling you I *know* he's a rat."

Graziano hesitated and turned to McDuff. "What do you think, Jack?"

"You know what I thought from the beginning, Joe. He's a rat."

"What about you, Ray?"

"He's a rat," Carrera agreed.

"Well, I guess that's what makes horse races, because I think he's good."

Ryan grabbed Graziano's arm. "Hey, we're not talking about horse races, and I'm not getting into a pissing contest with you. I don't care what you think."

"Lieutenant, at least let me talk to him, huh?"

Ryan recoiled, then sprang out. "You're outta here, Graziano. You're out of SIU. You know what's wrong with you? You think you're some sort of guinea don. Here I am telling you that prick is bad, and you're telling me he's good. I got it from reliable sources. The PC had no choice, he had to put Bucci back. The Knapp Commission ordered him to do it. Don't you understand? they put Bucci back into SIU to rat us out!"

"Boss, please."

"You know, Joe, it's a goddamn shame. We had a good run. No, I take that back. We had a great run together, but I can't trust you anymore. You can hurt me, you can hurt Jack, you can hurt Ray. I can't let that happen."

"Boss, please don't transfer me," Graziano pleaded.

"I have to, Joe. For your own good. I just can't trust you around that scumbag anymore. If I let you stay he'll suck you in just like he's sucking in those kids."

July 1971

DETECTIVE CHRIS MARIAN STRUGGLED WITH the Sunday *New York Times* crossword puzzle. Joe Graziano got up from his desk and stared out a rain-streaked window. He had been out of SIU for nearly a month, and he found it impossible to adjust to the quiet routine of the 107 Squad in Fresh Meadows, Queens. Most cops would have been delighted to work in such a country-club atmosphere, but Graziano told his friends, "It's like being sentenced to watch grass grow." He left the squad room, went downstairs to an empty office and telephoned Beninati at home. "Loo, have you seen the movie yet?"

"Lisa and I saw it Friday night."

"What did you think?"

"I thought it was a bit much, but Hackman did capture Egan perfectly."

"I couldn't agree more. The guy did a terrific job. So did Scheider. I just finished reading the papers. The critics think it's going to be the picture of the year."

"Jesus, we'll never be able to live with those two bastards. I wouldn't be surprised if they come up with a sequel, *The French Connection II.* Anyway, what's new with you?"

"Nothing, except I'm going out of my mind. It's been nearly four weeks. Have you been able to talk to anyone about me yet?"

"I mentioned your name to a few people over here but it's not easy. Everyone's afraid of SIU guys. They hear some of them are cooperating with Knapp."

"Bullshit. I'm sick and tired of hearing that crap. It's ridiculous."

"Joe, don't kill the messenger. I'm just telling you what I hear. Sit tight. I'll get you transferred as soon as possible. All I need is a little time."

"Please hurry, Loo. There's absolutely nothing to do. I'm going stir-crazy."

"Hey, Joe. I miss the real action every bit as much as you do. You have to learn to live with it. I suffered withdrawal pains for months. Homicide is no SIU either. I spend ninety-nine percent of my time chasing niggers all over Queens."

"It's still better than what I'm doing here."

"Let me ask you something. Have you ever given any thought of putting in for the new Joint Task Force?"

"Not really."

"Why not?"

"Lieutenant Stowe's the boss over there. Remember the stink he made with Bluth? He thinks all Narcotics cops are dirty."

"Not so. He's been actively recruiting Narcotics guys lately to work with guys from New York State and Federal agents. You know they want this to be a competition for SIU. Washington is pouring a lot of money into that."

"How do you know?"

"Louis."

"Your nephew, Louis?"

"Yeah. He's been on the task force for six weeks. He's the one who told me Stowe just took on several guys that used to be in Narcotics. According to Louis, Stowe's desperate. He promised the Feds he'd be able to build them another SIU within six months, but so far he hasn't delivered. Time's running out for him, and he needs experienced Narcotics detectives. Right now they couldn't catch a cold. Louis says two-thirds of the unit is made up of out-of-town Feds and state troopers. They still take out maps to get around the Bronx."

"Jesus, I'd love to work with the Joint Task Force."

"Joe, you'd knock 'em dead. Who knows narcotics better than you?"

"Do you really think Stowe would take on an ex-SIU guy?"

"You never know unless you ask. For Christ's sake, if Bucci could get back into SIU, you ought to be able to get on the Joint Task Force. Look, Joe, Louis and his girlfriend are coming over here for lunch today. Should I tell him to mention you to Stowe?"

"You bet. As a matter of fact, I'd like to talk to Louis myself."

"Where are you now?"

"At the 107. Where else would I have so much free time?"

"If you can slip away, join us for lunch."

AFTER BENINATI EMBRACED AND KISSED Graziano on the cheek, he led him into the den. "I hope you didn't' rush, Joe. After we spoke, Louis called and said he was running a little late."

"No problem. I got all the time in the world."

"Actually, I'm glad he's late. I want to talk to you about him."

"Go ahead."

"See, Louis is more than my nephew. He's like a brother. If you guys ever get a chance to work together, I want you to keep an eye out for him. I worry about Louis. He's a lot like his old man."

"What about his old man?"

"His father Mario was a wild son of a gun. He dated my older sister during the war when they were both teenagers. My parents almost had heart attacks when they started getting serious. You know the rest. Three months later, they're married. Early in '44, they went to see the movie *The Fighting Sullivans*. That was the tearjerker where the five brothers got killed when the Japs sank their ship. The next day Mario enlisted in the Navy. On October 19, 1944, the day Louis was born, Mario gets his ass blown up in the South Pacific. Denise got the news while she was still in the hospital. My parents wanted her to live with us, but she refused. She went back to her apartment to raise Louis. Eleven days later, a drunken hit-and-run driver killed her while she ran out to the store. My parents took Louis in and raised him as their own. I was twelve years old at the time. So you see, I'm both his brother and uncle. That's why he calls me 'Brunc.' "

A TRIM, FORTY-FIVE-YEAR-OLD CAPTAIN STOWE greeted Graziano. After shaking hands, Stowe waved him to a seat. He referred to his notes while Graziano sat in silence, looking at the framed family photos on the desk.

Stowe leaned back in his chair and looked across at Graziano."Now

I got you. I used to see you going upstairs to SIU but I never associated the name with the face."

"I remember you, sir. You headed up the Group 11 Field Team."

"I'm flattered. I thought I toiled in relative obscurity."

"Not at all, Captain. You were very well known. You enjoyed the reputation of being totally honest."

"That's an interesting observation, Joe. I thought honesty was a prerequisite for all policemen."

"It is, sir," Graziano managed. "It's just that you were very vocal about corruption when you were in Narcotics."

"Do you know what bothers me, Joe? I don't think things have changed one iota since I left there. I am of the opinion there's still a lot of corruption in the Narcotics Division. What do you think?"

"I'm sure things are going down, but I think most of the guys are honest."

"I don't. I think most guys illegally wiretap and perjure search warrants. I think most guys flake junkies. I think most guys take bribes and steal money. I think some guys fix court cases and sell drugs. I think Narcotics is a sewer."

"Captain, there's no doubt some of that's going on, but I don't think many of the guys are involved."

"Are you telling me you were never involved?" Stowe raised his eyebrows.

"That's exactly what I'm saying." Graziano replied, deadpan.

"I'm glad to hear that. However, with all due respect, I still think most of Narcotics is corrupt. Particularly SIU."

"Captain, I disagree with you about SIU. I believe a lot of people are jealous of SIU's successes, and they like to badmouth the unit."

"Maybe so, Joe. Incidentally, why aren't you there anymore? You were the king."

"I had a disagreement with Lieutenant Ryan."

"What about?"

"He thought a friend of mine was a rat, and I insisted he wasn't."

"Was he talking about Bob Bucci?"

"Yes, sir."

"There's a lot of rumors going around that Bucci's going to be the star witness when the Knapp Commission goes on TV."

"Those rumors have been floating around for weeks. I don't believe them."

"Did you ever work with Bucci?"

"Yes. For a few months."

"How do you feel about him?"

"He's the second-best detective I ever met. He wasn't nearly as good as me, but someone has to be second."

"That's what I heard, Joe. You're tops. I think we can get together. But first, I want to explain some ground rules." Stowe paused for effect. "There are to be no shortcuts. No perjured search warrants or illegal wiretaps. I won't tolerate crimes in this unit, and you know what my position on money is. If you arrest a junkie with five dollars in his pocket, you bring him in with five dollars in his pocket. If you find ten thousand dollars in a drug dealer's apartment, every penny gets turned in. I will not allow any deviations from this policy. If there are, you get locked up. Can you live by these rules?"

"Yes, sir. They're the same rules I've always followed."

"Joe, I have a specific role in mind for you. I don't need just another cop. I need a leader. A self-starter. Someone who is innovative, creative, results oriented. Someone who can help me get this task force out of the starting blocks. Someone who can teach my neophytes the difference between peddlers and major drug dealers. Someone with the hands-on experience to do it right. You've been there and back. Can I count on you?"

"Captain, I'll give it my best shot."

"Good. It will take me a week to get you transferred over here. Louis Di Lorenzo told me he wants to work with you if you come on board. Is that OK with you?"

"Fine with me, sir."

Stowe put out his hand. "Welcome aboard."

October 1971

MAYOR LINDSAY'S DISAPPOINTING POLITICAL TOUR through Indiana underscored a major problem hampering his newly launched presidential campaign: his strong identification with a crime-ridden New York City. The point hit home at Fort Wayne's Baerfield Airport during a late-night press conference. Earlier in the day, the former Republican and newborn Democrat Lindsay had endorsed local attorney Igor Lemacoff for Mayor of Fort Wayne, and Lemacoff was now returning the compliment by endorsing Lindsay for President.

A local reporter asked the absurdly toupeed Lemacoff, "Do you mind if I quote from your campaign literature, Mr. Lemacoff?"

"Of course not, Hal."

"Well, according to this pamphlet your headquarters issued last month, you made a stinging denunciation of New York City when you compared it to Fort Wayne."

"Hal, I think the description 'stinging denunciation' is an overstatement."

"Well, I'll read it verbatim: 'Let's examine New York City for a minute. It's a modern-day Sodom and Gomorrah. The people are virtually ignored. It's a cold and callous place. Newspaper strikes, garbage strikes, teacher strikes, police corruption, wholesale prostitution, blatant pornography, muggings and rapes. The people suffer. They scream but their screams are not heard.' "

The reporter lowered his notes. "Mr. Lemacoff, now that Mayor Lindsay has endorsed you for the Mayor of Fort Wayne, don't you find this statement somewhat hypocritical as it relates to your endorsement of Mayor Lindsay for the Presidency?"

Lemacoff smiled weakly at the small gathering of reporters and well-wishers. "I find no inconsistency in my criticism of New York City and my endorsement of Mayor Lindsay for President. After all, most of these incidents happened when the Mayor was a Republican."

The seven-member press corps chuckled dutifully. The newsman pressed his attack, "Mayor Lindsay, do you find it hard to accept Mr. Lemacoff s endorsement after his comments on New York City?"

"Not really," Lindsay replied, with an equally weak smile. "If New York City can be insulted by Johnny Carson on national TV, it certainly can be insulted by Igor Lomo . . .

The group howled as Lindsay forgot the name of the man he came to praise. "Lomocount," Lindsay belatedly yelled into the microphone as the politicos in both camps chuckled. Embarrassed, Lindsay stepped back from the microphone, cupped his mouth and whispered to one of his aides, "What's this moron's name?"

The aide shrugged. "Er . . . . Er . . . . Beats the shit out of me, Your Honor."

Lindsay frowned and returned to the microphone. "I think I've finally got it. How does the next Mayor of Fort Wayne, Indiana, sound?"

The amused well-wishers appreciated Lindsay's quick sense of humor. As the laughter subsided, he acknowledged a tired-looking reporter from the Associated Press who put up his hand. "Yes, sir?"

"Mr. Mayor, I know it's late, and you're about to catch a plane to Biloxi, but if you don't mind, I've got a question."

"Of course I don't mind. When you're Mayor of New York, answering questions at late hours is standard practice."

"I appreciate that, Mr. Mayor. With the Knapp Commission hearings in New York City entering their third week of exposing police corruption, why have you decided to run for President of the United States at this time? It appears to me you have your hands full just running New York City."

WHILE JOHN LINDSAY HOBBLED THROUGH several poverty-stricken Mississippi towns with the brother of slain civil-rights activist Medgar Evers at his side, the public Knapp Commission hearings became a "must-see" for New Yorkers. Businessmen, doctors, sales clerks, secretaries, city workers, housewives and cops stayed glued to TV sets. Makeshift schedules were planned according to Channel Thirteen's television programming agenda. Luncheon reservations were canceled. Sponsors complained angrily when regular daytime program ratings plummeted. Television audiences were mesmerized as cop after cop revealed incidents of corruption ranging from the trivial to the critical. The rogue cops described how brother officers, from probationary patrolmen to chief inspectors, routinely accepted free meals from restaurants; how tow truck operators "greased" uniformed patrolmen so they would bring cars involved in accidents to their repair shops; how construction-site foremen paid hundreds of dollars to precinct sergeants in order to avoid summonses for life-endangering practices; how brothels paid vice squad plainclothesmen in cash (and services) to stay in business; and how drug dealers escaped arrest by paying off thousands of dollars to station-house detectives.

By far and away, the disclosure that riveted audience attention the most was Police Officer William Phillips's testimony about the special relationships cops enjoyed with gamblers. Michael Carpenter skillfully played to the packed auditorium of the Association of the Bar of the City of New York.

"Officer Phillips, I'd like to take up where we left off this morning."

"Yes, sir."

"Can you tell me the names of some of the gamblers who paid off and befriended policemen? You don't have to go into details as to what they paid. We'll get to that later. Just tell me the names."

The well-rehearsed witness responded, "There was 'Eggy,' 'Spanish Al,' and 'Crappy.' "

"Excuse me, officer. Can you tell us why he's called 'Crappy'?" asked Carpenter, who was aware it was because the gambler ran a floating craps game.

"Because he always smells like he shit himself."

Carpenter instructed Phillips to go on.

"Then there's 'the Gimp,' 'Bonehead,' 'One-Eye Larry,' 'Johnny Cigars,' 'Elephant Ears,' 'West Indian Dave,' 'Leroy the Albino,' and 'The Snot.' "

"Officer, I wouldn't touch that last name with a ten-foot pole." After the gallery composed itself, the attorney continued, "I know everyone is anxious to learn what these men paid to the police, but if you could bear with me another minute, I think it more important we discuss some of the terminology commonly used by plainclothesmen, so the Commission and the general public can understand what we're talking about."

" Sure."

"Can you tell me what a 'bagman' is?"

"That's a policeman who makes the rounds to collect graft in behalf of a group of colleagues."

"What does it mean to 'flake' someone?"

"That's when you plant evidence on a guy."

"What's a 'pad'?"

"That's graft received at regular intervals and shared by a number of policemen."

"How about a 'kite'?"

"That's a complaint to police about an illegal operation."

"What's a 'cousin'?"

"That's a . . .

November 1971

TENSION WAS HIGH IN THE SIU Detectives' Room as the last rogue policeman was about to be introduced at the Knapp Commission TV spectacular. More than two dozen detectives gathered around a battered black-and-white TV set that McClellan had set up on a desk.

"Does anyone know how to fix this piece of junk?"

"Move the ears around. That always works."

"This ain't your girlfriend, Santiago."

"Screw you, Jiminez."

"Somebody do something about that picture or we'll miss him."

"It has to heat up, for Christ's sake."

"Santiago, I was wrong. It is just like your girlfriend."

"Fifty bucks says it's Bucci," yelled Carrera. "I'm giving two to one."

"You're covered!"

"You better be right, Koonce. You were told to stay away from that prick. If it's Bucci, you're going to be picking cotton on a Georgia chain gang for the rest of your life."

The camera zoomed in on a close-up shot of Michael Carpenter as he announced, "The Knapp Commission's final witness is Patrolman Waverly Jones."

Loud cheers exploded in the SIU room. Detectives leaped from their chairs and hugged one another. Voices clamored, "I told ya. Bucci's all right." "He's the absolute best." "A stand-up guy from day one." "SIU has dodged another bullet."

"We've dodged shit, Rafferty," boomed Jerry Lynch, sliding his backside off the edge of a desk and spitting a blob of cigar juice at the television screen. He took the cigar out of his mouth, dropped it at his feet and ground the smoldering stub into the floor.

"Jerry, he's the final witness, for Christ's sake. It's all over. Bucci never appeared!" yelled Detective Jimmy Simone.

"It's not all over. It's just beginning. Didn't any of you jerk-offs read the *Times* this morning?"

"What are you taking about now, Lynch?"

"Here's what I'm talking about, Simone." Lynch opened his leather attaché case and pulled out a folded copy of the *New York Times*. He held the paper up with his left hand and pointed to a front-page article with his right index finger. "For all you suckers who don't know how to read, it says, 'Bribery of Narcotics Detectives Widespread Here, Federal Prosecutor Charges.' Know what that means?"

"That's just Fed bullshit. They're trying to upstage Knapp."

"Simone, use your head. Don't you see what's happening? Don't any of you assholes see what's happening? Bucci's with the Feds."

"How do you figure? The rumors were that he was with the Commission."

"In the beginning, I thought he was. Know what? I think he was too big for them. I think they gave him to the Feds."

"You better check those cigars you're smoking."

"Go to hell, Snyder. I'm telling you he's with the Feds, and all you jerk-offs who've been hitting warrants and working with him are going to jail."

"I read that article this morning, Jerry. It never mentioned Bucci's name."

"It doesn't have to. Doug, you're a pretty sharp detective. I'm surprised you didn't figure it out."

"Jerry, don't hand me that shit. Why don't you just read the goddamn thing and let everyone else judge for himself?"

Lynch unfolded the paper and read, " 'An unidentified Federal prosecutor says a strike force against police corruption has obtained evidence that teams of New York City narcotics detectives have received bribes of up to twenty-five thousand dollars to let narcotics dealers avoid arrest. The alleged payoffs to policemen by narcotics dealers, which are described as widespread, are being investigated by a little-known group of Federal investigators . . .' "

"Need I go on?" Lynch glanced up at the uncertain faces.

"Jerry, I still haven't heard anything that mentions SIU or Bucci."

"Doug, read between the lines! Who else could they be talking about?"

"Jerry, never mind what's between the lines. Just read and quit editorializing."

Lynch sullenly continued, " 'The Federal prosecutor said the $25,000 figure was given to him by an active New York City narcotics detective. Asked if these payments went to individual policemen, the prosecutor said that the money was divided among teams."

Redmond spoke up. "I still haven't heard you mention Bucci's name or SIU."

"Doug, I can't believe my ears. Who else could they be talking about? It's got to be SIU!"

"Lynch, you're a lowlife."

The room fell silent as the men stared at Bucci standing in the doorway entrance. "Who are you to tell people I'm a rat? Ever since I came back to SIU, you've branded me as a rat. Show me one person I ever hurt."

Without warning, the bull-like Lynch charged through the startled crowd of detectives and viciously slammed Bucci against the wall. Bucci frantically clawed at Lynch's powerful thick fingers as they tightened around his throat. Several detectives grabbed the maddened Lynch's arms while Synder and Jiminez pried his fingers from Bucci's throat.

December 24, 1971

AN UNEXPECTED CHRISTMAS EVE STORM blanketed New York City under four inches of snow. Lynch and Beninati sat in Vinnie Catalano's living room. Catalano slowly paced the lush carpeted floor. "Jerry, are you sure Graziano can put this deal together?"

"He's always come through in the past. I don't know why he couldn't now."

"I just don't want to tell Capra we can do something and then not be able to deliver."

"Vinnie, I understand what you're saying. But I'm telling you for the tenth time, Joe said he got it."

"Ninety keys. That's unbelievable. The sucker must be working on some king-size junk over at the task force."

"All I know is he never had any trouble getting his hands on skag when he was in SIU."

"I wonder where he keeps it."

"I haven't a clue."

Catalano opened the blinds and peered out the window. "Jesus, I can hardly see you guys' car. We'll be snowed in for a month." He resumed pacing. "By the way, Jerry, did you tell Graziano that Capra wants the stuff on consignment?"

Lynch shook his head. "No way, Vinnie. I figure that's your problem."

"Thanks for nuthin.' " Catalano checked his watch. "When did he say he'd be here?"

"Twenty minutes ago."

A SHORT WHILE LATER, CATALANO poured a chilly Graziano a drink. "Joe, my man's ready to put this deal together right now." Lynch and Beninati fidgeted uneasily. "But he'll need a week or two to get your money together."

Graziano got out of his chair. "Are you nuts, Vinnie? You get me out in the middle of a blizzard on Christmas Eve and now you've got the balls to tell me you want ninety keys on consignment? There's no way I'd go for that. It's C.O.D. or no deal!"

"You know he's good for it."

"I know shit."

"Come on, Joe. He's good for it. It's not like you've never done business with him."

"No deal."

Catalano looked over at Beninati. "Maybe I can get you something up front."

"All the cash is up front or it's no deal."

"Joe, what is this, the fifth or sixth time we've done business? You've never been screwed."

"That's because I've always gotten my money first."

"Joe, I personally guarantee this deal."

"What is that supposed to mean?"

"Just what I said. I guarantee it. If my guy screws up, which he won't, I'll pay you the money."

Graziano threw back his head and sneered. "Holy cow! Now I feel a hundred percent better. I had no idea you were personally guaranteeing it. You should have said so in the first place. Wait here a minute. I'll run out to the car and get it."

Catalano's face reddened. "Go fuck yourself, Graziano."

"That's a lot better than you fucking me, Vinnie."

Lynch stood up and got between the men. "Sit down, Vinnie." Lynch then turned to Graziano. "It ain't necessary to break balls, Joe. Vinnie's just trying to put together a deal. A simple yes or no would have done the trick."

Catalano shouted from his chair, "Yeah, Jerry's right. That show wasn't necessary."

Graziano turned to Lynch. "Jerry, I have to tell you, I'm pissed at you and Loo. You guys should have told me about this instead of waiting and letting Catalano tell me."

Beninati touched Graziano's arm. "Our apologies, Joe. We were wrong."

"I know you want this deal to go down, and God knows I owe you. But this isn't like handing a guy a loaf of bread. This is heavy-duty. We're talking almost two million. Guys kill their mothers for a lousy fix, and you're asking me to let some guinea run around with my ninety keys."

"We've done business with him lots of times. You know the guy is good."

"Hey, two million."

"All right, Jerry and I will talk to him. I'll get him to put some money up front. Maybe half."

"I must be out of my mind for just listening to you guys."

"Graziano, I already told you I guarantee it."

"Don't underestimate me, Vinnie, and don't assume you're the only one I do business with. I know a lot of guys who would kill to be in your spot." Graziano put on his coat. "Loo, if we do it your way, how long before I see the rest of my money?"

"Two weeks. Three tops."

December 29, 1971

A COMMOTION IN THE SIU Detectives' Room caught Lieutenant Ryan's attention. Joe Graziano was being greeted warmly by everybody in the room. McClellan poked Sergeant O'Brien. "The prodigal son has returned."

Ryan rushed from his office with outstretched arms and embraced Graziano affectionately. The men separated for a moment, looked at each other, then embraced again.

Graziano's mind flashed back to the many times he and Ryan had broken bread together. How they wept when Detectives Billy Turner and 'Spider' Kniley were shot to death when a narcotics arrest went bad. How they laughed when they surprised Conner and Cahill playing "Hide the Weenie" at the Christmas party. How they locked a drunken Butera in a closet at his wedding. How the word "friendship" didn't begin to describe their relationship. And how the bad blood had surfaced.

Both men brushed away tears as Ryan steered Graziano back to his office.

"How's Eadie doing, Lieutenant?"

"Not well, Joe. It's only a matter of weeks now."

"I'm sorry to hear that, John."

"She'll be happy to hear we talked."

"I'm sorry I didn't come over sooner."

"Joe, I want you to understand something. Transferring you out was the hardest thing I ever had to do. You were like a son to me."

"Things worked out for the best."

"I heard you're doing well. How's the task force?"

"Great. I love it. It's a lot like SIU."

"You mean it's a lot like SIU used to be. Things have changed here, Joe. We've gotten a ton of supervision since the Knapp Commission. They don't want anyone making arrests. They think collars make dollars."

"I run into some of the guys now and then. I heard it was rough."

"Rough is an understatement, Joe. It's over. SIU is in its death throes.

You know what the shame of it is? A lot of good men are going to be hurt."

"John, not that tired old Bucci thing again."

"He's bad, Joe."

"Please, Lieutenant. Not again."

Ryan sighed. "All right, Joe. You're the last person I want to argue with. What brings you here, anyway?"

"I have an old case coming up. I lost the property clerk number and I have to look it up."

AFTER GRAZIANO LEFT RYAN'S OFFICE, he went over to McClellan's desk.

"Bernie, where are you hiding the log control book these days?"

"Right here in my file cabinet, Joe. Bottom drawer. I've got to keep it under lock and key. The guys are always leaving it all over the place."

"I need it for a few minutes."

"Sure thing. By the way, it was nice to see you and the Lieutenant getting together again. He's a great guy."

"The best."

"One favor, Joe. When you're finished with the log book, please bring it back to me."

"That's a promise."

Graziano took the inch-thick, hardcover book and carried it to a vacant desk. He scanned the columned 1970 entries until he found what he was looking for, the registration of a seizure of cocaine made on April 16, 1970, by the team of Novack, Daly and Ramos. Graziano focused on the pertinent data. Arrested: Jose Espinoza and Carlos Ruiz; Location of Arrest: 303 West 23rd Street; Precinct of Arrest: 10th; Arrest Numbers: 3604, 3605; Lab Number: L201-70; Property Clerk Voucher Number: M2794-70, Amount Seized: 90 kilos, cocaine (180 half-kilos in four suitcases).

Graziano jotted down M2794-70 on a small piece of paper, folded it and tucked it into his wallet. Finished, he returned the book to McClellan and went into Lieutenant Ryan's office to say good-bye. Ryan was on the phone. Graziano walked up to his desk and waited until he looked up. Graziano silently mouthed the words, "Tell Eadie I love her." Ryan nodded, stood up and cradled the phone with his left shoulder.

After the men shook hands, Graziano walked to the middle of the Detectives' Room, stopped and looked around.

He knew he had just made his last visit to the SIU.

As GRAZIANO WAS ABOUT TO open the door of his car he spotted Patrick Klyne walking up South Street. The young detective had not tied his trenchcoat although it was freezing cold. He wore olive-green corduroy slacks, a black-and-brown herringbone jacket, white dress shirt and a hydrant-red tie.

"Hello, stranger. Long time no see."

Klyne held onto Graziano's outstretched right hand after they shook hands.

"Joe, I'm glad to see you. I wanted to talk to you."

"What brings you downtown? All dressed up to boot."

"I'm on my way to see Lieutenant Ryan. My boss had told him good things about me, believe it or not. Now Ryan asked me to come for an interview. He said he would like me to join SIU."

"You know, kid, a year ago I would have said that's great. But now I think you'd better steer clear of the unit. Things have changed up there. Everybody is paranoid."

"That's what I heard."

"I got an idea. Why don't you come and work with me at the task force?"

"I wish I could, Joe, but I'm getting out of narcotics. I want to go to a squad. I've decided I'm going back to school. Law school. I start NYU in the fall."

All that Graziano, never at a loss for an answer, was able to say was "Wow."

"What I wanted to say to you, Joe, is—thank you. Without your. . . . financial aid . . . I could not have done it. Maybe something good will come out of something bad."

"That's a way to look at it. Good luck, kid. And come visit me at the task force."

Graziano abruptly turned around and walked back to his car. Klyne shouted, "I'll come by. Promise."

January 4, 1972

POWDERY SNOW SWIRLED BETWEEN THE buildings as Graziano cautiously guided his car to a stop in front of 400 Broome Street. Dominick Fiore, the uniformed cop responsible for keeping the front of the building free of all civilian and police cars, stopped on the driver's side of Graziano's vehicle. He vehemently pointed at several "No Standing" signs. Annoyed by the apparent lack of response, Fiore bent over to yell at the driver. Graziano rolled down the window and grinned. "Jesus, Joe. I didn't recognize the car. When did you get it?"

"Almost two weeks ago. I decided to give myself a little Christmas present."

"It's beautiful. But you'd better be careful driving a brand-new car in this kind of weather. There's going to be a lot of fender benders today."

"Can I leave it here for a few minutes, Dominick? I have to run upstairs and bring down a heavy load."

"Of course, Joe. Anytime. Where else would you park?"

Fiore took Graziano by the upper arm and helped navigate him through the gray slush leading to the entrance of the building. Freezing water instantly filled Graziano's low-cut Gucci shoes. "Next time I'll do what Mommy tells me and wear my galoshes," he joked.

Fiore held the front door of the building open for Graziano. "Mom's always right, Joe. I'll see you when you come down."

WILSON, THE BLACK ELEVATOR OPERATOR, stuck his head outside the half-filled car and watched Graziano stomp his feet on the wet marble floor.

"You're no Sammy Davis, Jr., Mr. Grazzio. You ain't got no rhythm. But I'll still take you for a ride." Graziano went over to the elevator and winked at the passengers. "Not today, Willie. I'm only going to the second floor. Anyway, the last time I took a ride with you, we were stuck for three days."

"Come on, Mr. Grazzio. It was only two hours."

Everyone in the elevator laughed. Pretending to be angry, Wilson banged the elevator door closed. Graziano could hear the muffled sound of Wilson's high-pitched voice yelling to him as the elevator creaked upward. "We ain't friends no mo', Joe."

Twenty-five minutes later, Graziano came out of 400 Broome carrying two suitcases. He gingerly tiptoed across the newly salted sidewalk towards his car, where Dominick Fiore held open the back door for him. "I think it's better if I put these two in the trunk, Dominick. I got two more upstairs."

Fiore watched Graziano pull out into the deserted street as the snow-fall intensified. Graziano turned on WINS radio and listened to the cheery broadcaster issue a traveler's advisory. Seeing driving conditions worsen, he drove cautiously across the Manhattan Bridge onto the Brooklyn-Queens Expressway for several miles following a slow-moving Department of Sanitation salt-spreader down the highway. Graziano grew uneasy at the increasing number of abandoned cars by the road-side and exited the expressway at Northern Boulevard. Stopping at a red light, he watched a car spin out of control and sideswipe an empty school bus.

That maniac could have killed someone, Graziano thought. *Suppose someone clobbers me like that? Do I leave two hundred pounds of cocaine in the car while I go for help? Or do I strap it on my back and carry it around like a mule? What if the cops impound the car?*

By early afternoon, a much-relieved Graziano pulled into his snow-filled driveway in Douglaston, Queens. He unlocked the front door of his house, stood in the hallway for a moment and heard the whirring of Anne's sewing machine coming from an upstairs bedroom. He quickly went back out to the car and carried the two suitcases from the backseat into his basement. He returned to the foyer, and, still hearing the sewing machine in use, went back out to the car and brought the two suitcases from the trunk down to the basement. He then shouted from the foot of the stairs, "Anne, I'm home."

Seconds later Anne came hurrying down the stairs. "Thank God. I was worried sick about you."

Graziano chuckled, "Worried about me or the new car?"

"Don't be silly. I was worried about you." She reached up and kissed his cheek. "By the way, is the car OK?"

"Just as I thought." He put his arm around her waist and they headed for the kitchen. "I'm starved. Anything to eat?"

"How about some leftover ziti and sausage?"

"Terrific."

"Joe, I hope you don't have to go out afterwards."

"No. I'm going to be home all day. I've got some paperwork to do. Where are the kids?"

"Over at the Von Hoffs'."

"Good." Graziano sat on a kitchen chair. "By the way, Lynch, Beninati and Catalano will be stopping by tonight."

"You're kidding. How are they getting here? By dogsled?"

AFTER LUNCH, GRAZIANO RETURNED TO the basement, opened the four suitcases, and removed the plastic bags from the suitcase. He carefully spread each plastic bag filled with cocaine side by side. He then carried the four empty suitcases over to the other side of the basement and laid them on the floor. He went into the furnace room and removed one of four leather suitcases he had stored by the furnace and brought it outside. He laid it on the floor next to one of the empty suitcases, opened it wide, and looked at the plastic bags of flour he had put inside it the previous day.

It took less than ten minutes for Graziano to switch forty-five half-kilo bags filled with flour from the leather suitcase to an empty Property Clerk suitcase. He repeated the process three more times and put the four Property Clerk suitcases filled with flour in the corner.

After lighting up a cigarette, he carried the empty leather suitcases to the spot where the 180 half-kilo bags of cocaine were stacked. *Those bastards better have at least half the money tonight,* Graziano thought.

Early February, 1972

NEW YORK CITY DETECTIVE JOHN Speaker and his Joint Task Force partners, Federal Agents George Murray and Al Gernhardt, drove up Sedgwick Avenue and observed Joe DiPalma's parked Pontiac in his driveway. DiPalma was a Bronx Mafioso whose history in narcotics trafficking dated back to his early days in Bay Ridge, Brooklyn.

Gernhardt continued driving up the street and double-parked in front of a five-story apartment house. Speaker left his partners in the car and went quickly into the basement. He unlocked a heavy metal door just off the boiler room and walked over to the far corner; everything looked the same as it had six hours earlier. He pushed aside a mattress angled against the wall and lifted an upside down empty television box off a voice-activated tape recorder. One incoming call had been made to DiPalma's home phone. He replaced the tape, covered the recorder with the box and returned the mattress to its original position.

Once back inside the car, Speaker handed the tape to Murray in the backseat. "Someone called."

Murray put the tape on a recorder and the three men listened to a gravelly voice: "Joey, meet me at my place tonight."

THE DETECTIVES FOLLOWED JOE DIPALMA'S maroon Pontiac over the Triborough Bridge into Astoria in two separate cars. DiPalma parked his vehicle underneath an elevated subway station on Thirty-first Street and walked a half-block past several Greek specialty stores to Ditmars Boulevard. He talked briefly to a couple of men standing outside a two-story building and went inside. Speaker waited a minute for the men to leave and drove slowly down the street. He read the chipped black-lettered sign on the window: "Astoria Colts Social Club."

At 2:15 A.M., DiPalma and Vincent Capra emerged from the club. Capra walked DiPalma to his car, where they talked for a few minutes. Speaker radioed Gernhardt and Murray, "Stay with Joey Baby when he leaves. I'll sit on the new guy."

"Do you know who he is?"

"How am I supposed to know?"

"Hey, you're the one that said you knew everybody."

"I said almost everybody. I'll try to take him home tonight. At worst, I'll get a plate number. We can start from there."

As soon as DiPalma's car was out of sight, Capra got into his Oldsmobile. He warily drove up the quiet Astoria streets, and immediately noticed the car following him. Fifteen minutes later, Capra went down Thirty-first Street to Astoria Boulevard and got on the Grand Central Parkway heading east. As he approached an emergency cutoff on the highway for disabled cars, he flipped on his right-turn indicator. Catalano, standing in the darkened shadows of the cutoff by his parked car, understood the signal.

Speaker tailed Capra onto the snow-cleared and nearly deserted Brooklyn-Queens Expressway, making sure he kept a reasonable distance between cars. Suddenly Capra's brake lights came on just before the approach to the Northern Boulevard exit. Speaker was forced to make an instantaneous decision: either pass Capra's car and stay on the highway, or get off at the exit. Speaker cursed and continued driving on the expressway as Capra waved at him tauntingly.

Once sure no one else was following him, Capra drove down the Thirtieth Avenue exit ramp and headed for the alternate meeting place he'd set up with Catalano, a desolate Bayside Marina lot.

CATALANO PUT A FINGER TO his lips as he approached Capra's Oldsmobile. Capra got out of his car and both men walked several yards in silence towards Catalano's car.

"Vinnie, you've gotta be careful what you say in that car. It could be bugged."

"Believe me, I don't say a word in there."

"I didn't like that guy following you tonight."

"It surprised me. It's been a long time."

"Just be careful. If you even think heroin or cocaine, the Feds will lock you up and put a Conspiracy on you." Catalano opened the trunk of his car, removed four suitcases and put them on the ground. "When do I see the rest of the money?"

Capra picked up two of the suitcases. "I told you. Two weeks. Maybe three."

After the men put the suitcases into the trunk of Capra's car, Capra carefully pulled out of the marina onto the Cross Island Parkway. He drove to the BQE and got off at the Queens Boulevard exit. At 65th Place, he made a right turn, went up to the top of the hill and parked behind a dark Chevrolet. After turning off the headlights, a silhouetted figure in the car in front of Capra's got out and started back towards him.

Capra opened the door and greeted his son, Luciano. He pressed a finger to his mouth. "Don't talk in my car. It could be bugged." The men walked up the street. "Is everything set?"

"Yeah, everything's set. Ragusa's waiting for us."

GIN!" SPEAKER CROWED.

Murray tossed his cards on the cardboard box which served as a table. "That does it. I'm outta here."

"Come on, George. Sit down. A couple more games won't kill you. Gernhardt's going to be here in a minute."

"John, I'm not like you. This isn't my whole life. I've got a wife and kid at home and I'd like to see them every now and then." Murray put on his parka. "Anyway, this wire's not going anywhere. Ever since that guy made you on the Queens-Brooklyn Expressway, this phone's been as dead as a doornail."

"That's the Brooklyn-Queens Expressway, and if you really want to sound like a New Yorker, call it the BQE. Furthermore, this wire's not dead. You gotta understand we're sitting on heavy hitters. These guys aren't niggers who move small packages every day. These guys are guineas, and guineas move heavy stuff every month or so."

"Come on, we don't know if these guys are heavy hitters."

Speaker opened a brown leather bag and waved a thick manila folder in Murray's face. "I assure you they are."

"Not the old manila folder routine again, John."

"You seem to have forgotten the guy's plate number I took. If you recall, the plate turned out to be registered to a Mildred Capra, who just happens to be the wife of one Vincent Capra, who just happens to be a well-known major drug dealer."

Murray sighed. "All right, I'll take your word for it. They're heavy hitters."

"No, no, no, Doubting Thomas. Don't give me that 'I'll take your word for it' bull. Let me read you some of his rap sheet. If you don't mind, I'll skip the minor incidents like the homicides, the armored-car robberies and assaults."

Murray covered both ears with his hands. "John, you've read it to me twenty times."

"Let's make it twenty-one. I want you to appreciate how big this guy is. In '57, Capra was arrested for possession of three keys of heroin, case dismissed; in '61, arrested with two others with nine keys of cocaine in a car, case dismissed; in '65, pleaded guilty to possessing a key and a half of heroin, six months. The prick had to have paid off the judge. Look at this. In '68, arrested by Balisteri of SIU with six keys, case dismissed. Knowing Balisteri, he probably sold the case.

"Now here's why the Feds consider Capra a major player. In 1960, '63, '66 and '70, the Feds arrested him with a ton of other guys for conspiracy to sell narcotics. All the cases against him were dismissed except the one where he pleaded guilty to some minor nonsense and got a year."

Murray leaned against the wall. "John, I get the picture. It's just that—"

Both men held their breath as the recorder activated. An outside number was being dialed. Speaker turned up the volume. After two rings, they heard the raspy voice of Vincent Capra respond, "Yeah?"

"It's Joey. Angela is here. She wants to see you."

"I'll see her after ten."

SPEAKER SLUMPED LOWER IN THE front seat of his car when the bright headlights appeared in his rearview mirror. After the vehicle passed, the detective looked up and recognized Capra's Oldsmobile. He watched the car continue for a half-block and pull into the driveway of 1908 Sedgwick Avenue. Capra got out and glanced around before proceeding up the steps to the front door. As soon as Capra was in the house, Speaker radioed Gernhardt and Murray: "Our boy's inside."

An hour later Capra slid behind the wheel of his car, reached over and unlocked the passenger side door. DiPalma opened the door, pulled up the button unlocking the back door, placed a large suitcase on the backseat, then got into the car alongside Capra. Speaker followed Capra's car down the street and radioed ahead to Gernhardt and Murray, "Cut him off at the end of the block. We don't want to get into a chase with this guy."

As Capra neared the intersection, Gernhardt sped out of a side street and screeched to a halt in front of the Oldsmobile. Guns drawn, Murray and Gernhardt scrambled to both sides of Capra's vehicle, ordered the men out and had them put their hands on the roof of the car. While they were searching the suspects, Speaker came up from behind, opened the rear door and took the suitcase off the backseat. "Whose is this?"

Capra shook his head. "I don't know. We stopped to make a telephone call and we found it in the booth. Somebody must have left it there. We're on our way to the police station to turn it in."

"What's in it?"

"I don't know. We just found it."

"You're lying."

"No. I mean it. We just found it."

Speaker turned to Murray and Gernhardt. "Put these guys in the back of your car while I take a look at this." He returned to his car with the suitcase, placed it on the passenger seat and opened it. He whistled as he saw at neat stacks of $100 bills.

While Murray kept Capra and DiPalma covered in the backseat, Gernhardt moved Capra's car out of the intersection and parked it. He returned to his car with the three men and parked by a hydrant. Speaker, with suitcase in hand, came over to the car and asked Gernhardt and Murray to step outside. The three investigators conferred. Gernhardt agreed to guard DiPalma and Capra while Speaker and Murray went back to the apartment house where the illegal wire was installed to count the money.

In the basement, Speaker opened the suitcase and he and Murray counted the money by wrapper amounts. For every $100,000 increment, Murray penciled a single line on top of a cardboard box. Twelve lines later the men shook hands.

"John, do you believe it? One million two. I've never seen so much money."

"We jumped them too soon. They had to be on their way to make a buy. I'd loved to have seen who was on the other end."

"Me, too."

Speaker walked over to the telephone recorder, disconnected it and turned to face Murray. "George, I'm not even sure we can arrest these guys for carrying money around."

"Me either. What should we do?"

"I think we should bring them in and call Captain Stowe."

"OK with me."

SPEAKER STARTED PUTTING THE MONEY back into the suitcase. "George, I want to ask you something, and I don't want you to take it the wrong way."

"What?"

"What would you say if I said we should keep some of the money?"

"I'd say how much are you thinking of?"

"A hundred thousand each."

"Oh my God. That's too much. I was thinking maybe ten apiece."

"Hey, if we're gonna do it, let's make it worthwhile. Don't forget, these guys claim they don't know how much is here."

"Yeah. But that's crap."

"You and I know that. They know that. But they're not going to squawk. They want no part of the money now that we've caught 'em with it."

"You're crazy, John. How about fifty?"

"Let's say we split the difference. Seventy-five apiece. OK?"

"Deal."

"Should we tell Gernhardt?"

"Absolutely. He's no problem. Don't worry about him."

"All right, I'll take your word for it."

Murray picked up a stack of hundreds. "That means we take two hundred twenty-five thousand and turn in nine hundred seventy-five."

"Not exactly. You always take a few extra bucks so you come up with a screwball amount. You never want an even amount, it looks bad. This way it seems legit."

SITTING IN A CAR IN Van Cortlandt Park by the boathouse, Lynch struck a match and looked at his watch. He showed it to Beninati, who looked around at Catalano. "Vinnie, it's after two. Are you sure he said one o'clock?"

"I'm telling you he told me one."

"I hope he didn't go somewhere else."

"No way. He knows the meet is here."

"Maybe he got into an accident."

"Not the way Capra drives. Something must be wrong."

Beninati bit his left thumb. A sure sign that his brain was shifting into overdrive. "Jerry, leave Vinnie and me here in case he comes. Go down to that bar on 238th and Bailey and call Graziano. Tell him our man hasn't shown yet and we're running late. Tell him when we're ready to meet him, we'll call."

"Good idea."

"While you're at it, check your office. See if anything's happening."

Lynch drove out of the park and double-parked outside Jimmy Joe's Bar. Once inside, he ordered a beer, then walked to the rear of the nearly empty bar and called Graziano at home.

Graziano answered on the first ring. "Hello."

"Joe, it's me, Jerry. We're running late. Our man hasn't shown yet."

"I don't think he's going to show."

"Why? Why do you say that?"

"I just heard on the radio that the Joint Task Force locked up Vinnie Capra and Joe DiPalma with a million bucks in their car. I figured they were with you."

"You're joking."

"I wish. It's all over the radio."

"I gotta go. I'll call you later."

"Jerry, for your sake, I hope your man is a stand-up guy."

"He's a rock. Anyway, it's no big deal. It's no crime to drive around with money in your car."

"I know. By the way, Jerry, do me a favor. Tell Catalano when you see him that I'm not worried about my money. I have his 'personal guarantee.' "

Lynch laughed, "Joe, don't hold your breath." Lynch hung up the phone.

February 23, 1972

TROUTMAN, THE SWITCHBOARD OPERATOR, WAVED a message pad. "Joe, I'm glad you guys showed up. Some freak's been calling for you all morning. He says it's very important you get in touch with him." Graziano glanced at the note and passed it on to Di Lorenzo, who read, "Joe, get in touch with me ASAP. It's very important. White Lover."

"Who the hell is 'White Lover'?" Di Lorenzo asked.

"A friend of mine. I'll tell you about him on the way to his place."

When Graziano and Di Lorenzo walked into the garishly decorated Sky Room club a bartender was busy setting up drinks for a middle-aged couple, while in the dining room, four attractive waitresses served the luncheon crowd. Di Lorenzo followed Graziano closely past the noisy diners. They went directly to the rear of the club, where Graziano knocked on a door.

Conrad Green looked through the peephole and cautiously opened the door. "I'm glad you're here, Joe."

"Long time no see. How's it going, Connie?"

"It could be better, Joe," Green said, staring at Di Lorenzo.

"I want you to meet my partner, Louis Di Lorenzo. Louis, shake hands with Conrad Green."

Green invited the men to be seated as he poured them coffee. "Joe, I appreciate you coming right over."

"What's up?"

"I've got a big problem. I need a favor," Green said.

"What's the problem?"

"Did you ever hear of a scumbag named Petey Mac?"

"Sure. He's a wiseguy. What about him?"

"He's been shaking me down for the past five months."

"For how much?"

"Four hundred a week. He says, 'It's for the privilege of staying open.' "

"Why didn't you let me know before?"

"Because I didn't want to start any trouble, Joe. I figured it was easier to pay."

"I'm sorry you didn't call me. I might have been able to do something. So what's happening now?"

"Three days ago, he sends a couple of his goons over here. They tell me Petey wants $750 a week now. I told them no way, I couldn't afford it. I gave them the regular $400. That night, the same two hoodlums came in with Petey and two other guys. They smacked me around in front of my people. One of my bouncers tried to help me and they slashed his face. Bad. More than a hundred stitches. All my customers ran out of the club scared. Petey said they'll put me out of business unless I come up with the $750 a week. I was so angry, Joe, I almost called Bruce Harper in the DA's Office. He's a close personal friend. But the more I thought about it, the more I thought I might get myself killed."

"You did the right thing, Connie. Believe me, talking to the DA would have been a bad move. If you had, your life wouldn't be worth a plugged nickel."

"That's what I figured."

"Connie, I'll try and get someone to talk to Petey Mac."

"Joe, that won't do any good. The guy is bad news. I'm afraid of him."

"Give me a day or two. I'll think of something."

"I already have. That's why I called you. I want you to lock him up."

"Come on, Connie. You know better than that. I just can't go out there and arrest him."

"I know that, Joe. I'm not talking about locking him up for shaking me down. I'm talking about busting him for narcotics."

"What are you telling me to do? Put a package on him?"

"No, even though I'd love that. You don't have to. He's putting down his own package tonight."

"How do you know?"

"A friend of mine is buying it from him."

"Who?"

"I don't think you know him. A guy named John Evans."

"John Evans? From the Bronx? A black guy with an ugly scar on his chin? Used to live with a good-looking Korean girl?"

"You're unbelievable. That's him."

"I thought he was still in the can!"

"He got out two weeks ago."

Graziano shook his head. "Sounds like he wants to go right back in again."

"Could be. Anyway, the deal was supposed to go down last night but it fell through. Evans couldn't come up with all the bread. He told Petey Mac he needed another twenty-four hours. Evans called me this morning. He wants to borrow fifty thousand dollars. He tells me it'll be worth my while. I asked him what for. He tells me he's getting a package from a guy named Petey Mac. I told him I'd let him know by four this afternoon. That's why I called your office and left a message."

"What do you want me to do?"

"I figure when Evans calls me back, I'll tell him I'll lend him the money. Then after he meets me, you follow him and lock them both up when the deal goes down. Not bad, right, Joe?"

"It sounds pretty good to me."

Green got up from behind his desk and walked around to Graziano's chair. "Naturally, I'd like my money back."

GRAZIANO AND DI LORENZO LEAPFROGGED each other's cars as they tailed Evans to the Jade East Motel near Kennedy Airport. It was nearly 10:00 P.M. when they watched Evans walk up the outside stairs of the motel to the second floor. Evans cautiously looked around before he knocked on the door of Room 227. The door opened and he entered the room.

When Evans opened the door to leave, Graziano and Di Lorenzo burst into the room with guns drawn. Di Lorenzo shoved Evans back into the room while Graziano lined Petey Mac, Tommy Demarco and his brother, Anthony, against the wall.

Petey Mac, AKA Peter Macharone, was a loud, fiftyish "made man" in the Columbo crime family. He ran the gamut of illegal activities from selling drugs to hijacking, loan-sharking to extortion. The highly visible "enforcer" could be seen three to four times a week dining and drinking at the Golden Chariot nightclub in Rego Park, Queens, with an entourage of pretty blondes, always seated at table number eleven. He had one ironclad rule that he lived by. He never would go anywhere without Tommy or Anthony Demarco by his side. He probably would have been well served to have his son follow this rule. Eight months earlier, his youngest son had been found dead in the trunk of an abandoned car, with what police estimated were fifteen to eighteen bullet holes in his head.

"Louis, bring Evans over here and toss 'em all," ordered Graziano.

Di Lorenzo skillfully searched the four men and disarmed the Demarco brothers. He joined Graziano and pointed at the backs of the Demarcos. "These two were carrying, Joe."

Still facing the wall, Petey Mac growled, "You're never going to get away with it, mothafuckers. You're dead men. I'm Petey Mac. I'll have the whole family on ya."

Graziano walked over and yanked Petey Mac's head back by the hair. "You ugly, fat guinea, who do you think you're talking to?"

Petey Mac rasped, "A coupla cheap rip-off artists."

Graziano laughed, "Evans, give 'Big Mouth' the bad news."

Embarrassed, Evans stuttered, "It's the po-police, Mr. Mac. His name is Joe Grazzziano. He's a narc-c-otics detective."

"How do you know?"

"He l-locked me up five years ago."

"They musta followed you, you stupid jerk."

"You're the stupid jerk." Graziano smashed Petey Mac's face against the wall. "You're the one that opened the door. You should have had someone outside to make sure he wasn't followed. Now, you're going to jail."

"Wait a minute. Take it easy. Isn't there anything we can do?" the gangster grumbled into the wall.

Graziano winked at Di Lorenzo. "Whadja have in mind, Petey?"

"Why don't you take twenty thousand dollars from the suitcase and go. You forget us, we forget you."

"Petey, that's mighty generous of you, but it's not quite good enough." He tapped Petey Mac on the shoulder and told him to turn around. "Petey, look at all this junk here. You've got a big problem, and there's no way you can afford to take a fall. This much heroin carries an automatic life sentence."

"Take thiry thousand."

"Petey, now you're pissing me off. What are you saying? Your ass is only worth $30,000? Put the cuffs on him, Louis. He wants to go to jail."

"Hold on. There's $150,000 in the suitcase. Why don't we split it?"

"That's better, Petey. But it's still no deal. One hundred-fifty thousand dollars is what it's going to cost you to have you and you friends walk out of here. Take it or leave it."

"We keep the drugs. OK?"

"Sorry, Petey, that goes with us too."

"Know something, mister? I was right in the first place. You're nothing but cheap rip-off artists."

February 24, 1972

A NIGHT BLACK AS A sewer. Graziano and Di Lorenzo sat slouched in Graziano's car in a corner of the Sky Room's parking lot. A bright light pierced the darkness. The rear door of the club opened. Green emerged with a tall, willowy redhead on his arm.

"Who's that with him, Joe?"

"Anita, the hatcheck girl. Good face, great body."

The couple walked over to her car and kissed. The girl opened her coat and Green put his right hand on her breast as they kissed again. Di Lorenzo watched disgustedly. "These niggers are all the same. Once they get money, they gotta get themselves a white woman."

"Don't blame him. Blame her. I don't see anyone twisting her arm."

Once the woman's car pulled out of the lot, Green headed towards his new gold-and-cream Cadillac. As he was about to unlock the door, Graziano rolled down his window and called, "Connie. Over here."

A startled Green jumped, then recognized Graziano's voice. He walked quickly to the side of Graziano's car. "How did it go?" he asked nervously.

"Pretty good, Connie. Get in."

"Only pretty good, Joe? That means it went bad, huh?"

"Connie, it went great. Just get in the car. I'd rather talk in here than out there."

Green slipped into the backseat. "Did you get my money?"

"Every penny and then some."

"Thank God." Green leaned forward. "Did you lock him up?"

"Not exactly."

Graziano watched Green's disappointed face in the rearview mirror as he slumped against the backseat.

"Joe, what do you mean 'not exactly'? You either locked him up or you didn't. Just tell me. Is he in jail or not?"

"No."

Green shook his head from side to side. "You just scored him. Didn't you?"

"Connie, we had no case. We had to let him go. We hit him in a motel room without a search warrant. If we locked him up, he'd have walked anyway."

"Come on, Joe. Don't bullshit me. If you really wanted to give him jail time, you could have. You wanted to score him all along." Green put his head in his hands.

"That's not true, Connie. We wanted to lock the sonofabitch up, but it made no sense. So we hit him where it hurt the most. In the pocketbook." Graziano took the attaché case from Di Lorenzo's lap. Without turning, he passed it to the backseat but Green refused to accept it. Graziano shrugged and tossed the case on the backseat. "Your fifty big ones plus twenty-five more."

"Joe, the money means shit to me. I wanted that prick locked up."

Graziano ignored Green and asked Di Lorenzo for the bag. Di Lorenzo reached down, picked up a paper bag from the floor and handed it to Graziano. "Connie, there's a key of pure heroin in this bag. It's worth at least thirty thousand wholesale. Give it a whack or two and you can retire for a while."

"Joe, you don't understand. You never understood. I needed him locked up. Now, he's going to shake me down forever. He'll never be happy until he takes my club."

"Come on, Connie, it's not that bad."

"Believe me, Joe, he is that bad."

February 27, 1972

IT HAD BEEN ANOTHER BUSY Saturday night. The last two wait-resses and a bartender left the Sky Room and hurried out to the parking lot. Once the bartender was sure the women were able to start their cars, he drove away. Inside the club, a pleased Conrad Green finished counting the receipts, loosened his cummerbund and took a sip of Chivas Regal. He looked up when he heard a light tap on the office door. "Who is it?"

"It's me, honey. Anita."

Green smiled. "Perfect timing, sweetheart. I'm hot. It's time for making whoopee."

He unlocked the door and started to open it. Without warning, he was driven backwards as the door crashed violently against his face. Blood spurted from his nose and mouth. Bewildered, Green instinctively threw his hands up to protect himself. Anthony Demarco rushed into the room and slugged Green on the side of the head with a blackjack. Green whimpered and fell to his knees. He swayed and pitched forward. Tommy Demarco dragged the terrified hatcheck girl into the room and roughly pushed her to the side. Petey Mac came in and locked the door.

The brothers stood over the fallen Green and repeatedly kicked him in the head and midsection while Anita screamed. Infuriated, Petey Mac picked up a large ashtray and slammed it into her face. Anita staggered against the desk and clutched at the night's receipts to try to break her fall. The money scattered when her head struck the floor. Tommy Demarco turned momentarily from Green and viciously kicked her in the head.

Anthony Demarco pulled the sobbing Green off the floor and pushed him backwards onto the couch. Petey Mac took out a black .38 caliber revolver and aimed it at Green's right eye.

"Nigger, you set us up with those cops the other night and now you're going to die!"

"Petey, what are you talking about?'

"Don't bullshit me, you know damn well what I'm talking about. Evans told you he had a deal going down with me."

"That's not true," Green stammered through bloody lips. "He told me he had a deal going down, but he never said it was with you. I gave him $50,000. He's supposed to get it back to me by Tuesday with an extra twenty-five."

"You're a liar. Evans told me he told you!"

"He's a liar, Petey. I swear on my daughter's life. He never told me anything!"

"Let's kill 'em, boss," Tommy Demarco said eagerly.

Green pleaded, "Please, Tommy. Don't say that."

"Shut up, Conrad. How much money is here?" said Petey Mac pointing to the money on the floor.

"Twenty-four thousand. Keep it. I want you to keep it."

Petey Mac picked up Green's crystal decanter filled with scotch and broke it against the desk. Anthony Demarco grabbed Green's short kinky hair and yanked it back hard. Mac pressed the jagged edge of glass firmly against Green's exposed throat. "Nigger, if I find out you set me up, you're dead. Now get down on that floor and pick up my money."

Green knelt and gathered up the money. He looked over at Anita's swollen and bleeding face and thought of Graziano. *Why didn't that greedy scumbag lock up this prick when he had the chance?*

March 13, 1972

GREEN STAYED AWAY FROM the Sky Room for several weeks nursing his assorted injuries. Badly shaken by the beating, he repeatedly telephoned the club's manager at all hours of the day and night to inquire if anyone was looking for him.

His options were limited. He either had to accept Petey Mac's terms or complain to the authorities.

Bruce Harper, head of the Organized Crime Bureau in the Queens District Attorney's Office, was lighting a cigarette when the phone rang. "Harper here."

"Bruce, it's Conrad Green."

"Connie, where are you? I've been worried sick. Word is out that you and Anita took a beating."

"We did, Bruce. A bad one."

"I'm sorry to hear that." Harper coughed. "Pardon me. These cigarettes are killing me. Connie, I'd like to see you. Can we get together?"

"Yeah. But not at your office. I'm afraid to be seen there. Is it possible you can come to me?"

"Sure. When?"

"Tonight."

"Where are you?"

"You can't let anyone else know."

"Connie, for Christ's sake. I know that."

Green paused. "I'm staying with my ex-wife and kid. They live in the Bronx at 1590 Underhill Avenue. Apartment 3C."

March 15, 1972

GREEN WAS JOKING WITH A couple of customers at the bar when the club manager, Gene Miller, came out of the dining room and whispered in his ear, "Petey Mac just came in. He wants to see you in your office."

Green went to his office immediately. Petey Mac and the Demarco brothers were waiting for him in the hallway. He unlocked the office door and the three men followed him inside. "Conrad, long time no see. Where have you been?"

"Recuperating from the beating you and your friends gave me."

"That was no beating, Conrad. Those were love taps. You don't wanna be around when I really let Tommy and Anthony loose."

"Petey, they were more than love taps. My girl needs twenty-two hundred dollars worth of dental work and she's still seeing double. That's what I call a beating."

"Conrad, the other day was business. It's over with. We thought you sent those two narcotics cops to rip us off. That nigger Evans told me you fingered us. Since he's on the run, we think he set us up. He's going to be one dead motherfucker when we get our hands on him."

"What do you want from me now, Petey?"

"Are you nuts? My money."

Green sighed and opened his wallet. He took out four $100 bills and tossed them on the desk in front of Petey Mac.

Petey Mac picked up the money between his forefinger and thumb and held it in the air. "Connie, Connie, Connie. What's this? Only $400. You must have forgot. The last time we were here, we told you it was $750 a week from now on. Anthony, how much is that? That's three weeks he owes us less $400."

"Gotta be around twenty-five hundred dollars."

Green didn't move a muscle. Suddenly, Tommy Demarco bolted from the corner of the room and smashed Green in the jaw with the heel of his hand. Stunned, Green fell against the wall.

"Jesus, Tommy, you didn't have to hit me." Green moaned.

"Shut up. You heard my brother. That's $2,500 more."

Green stumbled over to the closet, turned on the light and spun the dial of a Mosler combination safe. A moment later, he turned and started to count out $2,500 onto Petey Mac's open hand. Petey Mac then grabbed the roll of money out of his hand, went over to the safe and took out the rest of the money.

"Connie, next week have the $750 ready for me. I hate waiting around for my money."

A BLOCK FROM THE CLUB, Detectives Ed Romero, Peter Vousden and ADA Bruce Harper watched Petey Mac and the Demarco brothers get into a black Cadillac and drive away. Their blue undercover van rocked back and forth as the three heavyset men congratulated each other. The cramped Vousden reached over and squeezed Harper's shoulder awkwardly. "Conrad was terrific! Did you hear how he got it in about his girlfriend's twenty-two hundred dollar dental bill?"

"Yeah. That was beautiful. And I loved how he got both Demarco brothers on tape."

"You've got to hand it to the bastard. He's got some pair of balls. They could have killed him."

"Mark my words, Peter. When I prosecute this case, I'm going to get that scumbag Tommy a couple extra years for that smack."

Romero bent down and rewound the recorder. "Bruce, do you want to hear it again?"

"Nah, we've already heard it three times. Take the recorder with us. We'll play it inside for Conrad."

AT 6:45 A.M., THOMAS BARKELL hurried across the windswept street and rapped repeatedly on the Sky Room front door. A half-minute later, Detective Vousden appeared and admitted Barkell into the semi-darkened club. The Queens District Attorney glanced around at the arched walls covered with blue imitation velvet and silver stripes.

He elbowed Vousden. "Only a nigger could combo these colors." Vousden scoffed.

Barkell followed the beefy detective to the rear office where Green, Harper and Romero waited.

Barkell hugged Green. "Connie, how the hell are you?"

"Tired, sir."

"You should be. Tony told me you had a busy night. He said you did a great job."

"I'm still not sure I did the right thing."

"Believe me, you did the right thing. Those hoods would have never stopped bleeding you. They would have just kept on coming." Barkell turned to Harper. "Let me hear the tape."

Romero played the tape as Barkell closed his eyes and concentrated. When the tape ended, Barkell asked, "Bruce, how soon can you get Connie prepared to go before the grand jury?"

"Today's Tuesday. Sorry, Wednesday morning. He'll be ready on Friday."

"Good. Connie, for the next couple of days, I want you to tell Bruce everything you know about Petey Mac. Start at the beginning. Don't skip anything. Try to remember how many payments you made, for how much and approximate dates. Who was there? Who beat you? How many times? Who else did they beat? Do your best. The more you remember, the more jail time they'll get. Understand?"

"Mr. Barkell, I don't have to remember anything. I keep a ledger, and it's right up to date. I even have tonight's payment recorded."

"You're kidding me."

Green walked over to the closet, opened the safe and removed a small ledger book. He handed it to the District Attorney.

Barkell slowly fanned the pages. "It looks like all the entries are made on the first four pages. Is that right?"

"That's right. But forget the first two pages. That's something else. The Petey Mac stuff starts on page 3."

Harper looked over Barkell's shoulder as the District Attorney turned to page 3. The first entry read, "9/7/71, $400, P. Mac." Listed underneath the initial entry were twenty or so weekly entries indicating payments of $400 ending February 20, 1972. All payments were made to P. Mac. The first entry on page 4 read, "2/27/72, $24,000, Robbed. P. Mac—2 Demarco." The last entry in the ledger read, "3/15/72, $400 + $2,500 Owed P. Mac (3 wks) + $ 1,300 stolen from my safe. TBS."

"Connie, what does TBS mean?"

Green's right eyebrow arched and he smiled. It means, 'They'll Be Sorry.' I knew the conversation was being recorded."

"You can bet your sweet ass they'll be sorry!" Barkell sipped a cup of coffee and handed the ledger to Harper, who opened the book, scanned the pages and walked over to Green. "Connie, why didn't you let me know you kept a ledger?"

"I didn't think of it until Mr. Barkell said I should try to remember as many payments as possible."

"Well, I'm delighted you remembered. Connie, you told Mr. Barkell before to forget the first two pages. We can't do that. If we're going to successfully prosecute Petey Mac, we have to know what every entry in this book means."

Green shook his head. "Believe me, those entries have nothing to do with him."

"That may be true, but someday when we go to trial, Petey Mac's attorney is going to be allowed to see this book. He's going to ask you what every entry means and you're going to have to answer him."

"I sure hope not."

"What do you mean by that?"

"Bruce, you really don't want to know."

Barkell cleared his throat. "Connie, we have to know."

"Mr Barkell, if I told you, I'd get myself and some cops in trouble. We'd all wind up in jail."

"Are you saying the entries on the first two pages indicate corrupt dealings you've had with policemen?"

"Yes, that's exactly what I'm telling you."

"Then you definitely have to tell us everything. I can't prosecute Petey Mac and ignore your dealings with corrupt cops, Connie. If something like that was ever found out, I'd be impeached and thrown out of office, for Christ's sake. Connie, I have no choice. If you want me to help you, I have to know."

"Mr. Barkell, it's bad. Real bad."

"I still have to know."

"I'm surprised to hear you say that. I didn't think your office really wanted to know about crooked cops."

"You have no reason to say that."

"Weren't you a cop once?"

"Yes, and it's no secret how I feel about cops. It genuinely distresses me when I hear a cop is corrupt. But corruption is corruption, and I'll pursue and prosecute any crooked cop to the fullest."

"To be honest, Mr. Barkell, I watched your reaction when you listened to the tape. You never blinked when you heard Petey Mac say he thought I sent over narcotics cops to rip him off."

"I heard it, Connie. But by the way he talked, it sounded like some guy named Evans sent the cops over to rip him off. I didn't think you had anything to do with it. Are you telling us that you know the cops that ripped off Petey Mac?"

"That's exactly what I'm telling you. As a matter of fact, those scumbag cops almost got me and my girlfriend killed."

"Who are they?"

"I can't tell you, Mr. Barkell. If I did, they'd kill me."

"No, they won't. I promise you. No one will ever touch you."

Green nervously drummed on the desk. "Look. I'm not saying I did, but suppose I told you I sold drugs for cops. Would you prosecute me?"

Barkell moved around the desk and faced Green. "The answer is no. I won't prosecute you, provided you're willing to cooperate fully with us."

"I won't go to jail?"

"No, I'll grant you immunity."

"I won't have my liquor license revoked?"

"No. I'll take care of the State Liquor Authority."

"I'll be able to keep my club?"

"Yes."

Green stood up and took the ledger book from Harper. "Mr. Barkell, if I testify against Petey Mac and the cops, I'll need some sort of protection. I know them. They'll kill me for sure."

"No, they won't. Look, Conrad, the last thing you need right now is protection. Can you imagine fifty cops traipsing around your club? You'd be out of business in a week. People wouldn't come in here. Right now, no one knows you're cooperating with us. Let's get Petey Mac indicted first. We'll keep the indictment sealed for a month until we get other club owners to come forward and testify."

"What about the cops?"

"Don't worry about the cops. Bruce and I will work on them personally after we deal with Petey Mac."

"With all due respect, Mr. Barkell, as soon as Vousden and Romero here find out who the cops are, they're going to run outside and tip 'em off."

"Who the fuck—?" Romero snarled.

Barkell held up his hand. "I disagree with you, Connie, but you're entitled to your opinion. Don't say another word. Pete, Ed, please excuse us. Bruce and I will take the information."

Green waited until the detectives closed the door. "I take it you're telling me nothing is going to be said to them or any other cops."

"As God is my judge, nothing is going to be said."

Green took a deep breath and opened the book to the first page. "There are three sets of initials here, Mr. Barkell. You'll always see the initials GZ. He was in on all the deals."

"Who is GZ?"

"I'm not sure you want to know who it is. He's a friend of yours."

"I don't care. Who is it?"

"Joe Graziano."

Barkell couldn't mask his shock. His face blanched. "What?"

"You heard me right, Mr. Barkell. Joe Graziano."

Barkell inhaled deeply and shuddered as his eyes traveled to the next set of initials. "What does GZJL stand for?"

"Joe Graziano and Jerry Lynch."

"Jerry Lynch, the narcotics detective?"

"Yes. I sold drugs for Graziano more than a dozen times, and for him and Lynch eight times. Those are the dates and the amounts." Green turned the page and continued tracing the entries. "These last initials, GZD are for Graziano and his new partner. Delis . . . Delisi Delorenzer, Something like that. I'll know it if I hear it. Incidentally, it was Graziano and this new guy that ripped off Petey Mac. They told me that they were going to arrest him, but they scored him instead and gave me a key. Green sighed. "Used to be, you could trust cops like these."

March 23, 1972

THE WELL-WORN WOODEN FLOORS GROANED as Vousden and Romero entered the Queens Homicide squad room, where Beninati was pinning a notice on the bulletin board. When he heard heavy steps, he turned and motioned both men into his office. After shaking hands, the detectives cautiously lowered themselves onto rickety chairs.

"Hey Loo, if this thing collapses, I'm suing."

"Relax, Danny, that chair's held guys twice your size." Beninati hesitated. "On second thought, maybe both you pricks better stand up."

"Come on, Loo. I lost eight pounds last month."

"That's great, Peter. Only ninety-two to go." Smiling, Beninati walked behind the men and closed the door. "Danny, what made you guys call me at home this morning? It scared the shit out of me. I thought one of my men might have gotten shot."

"Sorry it was so early, Loo, but we wanted to make sure we got together today."

"What's so important?"

"Someone made a beef about a couple of friends of yours. We figured you might want to talk to them, but if you do, you gotta keep us out of it. It would be our jobs if anyone knew we talked to you."

"Who are we talking about?"

"You gotta swear, Loo. You won't tell anyone where you got this."

"I promise. Who's got the problem?"

Romero looked over at Vousden, who nodded. "Graziano and Lynch."

"Who beefed?"

"You've heard of Conrad Green?"

"Sure. He owns the Sky Room. What about him?"

"Last Friday, he testified before a Queens grand jury."

"About Graziano and Lynch?"

"No, no. Let me finish. Green told the grand jury he was being shaken down by Petey Mac and the Demarco brothers. Everything was on tape. Yesterday, the grand jury handed down a sealed indictment against them."

"Hmmph. That's one dead nigger. They better give him plenty of protection."

"That's what we thought, but Barkell convinced him it would be bad for business to have cops hanging around his place,"

"That was dumb. Anyway, where do Graziano and Lynch fit in?"

"You gotta understand, everything we're telling you Barkell and Harper told us in confidence."

"Go on."

"Evidently, Graziano and Lynch sold drugs to Green for a long time. The nigger kept a ledger with Lynch's and Graziano's names in it. It had dates, how much junk was involved, money. Everything."

"That black scumbag."

"That's not all. Graziano has another problem."

"What's that?"

"Green wore a wire to help us catch Petey Mac. On the tape, Mac mentioned some narcotics cops had ripped him off. Green told Harper and Barkell that Graziano and his new partner were the cops who did it."

"Jesus, Danny. Do I owe you and Peter a favor." Beninati rubbed his jaw.

"Why's that?"

"That new partner of Graziano's happens to be my nephew."

March 24, 1972

BENINATI WAS SANDWICHED BETWEEN SEVERAL boisterous drinkers when he spotted Graziano and Lynch making their way through the crowd.

"You guys must be nuts. An Irish bar on a Friday night," Beninati griped.

Graziano protested, "Don't break my balls. Jerry's the one who suggested we meet here."

They were seated upstairs in a corner booth. After a frazzled waitress curtly took their drink orders, Graziano looked at Beninati. "What's the problem, Loo?"

"Vousden and Romero from the Queens DA Squad visited me yesterday. Romero told me Conrad Green is spilling his guts to Barkell about you and Jerry. He told the DA he sold drugs for you guys. Worse, Green kept records. He supposedly has a list of about twenty deals he did with the both of you."

Lynch chomped heavily on his cigar. "Joe, I told you from day one that nigger was no good. You can't trust any of them."

Graziano sat back in the booth and inhaled through his teeth.

"Joe, he also told me that Green said you and my nephew ripped off Petey Mac."

"Jesus, that's not good. Did he say who caught the case?"

"Romero said Barkell and Harper are handling it personally. At the moment it's been put on the back burner, pending the arrest of Petey Mac."

Lynch removed the cigar from his mouth. "Whoa. Not so fast. What's Petey Mac being arrested for?"

"Extortion."

"Of who?"

"Green."

"Wait a minute. Are you telling me that crazy nigger went to the DA and complained that Petey Mac was shaking him down?"

"Yeah. And that's not all. Harper even got him to wear a wire and testify before a grand jury."

"Consider that one dead nigger."

"That's what I figure. Can you imagine Petey Mac's reaction when he finds out he's been indicted?"

"Loo, slow down. Are you telling me that Petey Mac doesn't know he's been indicted?"

"No. . . . er. . . . Yes."

"For Christ's sake, Loo, which is it?"

"He doesn't know yet. Barkell is sitting on a sealed indictment. He's trying to get more club owners to come forward and testify."

"Barkell's gotta be taking it in the ass. There's no way that's going to happen."

Lynch leaned back, folded his hands behind his head and looked up at the ceiling as the waitress served the drinks.

"Jerry, I can see the smoke coming out of your ears. What are you thinking?"

"I'm thinking someone should tell Petey Mac what's going on. Someone should tell him he's looking at ten years. Someone should tell Mac to whack that nigger."

The table was quiet for a moment. "Jerry, we can't go up to Petey Mac and tell him to murder someone."

"Easy, Joe. I didn't say we should do it. I said someone should do it."

"Who?"

"Someone who can get to these guys. Someone who speaks their language. Another wiseguy."

"Do you have somebody in mind?"

"Catalano."

Beninati reached across the table and grabbed Lynch's hand. "Of course. Of course, Jerry! That's brilliant!"

"Do you think he'll do it?" asked Graziano.

"For a fee." Lynch smiled.

"A fee? That's bullshit. It's the least he could do for us after his man lost my million two," Graziano groused.

"Joe, I think he would forget his fee, if you'd be willing never to bring up the subject again."

"It's a deal."

"I'll talk to him." Lynch winked at Beninati. "Corned beef and cabbage, gentlemen?"

March 30, 1972

EMBRACING COUPLES SWAYED ON THE undersized dance floor in time with the velvety music. Their reverie ended when the singer picked up the microphone and asked for attention. Unsuccessful in quieting the bar crowd, she turned to the drummer and signaled for a drum roll. The house lights dimmed and a blue spotlight followed a leggy waitress snaking her way across the supper club. She carried a large birthday cake adorned with a single sparkler over to a table where Conrad Green sat talking with a couple of local assemblymen and their girlfriends. As the waitress bent to place the cake on the table, the all-girl band struck up a very upbeat rendition of "Happy Birthday to You." Several patrons at nearby tables came over, shook Green's hand and patted his back. Well-wishers from all over the room yelled congratulations and an elated Green stood up and blew kisses to the applauding crowd.

IT WAS A LITTLE AFTER 4:30 A.M. when the last stragglers left the club. Green sipped a Courvoisier with the club manager at a rear table alongside three waitresses who were counting the evening's tips.

Suddenly, Bobby Greco, one of the club bartenders, rushed over to the table. "Connie, there you are!"

Green tensed. "What's wrong, Bobby?"

"The cops just called. Your daughter's been in a car accident!"

"Oh, no!" Green jumped up. "How is she?"

"I don't know. They took her to Morrisania Hospital in the Bronx."

"Gene, close up. I'll call you first thing in the morning."

The bartender followed the distraught Green to the office where he grabbed his car keys from the desk and draped a cashmere overcoat over the white tuxedo. As the two men rushed out the rear door, the bartender asked, "Do you want me to drive you, Connie?"

"No thanks, Bobby. I'll be OK."

Greco abruptly veered away from Green and darted towards the parking lot exit. Without warning, the powerful right arm of Anthony Demarco encircled Green's throat and viciously crushed his windpipe. The coat slid from Green's shoulders as the enforcer spun him around to face his brother Tommy. Green clawed at Tony's arm as the steel grip tightened. Tommy stepped forward and savagely kneed Green in the groin. In desperate pain, Green groaned hideously as vomit spewed from his mouth onto Demarco's slacks.

"You rotten nigger!" the older Demarco hissed, pistol-whipping Green on the side of the head. Startled at the ferocity of his brother's reaction, Anthony Demarco loosened his grip and Green tried to bolt. He ran straight into the bear-like arms of Tommy.

"Going somewhere, nigger?" He slammed Green to the macadam.

"Kill him. Kill that nigger!" spat Anthony.

Both gangsters began kicking Green in the face and ribs repeatedly while Green whimpered incoherently. Finally panting from the exertion, Anthony Demarco knelt on Green's chest and forcibly jammed a snub-nosed .38 caliber revolver into his mouth, shattering his front teeth. Green's eyes widened. The killer twisted the weapon upward and fired. The shot exited the back of Green's head.

"Hey, Tony, get off him. It's my turn."

Now Tommy pushed his brother aside and straddled Green, holding a .357 magnum an inch from his forehead. Green's mouth trembled involuntarily as Demarco squeezed off two rapid-fire shots. Green's head practically exploded.

Tony Demarco shivered with anticipation. "Turn him over."

Using his foot, his brother rolled Green over. "Look at this. The nigger shit himself."

Smiling, Tommy Demarco placed his revolver against the back of what was left of Green's head, and administered the Mafia execution imprimatur.

WHEN DISTRICT ATTORNEY BARKELL DOUBLE-PARKED in front of the Sky Room, he was immediately surrounded by a horde of screaming reporters. Detectives Romero and Vousden broke through the crowd and escorted Barkell towards the rear parking lot. Barkell watched stoically as a disinterested morgue attendant pulled back the gray blanket that covered the remains of Green's face. He looked at Vousden and asked if there were any witnesses. Before Vousden could respond, Bruce Harper appeared at the club's rear door and waved the men inside.

For twenty minutes Barkell and Harper huddled with Chief of Detectives Albert Spellman and Lieutenant Pat Beninati of Homicide, who was in charge of the investigation. After discussing various facets of the case, the men agreed to hold an impromptu press conference. Within minutes, uniformed police personnel turned the dining area of the club into a makeshift conference room.

Barkell, Harper and Beninati calmly seated themselves at a table facing the unruly reporters. Harper stood up and asked for quiet. The group reluctantly sat back and settled down.

"Ladies and gentlemen. For those of you who don't know me, my name is Bruce Harper, Chief of the Organized Crime Bureau for the Queens District Attorney's Office. I'm sorry we have to get together under such circumstances. Before making an opening statement, I want to make sure everyone knows District Attorney Barkell, who is seated on my right."

Heads nodded and murmurs of "Yeah" and "Hello, Bruce" rippled through the room.

"Good." Harper turned and extended his arm. "Seated to my left is Chief of Detectives Albert Spellman. Seated to his left is Lieutenant Pat Beninati of the Queens Homicide Bureau. Lieutenant Beninati will be in charge of the Green homicide investigation."

Harper paused and took a deep breath. "As I mentioned before, it is with a heavy heart that I stand before you. Conrad Green was not only a very respected businessman in the community, but a friend to all law enforcement. As you've probably heard by now, Green was a courageous and indispensable witness in our continuing war against organized crime in this county. His testimony against several mob figures regarding extortion led to an indictment that was to be unsealed by our office next week. Evidently these criminals got wind of the indictment and found out Green was going to testify against them. This morning's brutal murder shows they weren't just satisfied extorting his hard-earned money, they had to take his life. Well, I'm here to advise the citizens of Queens that the District Attorney's Office will continue to wage war against these and any other criminal elements in our society."

Harper stepped back and sneezed. After conferring briefly with Barkell, he stepped forward again, "Are there any questions?"

Mike Pearl, a poker-faced reporter for the *New York Post,* stood up and scratched the side of his head. "Mr. Barkell, if Mr. Green was such an indispensable witness in the war against organized crime, why was he left unprotected?"

Tom Barkell rose from his chair. "Mike, I want to make this perfectly clear. We offered Conrad Green police protection on several occasions. As a matter of fact, I personally urged Mr. Green to accept it. He adamantly refused, saying the presence of police would hurt his business. Had Mr. Green accepted our offer of protection, this heinous crime would never have been committed."

April 25, 1972

REPORTERS DASHED DOWN THE STAIRS of the Queens County Courthouse as a caravan of black Plymouths pulled over to the curb. Several detectives led by Lieutenant Beninati flanked Thomas and Anthony Demarco and Robert Greco. They allowed the suspects to cover their faces with jackets and escorted them into the building. Within a half hour, the men were arraigned before Judge Albert Buschmann and remanded to Riker's Island pending posting of bail.

Afterwards, a glowing Barkell, with Harper and Beninati at his side, boasted to reporters in the corridor outside the courtroom, "The relatively quick arrest in this case is the result of a great deal of hard work by the New York City Police Department. The number of witnesses they came up with to testify against these men will send a clear message to the underworld and organized crime that society can indeed fight back."

A youthful female reporter from the *Village Voice* squeaked, "Did these witnesses actually see the murder?"

"Sweetheart, I'm not going to discuss the merits of the case at this time. Suffice it to say, we have witnesses that place all the subjects at the scene."

"Sir, my name is Doreen Silverman, and I'm not your sweetheart. How many witnesses are there?"

"Several, Miss Silverman. And they are being given around-the-clock protection. My only regret is that Conrad Green refused such protection. If he had listened to us, he'd be alive today."

Early May, 1972

SPECIAL FEDERAL AGENT SPINA AND Detective Bucci arrived at the National Airport in Washington, D.C. on an early morning Eastern shuttle flight. As instructed, they proceeded directly to the Ionosphere Club, where an agent of the Federal Bureau of Narcotics and Dangerous Drugs met them at the entrance. The agent led the men through the airport to a black Ford illegally parked in a loading zone.

Forty-five minutes later, Bucci and Spina sat with Madison Pierpoint, the U.S. Attorney for New York's Southern District, in a large reception room outside Harrison Parker's office. Pierpoint, who was in charge of directing Bucci's and Spina's activities in New York, was uncomfortable because he had no inkling why Parker had summoned them to Washington.

A secretary served coffee when the large mahogany door opened and the diminutive Parker purposefully strode out of his office. Spina introduced Bucci to Parker, who curtly beckoned his visitors inside. He went over to his desk and sat down in his plush leather chair. "Gentlemen, don't get too comfortable. This won't take long. The reason I asked the three of you down here today is because I'm concerned." He looked directly at Pierpoint. "Madison, I frankly don't know what you guys are doing in New York."

Taken aback, Pierpoint floundered, "What do you mean, Harrison?"

"I mean where's the progress? Where's the meat? When are we going to start putting a dent in SIU and getting the heavyweights?"

"Harrison, I think we're making excellent progress. To date, we've got eight detectives and a sergeant on tape. We can indict them at any time."

"Come on, Madison. You haven't gotten any of the big players.. Not one." Parker then directed his attention to Bucci. "Correct me if I'm wrong, Detective. Are the eight men Mr. Pierpoint just mentioned not relatively new to SIU?"

"Not exactly. Two of them, Detective Koonce and Sergeant Goldman, have been in SIU for quite awhile, sir."

"Spare me, Detective Bucci. Koonce's IQ is 10 points below that of a moron's, and Sergeant Goldman would steal his dying mother's purse if given a chance. It's little wonder hardly anyone in SIU speaks to them, much less wants to work with them." Parker moved to the front of his desk and perched on the edge. "Gentlemen, I serve notice that I want the big guys. The McDuffs. The Belfrys. I want Redmond, Ramos, Santiago, Kiner."

Bucci spoke up. "It's not that easy, Mr. Parker. Everyone's laying low. Nobody's doing anything."

"Bucci, that's ludicrous. McDuff scored a guy in Brooklyn two weeks ago for over twenty thousand dollars. The week before, Ramos and his team pocketed fifty thousand dollars in the Bronx and ripped the dealer off a key of heroin."

"I never heard that," Bucci said firmly.

"I'm not sure about you, Bob." Parker moved away from the desk and hovered over Bucci. "Know what I think? I don't think you really want to catch any of the old guys."

"That's not true. I've tried everything, but they don't trust me."

"I don't believe you. I think you're deliberately keeping us in the dark. I think you're guilty of selective enforcement. I think you're deliberately steering your operation away from your so-called friends and sticking it to the new guys."

"No way."

" 'No way,' huh? Well, I'm going to give you an opportunity to prove me wrong."

Bucci stirred uneasily. "How's that?"

"In a few minutes, I'm going to bring a drug dealer named John Evans in here. He works for me. I got him out of jail a couple of months ago because he told me he could give me some real big junk people in New York. Right in the middle of our first operation last month, he and his connection were stuck up by an old friend of yours, who stole $150,000 and ripped off five keys of heroin. I want your friend, and I want you to give him to me."

"Who are you talking about?" Bucci didn't like where this was heading at all.

Parker grinned malevolently. "Joe Graziano."

Bucci gasped. "I can't give you Graziano! He's my best friend, my rabbi! Besides, he's not in SIU anymore. He works for the Feds in the Joint Task Force."

"Detective Bucci, I'm well aware where that scumbag works. But he's bad, and I'm going to give you a chance to show us that you're really sincere about helping us."

Bucci slumped in his chair. "What do you want me to do?"

"I want you to get in touch with Graziano and set up a meet with one of my operatives. He's a former dealer from Europe that I turned myself. He's done a lot of undercover work for me in the past. I want you to tell Graziano you're onto a big international drug dealer who just arrived in New York. Let him know there's big money to be made."

"No way, I'd never set up Graziano. He's almost blood."

Parker's words shot across the room like arrows. "Bucci, in six months SIU will be down the drain. Believe me, everyone of those miscreants is going to jail, including Graziano. But before they do, they're going to come crawling into my office trying to make a deal. The first thing I'm going to do is ask everyone of them if he's ever done business with you. If anyone says yes, he's going to be given the opportunity to save himself by testifying against you. I have to believe there's going to be a lot of takers, even though you claim you've only done five crimes. After they spill their guts about you, I'm going to personally lock you up. You better believe I'm going to make sure you do heavy time. Now get out of my sight. Your deal with us is terminated."

Bucci pleaded, "I just can't call Graziano up. He'd know something was wrong. The first thing he'd ask me is why I'm not working on the guy myself."

Parker glanced at the picture of a smiling President Nixon on his desk. "Tell him you're working with new partners and you don't trust them."

IN A CORNER SUITE AT the Americana Hotel, a Federal agent secreted a small listening device into the brass base of a table lamp. Parker, Pierpoint, Spina, Bucci and Parker's undercover "dealer," Carlo Pondolo, watched as the agent tested the apparatus. Assured it worked perfectly, he collected his tools and left.

Parker removed a clear plastic bag containing four ounces of heroin and a five-by-seven-inch manila envelope from his briefcase and handed it to Pondolo. "Write some Italian and French names and addresses on this." As Pondolo scribbled, Parker peered over his shoulder. "That looks terrific. Graziano will go for it hook, line and sinker. When he sees all these names and addresses and your Italian passport, he'll think he's onto another 'French Connection' case."

Pleased, Parker handed Pondolo a Quickunpic seam ripper, a needle and black silk thread. "Put the junk in the envelope and sew it in the lining of your coat, Carlo."

Pierpoint interjected, "How can you be so sure Graziano will find it there?"

Parker explained, "Don't worry, he'll look there. One of the first things a good detective does is check clothing." Bucci nodded in agreement and Parker continued his lecture. "Madison, the reason we're making it easy for Graziano is we don't want him tearing the place apart and accidentally finding the bug."

Pondolo eased himself into an overstuffed chair and turned his overcoat inside out. He carefully used the seam ripper to open several inches of stitching, flattened the plastic bag inside the manila envelope and placed it between the lining and the coat material. He held the coat away from himself and made sure no obvious impression showed through the garment. Pleased with his workmanship, Pondolo sat down and expertly sewed the lining back together.

Parker tossed him a thick wad of money. "Count it, please."

The undercover veteran snapped two thick rubber bands of the wad and counted 250 one-hundred dollar bills.

"There's twenty-five thousand dollars here."

"Right. You know what to do. When he finds the junk, offer him the money to let you walk. Let's see if he can pass the test. We'll be next door listening."

Pondolo put the money in his inside jacket pocket and said in perfect, unaccented English, "He'll take it. Don't they all?"

Bucci came up behind Parker. "This isn't a test. It's a setup, a cheap frame. Nobody could pass that kind of test."

Parker whirled around and said, "Who do you think you're talking to? Let me tell you how it is. I believe strongly in testing. Tests demonstrate how people react in real situations. So don't give me any more of your bullshit about this being a frame or a setup. And don't tell me no one could pass this test. I could. Now, get over to his house and make sure you get him here."

ANNE GRAZIANO EMBRACED BUCCI WARMLY. As they walked into the living room, she inquired about his wife and the children. Half-asleep in a recliner, Graziano struggled to his feet and hugged Bucci. Promising to return with sandwiches, Anne left the room. Graziano steered Bucci over to the couch. "So, Bob, how's everything going?"

Bucci felt the adhesive tape holding the miniature recorder against his groin pull several of his pubic hairs. "Considering the bullshit rumors that are being spread about me being a rat, things are pretty good."

"Why don't you just get out of SIU?"

"Joe, I don't want to. I love Narcotics. You know how it is. Didn't you jump at the chance to get on the Joint Task Force? I did the same thing when I got the chance to get back into SIU, and I'm not about to let any candy asses like Lynch and Ryan chase me out."

"Hey, if that's the way you feel about it, stick with it." Graziano leaned back. "What'd you want to see me about, Bob?"

Bucci stood up and started unbuttoning the front of his shirt. "Before we say another word, I want you to toss me for a wire."

"Bob, that's not necessary. I know you're not wearing a wire."

"I want you to search me."

"Bob, I'm not going to search you."

Bucci's shirt front was completely opened and he started unbuckling his pants. Graziano stopped him, "If you go any further, I'm going to throw you out of my house. I know you're not a rat."

Tears welled in Bucci's eyes as he put his arms around Graziano. "Thanks, Joe."

Graziano affectionately mussed Bucci's hair. "Now, what did you want to see me about?"

Bucci dropped his voice to a whisper. "Last night a Sicilian named

Carlo Pondolo checked into the Americana Hotel. He's in Suite 2002. He'll be there only for a day or two. He's big, Joe. International. Titanic."

"How do you know?"

"I got a stool that did business with him."

"Why tell me? Why don't you hit him yourself?"

"Because I just started working with a new team that I don't trust. I'm afraid if I did anything with him they'd give me up."

"What do you want me to do?"

"Hit Pondolo at the hotel. If you score him, take care of me."

GRAZIANO IDENTIFIED HIMSELF TO THE Americana Hotel manager and secured a maintenance man's uniform. Di Lorenzo stood off to the side while Graziano knocked on the door to Suite 2002. A voice called out, "Who?"

"Maintenance."

An eye appeared at the peephole. "Who?"

Graziano took a step backwards so he could be observed. "Maintenance. There's a leak downstairs. We think it's coming from your room."

Pondolo unlocked the door and opened it slightly. Graziano hit the door with his shoulder, forcing Pondolo back into the room. Di Lorenzo followed close on Graziano's heels.

Pondolo rubbed his jaw and asked in a heavy Italian accent, "Whatsa going on?"

Graziano pointed his revolver at Pondolo's head, "Shut up and get up against the wall. Search him, Louis."

Di Lorenzo quickly patted Pondolo down. "He's clean, Joe."

"Good. Have him lie face down on the floor and keep an eye on him. I'm gonna toss the bedroom."

Graziano found the twenty-five thousand dollars and Pondolo's Italian passport in a dresser drawer. He sat down on the edge of the bed, counted the money and leafed through the passport. It indicated Pondolo had recently traveled to France, Turkey, Hong Kong and Bangkok. Graziano left the money and passport on the bed and went to the closet.

Within minutes he had excitedly ripped open the lining of Pondolo's overcoat and found the envelope. His heart raced as he read the foreign addresses. He opened the envelope, took out the plastic bag, kissed it and said aloud, "Bucci was right. This guy is big."

As Graziano was about to walk back into the living room, an anxious feeling suddenly engulfed him. His dark eyes narrowed to slits and he scrutinized the room warily. Sitting back down on the bed, he stared at the envelope containing the heroin. His lips tightened as he looked at the passport. He tossed the passport aside and hefted the money in his left hand. The trained instinct of the experienced investigator flashed warning signals. He was uncomfortable. It was too easy. It could be a trap.

Graziano walked out of the bedroom, tapped the prone Pondolo on the arm with his foot and told him to get up. After Pondolo got to his feet, Graziano showed him the plastic bag. "What have we got here?"

Pondolo pointed to the money Graziano held in his other hand. "Take the money. It's yours. Just lemme go."

"Hey, paisan. If I wanted your money, I'd take it. The last thing I need is your permission."

"Yes, sir. I mean no disrespect. You letta me go?"

"I no letta you go. You a-going to jail."

A WEEK FOLLOWING PONDOLO'S ARREST, Graziano was ordered to report to the office of US Attorney Madison Pierpoint in downtown Brooklyn. Upon his arrival, a very business like secretary showed him into Pierpoint's office. The men shook hands and Pierpoint introduced Graziano to Parker, who was seated in a chair browsing through some papers. "Joe, Mr. Parker is in charge of the Bureau of Narcotics and Dangerous Drugs. He flew up from Washington this morning to talk to you about your arrest of Carlo Pondolo."

Parker shook hands with Graziano and smiled. "That's only partially correct, Joe. I really came here to congratulate you on your arrest of Pondolo, and to request your assistance in trying to turn him."

Graziano, relieved to hear that he was not the subject of an investigation, thanked Parker and said he would be glad to help in any way.

The three men moved over to an oval shaped, smoked-glass conference table. Parker opened a file folder, "Joe, I'm not sure if you realize how big Carlo Pondolo is."

Graziano blustered, "I know he's big."

Parker, parried. "I'm sorry, Joe. I didn't mean anything derogatory. Obviously, you knew a great deal about Pondolo, or you wouldn't have been there to arrest him. However, I'd like to fill you in on some background information about him that you may not be aware of. Then I'd like to talk to you about some specifics. OK?"

"OK."

"As you probably know, Pondolo is a major player in the European and Asian drug trade. When he first started, he worked out of Marseilles and Rome exclusively. With the pressure we put on the Turkish government to curtail poppy farming, he had to shift a large part of his operation to Southeast Asia. These days, he spends more than half his time in Hong Kong and Bangkok. Over the past fifteen years, he's been responsible for moving tens of thousands of keys of heroin into the United States."

Graziano ran his fingers through his hair. "To be honest, I had no idea he was *that* big."

"Suffice it to say, Joe, Pondolo is the tip of the iceberg." Parker turned over a sheet of paper in the file folder. "Pondolo's name resurfaced back in October of last year when we arrested a Frenchman named Roger Preiss at the Waldorf Astoria with eighty keys of heroin in his room. Preiss cooperated with us immediately. He told us how he was recruited in Paris by Pondolo to deliver the heroin to someone here."

Parker stood up and walked over to the window. "Madison, tell Joe what happened next."

Pierpoint leaned forward in his chair. "Joe, have you ever heard of Louis Cirillo?"

"Sure, he's big. In fact, didn't you lock him up in the Bronx a month or so ago?"

"That's correct. We wired Preiss and let him continue his operation. He delivered the drugs to Cirillo. As soon as Cirillo took the package, we busted him. But before we did, we got Cirillo on tape bragging to Preiss that he was getting ready to do a $10 million deal with Pondolo."

Graziano's eyes widened.

"A couple of weeks ago, we got word Pondolo was coming to the States. Our sources reported that with Cirillo out of the picture, Pondolo was trying to put together a deal with JoJo Manfredi."

"Manfredi! I've done a lot of work on him and his nephews in the past. They're heavyweights."

"We know they are. Anyway, we were setting up an operation to get all of them when you arrested Pondolo. Frankly, we were shocked."

Parker interrupted. " 'Shocked' isn't the word. We were flabbergasted. Not because you arrested Pondolo, but because he was carrying shit. Who would have figured? He must've wanted to personally show the Manfredis a sample of the goods."

Graziano frowned. "It's a shame I didn't get them all together."

"I wish you had, too, but all may not be lost. We can still get the Manfredis."

Graziano leaned forward. "How?"

"By turning Pondolo." Parker sat back down and lit a cigarette. "That's where you come in, Joe. Pondolo can help us. He can give us the Manfredis and a lot of other higher-echelon people both here and abroad. Now, Pondolo will be getting out on bail. I want you to go to court and set up a meet with him. Let him know you can help him with his case. Befriend him. Make things happen. Get him to turn."

THE FOLLOWING EVENING, GRAZIANO AND Di Lorenzo were sitting at a booth in the rear of Friar Tuck's restaurant in midtown Manhattan when Carlo Pondolo walked in. Graziano waved. Spotting Graziano, the rakishly attired Pondolo proceeded to the booth and sat down.

"Carlo, I'm delighted you could make it. Did you have any trouble finding the place?"

"No. No trouble. The taxi knew exactly where to go."

"That's a first." Graziano sat back. "You remember Louis?"

Pondolo glared at Di Lorenzo. "How could I forgetta, him? He helda gun to my head all night."

Di Lorenzo leaned forward. "Hey, pal, you were under arrest. What did you expect me to do? Dance with you?"

Graziano interjected, "Hold it. We came here to talk not argue."

Feigning annoyance, Pondolo scrutinized Graziano. "What did you wanna see me about?"

"Carlo, I think I can help you."

Pondolo's mouth twisted. "Helppa me! Don't you think its-a little late? You're the one that arrest me."

"I had no choice. I had to lock you up last week. My bosses knew we were hitting you."

"Come on. You coulda let me go. No one would have known."

"You're wrong, Carlo. If word leaked out that I scored you, Louis and I would have had big problems."

"So whatta you want now?"

"We can offer you a deal."

"What kinda deal?"

"One where you can stay out of jail."

"Jail? Whatta you talking about jail? Whatta I going to get, a lousy six months? Some deal."

Graziano grew serious, "Carlo, they're not talking about giving you six months. They're talking fifteen years."

"Fifteen years! I didn't kill no one. You caught me with a lousy coupla ounces!"

"Carlo, the government isn't going to give you fifteen years because I caught you with a lousy couple of ounces. They're giving you fifteen cause you're big time. Everyone knows about your operations overseas."

"Assurdo. I have no operations."

"That's not what your friends Louis Cirillo and Roger Preiss say. They claim your setup is one of the biggest in the world."

"Cirillo? Preiss? I never heard of them."

Graziano slid out of the booth and stood over Pondolo. "Carlo, I guess we got nothing to talk about. But before I go, let me tell you something. I don't know how the system works where you come from, but over here the judge works hand in glove with the prosecutor. I guarantee you, they're going to shove heavy time up your behind."

Graziano said, "C'mon, Louis." As he started to walk away, Pondolo grabbed Graziano's arm. "Where you going?"

Graziano stopped. Pondolo let go of Graziano's arm. "Sit down. Come on, sit down." Pondolo held out his palms face up. "Let's talk. Tell me what you can do for me."

Graziano squeezed back into the booth alongside Di Lorenzo. "Carlo, I can let you walk. No jail time."

"How's that?"

"By cooperating with us. Help us get the people you do business with."

Pondolo exclaimed, "I can't do that. I'd be killed!" Di Lorenzo gestured angrily. "Keep your voice down, please."

Graziano kept the iron aglow. "I know it's a risk, Carlo, but that's the way the game is played. You either give them up or you go to jail."

"Jesus Christ. You don't leave me much choice."

"It's the only choice I can offer you, Carlo. Take it or leave it."

"OK. But first you have to help me get back to Europe for a couple weeks. I have to take care of a lot of personal business."

"Are you kidding me? That's impossible. The prosecutors would never let you leave the country. That's why they're holding your passport."

"Look, I have a lot of business over there. Legitimate family business. If you can get my passport for me, I'll be back in two weeks. Then, I give you big people."

"They'll never go for it."

"Ask them."

"I'm telling you, Carlo. It is 'Mission Impossible.' "

"Do me a favor, just try it." Pondolo reached into his jacket and took out an envelope. He leaned across the table and slid it in front of Graziano. "This is for your trouble, Joe."

Graziano firmly pushed the envelope back across the table. "I appreciate that, Carlo. But it's not necessary."

Pondolo slid the envelope back toward Graziano. "Please, Joe. As a token of our friendship. We are all Italian here."

"No," Graziano said, putting his hand on the envelope.

Pondolo reached across the table and put his hand on top of Graziano's. "Joe, please take it. It's not much. Only a symbol. It shows you trust me." Getting up from the table, he kissed Graziano on the cheek and quickly walked through the restaurant.

Graziano was nearly ecstatic. "We hooked him. Let's get out of here. I'll call Pierpoint and Spina and fill them in."

As Graziano signaled for the check, Federal Narcotics Agents Grimes and Scroggins approached the table and flashed their identification. "Detective Graziano, we have bad news for you. You and your friend here are under arrest."

Graziano looked up blankly at them for a moment, then laughed, "Where are they?"

"Where is who?"

"The guys playing the joke on me."

Grimes scowled down at him. "This is no joke, Graziano. You just accepted a four thousand dollar bribe from a Federal agent."

OUTSIDE THE RESTAURANT, GRIMES AND Scroggins, were joined by six other Federal agents who roughly relieved the stunned detectives of their weapons and handcuffed them. Protesting loudly, Graziano and Di Lorenzo were unceremoniously shoved into the backseat of a waiting Ford, where their rights were read to them. Grimes and Scroggins led a caravan of four cars to a Bureau safe house at 400 East Fifty-second Street.

Leaving the other agents outside, Grimes and Scroggins escorted Graziano and Di Lorenzo to apartment 6E. Seated in the living room were Parker, Pierpoint and Spina.

Graziano jerked his arm free from Grimes grasp when he saw Parker. "Will you tell these jerks, to take these cuffs off me and that I work for you?"

Parker shook his head. "I'll tell them to uncuff you, but you ceased working for me the moment you accepted that $4,000 bribe from Pondolo."

"What do you mean 'bribe'? That was no bribe."

Parker instructed Scroggins, "Uncuff both of them and stay with 'em." He told Grimes, Pierpoint and Spina to accompany him into the bedroom, where Grimes handed him a small tote bag which contained the detectives' weapons, shields and ID cards. He then mounted the Pondolo-Graziano tape on a recorder. The men smiled and shook hands with each other as they listened to the conversation.

Carrying the tote bag, a grim-faced Parker returned to the living room with the others. He thanked both agents and dismissed them. As the front door clicked closed, Parker addressed the worried detectives. "You men are in big trouble. We have you on tape taking a bribe, clear as a bell."

Graziano shook his head. "Di Lorenzo had nothing to do with this, and I only did what you told me to do. You told me to befriend Pondolo and to make things happen. I got him to cooperate. I took his money so he would trust me. I was on my way to call Mr. Pierpoint when that asshole Grimes showed up."

A startled Pierpoint and Spina jumped when Parker exploded, "You're a liar, Graziano. You're nothing but a rip-off artist, Next, you'll be telling me that you and Di Lorenzo didn't rip off one of my agents a few months back."

Perplexed, Graziano asked, "What are you talking about?"

"I'm talking about you ripping off John Evans when he was with Petey Mac at the Jade East. You stole $150,000 and their heroin."

Graziano, now genuinely frightened, stammered, "That's not true. We were there, but we never ripped them off."

"Yes, you did. John Evans works for me. We got him out of jail to set up Petey Mac. I had agents sitting on the place when you barged in. You ruined my whole operation. And to make matters worse, you scored them."

"We didn't score them. The place was clean!"

"You're full of it, Graziano. My men watched you walk out of there with the package."

Graziano pulled himself together. "If that's true, why didn't they arrest me? Why didn't they stop me? Know why? Because they never saw me carrying any package. I never ripped off Evans or Petey Mac. I've never ripped off anybody in my life. Know something else? This case is bullshit. It's a setup. You know I didn't take any bribe. If I wanted Pondolo's money, I would've taken it the other night when I busted him at the Americana. I told you he offered me twenty-five thousand dollars to let him walk. Didn't I turn it in? Why would I fall now for a lousy four grand?"

"Because if you scored Pondolo that night, it would have been a one-time shot. This way you could have bled him anytime you wanted."

"That's ridiculous!"

"I don't think it's ridiculous, and by the time Mr. Pierpoint finishes prosecuting this case, I don't think a jury is going to think it's ridiculous either. Believe me, Graziano, he's going to get you and Di Lorenzo convicted."

"But we never took a bribe from Pondolo!"

"Oh, yes, you did. The both of you are rip-off artists. The only difference between you and Di Lorenzo is that you've been at it longer." Parker stood in front of Graziano, pointing a finger at his face. "Graziano, you were born a thief and you'll die a thief, But the worst thing is, you're a cop thief, the lowest of the low. You're supposed to be upholding the law and locking up drug dealers, but instead you're ripping them off and letting them walk."

"That's not true."

"It is true. And that makes you worse than any two-bit street pusher because you allow the dealers to go on peddling their poison. In fact, you're a murderer."

"Murderer?" Graziano was confused.

Angrily, Parker pulled out a slip of paper from his inside jacket pocket. " 'John Pollins. Stephen D'Agostino. Donald Harrington. Billy Turner. Spider Kniley. Timothy Riley. Ramon Gonzalez. Carmine Perrigine.' Recognize any of these names?"

Di Lorenzo stiffed uncomfortably as Graziano shrugged, "Yeah. They're dead cops."

"That's only half right, Graziano. They were New York City detectives who sacrificed their lives in the line of duty. To be exact, they were detectives killed making narcotics arrests. Men who probably would be alive today if you and the rest of SIU hadn't been shaking down every drug dealer you ever met."

Graziano paled. "That's a scumbag thing to say."

"Come on, Graziano. Everyone in this room knows you're a shakedown artist. Your name has been all over the streets for years. I'm here to tell you that Madison and I will do everything in our power to make sure you get heavy jail time."

"Jail time? I'm not going to jail. I never did anything wrong." Graziano struggled to keep his voice steady.

Parker paused and studied Graziano's twitching face for several moments. "Graziano, I might be willing to admit I made a mistake in this case if you could pass a simple test for me. If you want, I can give it to you right now."

Surprised at Parker's tactic, Pierpoint and Spina exchanged blank looks.

Graziano, seeing a silver lining on the horizon, brightened. "Sure, I'll take a test."

"Good."

"What is it? A polygraph? I'll take a lie detector test anytime."

"That's not quite what I had in mind, Joe."

"I don't care what kind of test you have in mind. I'll take it."

"I'm glad to hear you say that, because this test is important. If you pass, it'll go a long way in making me believe that you're telling the truth. Fair enough?"

"Fair enough."

"However, if you fail this test, I'll have to believe you're just another crooked cop. Agreed?"

Graziano hesitated.

"Graziano, yes or no? Do you agree or don't you agree?"

"I agree."

"Good." Parker circled the seated detective and stood over him. "Are you ready?"

Graziano shivered imperceptibly, "Go."

Parker took a stack of index cards out of his briefcase and handed them to Graziano. "As you can see, Joe, I believe in doing my homework. Each card contains a brief biographical sketch of everyone you've ever worked with in SIU. What I want you to do now is call some of your old partners and bosses. I want you to say, 'We have a problem. We're being investigated. We've got to meet and talk.' If they say, 'What possible problem could we have? We haven't done anything wrong,' then I'll believe you're an honest cop. But if they say, 'What's the problem? What case? Where should we meet?, or any hint like that, then I know you're just another dirty cop and I'll lock you up."

Graziano blanched; Parker had him and they both knew it. "Come on. That's not a fair test. Everyone would want a meet whether we did something or not."

Parker looked over at Pierpoint and Spina and winked. "You make a good point, Graziano. Instead, you set up meetings with them. We'll wire you and give you a script to follow."

"What, I'd never do that to my friends!"

"Why not?"

"Because . . ."

"Because why? They'll never know you're working with us. Anyway, even if they did, what difference would it make? All your Narcotics cop friends are honest. Right?"

Graziano was silent.

"Listen up, Graziano, before you call McDuff, Lynch, Beninati, Belfry, etcetera, I have a cop that I'd like you to call first. OK?"

Graziano leaned forward. "Who's that?"

Parker drifted towards Pierpoint and Spina. "First, I want you to call Sonny Grosso."

Graziano sat quietly for a moment, and then suddenly launched himself from his seat and screamed, "You no good sonofabitch!"

In a flash Spina's weapon was leveled at Graziano's chest. Parker's voice cracked, "Sit down! Sit down now or so help me God I'll put you in jail for the rest of your life!"

Graziano slumped back into his chair and put his head in his hands. Parker stabbed his finger at him. "Just as I thought, you're nothing but a lousy rip-off artist. 'Give me a test. Give me a test.' " he mimicked.

Graziano shuddered. "You call this a test? Ratting out my friends?"

"There was nothing unfair about it. You're nothing but a cop-thief. You've hidden behind that badge of yours for years and sold this city out. You've illegally wiretapped, shaken down drug dealers, perjured search warrants, framed innocent people, stolen money and sold drugs. Graziano, you make me sick. I can assure you, when you go to jail, you're really going to do hard time. Can you imagine what all those bad guys that you've put in there are going to do to you?"

"I hope your mother's rotting in hell for having a scumbag like you," Graziano sputtered.

Parker lashed back, "You'll know soon enough, because all you dirty cops that have been allowing these merchants of death to peddle their wares are going to wind up there. My mother may be in hell, but not because of anything I did. Your mother's alive, and her hell is about to begin when she sees your face on every TV station and newspaper in New York."

Not a muscle moved in Graziano's face.

"Now mark me well, Graziano. I'm going to give you a couple of days to think it over. That's more than you ever gave anyone. Be back here on Friday at 11:00 A.M. and be ready to cooperate, or you're going to jail. It's your choice."

Graziano shakily picked up his jacket and headed for the door. Di Lorenzo followed silently behind him.

Suddenly Parker yelled out, "Hold it, Graziano. Take your gun and shield. I want you to walk out of here a detective."

Graziano nearly dropped his jacket as Parker handed him the tote bag. "Graziano, you can stay a detective if you cooperate. If you don't, you're going to jail. It's as simple as that. He paused. "You can always take a third option if you don't like the first two."

"What's that?"

"You can always commit suicide."

ANNE CAME DOWNSTAIRS IN HER robe when she heard the front door being unlocked. Graziano looked at his wife and lowered his eyes without saying a word. He brushed past her and headed up the stairs. In the darkened bedroom he pulled off his shoes, fell back on the bed and stared up at the ceiling. Anne quietly slipped into the room and knelt by the side of the bed. She cradled Graziano's head in her arms and softly stroked his hair. The faint bathroom night-light betrayed an anguish in his expression that Anne had never seen before. He turned and hugged her. "Anne, don't worry. I'll be all right. I've just got to make some phone calls."

Anne put her hand to her mouth. "I almost forgot. Bob Bucci called just before you came home. He said it was important. He's going to stop by first thing this morning."

Graziano glanced at his watch. It was 6:23 A.M. Without comment, he went downstairs to the living room and stared at the phone. He wanted to talk to someone but was too deeply confused and ashamed.

What did Parker really know? Was his house bugged? Anne watched as he paced the floor, muttering, "I'm getting blamed for something I didn't do."

THE SCHOOL BUS HAD JUST picked up the children when the doorbell rang. A panic-stricken Anne led Bob Bucci into the living room.

Graziano, wildly gesticulating, was talking to himself. "They're all against me. Mother? The children? My friends? I'll kill Parker."

Anne whispered, "He's been like this for the last twenty minutes."

"Wait in the kitchen, Anne. Let me talk to him." Anne burst into tears and ran from the room.

Bucci grabbed Graziano's arm. "Joe, for Christ's sake, take it easy."

Graziano looked at Bucci. "Bob. What are you doing here?"

"Didn't Anne tell you I was coming over?"

"No . . . Oh, yeah. That's right. Is it morning?" Graziano tried to collect himself. "Did someone tell you I had a problem? Did Di Lorenzo call you?"

Bucci averted his eyes. "No. Parker did."

"Parker? How do you know Parker? Why would he tell you anything?"

Bucci steeled himself. "Because I work for him."

Whatever strength Graziano had been trying to summon now deserted him completely.

He sagged. " 'Work for him'? What are you telling me? You're a stinkin' rat?"

"Joe, I'm not a rat. Parker gave me a second chance to start my life over and I took it. And that's what I'm offering you."

Graziano had trouble speaking. "So Parker sent you over here to talk to me. What does he think? You can turn me?"

"Joe, he can help you."

"Isn't that nice of him? All I have to do is give up my friends, right? Tell Parker thanks, but no thanks."

"Joe, it's not like that at all. You don't have to give up your friends. Just new guys. Guys you hardly know."

"That's bullshit. This prick already told me the guys he wants me to setup."

"They'd never have to know. Parker would work it out."

"That's where you're wrong, Bob. They would know. And if they couldn't figure it out, I would know."

"They'd all be given the opportunity to turn."

"What about the cops that would rather go to jail than give up another cop? What happens to them? What about their families? What are they supposed to do, rot?"

"It's not like that."

Graziano, his voice rising to an infuriated crescendo, grabbed Bucci's arm. "It *is* like that. Tell your friends no deal. Now get out of my house. You're making me sick."

UNABLE TO SLEEP, DI LORENZO telephoned Beninati early that same morning. Guardedly, he related what had happened at Friar Tuck's the previous evening, and the subsequent encounter with Parker. Beninati hit the roof.

"Louis, I want you to meet me in an hour at the Seven Seas. In the meantime, I'm reaching out for Lynch. I want him to hear this."

In the diner, Di Lorenzo detailed the Pondolo incident and Graziano's downfall at Parker's hands. Lynch spoke first. "What a bunch of scumbags. They set you guys up!"

"I know."

"And those jerk-offs are beating their meat if they think Joe will turn."

"I wouldn't be too sure about that, Jerry." Di Lorenzo looked uncertainly at the two men. "Joe took it very bad."

Lynch's face reddened, and he reached across the table and grabbed Di Lorenzo's shirt. "What are you saying?"

Di Lorenzo tried to pull away. "Jerry, I didn't say he was going to turn. I said he took it very badly. It looked like something snapped in him."

"Snapped my ass. What do you know about Graziano anyway?"

"Enough to say he looked bad."

Beninati turned to Di Lorenzo. "How'd you leave it with him?"

"He was supposed to call me this morning. He never did. So I called his house a couple of times. Both times Annie said he was sleeping. Just before I came here, I called again. She said he was still sleeping."

Lynch stood up. "Come on, let's call him now." The three men went to the pay phones by the restrooms.

Di Lorenzo was about to pick up the phone when Lynch said, "Hold on, I'll call him."

Anne Graziano answered the phone on the third ring. "Hello."

"Hi, Anne, it's Jerry. Let me speak with Joe."

"I can't. He's sleeping, Jerry."

"Anne, it's important I talk with him."

"I don't want to disturb—"

"Who the hell is it!" roared Graziano in the background.

Lynch listened as Anne's voice broke. "It's Jerry. Jerry Lynch."

"Gimme that damn phone." A moment later, Graziano screamed into Lynch's ear, "What do you want? Why are you calling me again? I told you not to bother me!"

"I have to see you, Joe. It's important. I'm with Beninati and Di Lorenzo."

"What are you going to tell me to do? Cooperate? Stay away from me, Lynch. I don't want to see anybody."

"Joe, Joe, listen to me. We have to meet. Can we come over there?"

"Don't come here! You hear me? Stay away from me. I'll never turn. I'm going to bed. And stop bothering me!"

Lynch flinched as Graziano slammed down the phone. He slowly shook his head, dropped his cigar on the floor and kicked it across the tiles.

"Gentlemen, we have a problem. The guy's flipped."

LYNCH BANGED HIS ELBOW AGAINST the tiles as he slipped getting out of the shower. Sopping wet, he held a towel loosely around his middle and stomped down the hallway to the bedroom, where he angrily picked up the phone.

"Yeah?"

"Jerry, I'm sorry about this morning. Anne told me I was way out of line."

Heartened by Graziano's calmness, Lynch sat down on the edge of the bed. "Joe, forget it. You don't have to apologize to me. I just happened to be with Beninati and Louis this morning and we wanted to talk to you. We stopped by your house a couple of times this afternoon but nobody answered the door. We tried to call you, but the phone was busy."

"I heard you at the door, but I didn't feel up to talking with anybody. I had Anne take the phone off the hook." Graziano then assured Lynch, "I want to let you know I'm feeling much better. I was hoping I could get together with you and Loo and DiLorenzo, tonight."

"What time do you want us?"

'No. I'll come over to your place. I gotta get out of the house. I'll see you around eleven."

Di LORENZO AND BENINATI STOOD up as Lynch opened the door and admitted a haggard-looking Graziano, who hugged each of the men. He declined Lynch's offer to take his coat and sat down heavily on the couch. The three men stirred uneasily as the despondent Graziano incoherently began to describe his dilemma.

Suddenly, he looked wildly at Lynch. "Jerry, you were wrong about him. He's good people. He's trying to help me."

Lynch went over to the sofa, crouched and took Graziano's hands in his. "Joe, who was I wrong about? Who's trying to help you?"

"Bucci. Bob Bucci."

Lynch's brow knotted. "Bucci? What about Bucci?"

"He's not a rat." Graziano struggled to his feet and laughed, then began jabbering excitedly. "Lynch, the joke's on you. You always said Bucci was a rat. Well, you're wrong. He wants to help me. He only wants me to give up cops I don't know. No friends. He said absolutely no friends. I told him no friends. You know he's a Fed. He said you don't have to give up friends. A lot of cops would rat on friends but not me!" Graziano's face contorted and he started to weep.

Lynch took the sobbing Graziano's arm and led him back to the couch. "Joe, take it easy. I know you'd never give up a cop."

Wild-eyed Graziano pulled out of Lynch's grasp. "Oh, yes I would. I'd give up cops who would give me up. Never a friend. My friends wouldn't give me up. Bucci told me cops would hurt me. I know you'd never hurt me, but Lieutenant Ryan would give me up in a minute. He'd love to give me up. He's going to be sorry he threw me out of SIU."

"Joe, Lieutenant Ryan doesn't want to give you up. He loves you. You're like a son to him."

"He threw me out of SIU, didn't he? It's his fault this is all happening to me. Big deal, I stuck up for a friend. Now he's telling on me. What did I ever do to him?"

"Joe, relax." Lynch was trying hard, but he was out of his element.

Graziano raised his voice. "I'm getting out of here. Where is Anne? I don't want her talking to Ryan." Graziano pointed at Beninati. "Look at him standing over there!"

"What are you talking about? Ryan isn't here."

Graziano was babbling. "You're full of shit. I'm not blind. Do me a favor. Just ask Ryan where he put Anne. He hid her in the kitchen, didn't he? I told him she wasn't supposed to go to the kitchen without her sister. Ask him why he made her go in there without her sister. He made her go, didn't he? I want her and I want her now."

Graziano reached into his overcoat pocket and took out his service revolver. He pointed it at Lynch. Everyone froze.

"I understand it now. You're all against me. You're holding her hostage," Graziano mumbled.

Beninati took a step forward and Graziano swung the revolver towards him. "Ryan, if you take another step, you're a dead man."

Beninati slowly held his hands up. "Hold it, Joe, hold it. I'm not Lieutenant Ryan. It's me, Lieutenant Beninati."

"You're a liar, you Irish bastard."

"Joe, please come over here. Look at me. It's me, Lieutenant Beninati."

Graziano put the gun to his temple and asked uncertainly, "Where's Lisa?"

Beninati went for the opening, however brief it seemed, "She's not here, Joe. She's at home with the kids. There's just the four of us here. We're at Jerry's. We're trying to help you."

Graziano scanned their anxious faces. His face paled and his knees started to buckle. He dropped his revolver to the floor. Beninati rushed over, grabbed him and helped him over to the couch. Lynch pushed Graziano's service revolver under the couch with the side of his foot. Di Lorenzo ran into the kitchen and returned with a glass of water. After taking a few sips, Graziano attempted to stand but sagged back weakly against the cushions. A flushed Beninati knelt on one knee and implored Graziano to pull himself together. "Please, Joe. Snap out of it!"

"Fuck you, Beninati. Fuck all of you. What are you afraid of? Whadda ya think, I'd give you up? I know why you brought me here. You're afraid I'm going to tell them we sold drugs together. That you had Green murdered. Don't worry, I'll take the fall for us. I can do the time. They asked me about you guys. I told them you were my friends. I told them you were as good as gold, that you're straight, I told them I'd give them all the cops they wanted. But not my friends."

Di Lorenzo looked at Lynch, Beninati leaned closer. "Thanks, Joe, we appreciate that."

"What do you know about jail? Who's going to take care of my family? You guys think it's a big joke, don't you?"

"That's not true, Joe." "You're a liar. The only reason you came to see me tonight is because you think your ass is grass. Thank God I'm good, I don't give up friends. I bet you guys would give me up in a minute."

"Joe."

"Get out of my house. The Feds don't want me. They want you. They know about your drug dealing." Graziano pushed his way out of the seat. "Where's Anne? Where did my staircase go?"

Beninati looked helplessly at Lynch, who walked over and tried to embrace the sobbing Graziano, who pulled back. "They told me to blow my brains out, Jerry. Commit suicide. Can you imagine them telling a New York City detective to kill himself? Scumbags. They think I won't do it. I thought about it. I really did. Did you see my letter?" Graziano frantically patted his pockets.

"Anne must have it."

"Don't worry about it, Joe."

"No, no, no. I want you to see it. It's important. Here it is." He reached into his back pocket, and handed a letter to Lynch. "Read it to them, Jerry. Show them how messed up I was."

Lynch hesitantly unfolded the paper and read:

"Dearest Anne,

I remember the Chongchou River. Korea was so cold. Everybody was crying. The captain kept screaming at us to get up. I wanted to yell "Everybody's going to get killed," but I was afraid, He kept screaming at us. I told him I was shot. He kicked me and told me to get up. I was so tired. My stomach was on fire. I met him again yesterday. I'm not sure because I don't want to look at him. He told me to kill myself. I told him I couldn't, that I have a wife and kids. He said it was all right to kill myself. I'm afraid of him. I didn't do anything wrong. He shouldn't tell me to commit suicide. I'm a cop, My partner's a cop. He has no right to tell me to die. So I sold some drugs, big deal. They were going to use them anyway. The nigger was going to tell on us. We had to take care of him. What else could we do? Anne, do you remember my father when I came home? He was so proud of me. He loved to watch me play ball. Do you remember when he came to Minneapolis that weekend and I rode the bench? I wanted to die. He loved to watch me play base-ball. 'Joltin' Joe DiGraziano,' he used to call me in the house. He couldn't say that outside because everybody in Brooklyn hated the Yan-kees. Remember when I signed with the Giants? He held his hand over his heart and made believe he was having a heart attack. He told me the Giants hated Italians. He said even though he hated the Yankees they had a lot of Italians like DiMaggio, Berra, Raschi and 'the Scooter.' He even thought Charlie Keller's mother was Italian. I told him about Wil-lie Mays when he was at Minneapolis. I told him how great Mays was and he kept talking about 'the Duke' and Furillo. I'm sorry I never made it. I wanted to hit against Spahn, or Burdette and Johnny Sain. Why do I have to die? Does this happen a lot? Why do I have to cooperate? Why did I get my gun back? I told him to just arrest me. Please arrest me. Don't give me back my gun. I want to tell you here and now Grosso had nothing to do with this. He's good, you know that. Sure I've done a lot of things that I'm not proud of. If I do what they want me to do I could never live with myself. I'll never figure out why I have to die.

I love you more than anything and kiss the kids.

Joe"

Lynch returned Beninati's stare, folded the letter and put it in his back pocket. Graziano wiped his eyes and put his arms around Di Lorenzo. "Louis, I feel so bad for you. It's my fault. If it wasn't for me, you wouldn't be in this mess."

Di Lorenzo started to cry. He wrapped his arms around Graziano. "It's not your fault, Joe. We were set up."

Graziano pulled back. "Do me a favor, Louis. Pick me up early tomorrow. I want to go to Brooklyn to see my mother before we turn ourselves in. I've got to talk to her."

Di Lorenzo, Beninati and Lynch stared at each other, Then, slowly, Di Lorenzo spoke. "Sure. We have to be there at eleven o'clock. Is eight OK?"

"No. That's not OK. It's too late. Make it seven." Fighting back tears, Graziano smiled weakly at the three men. They did not smile back.

NATTILY DRESSED IN A CREAM-COLORED trenchcoat, Graziano slipped into the passenger side of Di Lorenzo's car. He appeared calm, even upbeat. Traveling on the Long Island Expressway, he recalled long-forgotten incidents.

"I'll never forget the time Inspector Cooper saw a Doberman licking his balls outside St. Patrick's Cathedral. In front of twenty guys, he turns to Lynch and says, 'I wish I could do that !' Lynch tells him, 'You better pet him first.' "

Di Lorenzo was laughing and crying simultaneously.

"One time Lieutenant O'Brien threw a Christmas party at his house. Nobody knew O'Brien's sister was a nun. She's dressed in civvies. You know Lynch, he starts telling her one of his half-ass jokes, only she don't *know* it's a joke. He tells her he was at the vet's earlier that day and there were two Siamese cats and a German shepherd in the waiting room. Lynch said he asked the vet, 'What's with the first cat?" The vet says, 'It's getting destroyed because it ate its owner's canary.' The nun bites and says to Lynch, 'That's terrible. What about the second cat?' Lynch tells her the second cat was getting destroyed because it ruined its owner's drapes. The nun says, 'People can be so cruel. What about the poor dog?' Lynch tells her the dog's owner was taking a shower when she dropped the soap. While she was bending over to pick it up, the dog jumped in the shower stall and mounted her. The nun says, 'Oh my God, she's destroying him for that?' Lynch tells her, 'No way. She's getting him declawed.' "

The two were still laughing when they exited the Brooklyn-Queens Expressway at Metropolitan Avenue. Driving into the run-down Williamsburg section of Brooklyn, they watched the streets come alive with activity. Neighborhood stores opened; delivery trucks started lining the streets; young Puerto Rican mothers held the hands of their kindergartners and first graders; commuters scurried towards the elevated subway station; properly dressed numbers men and sniffing junkies took up positions in doorways and on street corners.

Graziano rolled down his window. "Boy, how this neighborhood has changed. I wish I could get my mother to leave, but she won't. Look at all these dumb lowlifes. Can you believe none of them ever heard of 'Campy,' 'Oisk' or 'the Duke'? Before they let any of these seamy creatures into New York or at least into Brooklyn, they should be made to take a course in baseball history."

"Joe, not for nothing, and I don't want you getting mad at me, but who is 'Oisk'?"

Graziano shook his head. "Carl Erskine, you dummy. Haven't you ever heard of Erskine? Struck out fourteen Yankees in the '53 Series."

"I heard of Erskine, but not 'Oisk.' "

At the corner of Driggs and South Second, Di Lorenzo pulled the car over to the curb. Graziano tapped on his right hand, "Louis, my mother's place is on the next block."

"I just wanna run into Orlando's first and get a pack of cigarettes."

As he was about to open the door, Graziano leaned over towards the driver's side, "Louis, may I let you in on a secret?"

Di Lorenzo bent over. "Yeah?"

"I can't wait to tell Parker to go fuck himself."

Di Lorenzo smiled, "Me, too." Di Lorenzo shut the door and headed toward the bodega as Graziano leaned back in his seat and closed his eyes.

Seconds later he heard a noise outside the car and opened his eyes. "Vinnie. What are you doing here?"

Holding Graziano's service revolver in his gloved right hand, Vincent Catalano quickly reached in the open window and pressed the gun against Graziano's chest. A single shot ripped downward into Graziano's heart. Graziano's eyes and mouth opened as Catalano dropped the revolver and suicide note onto his lap. He then lowered his head, and walked briskly away.

ON THE DARK, TREE-LINED streets that surrounded Forcelli's Funeral Home in Douglaston, Queens, hundreds of civilian and police cars were randomly double-parked or indiscriminately blocking neighbors' driveways. In front of the funeral home, the sidewalk, narrow walkway and the five steps leading up to the front door were jammed with solemn-faced men in blue uniforms and white gloves. The vestibule inside the funeral home mirrored the outside except for eight young female classmates of Michelle Graziano.

Graziano's body was laid out in full uniform in the main viewing room, packed with hundreds of cops. Among them were Chief Crane, Captain Hughes, Captain Stowe, Lieutenant Ryan, Louis Di Lorenzo, Jack McDuff, Ray Carrera, Brogan Conner, Doug Redmond, Dick Belfry, Sonny Grosso and Eddie Egan. They cast their eyes downward as Police Chaplain Duane sprayed incense at the benediction.

The priest turned to the seated Anne Graziano, the children, Michelle and Joey, Graziano's mother, Theresa, and several other female family members. He slowly turned and looked at Graziano in his casket then made the sign of the cross and began, "Our father, who art in heaven, hallowed be thy—"

"My son no commit suicide, he was murdered!" yelled Graziano's mother as she slumped back in her chair. "My son no commit suicide!"

As family members consoled Graziano's mother, a commotion broke out in the back of the funeral parlor. Beninati had spotted Bucci in the long line of sympathizers, immediately approached him, and told him to get outside. Bucci looked straight ahead. Beninati grabbed Bucci's arm and snarled, "Get your ass outta here, you lowlife!"

Bucci yanked his arm out of Beninati's firm grip. "He was my best friend. I want to say good-bye. Leave me alone."

As Beninati again reached out for Bucci, several cops on line grabbed Beninati and ushered him out the vestibule. Lynch, talking in a corner, elbowed his way through the mourners when he saw the struggling Beninati being pushed out the front door. He confronted the young cop who corralled Beninati in a chokehold. "Let go of him or I'll put a bullet in your head."

The cop shoved Lynch aside. "Cool it, old man."

Lynch's left fist smashed into the face of the young man just above the nose. The cop let go and stumbled into the waiting arms of several bystanders.

Lynch grabbed Beninati. "What's up?"

"Bucci. He's inside."

Lynch shoved his way into the room where Anne Graziano was standing in front of Bucci. She raised her hand, "Jerry, please, I don't want any trouble here tonight. I'm going to bring him up to Joe, let him say his good-byes and then have him leave."

Lynch was not used to taking orders. "Anne. Don't."

"Please, Jerry, I know what I'm doing. Let him say good-bye."

All the cops stepped aside as Bucci walked up to the casket, blessed himself and knelt. A moment later, Lynch came up behind Bucci, took him by the hair and dragged him out of the room, through the vestibule, down the stairs and out into the front yard. While Beninati stood Bucci up, Lynch punched him twice in the stomach and then tried to bite him on the cheek.

Suddenly, a blackjack smashed against the side of Lynch's head while two Federal agents grabbed Beninati by the arms. Lynch, on one knee, watched the Federal agents shield Bucci with their bodies and push him into a waiting black car.

Lynch struggled to his feet, looked around at all the blank faces. He spotted Chief Crane who was standing on top of the steps shaking his head. He reached into his pocket, pulled out his shield and threw it towards Chief Crane and shouted. "I want to thank all of you assholes for coming to my retirement party tonight."

As he turned and walked towards the sidewalk, Beninati clutched his arm and also threw his shield on the ground. 'What do you mean *your* retirement party? You mean *our* retirement party!"

June 15, 1972

BENINATI DOUBLE-PARKED OUTSIDE a candy store to buy a pack of cigarettes. On the newsstand he spotted the *New York Times* headline: "U.S. LOOKING INTO HEROIN BRIBERY HERE—POLICE OFFICIALS ARE SAID TO BE IMPLICATED."

Beninati paid for his Camels and the paper, walked to the back of the store and crammed himself into a narrow telephone booth. He rapidly scanned the article, then dialed Lynch's phone number.

"Yeah?"

"Jerry, it's me, Loo. Have you seen today's *Times*?"

"Are you kidding me? I'm still in bed. What's the matter?"

"Brace yourself."

"What is it?"

"It's a big article about Bucci, and how he's been working undercover for the Feds for over a year."

"You're joking."

"I wish I was."

"Read it to me."

"I can't. It's too long."

"Hey, stop pulling my prick."

Beninati took a deep breath, "It's by that Burnham jerk-off who writes all their corruption shit." He started to read, " 'A Federal investigation into bribery of police officers by narcotics dealers has been under way for the past several months, and several indictments of New York City detectives and their superiors can soon be expected. Our sources indicated that the involvement of policemen is far more extensive and serious than what emerged recently from the Knapp Commission hearings. The undercover agent, Robert Bucci, who was the key operative in the investigation, is an experienced detective who served in the Narcotics Division for several years. He and his family were recently moved by the U.S. Atorrney's Office to a safe house in upstate New York as protection against possible retaliation.' "

"That scumbag."

"That isn't all. Listen to this, Jerry: 'For more than a year, wearing a tiny radio transmitter in his belt and driving a tan two-door Pontiac equipped with an elaborate system of hidden microphones, Detective Bucci has been collecting evidence for a special investigating team established in the spring of 1971 by United States Attorney Madison Pierpoint.' "

"They even mention Graziano later in the article."

"What does it say?"

Beninati searched the lengthy article. "Oh, here it is. It says, 'Detective Bucci cooperated in the investigation of rogue detective Joseph Graziano's activities which ultimately led to his suicide.' That's all."

June 16, 1972

HARRISON PARKER HURRIED THROUGH THE shuttle area at LaGuardia Airport to the waiting rank of cabs. He curtly directed the driver to Cadman Plaza in Brooklyn, and reread the article exposing Bucci in the *New York Times* en route. When he arrived at the Federal courthouse, he went directly to the US Attorney's Office on the third floor, stormed past the startled receptionist, and charged down the hall.

Pierpoint and Spina jumped from their chairs when Parker unexpectedly threw open the door. The man from Washington slammed the newspaper down on Pierpoint's desk and shouted, "What are you trying to pull?"

Pierpoint, ignoring the paper, asked, "Pull? What are you talking about? "

"I mean the deals you make with the press. You've made my office the laughingstock of Washington. We look like whores, for Christ's sake."

"Harrison, what was so bad about me talking to the *Times*? So I gave them a story, big deal."

"Big deal, huh? Well, the big deal is, I don't like my office being used as some self-serving launch pad. Furthermore, I don't like being called in the middle of the night by some asshole editor from the *New York Times* and asking me to confirm the story."

Spina leaned forward in his chair. "There weren't any secret deals. Everything was legit."

"Nick, don't insult my intelligence by telling me everything was above board. That's ridiculous. Everyone knows you two are going into private practice. Do you guys think you're the first attorneys to ever leave the Department that wanted some free publicity?"

"It wasn't like that."

"It *is* like that, Madison. And let me tell you, both of you are walking the edge ethically and I'm goddamn pissed off!"

Pierpoint exploded. "Ethics! Who are you to talk to me about ethics? After what you did to Graziano!"

Parker flared. "What are you talking about?"

"You know exactly what I'm talking about, the old Abbott and Costello trick you pulled with him. Heads I win, tails you lose."

"Madison, I'm asking you one more time. What are you driving at?"

"I'm talking about how you set up Graziano at the Americana. On one side of the coin you had Bucci encourage him to score Pondolo, and when he didn't, you turned the other side and had Pondolo try to hand Graziano twenty-five thousand dollars. That sounds pretty unethical to me."

"When you're catching corrupt cops, Madison, you sometimes have to give them a push. Everyone might not agree with the tactics, but that's the way it is."

"So you justify your actions by telling yourself it's OK to give corrupt cops a push? That's ethical? That's above board in your book?"

"Wait just a minute. Graziano was a rip-off artist, you know that."

"That still didn't give you the right to frame him."

"I never framed Graziano!" Parker yelled.

"What do you call having Pondolo leave four thousand dollars on a table at Friar Tuck's? We heard the tape. Graziano turned him down. He didn't want the money. You were the one who told Graziano to befriend Pondolo, to do anything to turn him."

"You think you're pretty cute, don't you?" Parker growled.

"No, I don't think I'm cute. But you know what I think you are?"

"I got a feeling I'm going to hear it whether I like it or not."

"You bet your sweet ass you are. To me, you're nothing but a murderer."

"A murderer?"

"That's right, a murderer. Don't forget, I was in the room the night you arrested Graziano."

"When we arrested Graziano?"

"No. When *you* arrested Graziano. Don't include me. It was your case from beginning to end. That man never took a bribe from Pondolo. You know it, I know it and Nick knows it. You murdered Graziano, all in the name of justice."

"You're crazy!"

"I'm not crazy. I watched Graziano go crazy right before my eyes. I'll never forgive myself for not having had the courage to stop you when you gave him back his gun and told him he could always commit suicide. He was a broken man, for God's sake!"

"He was a corrupt cop!"

"And *you're* a corrupt prosecutor." Pierpoint picked up the *New York Times* from his desk and threw it at Parker's feet.

July 4, 1972

THE SUN SENT SOME LAST rays of light through the trees and painted the granite angels, crosses and weathered headstones, some decorated with red, white and blue ribbons and bows, the color of melted gold. Little Stars and Stripes flags were stuck on many graves. The mourners had left the cemetery.

Patrick Klyne stood next to a plot covered with light green grass. He put both his hands on the gray headstone. "I promised you I would come by," he said in a hushed but clear voice. "I never really got to know you and I had a lot of questions to ask. None matter now. Anyhow, you already answered the most important one." He paused. "It wasn't worth it, right?"

Klyne stepped back, turned, stopped and looked back at the grave. Only then did he see a piece of paper, a page of a yellow pad, stuck to the headstone with scotch tape. He bent down. An American flag was painted on the paper and a girl's face, tears on the cheeks. Klyne had to lift the paper to read the words. "You missed the fireworks, Daddy. And I miss you. You are my hero. Michelle."

Klyne said in a whisper, "As they say, Joe, rest in peace. They can not get you anymore. Wherever you end up. You stupid son of a bitch."

August 1972

IT WAS A BALMY morning when Whitman Knapp and Michael Crowne, Governor Nelson Rockefeller's Chief Counsel, left the Governor's private jet in Seal Harbor, Maine, and stepped into a waiting limousine. A short ride later, Knapp ascended the terraced steps to Rockefeller's graystone mansion. Looking across the manicured lawn and past gnarled old pine trees fencing the property, he could see the spray from light waves crashing against the rocks. On the horizon, a lone two-master bobbed a seaman's invitation.

A uniformed black butler led Knapp and Crowne past the spectacular marbled reception area to the palatial library. Knapp stared up at the winding circular staircase and Viennese chandelier hanging from a fluted ceiling. Michael Crowne eased himself into a large leather chair and opened his briefcase, while Knapp wandered around the room examining bookshelves. He gently pushed a rollered ladder noiselessly down the sunken track runner and touched an exquisite leather-bound Gutenberg Bible. The adjacent shelf contained a collection of first-edition works by Sir Arthur Conan Doyle.

"Most people think he only wrote Sherlock Holmes mysteries," said Rockefeller from the open doorway.

Knapp backed away from the bookshelf. "They're magnificent."

Smiling, the Governor walked towards Crowne as the butler set down a Japanese lacquered tray with a cut-glass pitcher of iced tea and three heavy crystal glasses on a corner table.

"Madison, my pride and joy is that Remington Indian brave on the table next to you. It's one of a kind. My father acquired it in Chicago in the early 1900s. Rumor has it he won it from Andrew Carnegie in a poker game."

"Truly a treasure, sir."

Rockefeller's attorney leaned over and handed him a folder. The Governor turned to Knapp. "I want to express my gratitude for the untiring effort you and your Commission have rendered the citizens of New York City the past two years. We are deeply indebted to you."

"Thank you, Governor."

"Michael and I have reviewed the preliminary draft of your final report. Your remedial recommendations to curb future corruption are quite impressive."

"Thank you."

"There is one thing that bothers me, however."

"What's that, Governor?"

"It seems to me that on several occasions during your hearings, and as recently as ten days ago, you vigorously urged a special prosecutor be appointed to investigate the criminal justice system in the City. Is my understanding correct?"

"Yes, sir," Knapp responded.

"Well, I noticed this recommendation is conspicuously absent in your report. Are you now suggesting a special prosecutor isn't necessary?"

"Er . . ."

"Why did you change your mind?"

Knapp fidgeted uncomfortably. "To be candid, Governor, I didn't want to."

"What happened?"

Knapp dropped his eyes. "Last week, Mayor Lindsay summoned me to Gracie Mansion. When I got there, Hogan, Roberts and Gold were with the mayor. They're the DAs from—"

"I know the district attorneys from Manhattan, the Bronx and Brooklyn. As a matter of fact, I know them well."

"Well, sir, it was a difficult meeting, to say the least. I informed them we needed a special prosecutor because the public has lost confidence in their ability to prosecute officials for corruption. Hogan became emotional. He shouted at me, 'You worked for me eight years as one of my bureau chiefs. Did you ever once hear of any reluctance from my office about prosecuting anyone no matter what his position?' I tried to explain that I never claimed the DAs were doing anything wrong, but that the public perceives that the DAs are not prosecuting cops and politicians with the same fervor as they would an average citizen."

"So they changed your mind?"

"Yes, sir, they did. The mayor pointed out that installation of a special prosecutor would usurp the authority of his District Attorneys. He also reminded me that you would be responsible for the appointment of a Special Prosecutor, and would likely put in one of your hatchet men to tear the city apart. He says you still haven't forgiven him for switching political parties."

"The Mayor has a penchant for hyperbole. I'll even the score with him in good time, but never at the expense of the people of New York City."

"I know that, sir."

Rockefeller went over to Knapp, put his arm around his shoulder. "You've made a mistake, and I want you to correct it. As a fellow Republican, I insist you recommend the appointment of a special prosecutor. One who will not only look into police corruption, but one that will examine the entire criminal justice system, including how backroom politicians appoint judges and award contracts. Please understand my position. I'm not trying to force anything down your throat, but this is important to me. For years, the Democrats have been stealing New York City blind, and I want you to help me put a stop to it. Understand?"

"Yes, sir."

Rockefeller handed Crowne back the folder. "Michael, have you told Whitman?"

"No, sir."

"Good." Rockefeller proffered his hand to Knapp. "Yesterday I spoke with President Nixon, and he agreed with me that in recognition of your outstanding work, you be appointed to the Federal Bench at the earliest opportunity."

MAYOR LINDSAY SEETHED AS HE read the *Times* headline aloud to the five district attorneys assembled in his office: "KNAPP URGES ROCKEFELLER TO NAME SPECIAL PROSECUTOR TO LEAD CORRUPTION WAR.

"I can't believe I hired that pussy. A nobody. Now he goes and stabs me in the back."

Hogan nodded. "He promised us last week that the special prosecutor issue was dead. Now he's recommending one. The one thing we asked him not to do, he does. I should have known all along, he was a backbiter."

Lindsay spread the newspaper on the desk. "Something's wrong.

Rockefeller must have had something to do with this. Somehow, he got Knapp to change his mind. He's getting even with me for switching parties." Lindsay picked up the *Times*. "Just listen to this: 'The Knapp Commission recommends Governor Rockefeller appoint a special prosecutor to mount a five-year war among New York's policemen, prosecutors and judges.'"

"You have to admit, he has a good point regarding cops and judges" said the Brooklyn DA.

"Please, Gold."

"I'm sorry, Your Honor. I was only kidding."

Lindsay read further: "Knapp wants a special prosecutor because corruption is so widespread in the criminal justice system that neither the public nor honest policemen feel they can trust the city's prosecutors to handle the job.'"

Jay Kriegl, a special aid, opened the door. "Mr. Mayor, they're waiting for you in the press room."

A determined Lindsay led the way with the district attorneys trailing behind. The prosecutors took seats on the stage facing the media representatives as the mayor stepped to the podium. He removed his jacket and handed it to Gold.

Brandishing the Commission's report he stated: "I would like to say that I remain unalterably opposed to the Commission's recommendation that a special prosecutor be appointed to investigate the criminal-justice system in New York City. As the mayor of this great city, I have the utmost confidence in the abilities and integrity of the gentlemen seated behind me to ferret out and prosecute any corruption and wrongdoing that takes place within our system. As soon as Governor Rockefeller returns from his vacation, I intend to advise him of my position with respect to this matter, and request he not appoint a special prosecutor."

September 1972

ROCKEFELLER'S SEARCH COMMITTEE HAD NARROWED the field of candidates for the position of special prosecutor down to three men. Counsel Michael Crowne arranged for the Governor to participate in the final examination of each aspirant.

Aaron Nader was very much at ease as Crowne, seated beside his boss, conducted the interview. Rockefeller, visibly impressed with the forty-eight-year-old jurist's innate fervor and direct approach, listened with growing interest as he deftly fielded the counsel's questions.

Nader, a Sephardic Jew, had spent most of his adult life being a prosecutor in Manhattan and Suffolk Counties, His no-nonsense style was abrupt and to the point, and irritated his colleagues as well as his adversaries. While an ADA, he told a law class at New York University that a conviction of a cop, businessman or politician was "better than your last orgasm."

"Aaron, suppose you had to bring a judge, or a district attorney, say a friend of yours, before a grand jury as part of a corruption probe, could you do it?"

"Mr. Crowne, I worked as a prosecutor for fourteen years under Frank Hogan, and he's the only public official in New York City that I have any respect for. I consider him a friend. A close friend. That said, if I was the special prosecutor and I had the slightest inkling that Frank had done something wrong, I'd have him before a grand jury so fast his shit wouldn't have time to stink."

Rockefeller laughed as Crowne continued, "When you worked in Hogan's office, what was your relationship with the other ADAs you worked with?"

"I didn't like any of them. Most of them owed their souls to the Democratic Party."

"Suppose, down the line, you prosecuted one of them and got a conviction. What kind of sentence would you ask for?"

"The maximum. I have always adhered to the axiom that if you do the crime, be prepared to do the time. Our courts have traditionally sentenced cops, judges and politicos minimal jail time, a policy I find repugnant. In fact, I regard betrayal of public trust the most heinous of all crimes, and I think violators should be given significantly higher sentences than run-of-the-mill criminals."

"How do you feel about New York City judges?"

"Lots of smoke. There must be fires."

"Could you nail any of them?"

"Without question."

"What do you think of Mayor Lindsay?"

"Don Quixote with the brain of Sancho's horse."

Rockefeller guffawed, stood up and shook Nader's hand. "Michael, cancel the other interviews. We have our special prosecutor."

November, 1972

PATROLMAN MICHAEL BOLKOVIC PEERED AROUND the corner into the special narcotics cage. "Are you coming, sergeant?"

"I'll be right there, Mike. Just give me another minute."

For several days, Sergeant James Emburey had been puzzled by a small army of roaches marching across the floor and frenetically squeezing into a small opening at the bottom of a suitcase. Kneeling, he once again fingered the voucher tag hanging from the suitcase handle and checked the numbers against the logbook. Downstairs, he joined his impatient car-pool comrades for the arduous ride home to Long Island.

BEFORE DINNER THAT EVENING, THE concerned Emburey telephoned Internal Affairs. He identified himself and asked to speak with Inspector William Bonacum.

"He's not in, Sarge. Can anyone else help you?"

"No. I only want to speak to the Inspector," Emburey insisted.

"He should be checking in later, but if it's an emergency, I can try him at home."

"No, don't do that. It's no emergency. Just let him know that Sergeant Emburey from the Property Clerk called, and I'd appreciate him calling me back. Here's my home number."

While putting his two-year-old daughter to bed, the sergeant's wife rushed into the room and excitedly told him Inspector Bonacum was on the phone. Emburey hurried across the hall to the master bedroom. Without going into detail, he informed the IAD chief there might be a problem at the Property Clerk. Bonacum suggested they meet the following morning in the lobby of 400 Broome.

UPON ENTERING THE PROPERTY CLERK'S lobby the next morning, Emburey spotted Inspector Bonacum leaning against the far wall smoking a cigarette. He walked over and introduced himself. "Inspector, I'm Sergeant Emburey. My apologies for disturbing you last night, but I didn't know who else to turn to."

Bonacum dropped his cigarette on the floor and stepped on it. "How can I help?"

"I hope you don't think I'm crazy when I tell you this, but I think something's wrong upstairs."

"In the Property Clerk's?"

"Yes."

"What's the problem?"

Emburey took a deep breath. "Sir, one picture's worth a thousand words. Would you mind coming upstairs with me? It's easier for me to explain if I can show you."

Halfway up the flight of stairs to the second floor, Bonacum stopped. "Sergeant, does anyone else know what you're going to show me?"

"No."

"Not your commanding officer?"

"No."

"Why is that?"

"Because if I'm right about what I'm going to show you, even he could be in on it."

Bonacum nodded. "You impress me, Sergeant. Lead the way, please."

On the second floor, they pushed passed dozens of cops milling around in the reception area and were buzzed inside. Captain Wayne Toomey rose to attention when Bonacum and Emburey entered the room. "Inspector, it's a pleasure to see you."

"We'll see about that, Captain. Why don't you join us? The Sergeant here wants to show us something."

The three men left Toomey's office and proceeded past curious clerks to the special narcotics cage. Inside, the sergeant lifted a large cardboard box and exposed dozens of cockroaches skittering for cover. Startled, Captain Toomey jumped as the roaches scattered. "Christ, Jim, what are you trying to do?"

Emburey waited and looked to Bonacum for approval. "Proceed, Sergeant."

"Inspector, before I came on the job, I was a high-school science teacher."

"What's that got to do with this?"

Emburey bent down, his right knee on the floor. "Chief, do you see that suitcase where our little friends are crawling in and out?"

Bonacum squatted beside Emburey. "Yeah, what about it?"

"I checked the voucher number."

"I'm listening."

"This suitcase is one of the suitcases from the 'French Connection' case. It's supposed to be filled with heroin. Roaches wouldn't be going in that suitcase if it contained heroin. I think they're going in there because they're eating something."

The puzzled inspector stepped on a vermin. "Sergeant, what are you telling me?"

"I'm telling you I don't think there's any heroin in that suitcase."

The three men were silent for a moment, as full understanding of this statement sank in. Bonacum then ordered Emburey to bring the suitcase to the Captain's office. From there he phoned Captain Edward Rorke, the commanding officer of the police laboratory. "Captain, this is Inspector Bonacum. I'm on my way up there. I need some narcotics evidence analyzed right away."

BONACUM, TOOMEY AND EMBUREY WERE greeted by Rorke and a lab technician named Aaron Mintz at the reception desk. Rorke led the men into the laboratory. Bonacum took the suitcase from Emburey, put it on top of a Formica counter and opened it. He turned to Mintz and said, "Tell me what's in here."

Mintz randomly selected a plastic bag from the suitcase and opened it carefully. He then spooned some of the contents into a petri dish and started laughing.

The inspector moved closer. "What's so funny, Mintz?"

"Look at this." Mintz bent over and spread the powder around the shallow dish with the edge of the spoon. "Do you see all these red spots?"

Bonacum examined the tiny red dots in the powder. "Yeah."

"They're called *Trikalism ferrugineum.*"

"What the hell is trikkles fergum?"

Mintz laughed. "That's the scientific name for flour beetles."

"Flour beetles?"

"Yes. That's what these red spots are, flour beetles. They breed in flour."

"Flour? Are you telling me this shit is flour? There's no heroin here?"

Mintz stepped back and grinned. "That's precisely the message, sir."

ON THE FOURTH FLOOR OF police headquarters that evening a dispirited Police Commissioner Patrick Murphy slumped in his chair surrounded by First Deputy Commissioner William Smythe, Deputy Chief Inspector John Guido and Bonacum. Murphy asked Bonacum, "Are you sure it wasn't mislaid?"

"Not a chance, Commissioner. It was stolen."

"How much?"

"At least fifty pounds. Captain Rorke called an hour ago and confirmed the entire suitcase is filled with flour."

"What's the street value?"

"I'm not sure. About six or seven million."

"That's more what I make in a year." said Guido.

Nobody laughed.

Murphy snapped the pencil he was holding in two. "The goddamn place is only a block from here. Can you believe the nerve of those bastards?" Murphy threw the two pencil pieces at the wastepaper basket, missed and turned to Smythe. "What do you think we should do, William?"

Smythe stopped biting his hangnail. "Commissioner, the first thing we have to do is make an immediate disclosure. Go public right away. Too many people know about it already. If we sit on this and word leaks out, we'll be history."

Guido protested, "I disagree, Commissioner. At least let us set up a surveillance team on the place for a couple of weeks. Maybe they'll come back."

Murphy looked at Bonacum. "What do you think, Inspector?"

"I agree with John. We should sit on the place. We have nothing to lose. Before you make any sort of disclosure, let's make sure that we inventory the place, Without a complete inventory, you're liable to be making announcements every week."

Again Guido balked. "Wait a minute, Bill. We can't inventory it while we're watching the place. Everyone will know something's wrong."

"I didn't say inventory it now. I said conduct an inventory *before* we make any announcements."

Murphy leaned back and looked at his deputy. "I say we go along with John's idea. Let's sit on the place for a month. We just might get lucky."

December 13, 1972

At O'NEALS' BAR AND GRILL on the Upper West Side of Manhattan, Jerry Lynch squeezed out of a booth. "If that ugly waitress ever decides to come back to work, order me another drink, Loo."

As Lynch was walking to the bathroom, a television announcer appeared on the set over the bar and alerted audiences that the station would be cutting away from regular daytime programming and switching to New York City Police Headquarters where Commissioner Patrick Murphy was standing by to make an important announcement. Lynch stopped in his tracks and returned to the booth. He nudged Beninati and pointed to the television set. "Check this out."

Harsh klieg lights bounced off Murphy's balding head as he fidgeted nervously behind the wooden lectern and reviewed his notes. The camera scanned the large room and revealed assembled reporters sitting patiently with notebooks in hand.

New York's supreme law and order enforcer cleared his throat.

"Ladies and gentlemen of the press." His sad, watery blue eyes stared into the camera.

Lynch turned to Beninati. "I didn't know basset hounds had blue eyes."

Beninati quieted Lynch. "Let's listen to the jerk."

"It is my sad duty to announce that fifty-seven pounds of heroin, impounded in the 'French Connection' case, have been stolen. The heroin, which was stored in a vault on the second floor of the Manhattan Property Clerk's Office at 400 Broome Street pending its destruction, appears to have been stolen sometime between 1964 and 1969."

"Ha!"

"Shhh, Lieutenant."

". . . theft uncovered last month by the Property Clerk has been confirmed by the Police Department laboratory. I make the announcement today because I am of the opinion that continued secrecy would not now help the progress of the probe into its disappearance."

"Doncha love it, Loo?"

"Ssshhh!"

". . . I deeply regret that lax administrative procedures have permitted a corrupt act of such great magnitude to taint the genuine progress that we have made in the Department's thwarting narcotics trafficking."

As the police commissioner reached for a glass of water, the camera focused on several reporters shouting questions. Murphy turned back to the podium. "Gentlemen, please. I'll answer questions at the conclusion of my statement. Right now, I'd like to give you a little background as to how the drugs got to be in our possession and its storage history at the Property Clerk's Office. On February 19, 1962, Detectives Egan and Grosso made the first of two seizures of heroin smuggled in from Marseilles, France. On that day, they arrested Joseph Fuca and his wife after finding twenty-four pounds of heroin secreted in the ceiling of their home in Brooklyn in a suitcase. A week later, Egan and Grosso arrested Joseph Fuca's son, Tony, with eighty-eight pounds of heroin in two suitcases in his possession. These two seizures became world famous when the case became the basis of a book called *The French Connection,* and a movie by the same name.

A few days after the seizures, Egan and Grosso removed all the heroin from the police laboratory and placed the drugs in the custody of the Property Clerk. Since then, according to our records, the missing drugs were signed out of the Property Clerk four times and returned four times."

Lynch laughed. "This is better than the movie."

"The first seizure left the Property Clerk's on March 6, 1962, for presentation at an arraignment hearing in Criminal Court in Brooklyn. The drugs were returned to the Property Clerk later that day. The second occasion the drugs left the Property Clerk was March 30th of the same year, where it was again presented to a Brooklyn grand jury. Again, the drugs were returned to the Property Clerk later that day. Incidentally, ladies and gentlemen, what I'm going to tell you next does not count as an occasion when the drugs left the Property Clerk. In 1963, two bags of heroin were removed from the suitcase and delivered by New York City detectives to Oak Ridge National Laboratory in Tennessee for a neutron activation analysis. At that time it was hoped the heroin could be traced back to its original source in Marseilles."

As reporters howled with laughter, Lynch turned to Beninati, who was banging the table, "Loo, do you believe this moron?"

". . . test proved fruitless. The third occasion when the drugs were removed from the Property Clerk's Office occurred on July 23, 1964. The drugs were released to the US Treasury Department for display at a hearing on heroin trafficking which was being held in the United States Senate. The following month, for reasons only known to the Treasury Department, the drugs were returned unescorted to the Property Clerk by Railway Express. Obviously, ladies and gentlemen, the poor internal control procedures permitted under previous police administrations would not be tolerated today under mine."

Beninati pounded the table again. "Do you believe this? The stupid US government mailed it back to the Property Clerk!"

". . . September 29, 1969, a Property Clerk's receipt indicates a detective removed the narcotics for delivery to a Manhattan District Attorney and returned the drugs the following day. At this time, the signature of the detective is suspected to be false. Furthermore, the shield number reflected on the Property Clerk receipt has never been issued to any member of the service. From that date to the present, no further movement of the aforementioned narcotics is reflected on the Property Clerk's records. It is tragically apparent that the Department's procedures for the control of confiscated narcotics have been woefully inadequate. Accordingly, I have directed my First Deputy Commissioner, William Smythe, to develop controls that will ensure the integrity of all property held by the Department. Thank you." The Commissioner stepped back from the podium and conferred with Guido and Smythe.

After Lynch got the attention of the waitress, he laughed to Beninati, "Loo, I gotta believe the guys who ripped it off got a serious problem."

"That's an understatement, Jerry. They're gonna execute those guys."

A moment later Murphy returned to the podium. "I'll take your questions now."

A CBS reporter stood up and outshouted ABC's Bill Beutel. "Commissioner, are Detectives Egan and Grosso suspects?"

"Er. . . . everybody, both in and out of the Department, who had any contact with the heroin will be questioned. So the answer to your question is, Egan and Grosso will be questioned."

"Commissioner, that's not what I asked. I asked are Egan and Grosso suspects?"

Lynch smirked, "Those fags wouldn't have the balls."

". . . this moment there are no suspects. But we certainly will be talking to them."

Murphy pointed to Ramona Sheridan of the Associated Press. "Yes, Ramona?"

"Sir, is it possible additional narcotics are missing or stolen?"

"It's possible but unlikely. In any event, that's why I've assigned Deputy Inspector Michael Farrell of Internal Affairs the responsibility of inventorying all the narcotics in the possession of the Police Department. You have a question?"

Elaine Symington of Channel 11 asked, "Commissioner, I don't understand. Why were the drugs kept in the Property Clerk's all these years instead of being destroyed?"

"That's a good point, Elaine. The reason the drugs were not destroyed was because the foreigners responsible for bringing the drugs into the country escaped when we arrested Joseph Fuca. It was hoped they would be caught someday and made to stand trial. If this happened, it would have been necessary to produce the heroin at their grand jury proceedings as well as at their trials."

Marilyn Rawlings of the Village Voice looked up.

"Commissioner, what was the name of the detective who signed out the narcotics on September 29, 1969?"

"Marilyn, I hesitate to divulge the detective's name for several reasons. Firstly, the detective in question committed suicide some months ago and I don't want to give his family further pain. Secondly, we believe his name was forged. Thirdly, a full-scale investigation into the matter is currently being conducted, and it would be highly speculative on my part to make known any names."

Marilyn Symington's eyes widened. "Committed suicide some months ago? Was the detective's name Joseph Graziano, Commissioner?"

Beer spurted out of Beninati's nose and mouth as he watched Murphy reach for a glass of water. He desperately fought for breath.

"Oh, my God. I think I just figured out who those lads with the serious problem are."

". . . I can't comment on that. All I can say is that we believe the signature of the detective in question was forged."

"Wasn't Graziano the subject of a drug-related investigation, and that's why he committed suicide?"

"Marilyn, if you don't mind, I rather not continue with this line of questioning." Murphy pointed to Gabe Pressman. "Yes, Gabe."

"Commissioner, is the Bob Bucci investigation connected with this case in anyway?"

Lynch glowered at the TV screen.

The embattled Commissioner hesitated. "I can't answer that at this moment. Gabe, please bear in mind that our investigation is still in the preliminary stages. More questions, Gabe?"

"Just one. Will you ask Special Prosecutor Nader to join your investigation?"

"We don't plan to at the present time, but we'll certainly be talking to him. That's all the questions for now. You'll be advised as developments warrant."

Beninati sidled closer to Lynch. "Jesus, Jerry. No wonder Graziano was able to get shit anytime he wanted. The Property Clerk was his own private warehouse!"

January 1973

DEPUTY POLICE COMMISSIONER FOR PUBLIC Information Richard Kellerman, Bonacum and Deputy Inspector Farrell stood up as a frazzled Murphy walked into Kellerman's office. Kellerman skipped the welcoming protocol and sighed. "Commissioner, I've been trying to get in touch with you for hours."

Slightly annoyed, Murphy retorted, "I know, Richard. I got your messages. All fifty of them."

"I'm sorry, Commissioner. We—"

"I spent most of the afternoon with Aaron Nader. I asked him to join forces with us in the Property Clerk investigation."

"Smart move, sir. What did he say?"

"He went for it. He said he'd be glad to join us."

"Good. I'll put that in your announcement for tomorrow's press conference."

"What press conference?"

"Chief Guido didn't tell you?"

"No, Chief Guido didn't tell me."

"I'm afraid Michael here has got some more bad news for you, Commissioner."

The knot in Murphy's stomach tightened as he faced Farrell. "Michael. Not again. I can't take it anymore."

Farrell avoided Murphy's eyes. Commish—"

"Michael, this is ridiculous. I've already made two announcements. We're getting to look like the Keystone Cops."

Bonacum interjected, "Don't forget, Commissioner, I asked you to wait until a complete inventory was taken before you made any announcements."

"Inspector, I don't need you telling me when to make announcements."

"Sorry, sir."

Murphy turned back to Farrell. "How much is missing this time?"

"I'm afraid to tell ya."

"How much?"

"It is big."

"How big?"

Farrell referred to a piece of paper he took from his shirt pocket. "Another 198 pounds."

"Oh, my God."

"It was from one seizure. Ninety kilos of cocaine. Signed in by a Detective Ramos, SIU, in April of 1970."

"Who signed it out last?"

"Graziano, in January of 1972."

"Oh, my God. That Graziano again. How much does that make now?"

"Right now, it's up to 310 pounds."

"Oh, my God."

"And the bad news is we still have a lot more seizures to inventory and then we have to audit all the little shit."

Murphy raised his voice, "I want you to assign every available man you can get your hands on to the Property Clerk until you've inventoried and analyzed everything. I don't care if they have to work around the clock. We've got to get a handle on this." He put out his hand for the piece of paper Farrell held in his hand. "When did you say the last theft occurred?"

"Early January 1972."

"Shit!"

Kellerman faced Murphy with a touch of compassion. "What's the matter, Commissioner?"

"I was the PC then."

"Oooww. That hurts."

"*I know* that hurts, Dick. That's why I said, 'Shit.' "

WITH THE STAUNCH BACKING OF Mayor Lindsay and the other county district attorneys, a feisty Frank Hogan convened a special grand jury to investigate the thefts from the Property Clerk. He then issued a subpoena ordering Commissioner Murphy to appear before the grand jury and to bring all pertinent departmental records with him.

Upon receipt of the subpoena, the police commissioner called Nader for advice.

Nader made no attempt to mask his outrage. "Don't you dare appear before that grand jury. I'll take care of this."

Slamming down the phone, he called Hogan. "I'm not going to warn you again. Don't get involved in the Property Clerk case. The Governor has given *me* the mandate to probe police corruption in this city, and that means *I'm* the only one empowered to impanel a grand jury to look into the Property Clerk thefts."

Hogan bristled, "I've never seen anything saying you're the only one who can convene a grand jury in this case. Anyway, who says this is a case of police corruption? For all we know, these thefts could have been committed by civilians or members of the mob. You don't have one shred of evidence these thefts were committed by policemen. And until you do, this investigation falls under my jurisdiction."

Nader put through a call to the Governor in Albany and reported the incident. Rockefeller laughed. "Take it easy, Aaron. I'll call the little shit and straighten everything out." He pressed a button on his intercom. "Lois, get me Frank Hogan right away."

Within a minute the secretary buzzed back. "Governor, Mr. Hogan's on line four."

Rockefeller leaned back in his chair and rasped, "Frank, I'll get right to the point. I want you to dismiss your grand jury looking into the Property Clerk thefts. I asked Aaron to handle it."

"Governor, I fully intend to handle this case personally. And I'm not about to bow to any political pressure from you or anyone else. Furthermore—" Hogan stopped talking when he heard the dial tone.

Rockefeller calmly walked out of his office and strode down the hallway to his Chief Counsel's office. Crowne looked up as the Governor opened the door. "Michael, within the hour I want you to write an amendment to the executive order creating the special prosecutor's office. We grant Nader the sole authority to investigate the thefts from the Property Clerk's Office."

ARMED WITH ROCKEFELLER'S AMENDED EXECUTIVE order, an exuberant Aaron Nader led Police Commissioner Murphy and several of his high command on a grand tour of his very impressive office facility at Two World Trade Center. Upon entering the spacious, richly paneled meeting room, the group was greeted by Nader's Chief Assistant Prosecutor Joseph Phillips and Chief Investigator Walter Stone. As the group milled around the large conference table chatting, two plump miniskirted secretaries wheeled in a lavish collection of cold cuts and hors d'oeuvres.

Nader waited patiently for the nine men to take their seats. "Gentlemen, the purpose of this evening's meeting is to get an update from Inspector Bonacum, who has been working on this case from its inception. I'd like the inspector to outline his progress to date, and recommend the next steps to be taken so that we can start coordinating our activities. I want tonight's meeting to be as informal as possible and your input is welcomed. No suggestion will be considered unreasonable or farfetched. That said, the Commissioner would like to say a few words."

Murphy referred to his notes, then began speaking. "Gentlemen, without doubt, the theft of the drugs from the Property Clerk is the most cataclysmic incident of corruption ever experienced by the New York City Police Department. Its negative impact on our citizenry, as well as our own police personnel, will be with us for years to come. Therefore, it is paramount this case be solved at the earliest and the miscreants brought to justice swiftly." His blue eyes glistened. "I know it's frustrating and the trail is cold, but I don't want anyone giving up on this case. Something is bound to happen. Don't forget, all we need is one break and this thing could crack wide open."

He paused. "I am now going to turn the chair over to Inspector Bonacum, who will bring us up to date as to specifics regarding the investigation."

"Thank you, Commissioner. Before I tell you about some of our future plans that Mr. Nader alluded to, I'd first like to digress a bit and discuss my gut feelings about this case and some of the work accomplished to date. First of all, I'm convinced the crime was perpetrated by at least two persons, one of whom had to have been working in SIU when the thefts took place. Let me tell you why I've arrived at this conclusion. All the stolen drugs were from SIU cases. Aside from the people who worked in the Property Clerk's Office, only the men of SIU had access to the voucher numbers assigned to the missing drugs. Ordinary cops couldn't just walk into SIU or the Property Clerk's Office and get them.

Another thing: as you all know, Detective Joseph Graziano's name or an alias for it was used to sign out the drugs even though his name was misspelled. I believe the persons involved in the thefts knew Graziano's every move. Why? Can you imagine someone going into the Property Clerk's Office and forging Graziano's signature without knowing where he was at the time? Can you imagine the ramifications if Graziano happened to walk in on them while they were checking out the drugs? No, gentlemen, the perpetrators knew Graziano's every movement. They had to have worked with him.

"Moreover, I don't believe ordinary cops, or for that matter ordinary narcotics detectives, had the wherewithal to dispose of so much junk. It had to be guys with real contacts in organized crime, and only the men in SIU had that kind of exposure. I also—'

Phillips interrupted, "Whoa. Please, Inspector. Not so fast. If you don't mind, I'd like to backtrack on one of the points you just mentioned."

"OK. Which one?"

"You indicated Graziano's signature was a forgery. How do you know that?"

"Not only was his name misspelled, but the Department's handwriting expert analyzed the signatures. He readily determined the signatures on the vouchers were not Graziano's because the vouchers were signed by a right-handed person. Graziano was left-handed."

"That wasn't very smart of the guy that signed it out."

"I disagree. It worked."

Phillips contemplated the inspector's remark and concurred, "It sure did."

Bonacum continued, "While we're on the subject of Graziano being left-handed, there were a couple of things in the medical examiner's autopsy report that puzzle me." He looked at Murphy. "Do you mind if I talk about those issues relative to Graziano's suicide that I discussed with you?"

"Not at all."

Curious, Nader leaned forward. "I'd like to hear what bothers you, Inspector."

Bonacum leafed through several papers in his folder. He removed three yellow sheets of paper, scanned them briefly and held them up.

"After the discovery of the thefts, I reviewed Dr. DiMaio's report regarding Graziano's suicide. A couple of things struck me as peculiar. Firstly, the Medical Examiner reported that the bullet entered Graziano's heart in a downward spiral from the right side and exited his left side. I think that's pretty hard for a left-hander to do. Granted, the Medical Examiner concluded Graziano used his right hand, but if I were committing suicide, I'd do it with the hand that I had the most confidence in."

Most of the men seated at the table murmured in agreement.

"Secondly, Dr. DiMaio said he didn't find any gunpowder on either of Graziano's hands. Therefore, I don't know how he could have concluded that Graziano used his right hand. Finally, the thing that bothers me the most, and this is by no means scientific, is that it's been my experience that most suicides close their eyes before they pull the trigger. Graziano's eyes were wide open."

Phillips interrupted, "Inspector, are you saying you think Graziano's death wasn't a suicide? That it was murder?"

"No, I'm not saying that. I'm just saying I find these things odd. Another thing: if I was going to kill myself, I would have shot myself in the head with the hand I had the most confidence in. Not in the chest with my other hand."

"They found his gun and a suicide note in the car. The handwriting was verified as his."

"I know, Commissioner. All I'm saying—"

Chief Guido broke in. "Over the years, I've had dozens of suicide cases with that moron DiMaio. He's one lazy, dumb son of a bitch. If John Wilkes Booth had tossed a suicide note on Lincoln's lap, he would have ruled it a suicide."

When the chuckling subsided, Nader asked, "Do you have any suspects?"

"No. I just said I found it odd."

"I don't mean the suicide. I mean do you have any suspects relative to the thefts?"

"As a matter of fact, I do. A lot of them. Since discovering the thefts back in November, my office has gone over the background of every member of SIU who worked there at the time of the thefts. With the help of our new IBM computer, we've analyzed the personal and professional history of the 108 detectives and supervisors that worked in SIU during that period. As much pertinent data about the individual as possible was thrown into the computer. For example, when each individual entered the Department; where they worked during their careers; who they were partnered with, both in the field teams and SIU; the major cases they worked on; organized crime figures they worked on or arrested; allegations made against the individual; bank account records; how many accounts they had; how they paid for their homes; whether they paid off their mortgages; did their mothers suddenly pay off a mortgage; did they pay cash for their cars; did they purchase a lot of appliances; are they living a lavish lifestyle? Everything. Bottom line, with the help of the computer, we've got a list of thirty suspects. Well, actually, twenty-nine. One of the names the computer spit out was Graziano's, and we know he didn't do it." He took several sheets of paper from the folder and handed them to Guido and waited until everyone had a copy before resuming.

"The last name on the list, the one separated from the rest with the double asterisk beside it, is the name of an individual who used to work in Narcotics but never in SIU. I added his name. I guarantee he had something to do with the thefts. His name is Vincent Catalano. If there was ever a scumbag who had the balls to do something like this, it's him. After he was shot up by some of his mobster friends a few years back, I forced him out of the job. But he always remained close to a few guys in SIU. They're identified on your list with an single asterisk. As you can see, one of the three asterisks is next to Graziano's name. Catalano was very close to him. As I mentioned before, he was also heavily connected with the mob when he was a cop, and I hear he still does a lot of work for them. Somewhere down the line, I figure his name is going to pop up in connection with this thing."

Phillips stirred. "It's seems to me, Inspector, that you're putting all your eggs in one basket. That you're eliminating a lot of guys out-of-hand."

"I certainly didn't mean to give that impression. I can assure you we're taking a hard look at everyone. Not only from SIU and the field teams, but from the RDUs to organized crime figures."

"RDUs, Inspector?"

"They're police officers who are on restricted duty. Cops that can't work the street because they're sick or injured, You know. Car accidents, alcoholics, head cases. They're assigned clerical jobs."

"So why are you looking at these people?"

"Because RDUs were working the window at the Property Clerk's each time drugs were stolen."

Phillips turned to Murphy. "Do you mean to say you had alcoholics and head cases working at the Property Clerk's Office who could dole out millions of dollars worth of drugs to any cop, or for that matter, any organized crime figure who just happened to walk in off the streets and ask for it?"

The Commissioner stammered, "It wasn't like that at all."

"Well, it sure sounds that way to me!"

Nader touched Phillips's arm. "Joe, forget it. What's done is done. I happen to know the Commissioner has carefully reviewed past procedures and several new systems have already been implemented. Now let's move on."

Walter Stone pushed his glasses up onto his forehead. "Inspector, you mentioned that two or more persons pulled off the thefts. Why don't you think it was just one person?"

"First of all, it would have been virtually impossible for one guy to carry that last load out of the office. Don't forget, it was in four suitcases and weighed almost 200 pounds. The guy would have had to have made at least two trips. Can you see him asking the Property Clerk to mind a couple of suitcases full of drugs that don't belong to him while he takes the other suitcases to his car? But for argument's sake, let's say one guy did it. We know he couldn't have done it in one trip. He would have had to haul the drugs at least a couple of blocks to where he parked his car."

"Why couldn't he have parked right outside the Property Clerk's, carried two suitcases downstairs, put them in his car, and then have run back upstairs for the other two?" The police officials in the room roared with laughter. Stone was irritated. "What's so funny?"

Commissioner Murphy grinned. "Walter, you never met Dominick Fiore."

"Who's he?"

Murphy continued, "Excuse us for laughing, Walter. He's the day-tour cop assigned to make sure no one parks in front of 400 Broome. I mean no *one*. Not the Mayor. Not me. No one parks in front of 400 Broome."

Nader got up and walked around the table to where Bonacum was seated. "Inspector, where do you suggest we go from here?"

The Inspector stopped gathering up his papers. "The first thing we should do is sit on the guys on the list. Let them see us. We'll spook 'em. The pressure might make something happen. I'd also like to give a handwriting test to everyone whoever worked in Narcotics since the thefts. The same with the RDUs. Then I'd get in touch with the new US Attorney Curran that took Pierpoint's place and convince him to give us Bucci."

Nader shook his head, "They'll never give him to us. Once we ask—"

All heads turned as the conference room door opened. Nader moved towards the door. "Edna, I told you we weren't to be disturbed."

"I'm sorry. It's an Inspector Farrell on the phone. He says it's very important that he speak to Commissioner Murphy. He's on line four."

Guido got up. "I'll take it, Commissioner." He walked over to a small table in the corner of the room and picked up the phone. "This is Chief Guido. Go ahead, Inspector." All eyes watched as Guido rolled his eyes. A minute later he hung up the phone.

"Anything wrong, John?"

"Commissioner, Inspector Farrell just completed inventorying the Property Clerk's Office. He says the final total of missing narcotics is 570 pounds. It has a street value of over $87 million."

Murphy put his face in his hands. "Oh, my God."

August 1973

THE INSTANT THE DOORKNOB STARTED to turn, the two beefy men standing in the hallway pressed their backs against the wall and held their guns upward. As the door opened slightly, Detective John Speaker jolted forward, bursting into the room with his partner close on his heels.

Speaker directed three well-dressed black males to put their hands on top of their heads and face the wall. Detective Donegan stepped across the threadbare hotel room carpet and roughly searched the men while

Speaker kept them covered. After being informed that the men were un-armed, Speaker went over to a stained table and picked up the stack of money that lay next to a large plastic bag filled with white powder.

"OK, gentlemen. What have we here?"

When none of the men responded, Donegan slapped the smallest of the three men in the back of the head. "Hey, Rufus. He's talking to you."

The man mumbled, "Cocaine."

Speaker feigned being hard of hearing and cupped his hand to his ear. "What's that, Rufus? I can hardly hear you."

"Cocaine."

"That's better, Rufus."

"Yessur."

"Know what else, Rufus?"

"What?"

"You've got a lot of cocaine here. As a matter of fact, I'd say it's more than a pound."

"Yessur."

"You know what that means. Right, Rufus?"

"Yessur."

"Tell me, Rufus. What does it mean?"

"Life."

"I can't hear you, Rufus. What does it mean?"

"Life. It means life in prison."

"I'm proud of you, Rufus. Keeping up with the law and all that."

"Yessur."

"Well Rufus, it's time to stop beating around the bush. What's it gonna be? Do you wanna pay the fine or do the time?"

"I'd like to pay the fine."

Speaker cupped his ear again. "I can't hear you, Rufus."

"I'd like to pay the fine."

"Good choice."

"How much is the fine, sir?"

"Come on, Rufus. You know what it's going to cost you. It's going to cost your money and your dope. Any problem with that?"

"No, sir."

"I can't hear you, Rufus."

"I said, 'No, sir'. Take the money and the dope."

Speaker smirked and stuffed the money into his pants pockets while Donegan put the cocaine into a bright red Macy's shopping bag he had found on a chair. Sarcastically, Speaker thanked the men for their generosity and Donegan unlocked the door to leave.

Both men stopped in their tracks as they faced Inspector Bonacum and a half-dozen agents from Internal Affairs and the Special Prosecutor's Office, with weapons drawn. Speaker felt a nagging tap on his shoulder. He turned and a black face smiled. "It's me. Rufus. You're under arrest. Can you hear me OK?"

A TUXEDOED AARON NADER HURRIED into Internal Affairs Headquarters on Poplar Street in Brooklyn. The uniformed police captain immediately ushered him to a second-floor interrogation room where an obviously pleased Inspector Bonacum waited for him.

"I hope it's good news, Bill. You pulled me out of the Governor's party."

"It's better than good news, Aaron. It's great. The sting we set up at the Allerton Hotel worked perfectly. We got ourselves a live one, and he's spilling his guts."

"Terrific. Who is it?"

"A guy named John Speaker. He's a New York City narcotics detective assigned to the Joint Task Force. He hit the hotel tonight with a retired detective named Donegan, who used to be his partner when they worked Bronx Narcotics. Speaker convinced the asshole to join him for one last score."

"They must have been shocked when they found out the guys were cops."

"They practically died. You should have seen the look on Speaker's face when Johnson tapped him on the shoulder and told him he was under arrest. He broke down and started crying."

Nader laughed, "If the scumbag's crying now, can you imagine what he's going to do when I get him twenty years in jail."

"I don't think that's going to be necessary, Aaron."

"Why do you say that?"

"Because he's going to be a big help to us."

"How?"

"When I first heard Speaker's name, I knew I had heard it before. But I couldn't place it. So I asked him where I knew him from. He tells me I probably remember him from the newspapers. A year and a half ago, he grabbed a couple of guineas running around the Bronx with nearly a million dollars in cash."

Nader smiled. "Sure. I remember the incident. It was a big thing at the time. All over the media. If memory serves, some organized crime figures were involved."

"That's correct. Speaker told me their names were Vincent Capra and Joe DiPalma."

"Jeez, that rings a bell."

"It should. They're big junk people. As a matter of fact, I think the Feds popped them for a Conspiracy a while back. I believe they're in the can already. Anyway, when I was questioning Speaker, I asked him when he grabbed them. He said February of '72, and it hit me right away."

"What hit you right away?"

"The date. February 1972."

"Why?"

"Because the last Property Clerk theft took place in January of '72. It occurred to me Capra might have been on his way to buy the stolen drugs when Speaker bagged him."

"A month after the drugs were stolen?"

"It's possible. Say they got the drugs on consignment. Suppose Capra needed time to scrape up the money."

"That's a stretch, isn't it?"

"Ordinarily, I might agree with you, but Speaker said that a couple of days after the incident, he was approached by two cops who wanted to know what he had on Capra. They explained they were friends of Capra, and that he was good people."

"Who were the cops?"

"Lieutenant Beninati and Jerry Lynch."

Nader sat back. "Jesus, I know those names."

"I'll give you a hint. Both names are from SIU."

Nader slapped his knee. "I've got it. Beninati and Lynch are on the list you gave us as prime suspects in the Property Clerk thefts. They were the other two with the asterisks beside their names. You said they were close to that guy you had thrown off the job."

"Very good, Aaron."

Excited, Nader stood up and walked around the table. "What's the next step?"

"To find out if Capra and DiPalma are still in jail. If they are, let's go see them and offer them a deal. If they're not in jail, let's set up a task force to follow them around. If they're out, they're probably still doing business."

"What about Lynch and Beninati? Should we start watching them?"

"No. Not yet. Let's first find out where Capra and DiPalma are."

THE FOLLOWING EVENING BONACUM BROUGHT Nader up to date. "Capra was locked up in Atlanta Penitentiary, doing five years. He was arrested by Federal agents from the Organized Crime Strike Force for conspiracy to sell narcotics and violating Federal narcotics laws. The Feds had successfully turned two members of his organization and had built a solid case against him and three other mobsters. A few months after Capra's arrest, one of the two witnesses for the government left the US Attorney's office in Brooklyn and was never seen again. This unresolved mystery shattered the government's case, and they were forced to plea bargain.

"In September 1972, Vincent Capra pleaded guilty in Federal Court to conspiracy to import narcotics and to tax evasion. As part of his plea bargain arrangement of five years, all the charges against his co-defendants were dismissed."

NADER DISPATCHED PHILLIPS AND STONE to the Atlanta Penitentiary to get Capra to cooperate but the old trooper refused to budge.

Returning from Georgia, the two unsuccessful emissaries conferred with Nader and Inspector Bonacum at the Internal Affairs headquarters. They decided to get Capra out of prison and put him before the grand jury investigating the theft of the "French Connection" drugs. Should he answer Nader's questions, great; if he balked, they'd lock him up for contempt of court.

*   *   *

A WEEK HAD PASSED WHEN Nader and his investigators met outside the grand jury room with the notorious mob attorney Richard Vallone, who informed them, "I don't want you questioning my client before the grand jury."

Nader smiled. "As my investigators told Capra last week in Atlanta and as I assured both of you this morning, he has nothing to worry about. All he has to do is answer a few questions. He'll be granted immunity."

"I've advised him not to answer any of your questions."

"That's too bad, because when he finishes doing the five he owes the Feds, he's going to do another five for contempt." He then nudged one of his investigators, who promptly put his hand on Vallone's arm and moved him aside. The two Federal marshals, who had accompanied Capra to New York for the grand jury proceedings, grinned.

When Nader entered the grand jury room, a sullen Vincent Capra was sitting in a straight-backed chair facing the twenty-three members of the panel. A matronly court reporter put down a container of coffee, adjusted her dress and nodded that she was ready. The foreman of the jury swore in Capra who wore a green prison uniform and a three-day growth of stubble.

Nader opened the skirmish: "Mr. Capra, as I advised you and your attorney this morning, you will be testifying under a grant of immunity. This means that any information you provide this grand jury cannot be used against you in a court of law at any time, understand?"

"I understand."

"Furthermore, if you refuse to answer the grand jury's questions, you can be held for contempt, and that carries a penalty of up to five years in jail. Do you understand?" Capra glared at Nader without responding. Nader took a step closer to Capra. "Do you understand?"

"I understand."

"Please tell us your full name."

"Vincent Capra."

"Where do you live, Mr. Capra?"

"In Atlanta Penitentiary."

"When you're not in jail, where do you live?"

"Queens."

"Where in Queens, Mr. Capra?"

"Astoria."

"Your exact address, sir?"

"121-34 37th Street."

"Now, that wasn't too difficult, was it?" The members of the grand jury tittered as Nader rolled his eyes. "Mr. Capra, isn't it a fact you participated in a number of illegal narcotics transactions with several New York City police officers over the past few years?"

"On the advice of my lawyer, I will answer no questions."

Nader moved closer to the jury and continued, "Mr. Capra, isn't it true that on or about March 21, 1969, you took into your possession approximately twenty-four pounds of heroin that had been sold to you by a member or members of the New York City Police Department?"

The calm Capra responded, "On the advice of my lawyer, I'll answer no questions but my name and address."

"Mr. Capra, isn't it true that on or about September 29, 1969, you took into your possession approximately eighty-eight pounds of heroin that had been sold to you by a member or members of the New York City Police Department?"

Capra stared straight ahead. "On the advice of my lawyer, I'll answer no questions."

"Sir, isn't it a fact that on or about May 25, 1970, you took into your possession approximately ninety-seven pounds of cocaine and thirty-five pounds of heroin that had been sold to you by a member or members of the New York City Police Department?"

"On the advice of my lawyer, I'll answer no questions."

"Sir, isn't it true that on or about August 12, 1970, you took into your possession thirty-one pounds of heroin that had been sold to you by a member or members of the New York City Police Department?"

"On the advice of my lawyer, I'll answer no questions." Capra had his lines down pat.

"Sir, isn't it a fact that on or about January 20, 1971, you took into your possession twenty-four pounds of heroin that had been sold to you by a member or members of the New York City Police Department?"

"On the advice of my lawyer, I'll answer nothing."

"Sir, isn't it also a fact that you and Joseph DiPalma had close to

$1 million in your possession on the night of February 4, 1972, when you were stopped by the police?"

"On the advice of my lawyer, I'll answer no questions."

"Mr. Capra, on the night of February 4, 1972, when you were stopped by the police with approximately $1 million in your possession, wasn't the money to be used to pay for more than 198 pounds of cocaine which had been stolen from the New York City Property Clerk's Office?"

"On the advice of my lawyer, I'll answer nothing."

Nader walked across the room and held the door ajar. He signaled his two investigators and the two Federal marshals that accompanied Capra from prison, to come inside. "You're dismissed, Mr. Capra. Please wait outside with these gentlemen."

As soon as Capra exited the room, Nader requested the panel to immediately vote a true bill indicting Capra for contempt. Five minutes later, he went into the reception area and instructed his investigators to arrest Capra, take him to court, and arraign him. He then told them to have the judge return Capra to the Federal marshals so they could take him back to prison in Atlanta. Over the heated objections of Richard Vallone, Nader told Capra, "You're under arrest."

MISSION ACCOMPLISHED, THE EBULLIENT special Prosecutor held up his hands to quiet the throng of journalists cramming the press room.

"Ladies and gentlemen, I'd like to make a brief but very significant announcement." When the crowd hushed, Nader stepped back up to the microphone. "Thank you. Thank you very much. A little more than a half hour ago, the special grand jury to hear evidence regarding the theft of narcotics from the New York City Property Clerk, handed down a seven-count indictment for criminal contempt against one Vincent Capra of Astoria, Queens. Mr. Capra, who is currently serving five years in Atlanta Penitentiary for conspiracy to sell narcotics and income tax evasion, was indicted today because of his refusal to respond to questions posed by the special grand jury concerning his purported purchase of stolen Property Clerk drugs from members of the New York City Police Department. As a result of this indictment, I have ordered agents from my office to arrest and arraign Mr. Capra before returning him to Atlanta Penitentiary. The arrest of Mr. Capra is the first of several we anticipate making over the next couple of months regarding the Property Clerk thefts. Are there any questions?"

Hands flew in the air as several reporters screamed questions. Nader stepped back. "Hold it. One at a time, please." He pointed to the representative of Channel 5 in the first row. "Miss Sugawara."

"Are you saying that the Property Clerk thefts are solved?"

"Chako, that's exactly what I'm saying."

PRIOR TO HIS ARRAIGNMENT IN Criminal Court that afternoon, a stoic Vincent Capra leaned heavily against the iron mesh of his holding pen, while his attorney silently read the questions Capra had refused to answer in front of the grand jury. Vallone shook his head and looked up. "Vinnie, I want the truth and I don't want any bullshit. Did you ever buy drugs from cops, and if so, who are they?"

"Why?"

"Because every question they asked you in the grand jury was about you buying drugs from cops."

Capra hesitated. "Richie, I can't tell you that."

Vallone drew closer to the enclosure. "Vinnie, I'm your attorney. If I'm going to help you, I have to know what went down. Right now, Nader knows more than me." Capra turned his back to the attorney and walked to the middle of the cage, "Vinnie, you better pay attention to me. You're in big trouble."

Capra faced Vallone. "I told them I would never say anything to anybody."

"Vinnie, don't be stupid. You're not just saying anything to anybody. I'm your attorney, for Christ's sake. I'm here to help you. I have to know what's going on. I might have to see these guys."

Capra wavered. "Richard, you better not screw me."

"I'm not going to hurt you. I'm here to help you."

Capra moved back to the side of the cage and faced Vallone. "I bought drugs from Vinnie Catalano when he was a cop."

"My brother-in-law?"

Capra leaned forward and glared. "Yeah, your brother-in-law."

Vallone sagged. "Damn it to hell. Who else?"

Capra hesitated a moment. "A coupla friends of his, Lynch and Beninati."

"Lynch and Beninati? Who are they?"

"Narcotics cops I met a few years ago."

"How did you meet them?"

"They shook me down. Later, we talked and became friends. They looked out for me in Narcotics. They let me know if anybody was working on me."

"They sound like real honorable guys."

"They are."

"How much did that cost you?"

"Twenty-five grand."

"How did you get to buy drugs from them?"

"One day they asked me if I wanted to move a package. I said OK. Then I just kept buying."

"I'm sorry you did, because they obviously stole it from the Property Clerk. Now you've become the main suspect."

"What do you mean I'm the main suspect? I don't even know where the Property Clerk is!"

"It doesn't matter. The point is, you're the main suspect. In fact, it wouldn't surprise me if Lynch and Beninati were the ones that gave you up."

Capra banged the iron mesh in front of Vallone's face with the heel of his hand. "Don't ever say that again. They'd never give me up!"

"Hey, maybe they got caught doing something and turned on you."

"No way. These guys are friends. They'd never give me up."

"Well, somebody had to have said something."

Capra, his anger boiling, barked, "Not them."

Vallone attempted to soothe Capra. "Take it easy, Vinnie. I'm not arguing with you. I'm glad to hear you stick up for them, because I've got to talk to them."

"Why?"

"Because I don't want them getting panicky and doing something stupid when they hear you've been arrested. My problem is I don't really know these guys. If I approach them, they might think I'm setting them up."

"That's no problem. Have your brother-in-law set up the meet. He's close to them."

Early September 1973

CATALANO AND VALLONE LED a parade of slow-moving un-marked police cars to Garguilo's restaurant on West 15th Street off Mermaid Avenue in Coney Island. Catalano handed the red-jacketed parking valet a five-dollar bill, turned and saluted the cars of the trailing detectives with a raised middle finger. Inside the restaurant, the two men proceeded to the crowded bar, where Catalano introduced the law-yer to Lynch and Beninati. The maitre d', spotting Catalano, hugged and kissed him on both cheeks and led the party to a reserved table in the rear of the ornate dining room.

En route, the group stopped at a table where Catalano and Vallone embraced Philip Rastelli, acting boss of the Bonanno crime family, and Natale Evola, a highly respected Mafia don. Before being seated, Val-lone blew a kiss to an attractive young couple seated in a corner booth. Under his breath, he muttered to Beninati, "Pat, That nitwit owns half the pizzerias in Brooklyn."

"Counsellor, do me a favor. Call me Loo—everybody does—it's from my days on the P.D. It's short for Lieutenant."

After Catalano ordered two bottles of Pinot Grigio, he turned to Ben-inati. "Were you followed tonight?"

"Of course, I was followed. Like I told you last week, Jerry and I are followed everywhere we go. What about you?"

"I had three cars on me tonight. They were so close they were looking up my asshole." Catalano glanced at Vallone. "The guy I feel sorry for is Richard here. Now that he's been seen with us, they'll probably follow him all over."

The attorney shrugged. "Vinnie, ever since I defended Johnny Or-mento and Vito Genovese back in '62, I've been shadowed. I'm used to it. The only difference between you and me is that I don't give them the finger every time I get out of my car."

Beninati and Lynch laughed as the waiter approached the table with the wine. Enjoying playing the role of connoisseur, Catalano chewed a small piece of bread and sampled the wine. Satisfied, he gestured for the waiter to pour.

After waiting patiently for the waiter to leave, Catalano looked at Beninati and Lynch. "As I told you before, not only is Richard my brother-in-law, but he's Capra's lawyer. He asked me to set up a meet with you."

Lynch flicked his cigar ash to the floor. "Why'd you want to meet us, Mr. Vallone?"

Vallone put down his glass. "Call me Richard." He then leaned forward and signaled the three men to move closer. "Gentlemen, I appreciate you coming on such short notice. I'm also aware that you might have concerns about this being some sort of a setup. So I'm saying to you up front, you don't have to say a word. All I want you to do is listen. Fair enough?"

Lynch looked at Beninati and then back to Vallone. "Keep going."

"As you know, Nader arrested my client recently for refusing to answer questions in the grand jury. What you may or may not know is Nader kept asking him if he bought the Property Clerk drugs from cops. When I spoke to Capra he said he knew nothing about the Property Clerk thefts. I believed him. Then I asked him if he ever bought drugs from cops. Naturally, he claimed he hadn't. To be honest, I didn't believe him, so I spoke to him at length. I convinced him how important it was that I know the truth, because I probably would have to reach out for those guys he did business with and assure them he would never give them up. That's when he told me he did business with you three. Hence this meeting. I wanted to let you know what's going on. I didn't want you getting spooked when you heard Capra was indicted in connection with the Property Clerk thefts."

Beninati reached across the table and shook hands with Vallone. "Thank you, counselor."

Vallone held Beninati's hand tightly. "Just one more thing. If you or Jerry are ever questioned, indicted or arrested, I want your lawyer to contact me immediately so we can coordinate our efforts. Agreed?"

"Agreed." Beninati sipped his wine. "You make it sound like we're at war."

"We are."

January 1974

Having made little progress solving the thefts despite Capra's indictment, an irate Aaron Nader glowered at his chief investigator. "Walter, that's got to be the stupidest idea I've ever heard." Irritated, Nader looked down the length of the table. "Yes, Inspector?"

Newly transferred from the Chief of Detectives' Office to Internal Affairs as Bonacum's chief aide, Deputy Inspector Warren Creighton spoke up. "Why don't we bring Lynch and Beninati in for questioning? Maybe they'll break."

Nader closed his eyes, grimaced and sighed quietly. "Why me, God?" He looked at Creighton. "I'm sorry, Warren, I don't mean to be rude, but that's the first thing we tried to do after we indicted Capra. Their attorneys told us to get lost. Anyway, when you really think about it, what do you think the chances are that the men who stole $87 million worth of narcotics would just walk in here and confess?"

Chief Guido agreed. "About one in a million."

Nader lit a cigarette and scanned the faces of the other eight men seated quietly at the table. "Gentlemen, we better come up with something quick. There are rumors the US Attorney is finally going to arrest the SIU guys that Bucci set up. Once that happens, he's going to get those scumbags to turn on each other. When the rest of the guys see what's going on, they're going to start panicking and running down to the US Attorney's Office to make deals. It's going to be a stampede. Guys will be climbing on each other's backs and confessing in order to save their asses. Sooner or later, one of them is going to give up the Property Clerk thefts."

Bonacum answered with a question. "Why don't we offer our own deals?"

"What do you mean?"

"I figure the US Attorney is going to work his way up the SIU ladder by having detectives give up bosses. I say we beat him to the punch by reversing the process. Let's work our way down the ladder. If we can turn Hughes and Ryan, lure them with a deal of no jail time and their pensions, they may help us."

Murphy looked up from his notes. "Hughes and Ryan? What makes you think you can approach Hughes and Ryan? They've never been accused of anything."

"Come on, Commissioner, both men had to be involved. The entire unit was corrupt."

"Inspector, you haven't one iota of evidence to back up that statement. And that's a terrible thing to say about someone who just lost his wife."

"We all sympathize with Ryan. Most of us have known him for years. As a matter of fact, Warren here was an honorary pallbearer at Edith's funeral. But that doesn't mean Ryan's not corrupt. He looks like dear old Santa Claus, but he was a boss in SIU a long time and he had to know what was going on. The same is true of Hughes. I say we offer them a deal to turn before the Feds lock them up. A deal that will benefit them as well as us."

"What kind of a deal?'

"As I said, no jail and their pensions if they come clean."

"That's assuming they've done something, Inspector."

"That's assuming they've done something, Commissioner. But we'll never know unless you give me permission to talk to them."

AFTER THE MEETING, BONACUM CALLED Ryan's and Hughes's respective precincts. He was advised by both desk sergeants that each of the commanders had left for the day, but both were scheduled to be on duty the following morning. Before Bonacum and Creighton left the World Trade Center, they agreed to meet at 07.45 hours the following morning in front of the 46th Precinct in the Bronx.

As they parted, a worried Warren Creighton walked quickly to the garage where his car was parked. Moments later he was speeding northward on the West Side Highway to the Sawmill River Parkway. Exiting at Hastings-On-The-Hudson, Creighton drove west through the quiet little town until he pulled into a graveled driveway. He breathed a sigh of relief when he saw lights on the ground floor of the house. He got out of the car, looked around nervously and rang the bell impatiently. A tired-looking John Ryan opened the door.

Over coffee, Creighton explained what had happened earlier that afternoon in the Special Prosecutor's Office. Ryan's expression hardened as he listened. "So far they ain't got nothing, but Bonacum seems to feel the US Attorney is eventually going to come down on you. He wants to outfox him by striking a deal with you. He's going to offer you your pension and no jail time if you turn. So tomorrow morning, act surprised when we meet you at the Four-six."

"I'll act surprised, but I'm not going to turn," Ryan said firmly.

"John, that's up to you. All I wanted to do was warn you and make sure you don't mention anything about me or how you used to funnel money downtown." Creighton stood up. "I've got to run. I have another trip to make."

MINUTES AFTER CROSSING THE WHITESTONE Bridge, Creighton got on the Long Island Expressway and drove east towards Captain Hughes's home in Northport, Long Island. Upon his arrival, Allison Hughes warmly greeted him and called her husband, who was watching television in the family room.

Hughes's color drained from his face when he saw Creighton standing in his hallway. "I got to talk to you, Dan." Hughes nodded and led him into the kitchen. Once the door shut behind them, Creighton spoke in a hushed tone. "Tomorrow morning, Bonacum is coming to your office. He will offer you a deal of no jail time and your pension if you cooperate. He has nothing on you, but he thinks you may be able to help him with the Property Clerk thefts. He's fishing but he hopes you can give him a lot of guys." He walked over to the sink and poured himself a glass of water.

"Dan, I know it's not an easy decision. All I'm asking you to do is not to say anything about me or downtown."

Hughes trembled. "I can't believe this is happening to me. Here I was, the youngest captain ever on the job, and now my career is over. I guess you were wrong a few years back."

"Wrong about what?"

"You told me my star was going to shine like the one long ago in Bethlehem."

AT 7:52 A.M., A FRAZZLED Deputy Inspector Creighton hurried down the wet pavement and got in the passenger side of a department vehicle parked across the street from the 46th Precinct. Bonacum half turned and glared at Creighton. "Warren, don't ever hang me up like this again. When I say 0745 hours, I mean 0745 hours. Not 0746. Not 0747. Not 0748. Understand?"

"Inspector, I got tied—"

"Warren, I don't care what happened. That's your problem. All I know is you're late, and I won't tolerate it."

"Inspector—"

"Warren, lateness indicates a lack of discipline and disrespect. And as far as I'm concerned, you've stolen seven minutes out of my life."

"I'm sorry, Inspector. It won't happen again."

"I hope it won't." For several minutes, the two men silently watched the uniformed day shift patrolmen filter down the precinct stairs to their assigned vehicles. Many of the patrol cars were randomly double-parked, or left abandoned on the sidewalk by the men of the midnight shift.

"Warren, see all those patrol cars illegally double-parked and on the sidewalk?"

"Yeah."

"That's a telltale sign. Cops that would leave their cars like that are very susceptible to corruption."

"How do you figure, sir?"

"Because they think they're above the law. If a civilian committed the same violation, he'd have a ticket shoved right up his ass. Yet cops park like that without a second thought. They think they can do whatever they want."

"I never thought of it like that, Inspector, I figured they parked that way because it's tough to find parking spaces around a station house."

"Believe me, if they wanted to, they could find a legal parking spot." As Bonacum opened the door to leave, he paused. "Warren, mind if I ask you a question?"

"No, sir."

"By any chance, did you visit Ryan last night?"

Caught off-guard, Creighton stammered, "No. Of course not."

"You didn't call him and warn him we were coming to see him this morning?"

"No, sir. Why do you ask?"

"I know you're close to him. I figured you might have warned him. After all, didn't you help bury his wife a few weeks back?"

"Inspector, I helped him bury Eadie. But I assure you, I never warned him we were coming here this morning."

"You're a better man than I am, Warren. If he was my friend, I would have warned him." He got out of the car and walked across the street. A disconcerted Creighton pulled up the collar of his raincoat and followed a half step behind.

At the top of the station house stairs, Bonacum stopped. "If you feel uncomfortable about seeing Ryan, you can wait in the car."

"I'll go in with you. But first I think I should park your car legally."

Inside the station house, Bonacum walked to the switchboard. The desk officer saluted and asked "Should I get the captain, sir?"

"No. I'm waiting for someone. He'll be right here, And, anyway, I'm here to see Lieutenant Ryan."

Several minutes passed before a soaked and out-of-breath Creighton entered the station house. As they neared Ryan's office, Bonacum stopped a few feet from the closed door. "Warren, you know Ryan. What do you think he's going to say when I ask him to turn?"

Creighton smiled. "Inspector, I think he's going to tell you to go fuck yourself."

AFTER THEIR TURBULENT MEETING WITH Ryan ended, Creighton chauffeured the seething Bonacum across the 155th Street Bridge into Harlem. A block away from the Twenty-eighth Precinct, he pulled the car over to the curb and turned off its engine. Bonacum turned in his seat, wiped the steamy side window with his hand and peered out. "Warren, where are we?"

"At 122nd Street and Seventh Avenue."

"This may come as a surprise to you, but I'm not a duck. Pull the car in front of the station house."

"I don't think we'll get a legal spot up there, sir."

"Just pull the car up."

Restarting the engine, Creighton slowly navigated the car passed double-parked patrol cars to the front of the station house. As Creighton was about to turn off the ignition, Bonacum touched his arm. "Stay here and watch the car." He slammed the car door shut, stepped over a puddle and went into the Twenty-eighth Precinct.

IN HUGHES'S OFFICE, BONACUM LEANED back in his seat. "Dan, think it over and call me tomorrow. Let me know what you decide."

"Inspector, if I agree to think it over, it would be tantamount to an admission of guilt."

Bonacum grinned. "I know."

Hughes got up and paced the wooden floor. "This isn't an easy decision, Inspector. I have a wife and two kids to think about."

"And Brogan."

Annoyed, Hughes snapped back, "That's right, Inspector. And Brogan. And before I'd make any sort of deal with you, she'll have to be part of the equation."

"What do you mean, 'be part of the equation'?"

"I mean she'll have to be granted immunity, and given her pension too."

"Why does Brogan have to be given immunity? Are you saying she's dirty?"

"No, I'm saying if I start naming people, they might turn around and say they did business with her just to get even with me."

Sensing a breakthrough, Bonacum decided to back off. "Look, Dan, I can't give you a decision on her immunity and pension. I'd have to check with Nader and the Commissioner. But I've got to tell you, before they'd agree to anything like that, they'd have to know you can give them a lot."

"Tell them I can."

"Are you saying you can give me the guys that did the Property Clerk?"

"Come on, Inspector. You know I had nothing to do with that. I can't help you there, but I can give you enough."

"Can you give us Lynch or Beninati?"

"No. As a matter of fact, the first thing I did when I got to SIU was throw Beninati out. As for Lynch, I never liked the guy or did anything with him personally."

"What do you mean, 'personally'?"

"I once got five thousand dollars from him in a roundabout way. It came through Lieutenant Ryan."

Hughes's visitor smiled, stood up, and draped his raincoat over his arm. "Then I assume you can give me Lieutenant Ryan?"

"On a silver platter."

THE FOLLOWING AFTERNOON, A DISCONSOLATE Commissioner Murphy sat next to Inspector Bonacum in the Special Prosecutor's Office and listened to Nader respond to Hughes's question. "Captain, I appreciate your cooperating with us, but that doesn't mean I can automatically grant Conner immunity. I just can't do it. She's going to have to earn it like everyone else."

"I don't want her testifying."

"Look, Captain, she worked with Belfry and Redmond for years. She had to have known what was going on."

"Believe me, she wasn't involved. She never took a cent."

"Captain, whether or not she took money is only part of the issue. She had to have known about illegal wiretaps, perjured search warrants, rip-offs."

"I don't think she did."

"Please, captain. Brogan's a very bright detective. Don't insult our intelligence by telling us she didn't know what was going on."

"All I know is that she never took money."

Nader disagreed. "I'm not so sure about that, captain. I heard she sold a wiretap to Lieutenant Ryan for $25,000 a few years back."

"Wait a minute. I know the incident you're referring to, and she had nothing to do with it."

"How do you know?"

"Because I investigated it."

Nader looked dubious. "Captain, I've gone through every piece of paperwork from SIU I could lay my hands on, and I never saw anything indicating you conducted an investigation on that case."

"It was an unofficial investigation. I didn't write anything down."

Nader sighed. "Go ahead, Captain."

"I had just returned from the FBI Academy in Virginia. There were rumors floating around the office that Brogan took fifteen thousand dollars with Belfry and Redmond to kill a wiretap for Lieutenant Ryan. I was shocked when I heard the rumors, and I called her into my office. When I asked her about it, she became very upset. She swore she never took a dime. Later, I went to Belfry and Redmond and asked them about it. Both confirmed that they kept her share."

Nader watched the tape on the recorder slowly turn. "Go ahead, Captain."

"You're sure I have immunity?"

"Absolutely. As I told you before, you have immunity as long as you tell the truth, and you're willing to testify before the grand jury."

Hughes looked over at the pained expression on Commissioner Murphy's face. "I'm sorry, Commissioner, but when I was in SIU, I participated in a lot of scores. When I first took over, I never intended to take any money, but things just happened. I know that's no excuse, and I have no one to blame but myself." Murphy's eyes grew moist as Hughes turned to Special Prosecutor Nader. "Before I go on, may I go back to the Conner incident a minute?"

"Certainly."

"If I'm going to start confessing, I might as well start there. I made five thousand dollars on that case." Hughes turned to Bonacum. "That's the five thousand dollars from Lynch that I was telling you about last night."

Bonacum looked perplexed. "I thought you just told us you were at the FBI Academy when everything went down."

"I was, but Ryan gave me five thousand dollars from the case when I got back."

Nader took off his glasses. "Why'd he do that?"

"We had made an agreement before I left. Ryan was to hold out my share from each score made by a team. When I returned, he met me at the airport and gave me over $100,000."

"A hundred thousand! That's a lot of money."

"I was at the FBI Academy for six months."

Nader shook his head and looked at Murphy. "Go on."

"Ryan read me a list of teams that gave him money and how much each one paid while I was away. I remember him telling me five thousand dollars of it came from Belfry's team. Naturally, my ears perked up because Brogan worked with Belfry. Ryan told me Jerry Lynch had given him twenty-five thousand dollars to give to Belfry's team in order to forget about putting a wire on some guy in Queens."

"Did you ever mention anything to Lynch about the five thousand dollars you received?"

"No."

"You never thanked him?"

"No. I had nothing to thank him for."

"A guy gives you five thousand dollars and you don't thank him?"

"Mr. Nader, I thanked the guys who gave me the five thousand dollars. 1 thanked Belfry and Redmond."

"Did Jerry Lynch ever give you money on any occasion?"

"No."

"Are you sure?"

"Positive."

"Did you ever go to any location and see Lynch illegally wiretap anyone?"

"No."

"Did you ever see Lynch take any money?"

"No."

"Did you ever see anyone give Lynch money?"

"No."

"Did you ever see Lynch do anything illegal?"

"No. As I told Inspector Bonacum yesterday, I didn't like the man personally, so I had as little contact as possible with him. I let Lieutenant Ryan deal with him."

Bonacum looked up from his notes. "Incidentally, Captain, did anyone ever mention the name of the person Lynch didn't want wiretapped?"

"Yes, Inspector. Ryan told me. His name was Vincent Capra."

*   *   *

FOR THE NEXT TWO HOURS, Hughes painstakingly described dozens of corrupt acts he participated in while Commander of the Special Investigation Unit. Crimes ranged from the ordering of illegal wiretaps to the stealing of hundreds of thousands of dollars; from suborning perjury of search warrants to allowing confiscated drugs to be sold. When Hughes indicated he wanted to go to the bathroom, Nader excused him and Bonacum turned off the recorder.

The moment Hughes left the room, Murphy spoke up. "Aaron, I think what we're doing is disgraceful."

Stung by the comment, Nader stared at the Commissioner. "What are you talking about?"

"This whole thing with Hughes. Letting him off scot-free by permitting him to implicate subordinates."

Nader parried the attack. "Have you forgotten what this man's 'subordinates' did to you? Have you forgotten it was this man's 'subordinates' who walked out of the Property Clerk's Office with 87 million worth of drugs?"

"But the idea of—"

Nader interrupted. "Do you think I like the idea of letting Hughes walk free? You've got to understand, he's our last hope! If Hughes doesn't cooperate, you're left with the legacy that while you were supposed to be watching the Property Clerk's Office, the men of SIU cleaned it out."

Murphy's eyes filled. "That's not true. Most of the thefts took place before my time."

"It doesn't matter when the thefts took place, Commissioner. The thefts were discovered on your watch, and you're the one that's stuck with them."

Murphy stood up and started toward the door. "Stolen drugs or not, I still think it's an outrage to give immunity to a traitor like Hughes."

Nader pushed his chair back from the table. "I don't care what you think! I'm going to give immunity to whomever I think can help me get to the bottom of the Property Clerk thefts! I don't care who I have to knock over, who I have to hurt and who I have to give immunity to. I want Lynch and Beninati. And if it means giving immunity to a thousand Hugheses to get them, then so be it!"

"Well, I'm not going to be part of it." Murphy opened the door and came face to face with Hughes.

He stared at him for a moment and said, "I'm ashamed of you, Dan. You've betrayed every member of this Department. You're a disgrace."

Hughes lowered his eyes as Murphy pushed by him and hurried down the hallway.

Visibly hurt by the Commissioner's remarks, Hughes stood in front of Bonacum. "You can hardly blame the man. He's heartbroken. He sees his whole Department going up in smoke."

Slowly regaining his composure, Hughes sat down and reviewed his previous disclosures. At the conclusion of the interrogation, Nader advised him that he wanted to meet with him again in the morning. As Hughes got up to leave, he grasped his arm. "I want you to reach out for Brogan and bring her with you tomorrow. Convince her to cooperate with us. Tell her how important it is she give us Ryan and Lynch."

As THE SMOKE FROM HUGHES'S cigarette spiraled upward, Brogan Conner turned in bed. She kissed his shoulder and whispered, "Dan, I'm afraid. I don't want to go to jail."

"How many times do I have to tell you? You won't go to jail if you listen to me. They want Lynch and Beninati for the Property Clerk and they know you can help them."

"But I can't help them with the Property Clerk. I don't know anything about it."

"Nader knows that, but he also knows you, Belfry, Redmond and Ryan killed a wiretap on Vincent Capra a couple of years back for Lynch."

"So what does that have to do with it?"

"They want all of you to testify against Lynch. They're having trouble getting Lynch for the Property Clerk, so Nader wants to start putting together another case against him. That's where you come in. He wants you to tell him what happened."

"But I don't want to give up Belfry and Redmond. I love those guys."

"Brogan, you have no choice." Hughes leaned over and stubbed out his cigarette in the ashtray on the endtable. "Belfry and Redmond are going to be given the same opportunity as you to turn, and you better believe they're going to give you up."

"But I never did that much with them. And they know I never took any money."

"Yeah, but you were in on all their other shit, and they're going to tell Nader this. And you better believe he going to stick it up your ass if you don't cooperate with him because he knows you can help him get Lynch."

"But I can't help him with Lynch. I wasn't there when everything went down. I came in afterwards. I met Lynch when he was coming down the stairs."

"Just say you were in the office when everything went down. Who's going to remember?"

"I'm not going to say that. Belfry and Redmond know I wasn't there. If I'm going to tell what happened, I'm going to tell the truth. I'm going to say how I walked in while Belfry, Redmond and Ryan were dividing the money."

"It would be better if you told them you saw Lynch hand them the money, or you heard them discuss the money was from Lynch."

"No. I'm not going to say that. It's just another lie." Conner began to cry.

Hughes pulled her into his arms and gently rubbed her back. "Stop worrying, honey. Everything will be all right."

THE FOLLOWING MORNING, BROGAN CONNER accompanied Captain Hughes up the granite steps of the New York City Public Library. Hand in hand, the pair took the elevator to the third floor and headed for the Reference Room.

Standing on tiptoes, Hughes spotted Nader and Bonacum sitting at a comer table in the rear of the room. Both men stood as the couple approached.

Once everyone was seated, Nader turned his attention to Conner.

Aware of the library's rules, he spoke in a low voice. "Detective, I was delighted when Captain Hughes called me last night and said you were willing to meet with me."

"Yes, sir."

"And I certainly can understand your reluctance to meet with me at my office. I assume Captain Hughes told you he's cooperating with us."

"Yes, sir."

"Did he also tell you that I probably will want you to appear before the grand jury and tell them everything you know? That you'd be granted immunity?"

"Yes, sir, he did. But I really don't have that much to tell."

"Let me be the judge of that. OK?"

"OK."

"Brogan, before we begin, why don't you tell me what you've been doing since you left SIU? As a matter of fact, why were you transferred out of SIU?"

"I was promoted to sergeant. I wanted to stay in SIU but it's Department policy that you get transferred after a promotion. They don't want you supervising people you just worked with. I was assigned to Manhattan Robbery. A few months later, Commissioner Murphy called me in and asked if I would start a new unit for him."

"Was that the Sex Crimes Unit?"

"Yes, sir."

"Tell me a little bit about it."

Conner enthusiastically described how she had created an office of mostly female police officers so the Department could better communicate with raped and abused women about their emotional and physical trauma. "There's really not that much difference between the needs of a teenager and an older woman when it comes to rape. Both have been brutalized, and they need to talk to a person who understands if they're going to start to recover."

Bonacum turned his head and rolled his eyes heavenward as Nader agreed. "The Sex Crimes Unit was long overdue, and, believe me, I've heard nothing but good reports about you and the unit."

"Thank you."

Nader reached for his briefcase. "Brogan, I think we best talk about your activities in SIU now."

"All right."

"I understand when you worked with Detectives Belfry and Redmond, you participated in the installation of several illegal wiretaps and perjured many search warrants. Is that correct?"

Nervous, Conner took a tissue from her purse and gently dabbed her upper lip. "That's correct. However, I never stole or took money. Never."

"But you knew Belfry and Redmond were stealing money?"

"Yes."

"You saw them?"

"Yes."

"You never tried to stop them?"

"No."

"You never said anything to them?"

"No."

"Why?"

"Because that's the way it was. If you wanted a share, you took it. If you didn't want a share, you kept your mouth shut."

Nader referred to his notes. "Tell me about the Capra incident. What happened there?"

Conner looked at Hughes, who nodded. "Ryan told me not to install a wire on him because Lynch was already working on the subject."

"Did you install the wire?"

"No. Lieutenant Ryan said not to."

"What happened next?"

"The following day, Ryan left word for us to meet in his office that night. The guys went upstairs while I parked the car."

"Guys?"

"Yes. Belfry and Redmond."

"OK. I just wanted to make sure who we're talking about. What happened next?"

"As I was going upstairs, I met Lynch."

"Jerry Lynch?"

"Yes."

"What happened?"

"Nothing. We just said hello."

"He didn't say anything about leaving some money upstairs for you?"

"No, he didn't."

"And then?"

"I continued upstairs and went to Lieutenant Ryan's office. He was handing Redmond an envelope with money in it."

"Who was handing Redmond money?"

"Lieutenant Ryan." Conner put her hand over Hughes's and squeezed it gently. "Ryan said it was twenty-five thousand dollars. He said it was a thank-you card from Jerry Lynch for killing the wire on Capra. Redmond then counted out ten thousand dollars and gave it to Ryan. I excused myself from the room because I didn't want any part of it."

Nader smiled, glanced at Bonacum, then back to Conner. "Ryan said it was a thank-you card from Jerry Lynch?"

"That's what he said."

"That's terrific, Brogan. By the way, did you ever ask Redmond why he gave $10,000 to Ryan?"

"No, I knew why. Ryan got the $10,000 because he was the intermediary."

"Do you know what Ryan did with the $10,000?"

"No."

"Do you know if he split it with anyone?"

"No."

"Do you know what Redmond did with the fifteen thousnad dollars he got from Ryan?"

"I assume he divided it with Belfry."

"Do you know. . . .

February 1974

TWO DAYS AFTER HUGHES, CONNER, Belfry and Redmond testified before the special grand jury investigating the Property Clerk thefts, Lieutenant Ryan nervously paced the reception area outside the room. Mike Washow, Ryan's attorney, watched him. "John, you're acting like an expectant father. Relax." Apologizing, Ryan sat down on a bench next to Washow. A moment later, both men looked up as they heard the grand jury room door open. Nader stepped out into the reception area and curtly acknowledged the lawyer.

When Washow stood up and attempted to shake Nader's hand, the Special Prosecutor ignored the gesture. "Counselor, before Lieutenant Ryan testifies before the grand jury this morning, I want you to know several former members of SIU have already testified against him. Some say they gave your client money, and some say they received money from your client."

Washow remained expressionless. "Why are you telling us this? Why don't you just bring him inside and indict him?"

"Because I have no interest in putting your client in jail. I need his help. I want him to cooperate."

"Cooperate? My client's always been willing to cooperate."

"I was advised differently. I was told Ryan refused to cooperate."

"Mr. Nader, Inspector Bonacum didn't want my client to cooperate. He wanted him to lie about police officers. My client would never do that."

"Obviously, Counselor, there's been a misunderstanding. I can assure you Inspector Bonacum did not want Lieutenant Ryan to lie about cops. He wanted him to tell the truth."

"Perhaps there was a breakdown in communications. If that's the case, why don't you ask Ryan yourself to cooperate?"

"Is that OK with you?"

"Of course."

Nader turned to Ryan. "Lieutenant, I'm sorry about the misunderstanding between you and Inspector Bonacum. Let me assure you he didn't want you to lie about anybody or anything. He approached you because we want your cooperation in our investigation of the Property Clerk thefts. If you agree to cooperate, you won't be indicted, and you'll be granted immunity."

Ryan grinned at Washow, turned to Nader and said, "Go fuck yourself"

WITHIN SEVENTY-TWO HOURS NADER STOOD before a battery of microphones in his World Trade Center press room. "As I speak, investigators from my office are arresting a New York City Police lieutenant on a five-count indictment for perjury. The special grand jury looking into the Property Clerk thefts has charged Lieutenant John Ryan with giving conspicuously unbelievable and evasive answers when asked if he ever received or passed along moneys to subvert a planned court-ordered wiretap on the phone of reputed mobster Vincent Capra. Incidentally, this is the same Vincent Capra who is currently under indictment by the special grand jury for contempt. The indictment of Ryan brings to two the number indicted by the special grand jury, and it brings us one step closer to formally charging the principal brain behind the thefts."

C OME ON IN, GENTLEMEN." LYNCH AND Beninati shook hands with Richard Vallone, who was standing in his office doorway. "I've got a feeling I know why you're here." The attorney, who had a copy of the *Times* on his desk, read the caption aloud: " 'NADER CLOSING IN ON PROPERTY CLERK THEFTS—INDICTS POLICE LIEUTENANT FOR PERJURY.' What a headline. It makes it seem like Ryan stole the drugs."

Lynch scowled, "Yeah, until you read the article."

Vallone pointed at Lynch and Beninati. "There's no doubt they think you guys did it. They practically name you. Listen to this. 'Both men retired from the Police Department shortly after the death of Detective Joseph Graziano'."

Beninati laughed. "I don't know why they just didn't put our names and addresses in the paper instead of fooling around. It's no secret who they're talking about."

Lynch leaned forward. "We both got calls from the *Daily News* this morning. A guy named Kirkland wanted to know our reaction to the article."

"What did you tell him?"

"Nothing. I told him I hadn't read it."

"How about you, Loo? What did you tell him?"

"Lisa answered the phone. She told him I wasn't in."

"Good. That was smart of her."

Lynch pushed back his chair and took out a cigar. "Where do we go from here, Richard?"

"It depends on Ryan. Can he hurt either one of you?"

Beninati spoke up immediately. "He can't hurt me. I never worked with him."

"Jerry?"

"He can hurt me, but he never would."

"So you've done things with him?"

"Yeah. Lots of times. But believe me, Richard, Ryan would never hurt me. He's stand-up."

"Are you sure?"

"Positive."

"OK. What about Hughes and Conner? Can they hurt you?"

"No. I never did anything with Hughes. I never trusted him. I did everything through Ryan. Conner, I never worked with."

"Good. What about you, Loo? Did you ever do anything with Hughes or the girl?"

"No, I never worked with either of them, As a matter of fact, the first thing Hughes did when he got to SIU was throw me out. He said he wanted to clean SIU up. What a joke. Look at the rat pack now."

Vallone stood up and walked around his desk. "You asked me before where do we go from here. I think they're bluffing. They're trying to stampede us. I say we take the bull by the horns and force the issue. I want you guys to call back that guy from the *Daily News* and tell him you want to meet him. Tell him you had nothing to do with the thefts. Put Nader on the defensive. Make him put up or shut up."

"Do you want to go with us?"

"No. It would look bad, me being Capra's attorney and all that. Anyway, I have to fly down to Atlanta and prop him up. He said Nader's men came down again this week and offered him another deal."

March 1974

PARKER PRESSED THE INTERCOM BUTTON. "Bring them in."

He circled the *Washington Post* headline "NIXON WILL NOT RE-SIGN" with a red marker when his secretary escorted two Federal marshals, the handcuffed mobster Joseph Ragusa and his attorney, Bernard

Monterosa, into the office. Parker thanked the marshals and requested they wait outside.

Bernard Monterosa sat down next to his client. "As I told you on the phone yesterday, my client is willing to testify against Capra, providing you get him out of jail and place him and his family in the witness-protection program."

"What makes you think I'm interested in making a deal to get Capra? We've got him where we want him."

"We read the papers. Everybody knows Capra had something to do with the Property Clerk thefts."

"Are you telling me your client can give us Capra for the Property Clerk thefts?"

"Not exactly. Everyone knows cops did that. But my client can tell you about the time Capra had four suitcases filled with junk."

"When was that?"

Monterosa grinned. "Early January 1972. The time when the last Property Clerk thefts occurred."

Parker looked at Ragusa. "You actually saw the narcotics?"

"Yeah. I saw him and his kid with it."

Monterosa held up his hand. "Don't say anything more, Joey." Monterosa turned to Parker. "Do we have a deal?"

"If we convict Capra and—"

Monterosa held up his hands. "Hold on. As I told you yesterday, my client will cooperate fully and testify to the best of his ability. The rest is up to you. Do we have a deal?"

Parker tapped his teeth with his thumbnail and stared at Ragusa for several seconds. Then he looked back at Monterosa. "We have a deal."

"Good. Joey, tell Mr. Parker what happened that night."

Ragusa rubbed his left wrist. "Can you take these handcuffs off me?"

Parker ignored the request. "Just tell me what happened."

"Luciano called me one night and told me his father didn't want me to leave the house. He said he and the old man would be over later. About four or five in the morning they came over with four suitcases. They told me they wanted me to sit on the suitcases for a couple of days."

"Go on."

"We went in the bedroom and the old man opened up the suitcases and counted the bags. I never saw so much cocaine."

Parker stood up and removed his jacket. "Before we go any further, let's start at the beginning. When did you first meet Vincent Capra?"

Late March 1974

CAPRA, ACCOMPANIED BY A GUARD, slowly limped past dozens of prisoners watching them through cell bars. Taunts followed them down the cell block: "Make sure he doesn't kiss ya, Vinnie." At the guard station, they stared up at the camera and waited until they heard the mechanism loudly engage the gears of the rollback iron gate which admitted them into a long, windowless corridor. At the end of the passageway, they again looked up at a camera and waited until the gate opened into a large, well-lighted visitors area.

Capra's eyes narrowed as he tried to identify the man seated at a table in the center of the room. Arriving at the table, the guard advised the visitor to wave up at the window if he needed anything. The visitor looked up at two uniformed armed guards who waved down at him from behind the bulletproof-glass-enclosed room.

Parker motioned for Capra to be seated and waited for the guard to leave. He took out a box of Marlboros and pushed it toward Capra. Capra pulled out a cigarette and leaned forward for a light. Exhaling, he said, "I don't know why you people keep coming down here. I told you I don't know anything."

Parker leaned forward. "What are you talking about? I never spoke to you."

"You haven't personally, but guys from your office have."

"What office do you think I'm from?"

"Nader's."

Parker shook his head. "I'm not from New York. Let me introduce myself. I'm Harrison Parker. I am the Director of the Federal Bureau of Narcotics and Dangerous Drugs in Washington."

"Too bad. I was hoping you were from the parole board and you were bringing me good news."

"No such luck. As a matter of fact, nothing could be further from the truth. I'm here to tell you you're getting locked up again unless you cooperate."

"Locked up again? What for?"

"For selling the drugs that were stolen from the Property Clerk."

"That's crazy. I had nothing to do with that."

"That's not what I heard. Remember Joey Ragusa? He told me a lot about how you and your son brought 200 pounds of cocaine to his house and asked him to keep an eye on it for a couple of days. He said you gave him ten thousand for his troubles." Capra lowered his eyes as Parker continued. "That's the reason why you were driving around with a million dollars. You had just sold the stuff."

"That's not true. I found the money in a phone booth."

"Bull. No jury in the world is going to believe that. Not only are you going to get twenty more years in jail, but your son is going to get twenty as well."

Capra's snuffed out his cigarette in the ashtray. "My kid had nothing to do with it!"

"That's not what Ragusa said."

"Ragusa's a liar!"

"No he's not. He's smart. He's getting out of jail by giving up you and your kid. You could do the same thing. You could get out and save Luciano by giving up the cops who did the Property Clerk. Those guys are going to be walking around free while you and your kid are doing twenty."

Capra hammered the table with his fist. "I don't want to hear any more of this. I wanna see my lawyer."

Parker remained unmoved. "Look at yourself. You're fifty-something years old and you're sick man. Is this how you want the kid to wind up? Rotting away behind bars?"

"I wanna see my lawyer!"

Parker pushed away from the table and signaled the guards. "And don't think those guys from SIU are invincible either. In fact, we're going to lock up a dozen of them this week. Sooner or later, they're all going to turn on each other and I'm going to find out who did the Property Clerk." The heavy steel door opened. Parker reached over and put his business card into Capra's hand. "Think about it. And don't wait too long."

Early April 1974

TWENTY YEARS. HE WANTS TO give me and Luciano twenty years!"

Vallone opened his folder.

"Who said that?"

"Parker. He's the head of something. He says he's going to indict me and Luciano." Capra stood up and fumbled through his pockets. "Here's his card. Do you know him?"

"Yeah, I've heard of him."

"Who is he?"

"Like his card says. Harrison Parker. He's the head of the Bureau of Narcotics and Dangerous Drugs in Washington."

"He says he turned Joey Ragusa, and he's now going to lock me and my kid up for selling the Property Clerk drugs!"

"Who is Joey Ragusa?"

"A guy that held packages for me sometimes."

"How many times?"

"Twenty, thirty, forty times. How am I supposed to remember?"

Vallone looked up at the overhead guard station. "What exactly did Parker say?"

"He said if I cooperated and gave him Lynch and Beninati, me and Luciano could walk."

"He mentioned Lynch and Beninati by name?"

"No. He said if I gave them the guys that did the Property Clerk, we could walk."

"Who told you Lynch and Beninati did the Property Clerk?"

"Everybody knows they did it. For Christ's sake, didn't they go to the newspapers and tell them they were the main suspects?"

"That doesn't mean they did it."

"They did it. Believe me, they did it. I bought the drugs from them and Catalano."

"How do you know it was the Property Clerk drugs?"

Capra winced in pain. "Why are you sticking up for them? Is it because Catalano's your brother-in-law? Aren't you supposed to be my attorney?"

"I'm not sticking up for them and I am your attorney."

"You sure don't sound like it!"

"Calm down, Vinnie."

"I am calm!" Capra hissed.

"Good. Now, what do you want me to do about Parker?"

"I want you to call him and tell him I want to cooperate. Make a deal. I don't want to do any more time. I'm tired, and I don't ever want my kid to do any time. I want you to work out a deal with this guy."

"Vinnie, I don't think that's a good idea. Let's play it cool and see what he really has."

"Listen. This guy says he's going to start indicting some SIU guys. He says when that happens, they're going to start turning on each other, and he's going to solve the Property Clerk thefts. He says then it's going to be too late for me and my kid to cooperate, and we'll never get out of here."

"Vinnie, listen to me. I've been through this a thousand times. He's trying to spook you. We have plenty of time to decide if you should turn. Believe me, if he didn't need you, he wouldn't be coming down here hat in hand, offering you a deal. He's still a long way from solving the thing."

"What are you telling me to do?"

"Just sit tight. I'll think of something"

Mid-April 1974

A FLASHLIGHT IN HIS LEFT hand, Detective Bob Buhl led Detective Del Sieburn down the pitch-black hallway. Buhl fixed the narrow beam on the door to Room 517 while Sieburn inserted a lockpick into the key hole of Richard Vallone's office door and quickly worked the lever against the tumblers. A deep breath later, Sieburn turned the knob and gently pushed the door open. Buhl grinned, "You're better than Willie Sutton."

After surveying the reception room, Sieburn browsed through a stack of papers on Vallone's desk, while Buhl picked up the phone and dialed the number on a slip of paper he had taken out of his pocket. Bonacum answered on the first ring.

"Yeah?"

"It's me. We're in."

Standing in a room four blocks away, Bonacum watched the tape monitoring their conversation turn on a large recorder. "Any trouble getting in?"

"Piece of cake. Sieburn's the best."

"How much longer is it going to take?"

"Ten minutes or so. We'll put a couple of bugs in his office and one in the reception area."

"Do you think that's enough?"

"If it's not, we can always come back tomorrow."

May 1974

VINCENT CAPRA CLOSED HIS EYES and clenched his teeth as the Eastern Airlines jet bumped down on the windswept runway at New York's LaGuardia Airport. The two US marshals escorting Capra smiled when they saw his reaction. As the plane slowly taxied towards the terminal, the older officer leaned over and recuffed Capra's wrists. "Stop worrying, Vinnie. After you get back to Atlanta, you won't be flying again for another twenty years."

AT 9:30 A.M. THE FOLLOWING morning, two prison guards walked slowly beside a limping Capra as he made his way from the third-floor holding pen to the courtroom. Capra's eyes moistened when he saw his handcuffed son standing by the door, The guards escorting Luciano Capra were taken by surprise as the young man bolted from their grasp and greeted his father. Tears flowed unabashedly as they faced each other. The guards quickly separated their prisoners and led them into the courtroom.

The four guards stood a discreet distance behind the defense table and watched both Capras confer with their attorneys as they waited for the judge. Jerry McEldery and Richard Vallone were busy talking to their clients about their pending indictment when Capra asked Vallone if he could talk to his kid alone. Before stepping away, Vallone bent down and in a low voice advised Capra to hurry because the judge would be out in a minute.

Capra looked around and made sure he couldn't be overheard. "Luciano, I can't stand the thought of you going to jail. It makes me sick to see you in handcuffs."

"It's all right, Papa. We're going to win. McEldery says the case is *nullo*."

"What does he know? I hate these lawyers who say everything's OK. It means nothing to them. If they lose, they should do the time."

"I've never seen you so upset."

"I've never seen my kid in handcuffs before. I don't like it."

"There's not much we can do about it now."

"That's not true. There is something I can do. The head of the Federal investigation has been down to see me. He wants me to cooperate with him."

"You can't do that." Luciano Capra's face tightened. "Vito and the guys would kill you."

"I'm not telling on them. The Feds want me to give up Lynch and Beninati. It would mean the both of us walk."

"Jesus Christ, Lynch and Beninati. That's worse than Vito. What does Vallone say?"

"He wants me to sit tight and see what happens. He thinks the Government has nothing."

"I told you that's what McEldery says."

"Yeah. But in the meantime, we're the ones sitting in jail."

The sharp voice of the court attendant interrupted the conversation.

"All rise. Court is now in session. Judge Weinstein presiding." The tall jurist strode out of his chambers followed by U. S. Attorney Paul Curran and Andrew Parker. The judge stood behind the bench while Curran and Parker took seats at the prosecutor's table. All eyes focused on the court attendant as he read, "Indictment number B8545/74. The United States Government versus Vincent Capra and Luciano Capra."

June 1974

For THE NEXT SEVERAL WEEKS, an astonished public watched in disbelief as Special Prosecutor Nader and US Attorney Curran attacked each other. From press conferences announcing indictments of SIU detectives to televised Sunday morning interview programs, they blamed one another for "retarding" their respective investigations into the Property Clerk thefts.

The media ridiculed and berated both agencies as self-aggrandizing and greedy. A spokesman for Channel 2, declared, "The shocking public-be-damned attitude of these two arrogant law enforcement agencies shows they are as avaricious as the Property Clerk thieves they are pursuing. A pox on both their houses."

Steve Dunleavy, a respected columnist of the *New York Post*, wrote, "I can visualize the thieves that stole the Property Clerk drugs sitting at home, watching a ball game and sipping a beer. They're not at all concerned these two inept agencies run by publicity-seeking buffoons could ever catch them."

The *New York Times* contributed a stinging editorial condemning both law enforcement agencies and Governor Rockefeller's lack of leadership for not getting these public servants to merge their efforts. Under the caption, "GOVERNOR, GOVERNOR. WHEREFORE ART THOU GOVERNOR?' the *Times* asked Rockefeller "to wake up and invite both warring parties to Albany without fanfare or publicity and mediate their dispute. Once this occurs, the Property Clerk thieves will be put on notice they are being sought on a united front and they soon will be apprehended."

July 1974

Governor ROCKEFELLER WAS WATCHING HIS secretary clasp her bra underneath her breasts, when Michael Crowne opened the door without knocking.

"I'm sorry to disturb you, Governor, but they just showed up. I left them in there with Nader.

After looking in the mirror and adjusting his tie, Rockefeller slipped into the jacket Crowne was holding for him.

The governor shook his head when he saw Parker and Curran seated at the table and Nader reading a newspaper at the other end of the room. "No wonder you can't resolve your differences. You won't even talk to each other when you're left alone in the same room."

Moving towards the table, Rockefeller took off his jacket and draped it over the back of a chair. "I was hoping everything would be resolved by the time I got here." Feigning annoyance, he stood at the head of the table, and waited while Crowne and Nader seated themselves opposite Parker and Curran.

Crowne removed several press clippings from a folder, handed them to the Governor and distributed copies to the rest. Rockefeller rasped in a gravely voice, "Gentlemen, I'm happy to say I'm never going to see crap like this again. You three selfish douchebags have embarrassed me for the last time. Since you people couldn't resolve your differences, I did it for you." He tossed the clippings on the conference table.

"Yesterday, I spoke to the President and the Attorney General. They, as God and we all know, have more pressing problems to address. Both agreed with me that Aaron here should be in charge of the Property Clerk investigation. The Attorney General will confirm this by letter."

Rockefeller pointed to Parker. "You are to turn over all pertinent information, informants and whatever to Aaron here as soon as possible. Do you understand?"

Parker nodded. "Yes, sir."

Crowne smiled thinly as he watched New York's Chief Executive walking behind Parker and Curran and put a conciliatory hand on each of their shoulders. "Men, Aaron and I have a lot at stake here. Our reputation is riding on this case. Since Aaron has been investigating the Property Clerk thefts from the beginning, I don't want his authority usurped by any outside agency no matter how well-intentioned its efforts. So here's what I have in mind. I don't want your men out of the case or your valuable efforts wasted. I want you to join forces with us and form a task force with Nader in charge. Pool your resources, your

expertise, your knowledge, your informants. Let's solve this case together."

August 25, 1974

THE BLACK-AND-GRAY SENTRY ARMORED TRUCK pulled off the
Deegan Expressway, turned left onto the crate-strewn cobblestone
streets of the Bronx Terminal Market. In front of Giogaia's Wholesale
Fruit Company, the burly middle-aged driver reached up and pressed
an overhead button which released the lock on the rear door of the
truck. Hearing the sharp clank of the lock unlatching, the armed guard
inside the truck pushed the door open and jumped to the pavement,
holding a large empty canvas bag.

He then visited the offices of eight produce companies and picked
up their daily bank deposits.

After he had collected the last of the pouches, he walked to the front
of the truck and signaled for the driver to push the release switch for
the rear door. At the back of the truck, the guard heard the lock release.
He opened the door and tossed the canvas bag filled with cash and
checks inside the truck. After securing the door, he returned to the
front of the truck and waved for the driver to get out. "Let's get something to eat."

As the two security guards started towards Ramon's Luncheonette,
three men in rumpled white jackets and dirty aprons approached them.
As they were about to pass, two of the men drew handguns and pressed
them against the guards' stomachs. After the guards' weapons were
removed, the shortest of the three assailants said, "Give me the keys
or you're dead." He took the truck keys from the driver and hurried
over to a parked car. He put his hand in the open window and dropped
the keys onto the driver's lap. "You know what to do, Lucky."

Luciano Capra, dressed in a Sentry guard uniform, got out of the car
and headed towards the armored truck. He was about to put the key in
the lock when his face was viciously slammed against the side of the
car. Dazed and bleeding, he was roughly spun around and faced the
barrel of a black snub-nosed .38. Two detectives quickly disarmed and

handcuffed him. Inspector Bonacum's revolver pointed at a spot between two horrified eyes. "Capra, you and your friends are going to jail. And this time, *there ain't no bail.*"

August 26, 1974

BONACUM'S CIGARETTE SMOKE DRIFTED LAZILY in the air as he watched the reels of the tape recorder start to rotate the moment Vallone's secretary answered the phone. Vincent Capra snarled, "Put Vallone on."

"Richard, it's Mr. Capra. He sounds angry."

"What else is new? The jerk's always angry." Vallone's chair squeaked as he leaned forward to pick up the phone. "What's happening, Vinnie?"

"What do you mean? Didn't you hear?"

"No, I just got in. What are you talking about?"

"My kid! They locked up my kid!"

"What happened?"

"Jesus, I'm a thousand miles away in a jail and I hear things quicker than my lawyer. Luciano got locked up there yesterday for an armored car robbery!"

Riffling through a stack of telephone messages on his desk, Vallone paused. "I heard something on the radio this morning but they didn't give any names. Hold it, here's a message from Luciano's lawyer. I guess that's what he called me about."

"I can't believe you, Richard. You're not on top of things like you used to be. I get the feeling you're forgetting about me."

"I'm not forgetting you, Vinnie."

"Know what? I think you've been hanging around with Lynch and Beninati too much. I think you're trying to protect them and screw me!"

"I'm not trying to screw you."

"Well, if you are, I've got to tell ya I'm not about to stay in here while your buddies walk free."

"You're becoming paranoid."

"Don't think I don't know what's going on up there."

"Nothing's going on up here. Believe me, nothing's going on."

"Then get your ass down here and get me out of here! Bring the card of this Washington guy with you. I want you to make a deal with him, and I want you to get me and my kid out of jail. I'm going to give up Lynch and Beninati. I'll even give them your brother-in-law if I have to, but just get me out of here! Now!"

"Vinnie, *relax*, for Christ's sake. Why don't you let me call McEldery first and find out what's happening with Luciano? Call me back about seven tonight. No, you better make that eight o'clock. I'll make sure your kid is being taken care of properly, and then I'll make arrangements to come down and see you."

PAUL CURRAN AND AARON NADER greeted Harrison Parker as he stepped off the Eastern shuttle from Washington. Nader cautioned, "We better step on it if we want to be at the plant by eight o'clock."

The three men immediately hurried out of the terminal to a waiting black Chrysler where Deputy Inspector Creighton sat behind the wheel. Sirens blaring, the car sped out of LaGuardia airport, bound for downtown Brooklyn.

At exactly 7:40 P.M., the three men stepped off the elevator onto the eighth floor of 32 Court Street and walked down the hallway. Nader knocked on the door of Room 841 and was greeted by Chief Guido. "You guys sure know how to cut it close."

Inside the room, agents from the Special Prosecutor's Office and the US Attorney's Office huddled around several sets of sophisticated electronic equipment. Bonacum, holding a container of black coffee, was introduced to Parker by Nader. "I'm getting worried. No one's been in the office since his secretary left at five-thirty. As a matter of fact, the phone hasn't even rung."

Nader checked his watch. "It's already ten to eight." While Bonacum updated the three men on the day's events, Federal Agent Harris called: "Inspector, somebody just came in."

Bonacum hushed the excited investigators and stepped over to the recorder where Harris sat wearing earphones. "Put it on the speaker, Tim." Harris leaned over and flipped a switch. A gruff male voice came over the speaker.

". . . damn traffic. I hope he didn't call."

"Take it easy, Jerry. There's nothing on the answering machine. Why don't you make Vinnie and Loo a drink while I take a leak?"

Bonacum waved his hand to silence Chief Guido, who was about to say something. He then turned to the others and whispered excitedly, "That's Vallone. It sounds like Lynch, Beninati and Catalano are with him." All eyes looked at the speaker as the conversation from Vallone's office filtered into the room.

"Tell Capra, if he turns he's dead meat!"

"Vinnie, I know what to tell him. I've been through this dozens of times."

"I want to speak to him."

"Vinnie, I told you before. You can't talk to him. I don't want him to know you're here."

"Why not?"

"Because he thinks I'm screwing him. He thinks the only reason I don't want him to turn is to protect you guys."

"I still—"

Beninati's voice interrupted: "Vinnie, why don't you shut up and let Richard handle this?"

"Because I don't feel like going to jail for the rest of my life. And don't talk to me like I'm some sort of—" Catalano's voice stopped when the telephone rang.

Harris looked at the recorder monitoring the phone and saw the tapes start to rotate slowly. He immediately adjusted the volume so the conversation could be heard throughout the room.

"Vallone here."

"It's me. Vinnie. What's new with Luciano?"

"Everything's fine. Right after I spoke with you this morning, I got in touch with McEldery. We met at the Bronx County courthouse before Vincent's arraignment. He let me speak to the judge about Luciano's bail. As it turned out, Judge Sandler handled the arraignment. He's an old friend. I told him you were a very sick man, so he let Luciano out on fifty thousand dollar bail. He also gave me permission to bring him down to Atlanta to visit you. You should have heard the jerks from the Special Prosecutor's Office scream. They wanted Luciano held without bail."

"Good work. When are you coming down?"

"I'm jammed up tomorrow. I figure we'll be down Thursday."

"There's no way you can come down tomorrow?"

"I can't. I'm tied up in Federal Court with Angelet and Texeira."

"Well, don't forget. When you come down, bring that guy's card with you."

"What are you talking about?"

"Parker. The guy that's the head of the Feds. I told you before, I want to cooperate. I want to get me and Luciano out."

Everyone in the plant looked at Parker as Vallone responded to Capra. "Why don't we talk about this Thursday when me and Luciano get down there? OK?"

"All right, I'll see you then." But don't forget, bring that guy's card with you."

After they hung up, Bonacum lowered the volume of the recorder monitoring the phone. All eyes concentrated on the speaker when they heard Vallone's voice. "We got a problem. He's definitely going to turn."

"I told ya I shoulda talked to him."

"Vinnie, nothing you could have said would have changed his mind."

"I don't know about that, Richard. I'm close to him. Anyway, I don't know what makes you so smart. Am I right, Jerry?"

"You're wrong, Vinnie, and I think you should stop hassling Richard. He's been doing a great job for us. And if you're asking me what we should do next, I think we should stop all the bullshit and order in some Chinese. I'm starved."

Vallone stood up. "I'm starved too, Jerry, but if you don't mind, I'd rather not talk in my office. The walls might have ears. I know a great place a couple of blocks from here. We can talk there."

"Jerry, I say we put a cannon up Capra's ass."

"Vinnie, shut up."

NADER WAS NOT A HAPPY CAMPER after he heard the door to Vallone's office slam shut. "Do you believe this? Here they are about to spill their guts and that ugly Irish scoundrel gets hungry!"

Parker touched Nader's arm. "Why don't you, me and Paul go somewhere that we can talk privately? And bring Bonacum."

In a spacious kosher delicatessen, Parker, Curran, Nader and Bonacum went to a table where an elderly waiter took their orders as soon as they were seated. Parker reached over and selected a dripping dill pickle from a glass dish. "Aaron, I can understand you getting angry upstairs, but all in all, we've had a great day with Capra wanting to turn and all that. The question is where do we go from here? Do we go to Atlanta tomorrow and see Capra, or do we risk waiting until Vallone sees him on Thursday?"

Nader shrugged. "Risk waiting? What's the risk?"

"Suppose Vallone talks him out of turning?"

"That could happen, but Capra doesn't sound like a guy that could be talked out of anything. If we run down there tomorrow, we might spook them. We'll be tipping our hand. Vallone will know his phone is tapped, and weeks of hard work will go down the drain. Don't forget, we have a lot of leverage with Capra. We got his kid by the balls."

Parker wiped his chin. "What do you think, Paul?"

"I agree with Aaron. I don't think we should tip our hand and what better ace in the hole can we have than his kid?"

"How do you feel, inspector?"

"I remember when I was a young cop in plainclothes. Some broken-down hooker once told me that it was a lot easier to strike a deal when a guy's cock is hard than when it's soft. Capra's cock is hard now."

"So what are you trying to say?"

"If it was up to me, I'd be on a plane to Atlanta tonight. If you wait until Thursday, Vallone might talk him out of turning."

Nader finished his hot pastrami sandwich. "What do you think, Harrison?"

"The inspector has a valid point about striking while the iron is hot, but I also agree with you and Paul. We sure don't want Vallone to wise up and start looking for the bugs in his office. I say we wait and see if Vallone contacts us after he talks to Capra." He signaled for the check.

The waiter pointed across the restaurant. "The gentlemen over there picked up your bill."

Sitting in a booth, Vallone, Lynch, Beninati and Catalano mockingly bowed, each holding up the middle finger of his right hand.

August 28, 1974

TWO GUARDS HELPED CAPRA, WHO WAS VISIBLY in pain, into a wooden chair. He straightened out his leg and acknowledged his son and attorney. After the guards had left, Richard Vallone shook his head. "I don't know how you do it, Vinnie. Your own private room."

"For the right price, anything can be bought in here." Capra held onto the sides of the chair, shifted his weight and examined his son's face. "What the hell were you thinking of? Sticking up an armored car!"

"It would have worked if someone hadn't tipped off the cops."

"It wouldn't have worked. *Nobody* sticks up an armored car and gets away with it. I oughta know. I tried it twice. Somebody always talks." Capra rubbed his leg. "What does your lawyer say?"

"He says I caught a break. Since I never got into the truck and no one got hurt, I shouldn't have to do more than a year or two."

"He's wrong. What does he think is going to happen when they find out you're my kid? Or the Feds just indicted you for the Property Clerk's thefts. They're gonna stick it right up your ass."

"Hey, I'm only telling you what McEldery told me."

"All these lawyers do is look out for themselves and take your money." Capra faced Vallone. "Did you bring that Washington guy's card with you?"

"Yeah. I got it."

"Give it to me."

What are you going to do with it?"

Capra shifted in his chair. "I'm gonna make myself a deal, one that'll get me and Luciano out of this mess. A deal where we won't have to go to jail."

"Vinnie, why don't you let me do it? If you do it, they'll burn you. I promise I'll get right on it."

Capra glared at Vallone, "OK, but this is your last chance. I think you've been too busy hanging around with those cops."

"That's not true."

"Don't make a mistake. Do not underestimate me. I may be in jail, but I am not out of the game. I heard you had dinner with Lynch and Beninati at Trinchi's last week. Bucetta and Sartaretti saw you."

"Hey, I'm not denying it. I was at Trinchi's, but I'm not hanging around with them. They called me and asked what was happening with you. We met and had dinner together once."

"What did you tell them?"

"I told them you were doing fine."

"Did you tell them I wanted to turn?"

"Of course not. I'm your lawyer, not theirs."

"I'm glad to hear you say that, because here's what I want you to do. I want you to get in touch with that guy in Washington and make a deal for me and Luciano."

"I still don't think it's a good idea."

"I don't care what you think. You don't have to sit in here for the rest of your life. Now are you going to make the deal or do I have to?"

"I'll do it. But give me a week or so to set it up."

"A week or so? Why?"

"Because deals like this can be very tricky. You can't take the Government's word for anything. You've got to get everything in writing."

"You're not trying to cross me, are you?" There was an edge to Capra's voice.

"No, believe me, but these things are difficult."

"OK. Go ahead and make the deal. Just don't take too long." Capra reached down and kneaded his calf. "Do me a favor, Richard. Knock on the door and have the guards let you out. I want to talk to Luciano alone for a couple of minutes."

August 31, 1974

DR. WEBER TRACED HIS FINGERS gently over the inflamed vein in Capra's left leg. "You've got phlebitis."

"It hurts like a son of a bitch. Is there anything you can do for it?"

"Sure, several things. But first I'm going to put you on antibiotics to get the inflammation down. However, the best prescription I can give you is to stay off the leg as much as possible and keep it raised when you sleep."

He opened a cabinet and removed a small plastic vial filled with tablets. "I want you to take one of these every twelve hours and I'll see you in a couple of weeks." Dr. Weber helped Capra off the examination table and watched him slowly hobble out the infirmary door.

Holding on to the railing, the ailing Mafioso carefully made his way down the six wrought-iron steps to the sidewalk. He squinted in the warm morning sunlight and checked his watch. With more than an hour and a half to go before lunch, Capra decided to ignore the doctor's advice and headed off to the recreation field. Passing several buildings, he stopped in front of Cellblock B and talked for a few minutes with the prison chaplain. Thanking the priest for his concern, he headed for the pathway separating the recreation area from the cell blocks. Capra sighed as he started down the football-field-length pathway bordered by eight-foot walls. Several passing inmates solicitously offered their arms to help him walk, but he refused.

Exiting the pathway, Capra could see hundreds of screaming prisoners jumping up and down around Basketball Court No.4 as they watched a match between Cellblock A and Cellblock E. Limping past crowded handball and basketball courts, he leaned against a fence and watched a group of sweating inmates pump iron.

After taking a drink from a water fountain, Capra made his way over to a group of high-level mobsters sitting on the first row of the softball field bleachers. Bobby Franchese and Carmine Persico slid over as Michael Viggiano moved up to the second row, allowing Capra to sit down next to the powerful New York boss, Carmine Tramunti.

"What'd the doctor say?" Tramunti's voice was a low rumble.

"He told me I had phlebitis and to stay off my leg."

Tramunti swatted at a bee. "I like Doctor Weber, but sometimes he can be a little strange."

"What do you mean?"

"The last time I went to him, he asked me for a urine specimen, a feces specimen and a semen specimen."

Capra scratched his chin. "Jeez, what'd you do?"

"I gave him my undershorts."

While the men were laughing, a thin black man trotted up to Capra. "There's three guys in the warden's office asking about you."

"Did you ever see any of them before?"

"Yeah. One of them visited you a couple of weeks ago."

"That must be that Fed that thinks I can give up the Property Clerk! He doesn't understand English."

As Capra struggled to his feet, a voice boomed over the public-address system. "Vincent Capra. Number 461876. Report to the warden's office."

As CURRAN AND PARKER CHATTED with the warden, Nader walked over to the window. He pulled up the blinds and stared out at the grounds. "How big is this place, warden?"

Matthew Washburn got out of his chair and joined Nader by the window. "About twenty-eight acres. We house over two thousand inmates."

He opened the window. "If you look over to your right, you can see our new drug rehab building. It's the one with the flag on it next to the cellblocks. Every new inmate is tested for drugs there before he's admitted into the general population. If he tests positive, he's assigned to the drug rehabilitation program until he's clean."

"When was this place built?"

"Around the turn of the century. Construction started in 1898 and it was finished in 1901. Teddy Roosevelt dedicated it."

Nader put his hands on the windowsill and cautiously leaned forward. His eyes surveyed the grounds. "I can't believe the size of that wall. It's incredible. It's like the Great Wall of China."

The warden proudly agreed. "That stone wall is thirty-seven feet high. Solid granite. They don't make walls like that any more."

Curran stood up. "You must have had some big shots in here."

"I've only been here four years, but they tell me they had some doozies stay here during the twenties and thirties. Al Capone, 'Machine Gun Kelly,' 'Legs' Diamond, Dillinger when he was young,"

"What's over there?"

"That's the recreation area. As you can see, it's a mob scene today because it's Sunday. Monday through Saturday it's not nearly as crowded because most of the men are at work."

Nader pointed toward the pathway separating the recreation area from the cellblocks. "What's happening in that alley over there?"

"Where?"

"Over there. Where the inmates and guards are running."

Nader stepped back and allowed Washburn to lean out the window. "Jesus. I don't know but I'll check." The warden went over to his desk and pressed the intercom button. "Reynolds, what's happening in Finnegan's Alley?"

The voice answered, "Nothing as far as I know, but I'll check on it."

The warden went back and closed the window. "Too many flies this time of year." When Washburn sat down, Parker again thanked him for letting them see Capra on a Sunday. "We were going to come down this past Wednesday—

The intercom buzzed and the warden answered, "Yes, Reynolds. What happened over there?"

"It's Vincent Capra, warden. He was just stabbed to death."

September 2, 1974

CAPTAIN PETER COCHRAN ADJUSTED the volume on the telephone recorder as Vallone started speaking with Capra's widow. Federal Agent Osgood Harris and Sergeant Dennis Frawley stepped closer to the recorder.

"Mildred, I know the undertaker is waiting but there's nothing I can do. They have to do an autopsy, and by the time those crackers get the body shipped up here, it'll be Thursday."

"He'll be decomposed by then!"

"He won't be decomposed, Mildred. They treat the body with special solutions."

Frawley started laughing. "Special solutions? He should tell her they're just going to drain the blood out of the sucker."

". . . are you sure they know where to mail him?"

Frawley howled, "What does she think they're going to do? Stick him in an envelope and put a stamp on his dick?"

Cochran held up his hand and frowned. "Please, Sarge. I want to hear this."

"Don't worry about a thing. Everything's being worked out. Now get some rest and I'll talk to you in the morning. Incidentally, is Luciano there?"

"No, I haven't seen him since the prison called and told us Vinnie was murdered."

"When he comes in, would you please have him call me? It's important."

The three investigators heard the telephone line click off. Captain Cochran bent over the table and noted in the telephone log, "Conversation between R. Vallone and Mildred Capra ends 18:14 hours." He picked up a three-day old copy of the *Sporting News* and sat down while Frawley and Harris traded copies of *Playboy* and *Penthouse*. The investigators relaxed as they heard the click of Vallone's shoes crossing his office floor and a toilet flushing.

Cochran jumped when he heard the attorney yell, "Luciano! What are you doing here?" Cochran snapped his fingers to alert Harris and Frawley.

"I tried to reach you last night and tell you how sorry I was about your father. In fact, I just got off the phone with your mother."

"Whadda mean you're sorry? You're the one who had my father fingered."

"What are you talking about? I loved your father. Why would I want him killed?"

"Because you're protecting those cops. My father wanted to give them up but you wouldn't let him."

"That's ridiculous. Who told you that?"

"My father. Do you remember when he had you leave the room when we visited him?"

"Yeah."

"Well, the last thing he told me was if anything happened to him, you, Catalano, Lynch and Beninati were responsible."

"Lucky, don't be stupid. Put down that gun."

Sergeant Frawley immediately picked up his portable radio and contacted the surveillance team assigned to Vallone. "Skip, where are you?"

A voice crackled over the walkie-talkie. "About a block from Vallone's office."

"Get upstairs. Lucky Capra's up there with a gun."

"Ten four. I'm on my way."

Frawley squeezed his Motorola tightly as he heard Vallone scream, "Luciano, it wasn't my idea. It was Lynch's—" The three men cringed as they heard the shots.

AFTER FIRING A FOURTH BULLET into Richard Vallone, Luciano shoved the revolver into his waistband and hurried out the front door towards the elevator bank. Seeing several curious onlookers standing in neighboring office doorways, Capra took the fire stairs down to the street. At the lobby level, he opened and quickly shut the heavy metal door when he observed several men with drawn weapons running into the building. He turned and raced down the staircase. Pushing open the door to the basement, he surprised three uniformed maintenance men playing cards. Capra took his gun from his waistband and pointed it at the face of the closest man. "How do I get out of here?"

The man wheeled and pointed. "Over there, suh. That door goes to the alley."

THIRTY-FIVE MINUTES LATER, LUCKY PARKED his car on a quiet residential street in Whitestone, Queens. He went up the walkway of a house with the statue of a Blessed Virgin Mary on the lawn and rang the doorbell. A plump girl answered the door. "Yes?"

"Is your father home, sweetheart?"

"Yes, he is. Won't you please come in?"

"No, I'll wait here. Just tell him Luciano's here."

The little girl disappeared and seconds later, her father came to the door. "Luciano, what are you doing here?"

Luciano Capra fired five shots into Catalano, who clutched his stomach in agony and crumpled in a heap in the doorway. Capra looked over at the horrified little girl standing in the living room with her hands over her ears. He stepped over her father's still body and put the tip of the barrel between his eyes. "You used to brag to me and my father how you once survived a guy shooting you five times. Let's see you survive six." He pulled the trigger.

"THAT'S NO EXCUSE, CAPTAIN. I should have been notified first. I would have sent cars to Catalano's house right away!"

"But, sir—"

"Captain, I'm the boss! You shouldn't have done anything until you notified me!" Bonacum shook his head in disgust. "Another thing. Who gave you the authority to send the surveillance team up to Vallone's office?"

"Nobody. We heard Lucky Capra threatening him."

"You had no right to send men up there. You could have blown everything! Suppose nothing had gone down? Months of hard work would have gone done the drain."

"But a man was being murdered up there!"

"That's irrelevant. The point is, you made a bad decision."

"Well, actually, I didn't send them up there. Sergeant Frawley called 'em before I had a chance to stop him."

"I don't care who did it. You're responsible. I want both of you morons to report to my office tomorrow morning at 0800 hours, and be in uniform." Bonacum slammed down the phone and turned to Creighton.

"Get radio cars stationed outside Lynch's and Beninati's homes right away. I want them and their families protected. Then seal off the city. I want you to cover every airport, train station, bus terminal, bridge and tunnel. Circulate Lucky Capra's picture to every rent-a-car depot, taxi, limousine service, hotel, motel and flophouse. I want every one of his friends and associates checked and double-checked. I want every rumor and whisper followed up until we nail this prick."

Creighton started for the door and turned. "Isn't it ironic, Inspector?

For the longest time, you've been trying to put Lynch and Beninati in jail. Now you're trying to save their lives."

THE MEN STANDING IN FRONT of St. Luke's Roman Catholic Church bowed their heads as the hearse carrying Vincent Catalano's body pulled away from the curb. It was followed by several highly polished black limousines and dozens of cars with their headlights on.

Beninati shook his head. "What a shame. Only eight cops with the balls to come to his funeral."

Detective Johnny Biaggi, a lifetime friend of Catalano, touched Beninati's arm. "Loo, why don't we go somewhere and get a drink?"

I wish I could, Johnny, but I can't. Jerry and I are on our way to another funeral."

"That lawyer's?"

"Yeah."

"You guys better be careful. We don't want to read about you getting killed by that maniac too."

Beninati snickered, "Not a chance, Johnny. When we leave here, there's going to be a hundred cops tailing us."

As Beninati pulled out of the parking lot, Lynch twisted in his seat and looked out the rear window. "Let's lose these clowns."

"Done." Laughing, Beninati stomped down on the accelerator, raced through a red light and sped down Utopia Parkway. "I told them it was OK to sit on my family, but not to follow me around. It's embarrassing." At the entrance to the Clearview Expressway, Beninati checked the rearview mirror. "We lost them." After shooting down the ramp to the highway, he grumbled, "Jerry, I think I'm going to send Lisa and the kids to Florida."

"To her sister's?"

"Yes."

"Are you sure you want to do that?"

"I'm not sure what I want to do. But all of a sudden, I'm getting bad vibes. I'm not sure they're gonna catch Lucky right away. You know as well as me, if they don't catch someone in the first forty-eight hours, it could go on for months. And if the kid's anything like his father, he's probably zeroing in on us right now."

September 24, 1974

AARON NADER PUT HIS HEAD BACK and stretched his neck until he heard a crack. "Now we can get down to business." He came around from behind his desk and sat with Parker and Curran. "I appreciate both of you coming here on such short notice."

Curran smiled. "No problem, Aaron. Harrison loves catching the 7:00 A.M. shuttle."

Parker reached for his briefcase. "Aaron, before we start, do you mind if I bring you up to date on what's happening in Atlanta?"

"Not at all."

"Last night the warden called me and said they locked up two inmates for Capra's murder. He says one of them claims Carmine Tramunti paid him five thousand to do the hit."

"Figures. Who are the guys?"

"Two Muslims from Detroit. A Mohammed Something and a Mohammed Whoknows. And it ties in because after Vallone talked to Capra, he visited Tramunti."

"Can we charge Tramunti?"

"Not a chance. It's one nigger's word against the other."

Curran covered his mouth and stifled a yawn. "At least that's solved. Now if we could only come up with the kid."

Parker crossed his arms. "What's the latest on him anyway?"

"We still have a task force of fifty men trying to find him. According to Guido, he's been spotted all over the world, from Tokyo to Palermo. They're going crazy trying to check out leads."

"What you're telling me is they have no idea where the guy is."

"That's what I'm telling you." Nader stood up and moved behind his desk, "Gentlemen, the reason I asked you here today is to tell you that I now agree with you. Trying to nail Lynch and Beninati for the Property Clerk thefts is an exercise in futility."

Parker sympathized, "I know how you feel, Aaron. It wasn't easy for us to accept it either. How do you want to approach it?"

"As you suggested, indict as many SIU guys as possible. Offer them and the guys we already have under indictment, immunity and incentives if they can give us Lynch and Beninati for any-thing."

Curran spoke up. "Anything?"

"Anything."

"What kind of incentives?"

"Besides no jail time, offer them their pensions."

"A lot of guys might lie to get out from underneath their indictments."

"That's not our problem, Paul. That's Lynch's and Beninati's."

Nader pulled his necktie tight. "That's about it. Thank you again. May I invite you gentlemen for breakfast?"

Parker sighed, "I was afraid you'd never ask."

FOR THE NEXT SEVERAL WEEKS, Nader and Curran worked to-gether implementing the new strategy. They brought Bucci, as well as several old and new SIU turnarounds, before state and Federal grand juries to testify against former SIU investigators. Newspaper headlines chronicled the indictments on a regular basis:

"2 IN ELITE NARCOTICS UNIT CHARGED WITH TAKING BRIBE"

"A retired sergeant and a former detective, once members of the SIU, were indicted yesterday by the Special State Prosecutor for ac-cepting a nine thousand six hundred dollar bribe to release a reputed underworld figure picked up during a narcotics transaction in the Bronx. Former Detective Robert Bucci is the . . ."

"10 POLICE FACE DRUG RAP"

"Ten more former SIU narcotics detectives were indicted yesterday by the Federal grand jury investigating how the drug underworld bought off police here. It was learned that seven of the ten former narcotics detectives indicted have been cooperating fully with Federal and state prosecutors investigating widespread corruption in the once-elite Spe-cial Investigating Unit of the Narcotics Division. One of the officers, Second Grade Detective Carl R. Ramos . . ."

"4 EX-SIU MEMBERS ACCUSED
OF RECEIVING $80,000 BRIBE"

"A special state grand jury has heard evidence that three detectives and a police lieutenant accepted an eighty thousand dollar bribe to free two major narcotics dealers they had arrested. According to the ten-page indictment, Detectives Richard Belfry and Douglas Redmond have been named as unindicted co-conspirators along with . . ."

"THREE FORMER ELITE DETECTIVES INDICTED
IN SHAKEDOWN SCHEME"

"Three former detectives assigned to the Special Investigating Unit were indicted yesterday by a grand jury on charges they installed illegal wiretaps on the homes of three suspected narcotics dealers and later illegally took nearly $100,000 from them and other suspects. Those named as defendants were John McDuff of Belle Harbor, Queens; Ramon Carrera of the Bronx and Edward Santiago of West Islip, L.I.

"Also yesterday a former head of the elite police unit, Captain Daniel Hughes, agreed to pay twenty thousand dollars to the Police Department pension fund and agreed to retire with half-pay after pleading guilty to Department charges he shared bribes to hinder narcotics investigations. According to a Police Department spokesman, Captain Hughes was very instrumental in the above indictment of the aforementioned detectives, saying he had received a total of twenty-four thousand dollars from the three men. The spokesman also said Captain Hughes has been quietly cooperating in several other corruption investigations, and this was taken into account in the decision to have him pay a fine in lieu of prosecution. Captain Hughes . . ."

NADER GLANCED ENCOURAGINGLY AT PAUL Curran as the attorneys for former SIU Detectives Robert Wong and Michael Andrews huddled with their clients. Wong's attorney, Aaron Moscowitz, looked over at Nader. "Mr. Rosenberg and I agree. You have a deal. Wong and Andrews will tell you everything they've ever done in Narcotics, in exchange for their pensions."

"Good. They've made a wise decision. Out of the sixty-seven the US Attorney and I have indicted, this now brings to forty-nine the number cooperating with us." Nader turned and faced Wong and Andrews. "You've heard the deal, gentlemen. I expect you both to tell me everything you've ever done in Narcotics. If you lie or omit anything, you're going to jail."

Andrews dabbed the beads of perspiration from his forehead. "Don't worry, Mr. Nader, we'll do our part. Where do you want us to start? On the case you just indicted us for?"

"No. We'll get to that in a few minutes. First I want to talk to you about the time Lynch gave you fourteen thousand dollars when you hit a search warrant with him and his team. Don't omit a single detail."

November 18, 1974

JERRY LYNCH, NURSING A HANGOVER, stumbled down the hallway in his shorts and peered through the peephole. Seeing Inspector Bonacum's face, he opened the apartment door.

As several investigators from Internal Affairs pushed past Lynch, the Inspector ordered, "Tell these men where your guns are. You're under arrest."

Lynch scratched his groin. "They're in the top drawer under my shirts."

After Sergeant Lear of IAD removed two revolvers, Bonacum told Lynch to get dressed. Lynch pulled on a faded plaid shirt he removed from the back of a chair and staggered into a pair of wrinkled blue slacks he retrieved from the floor. He then sat heavily on the edge of the bed and violently sprayed a sneeze before slipping into a pair of worn brown loafers. Lynch's wrists were tightly cuffed behind his back and he was hurried downstairs to a squad car. With sirens blaring, the black Plymouth screeched away from the curb.

*   *   *

IN FRONT OF THE WORLD Trade Center, Deputy Inspector Creighton pulled the bulky Lynch from the backseat of the car and shoved him past shouting newspaper and television reporters.

"Did you steal the 'French Connection'?"

"What did you do with the money?"

"Did you have Vincent Capra killed?"

An elevator door pinged open and Lynch was pushed inside.

On the ninety-second floor, he was uncuffed in front of the reception desk and ushered to a room guarded by two uniformed officers. Creighton motioned to Lynch, "Wait in there with your friend until I get back."

Inside, Pat Beninati stood up and embraced Lynch. "Don't say a word, Jerry. The room's gotta be bugged." Both men sat down. Beninati continued reading a newspaper while Lynch put back his head and dozed.

Twenty-five minutes later, Beninati nudged the drooling Lynch awake when Nader, Parker, Curran and Bonacum entered the room.

Nader tossed two thick blue binders of bound paper on the table. "Gentlemen, you've been indicted for illegal wiretapping, perjury, extortion, bribery, bribe receiving and ripping off drug dealers. All told, 185 counts."

Lynch opened his bloodshot eyes. "Suck my dick."

Nader stayed cool. "I want to tell you something, Lynch. When I get finished with you and Beninati, you are going to jail for the rest of your lives. When you go to trial, there's going to be more than sixty witnesses testifying against you, most of them cops. Belfry, Redmond, McDuff, Koonce, Kiner, McCrorie, Wong, Andrews. They're just a few of your friends that are going to stick it up your asses. And then there's Anthony Oliveras and his old lady from 116th Street, the ones you clowns ripped off for $40,000 with McDuff. They'll be testifying too. And remember Akki from Brooklyn? The guy you framed with Matrone and Oliva? You planted half a key of cocaine on him and got him nine years. He'll be there too. Remem—"

"Go fuck yourself."

Nader stepped back. "One more thing." Lynch and Beninati looked up as the four men laughed and raised the middle fingers on their right hands.

March 31, 1976

A BLUSTERY COLD WIND LIFTED several pages of an abandoned newspaper skyward as Lynch, Beninati, and their attorneys ignored jostling reporters outside the Criminal Court building in lower Manhattan. As the men filed out through the revolving door into the lobby, several well-wishers shouted encouragement. Lynch waved and headed for the newspaper kiosk as Beninati and their attorneys proceeded towards the elevator bank. Lynch placed a ten dollar bill in the hand of the blind newsstand owner and said, "That's a hundred, Leroy. Gimme a pack of my cigars and keep the change."

"Thanks, Mr. Jerry. And good luck today. My wife and I are praying for you."

As the man felt for a pack of Antonio & Cleopatra's, Lynch caught the headline of the *New York Times:* 'LYNCH-BENINATI TRIAL STARTS TODAY; JURY SELECTION COMPLETE, NADER TO TRY CASE PERSONALLY.'

Lynch folded a copy of the newspaper under his arm and joined Beninati and the attorneys by the elevators. On the thirteenth floor they were met by six court officers who quickly shepherded them down the crowded corridor to Room 1313. The courtroom buzzed with excitement as the men proceeded down the aisle, past the railing and took their seats at the defense table.

Every head in the room turned and looked back when Aaron Nader, accompanied by two young assistants carrying oversized briefcases in each hand, entered the courtroom and purposefully made his way towards the prosecutor's table.

At precisely 9:30 A.M., the loud voice of the court clerk boomed, "All rise. Court is now in session. The Honorable Jack Sapperstein presiding."

SAPPERSTEIN WAS A VETERAN JURIST, whose political influence reached right into the Governor's mansion. He was one of only three judges carefully selected to exclusively hear Nader's corruption cases.

His role was simple: help Nader through his cases, give him the benefit of the doubt, and his appointment to the highest judicial position, the New York State Court of Appeals, was assured. It was under this prearranged backdrop that Lynch's and Beninati's attorneys had to labor.

With black robes flowing, Justice Sapperstein emerged from a side door and took his place behind the bench. After briefly conferring with the five attorneys involved, he signaled the court clerk to bring out the jury. Everyone in the court measured the panel of seven men and five women as they were slowly led across the front of the room and took their places in the jury box. The jurors' eyes were fixed on the severe face of the white-haired judge whose black eyebrows pyramided sardonically.

Sapperstein sternly cautioned the jury to pay attention to his instructions during the trial, and "not to form any opinions as to the guilt or innocence of the defendants until all the evidence has been presented. And please do not be influenced by the theatrics or personalities of these very capable attorneys. Judge the case on its merits." Satisfied that the jury was properly instructed, the judge signaled the prosecutor to make his opening statement.

Nader rose and dramatically strode to the podium. With great passion and flamboyance, he thoroughly outlined to the jury the indictment against Lynch and Beninati and explained the type of witnesses he would be bringing in to testify. "I couldn't go to neighborhood churches to get my witnesses. I had to dig them out of the sewer of corruption where Lynch and Beninati resided with them."

Angry yells of "Objection!" from both defense counsels caused Sapperstein to admonish the Special Prosecutor.

"Mr. Nader, limit your opening remarks to outlining your case only, and please refrain from attacking the defendants personally."

Rephrasing his opening statement, Nader pointed at the defendants. "Ladies and gentlemen, during the course of this trial, we will prove to you beyond a reasonable doubt that Lynch and Beninati oversaw a veritable cesspool of corruption."

Fallek and Washow immediately leaped to their feet demanding a mistrial. A heated argument among the three counsels erupted in the courtroom.

Sapperstein angrily called for a short recess and ordered all combatant attorneys into his chambers. "Mr. Nader, I will not tolerate any further inflammatory rhetoric. And as for you, Mr. Fallek, and you, Mr. Washow, when you object, just say 'Objection.' There's no need for both of you to jump out of your chairs screaming and waving your arms. Gentlemen, I warn you, just present your case and get on with it."

Just prior to lunchtime, Nader concluded his opening statement with many objections but few major incidents.

AFTER THE LUNCH BREAK, JUDGE Sapperstein asked Lynch's attorney, Joe Fallek, if he wished to make an opening statement. The distinguished-looking Fallek paced in front of the jury box. He warmly eyed the twelve faces seated before him and in a rich, resonant voice began: "Ladies and gentlemen, for the next several weeks, Mr. Nader is going to try and sell you a bad product. He's going to try and sell you a bunch of rogue cops and drug dealers. I want you to inspect his product carefully. Examine his product like you're buying a pair of shoes. Check the leather, the soles, the heels, the stitching. Put the shoes on. Make sure they fit properly, that they're comfortable, that you're completely satisfied."

He then walked over to the prosecutor's table, stood behind Nader and raised his voice. "Mr. Nader wants to put the shoes in a pretty box and have you take them home without looking at them. The last thing he wants is for you to examine his product. He knows you'll see the holes in it. You'll see the heels are worn down, that the tips are scuffed, that the stitching is falling apart. That these shoes have been worn many, many times by corrupt cops who have paced these halls of justice seeking to make deals for themselves to stay out of jail and save their pensions. I ask you ladies and gentlemen . . ."

At the conclusion of Fallek's remarks, the nattily dressed Michael Washow, Beninati's attorney, emotionally addressed the jury. "Bear in mind, ladies and gentlemen, the prosecutor is going to parade before you, a line of admitted perjurers, rip-off artists, extortionists and drug dealers who are seeking to climb over jail walls on the backs of these two highly decorated and highly respected former narcotics detectives. Also bear in mind as you listen . . ."

After Washow took his seat. Judge Sapperstein glanced at his watch, stood up and looked at the counselors. "It's almost 4:30. I suggest we adjourn till 9:30 tomorrow. Be on time, and Mr. Nader, be prepared to call your first witness."

MANY IN THE GALLERY STRAINED to hear the soft-spoken Jack McDuff respond to the well-rehearsed questions put to him by the Special Prosecutor. The detective spoke confidently as the prosecutor led him through his police career, starting with his first uniform assignment.

When McDuff finished his background-testimony, Nader turned and looked in the general direction of the defense table. "Detective McDuff, do you see Jerry Lynch and Patrick Beninati in the courtroom?"

McDuff nodded. "Yes, sir."

"Will you point them out?"

"Yes, sir." McDuff pointed in the direction of the defense table. "They're sitting at that table, between their attorneys."

Nader resumed. "Detective McDuff, did there come a time when you worked with Jerry Lynch?"

"Yes, sir. The first day I transferred into SIU, Lieutenant Beninati assigned me to Lynch's team. Beninati told me he had heard good things about me. He had been told I was trustworthy and that was the reason he was assigning me to Lynch."

"When Beninati referred to you as 'trustworthy' what did he mean?"

Washow shouted, "Objection!" and bounced from his seat.

Sapperstein curtly overruled the objection. "You may answer the question, Detective."

"He meant that I was good. That he had checked me out with my previous boss in the Field Team Unit and he told him I was stand-up."

" 'Stand-up'?"

"Yes. My boss told him if I was ever questioned about taking money or doing anything illegal, I would deny it."

"When did you first meet Jerry Lynch and the rest of his team?"

"Later that same day in an apartment-house basement in the Bronx. Lieutenant Beninati brought me up there and personally introduced me to my new team."

"Who was on the team?"

"Detectives Lynch, Matrone and Oliva."

"When you got to the apartment-house basement, what were they doing?"

"They were monitoring an illegal wiretap on a drug dealer named Jose Guzman. We sat on the place for about a week. Then Guzman got a phone call from a guy named Johnny Akki. Akki was going to bring over a key of cocaine that night. When Akki got there, we hit the place. We ripped them off for twenty-two thousand dollars and locked them up."

"Was Lieutenant Beninati present when you hit the apartment?"

"No."

"What happened to the money?"

"We divided it up five ways."

"Who got the money?"

"Me, Lynch, Oliva, Matrone and Beninati."

"I thought you said Beninati wasn't there when the money was divided."

"He wasn't. Lynch held his share."

"Why would Beninati get a share?"

"Because he was the boss. He was an equal partner."

"How do you know Beninati got his share?"

"I saw Lynch hand it to him the next day in the office, forty-four hundred dollars"

For the rest of the morning, Nader had McDuff detail all instances of corruption he had participated in while assigned to the Narcotics Division, including the several instances he shared money with Lynch and Beninati. Satisfied he had examined his witness completely, Nader concluded his direct examination.

WHEN THE TRIAL RESUMED THAT afternoon, McDuff was seated in the witness chair. Fallek was asked by Judge Sapperstein if he wished to cross-examine McDuff. The attorney responded affirmatively and stood up. He slowly crossed the room and positioned himself near the jury box.

"Detective McDuff, let's go back to your first day in SIU. OK?"

"OK."

"When you were first assigned to SIU, you didn't know Lieutenant Beninati. Did you?"

"That's correct."

"You had never seen him before had you?"

"I had seen him around, but I never spoke to him."

"So for all Lieutenant Beninati knew that first day, you could have been a plant from Internal Affairs. Correct?"

"That's correct."

"And later on that day, Lieutenant Beninati brought you up to the Bronx and introduced you to three detectives who just happened to be monitoring an illegal wiretap. Is that correct?"

"That's correct."

"And you had never met any of these detectives before. Is that correct?"

"That's correct."

"And you could have arrested these detectives on the spot for that illegal wiretap. Is that correct?"

"Yes."

"And they could have all gone to jail. Isn't that true?"

"Yes."

"For a considerable amount of time?"

"They could have."

Fallek half-turned and held out an open hand. "Detective McDuff, are you telling me that you expect this intelligent group of men and women to believe that three experienced investigators and a lieutenant exposed themselves to years in jail the first day they met you? That you, a detective they had never met before, a man sworn to uphold the law, would be shown a place where they were conducting an illegal wiretap?"

"Objection, objection, objection!" screamed Nader.

Over the banging of Sapperstein's gavel, Fallek continued relentlessly, "Detective McDuff, do you honestly expect this jury to believe that a few days after you came into SIU, three experienced detectives who hardly knew you handed you forty-four hundred dollars?"

"Objection! Objection! *Objection!*"

*   *   *

THE FOLLOWING DAY, DETECTIVES OLIVA and Matrone fully corroborated McDuff's recollection of events. Lynch's former partners recalled Beninati bringing McDuff into the basement of Guzman's apartment house and introducing him to the team. Matrone remembered taking Beninati aside and asking, "Are you sure this guy's kosher? He could hurt us with this wire. Beninati told me he had checked him out and he was as good as gold."

When Nader questioned Oliva about the money incident, Oliva laughed. "I remember it well. We each got forty-four hundred dollars, but since McDuff was the new man, he got fouteen hundred dollars of it in singles."

JOSE GUZMAN FOLLOWED THE DETECTIVES to the stand. In halting English he explained, "I remember them knocking down my door. The big red-faced man, him over there, punch my wife in the mouth and break her tooth. He took all my money and they lock me up. I asked him if we could have a coupla hundred dollars for the kids. He tell me, 'Fuck you.' "

"I WAS JUST LEAVING JOSE'S apartment when this group of men came running down the stairs," testified Johnnie Akki. "They brought me back into Jose's apartment and they took all his money. The Lynch guy, the man sitting over there, said I had a pound of cocaine on me. He put me and Jose in jail. Thank God, the Special Prosecutor got us out."

IN THE THIRD WEEK OF the trial, as cop after cop testified against the two men, the animosity between Special Prosecutor Nader and the defendants reached the boiling point.

Following an extremely damaging morning session wherein Detective Wong confirmed Detective Andrews's earlier testimony, Lynch started with Nader: "Hitler should have gotten all you Jew mothafuckers." In the presence of Fallek, Washow, Nader and his two assistants, Sapperstein severely reprimanded Lynch in his chambers.

As the jury was led back into the courtroom, Nader smiled imperceptibly at Lynch. Enraged, Lynch bolted from his chair, dragging two startled court officers across the room. After a third court officer pinned Lynch's right arm behind his back, Lynch tried to kick Nader in the groin. Five court officers finally wrestled the powerful Lynch to the floor. When order was restored, an angry Sapperstein ordered the jury from the courtroom. Fallek's request for a mistrial was dismissed out of hand. Judge Sapperstein raged, "There's no way this trial is going to be stopped now. Mr. Lynch has made his bed and he's going to sleep in it." Sapperstein pointed his finger at Lynch. "Any further threats or outbursts directed at the Special Prosecutor or his assistants, the jury, myself or anyone else connected with this case will result in me remanding you to jail and your being tried in absentia."

IN THE TWO MONTHS THAT followed, a parade of fifty-two turn-around cops and admitted drug dealers followed Akki to the stand. Roberto Cavalaro, a Sicilian of many passports and the Mafia's main South American connection before being apprehended by Federal agents, explained how he was once shaken down by Lynch and Beninati for thirty-five thousand dollars: "When I was eating in the hotel restaurant one night, these two guys pulled up chairs and sat down. They told me they knew who I was and what I was up to and if I didn't pay them $50,000, they were going to lock me up. The big man opened a bag and showed me some white powder. He said it was going to be mine unless I came up with the money. He let me make a call. I told him all I could get that night was thirty-five thousand dollars. He said that would be good enough."

Willie "Goldfinger" Stepney, a Harlem trafficker and Mafia middle-man, testified: "I had just picked up eight keys of coke in Jersey and had come over the George Washington Bridge when Lynch and Beninati pulled me over. Beninati got in my car, put a gun to my head, and took my money and drugs."

Detective John Speaker testified, "A couple of days after I stopped organized crime figures Vincent Capra and Joe DiPalma carrying almost a million dollars, Lynch and Beninati approached me. They gave me thirty thousand dollars and said it was from Capra. They wanted me to say if his case ever went to trial or the IRS ever asked that I thought the money was DiPalma's, not Capra's."

Joe DiPalma's face revealed a prison pallor. "Many times I used to go with Vincent Capra to meet with Lynch and Beninati. They used to sell him drugs. Capra told me they were stealing it from the Property Clerk.

Detective Joe Fasanello told how after separating from his wife, he had lived with Lynch for a month. "One night I woke up and Lynch and Beninati were in the living room with an open suitcase. It was filled with bags of white powder. I asked Lynch what was going on. He said not to worry about it because he was getting rid of it in the morning. I asked him where he got it. He told me out of the Property Clerk. I thought he was kidding."

The final witness, a confident Detective Doug Redmond, asserted, "Belfry and I met Lynch in Lieutenant Ryan's office. Lynch handed me twenty-five thousand dollars to kill a wiretap on Vincent Capra. I gave ten thousand dollars to Ryan, and told him to give five thousand dollars to Captain Hughes. Belfry and I split the rest."

AFTER TWO DAYS OF FIERY summations by Nader and the two defense attorneys and three days of jury deliberations, eight excited uniformed court officers hurried from the almost empty courtroom and assumed positions around the metal detector.

Word quickly spread the length of the crowded, smoke-filled hallway: "There's a verdict"; "Let's get inside"; "It's over." The weary press corps and shoving spectators swarmed around the metal detector. A tall, blond-mustached court officer with long straggly hair stepped forward and raised his hand. "Yes, there's a verdict, but nobody's getting into this courtroom until a single line is formed. We'll get as many of you in there as possible. For those of you who can't make it inside, we'll advise you immediately as to the jury's decision."

Lynch and Beninati twisted in their seats and looked at the anxious spectators. Anne Graziano, standing next to Lisa Beninati, gave two thumbs up to both of them. Beninati smiled, caught his wife's eye and winked. Lynch adjusted his chair and glanced over at the confident Nader and his two assistants, who had just finished chatting at the prosecutor's table with Inspector Bonacum, Parker and Curran. Lynch then reached out and put his hand over Fallek's. "Joe, win, lose or draw, you were absolutely great."

Tears welled in Fallek eyes. "Jerry, I truly appreciate that. But I'm worried. It's always the ones that you want to win the most that you lose."

Moments later, the crowd tensed as Judge Sapperstein entered the courtroom. The clerk's voice boomed, "All rise. This court is now in session. The Honorable Jack Sapperstein presiding."

Standing behind the bench, Sapperstein's steel-blue eyes surveyed the packed courtroom. "Be seated." Waiting for the crowd to settle down, Sapperstein patiently adjusted the sleeves of his robe. "Before I bring out the jury, I want to warn everyone that I will not tolerate any outbursts in this courtroom regardless of the verdict. For those reporters standing in the rear of the court, I don't want you running out of here and calling your offices until the jury has completed its work and left the courtroom." He then ordered the court clerk to bring in the jury.

The squat clerk's eyes dropped as he stepped passed the defense table to the side door. He turned the ornate brass handle, pushed open the heavy door and disappeared from view. Seconds later, he reappeared leading the group of tight-lipped jurors across the room. The jury slowly filed past the defense and prosecution tables without looking at any of the participants. They quietly slipped into their seats in the jury box and stared at the still-standing judge. who addressed the jury foreperson. "I understand you have reached a verdict. Would you please rise and give it to the clerk." The court clerk moved around in front of the matronly foreperson. "Madame Foreperson, how do you find as to defendant Lynch on Count One?"

The buxom grandmother of eleven removed her eyeglasses and folded them in her hand, "Mr. Court Clerk, there's no need to go through all these Count Ones, Count Twos, Count Threes and all that. We find the defendants, Lynch and Beninati, not guilty on all counts."

FOR A SPLIT SECOND THE room seemed frozen in suspended animation. Lynch shattered the stillness first with a ear-piercing "YYY-YYEEEEESSSSSSSS!" as he leaped up and punched the empty air. As reporters crashed out the rear doors, Beninati bolted from his chair and embraced his sobbing wife. Lynch again threw a fist in the air and screamed, "OOOOHHHHH YYYYYYYEEEEEEAAAAAA-HHHHHHH!" He separated Fallek from Washow's embrace, kissed him several times on the lips and carried him like a rag doll over to the jury box. The jurors clamored out of the box and surrounded Lynch who still held Fallek several inches off the ground. In a rush, they charged the cavorting Lynch and engulfed him. Lynch staggered under the weight of the group and fell playfully to the floor howling. Several bodies lay piled across his midsection.

Beninati pushed his way over to the crushed Nader who sat with bowed head. When the prosecutor lifted his eyes Beninati stuck out his middle finger.

Judge Sapperstein gaveled futilely trying to restore order. Shrugging, he decided to wait the celebration through.

From the back of the room, a single court officer pushed past euphoric well-wishers, celebrating in the aisle. As the man neared the writhing Lynch, Judge Sapperstein called out, "It's all right, officer. Let them be."

Unholstering his revolver, the court officer bent over and pressed his weapon forcefully against Lynch's forehead. Shocked, Fallek and the celebrating jurors scrambled away from Lynch.

The room quieted as Luciano Capra screamed at Judge Sapperstein, "He had my father murdered. I'm going to kill him."

Capra whirled and pointed his gun at Beninati. "Get over here. You're going too." When Beninati hesitated, Capra cocked his revolver. "I told you. Get your ass over here."

Nausea gripped Beninati as the color drained from his face. "Take it easy, Luciano. We had nothing to do with your father's murder." Hate contorted Capra's face when Beninati inched forward. Lynch stirred slightly and Capra immediately pointed the gun down at his face.

Suddenly, the uneasy stillness was shattered by a deafening shot. Lynch saw Capra's head explode above him.

Inspector Bonacum stepped over Capra's lifeless body and holstered his weapon.

From the floor Lynch gasped, "Jesus Christ. What took you so long?"

Bonacum laughed, "I was deciding which one of you three scumbags to shoot."

The Surprise

A s the mid-morning sun warmed the air of Crown Heights, Myron Katzman hurriedly pushed out his apartment door. On the street below, hundreds of bearded Hasidic men wearing hats scurried down the street, many heading towards the Lubavitch at 770 Eastern Parkway in Brooklyn. Myron barked orders in Yiddish to his brother Irving to start his car. The exasperated pair then drove to Kingston Avenue, made a U-turn on Eastern Parkway and headed towards Flatbush Avenue.

Every few weeks, Irving asked Myron to help him out with his business. Irving called himself a "salvage retailer"; Myron called him a junkman, which was closer to the truth. Irving resold salvaged junk to thrift stores, garages, relief agencies and any other buyers he could find. Irving proclaimed he had more business savvy than his brother because of his tactic of "making something of nothing"; Myron thought his brother was a schmuck who didn't have the brains to sell junk unaided.

Still, family was family, and so, when Irving called, Myron grudgingly agreed to make the rounds of the local auctions of forfeited and seized property to help find some cheap junk for his brother to sell. Myron usually just took his cues from the seizure reports in the *Times*. However, the night before, Irving had tipped him off about a warehouse in Queens which was holding an auction on some secured spaces their renters had let lapse.

In an isolated lot in Long Island City, a large crowd had already gathered in front of the Spectrum Warehouse on Starr Street for their annual auction of unpaid rental space. The auctioneer standing behind a podium in front of the building raised his hand. "Come on, folks, $27 isn't nearly good enough for what might be in room 216! You can do better than that." After much prodding, the room was sold for thirty-five dollars to a group of Hispanics. Six other rooms' contents, were also auctioned off sight unseen over the next forty minutes without the Katzman brothers once uttering a sound.

The auctioneer banged his gavel down again. "Room 319 is the next up for bidding. The room was rented over six and a half years ago by a man named Mike DiSalvatore for a period of five years. As you know, by law, I have to issue the following disclaimer: we tried in vain to reach the subject Michael Di Salvatore through registered mail to the address he had left with us when he rented the space, and we also tried to contact him by phone. We have now waited over one year, the legally prescribed period of time, and Mr. Di Salvatore is in default of the rent and we are now going to auction off the contents of the room." The auctioneer took a quick sip of water and resumed. "What is my opening bid for Room 319?"

When the final bid of thirty-seven dollars was accepted as the winning bid, the Katzmans jumped up and paid the cashier.

Inside the warehouse, the brothers were led to Room 319. There the attendant slipped a black crowbar under the latch and popped the door open. He then shook hands with Myron and walked away.

Myron flipped on the light switch and closed the door behind them. He looked, disappointed at thirteen suitcases on the floor and then at Irving, who shrugged, muttered a quick prayer, knelt down and opened one up.

The suitcase he slowly opened was filled with plastic bags containing white powder.

Irving looked at Myron quizzically. He opened another suitcase and saw row upon row of hundred-dollar bills.

The Katzman brothers looked at each other, scratching their side curls in unison, before Myron said, "There's an El Al flight to Tel Aviv leaving at six."

The Summary

Of the seventy-four SIU narcotics detectives at the time of the Property Clerk thefts, only eight escaped indictment; fifty-one cooperated with Federal and state prosecutors; fifteen were put on trial; eight were convicted and served time and seven were found not guilty.

Bibliography

New York magazine
"Further Developments in the 'French Connection' Case" by
Nicholas Pileggi
January 8, 1973

The New York Times
"The Stone Wall of Silence" by Bob Herbert
July 23, 1998

The Knapp Commission Report
Published by New York City, 1973

*The Comptroller General's Report to the Honorable Charles B. Rangel,
House of Representatives*
Published December 1972

Cop Hunter
by Vincent Morano with William Hoffer
Simon and Schuster
New York, 1990

The Marseilles Mafia
by Pierre Galante and Louis Sapin
W.H. Allen, London, 1979

The French Connection
by David Moore
Bantam Books,
New York, 1970

Crusader
by James Lardner
Random House
New York, 1996

Prince of the City
by Robert Daley
Houghton Mifflin
Boston, 1978

The Pleasant Avenue Connection
by David Durk with Arlene Durk and Ira Silverman
Harper & Row
New York, 1976

The Underground Empire
by James Mills
Doubleday & Company
New York, 1986

Beneath the Badge
by Herbert Beigel and Allen Beigel
Harper & Row
New York, 1977

Serpico
by Peter Maas
Viking Press
New York, 1973